An Ancient Solution

by

NEIVE DENIS

COPYRIGHT

Cataloguing-in-publication data
Creator: Denis, Neive, author
Cataloguing-in-Publication details are available from the National Library of Australia www.trove.nla.gov.au

This is a work of fiction. All characters and events are purely the imagination of the author. All locations are fictitious. Any resemblance to a particular location, or anyone, living or dead is coincidental.

ISBN: 978-0-9953533-1-2 (paperback)

Cover design: T A Marshall, Mackay, Queensland

Contents

Also by the Author

A public Service
Missing!
Connections

Acknowledgments

While the actual writing of a book might be a solitary activity, a writer trying to work completely in isolation has a difficult, if not frustrating, road ahead of them. It is the interaction with and support of others that assist in making the journey both enjoyable, satisfying and ultimately productive. Any number of people has provided support, encouragement and inspiration along the road to publication of this book. In acknowledging all those who have contributed in some way to this work, my heartfelt thanks go to all of them.

My admiration and deepest gratitude go to Tom Marshall for his ability and skill in in taking my sketchy ideas and producing a cover far beyond my expectations. To my husband for keeping a watchful eye over my well-bring as well as providing writing encouragement and support, thank you. Thanks to Elaine Ouston for reviewing my work and providing invaluable feedback, which can only serve to strengthen my writing. My heartfelt gratitude goes to all those others, too numerous to mention, who have taken the time to interact, review, comment and support me in some way with my writing endeavours.

Prologue

A car came up the driveway too fast; the loud 'thunk' of a slammed car door. Sonoma (Sonny) Whittington was back from today's surveillance job. James Harris looked up to greet his partner as she marched into the office.

After throwing my bag on my desk and dropping onto the chair, I faced James. "I have to get away for a while. I need to get away now."

"What's happened? What went wrong today? Should we be talking to the police?"

I shook my head as I wondered how to begin what I knew would be a difficult conversation.

A different situation occurred to James. "You're not bailing out on me are you? You're not looking to leave the agency?" The thought of losing Sonny, an invaluable business partner and someone he might need to depend on even more in the future, was frightening.

Emphatic head shake again, and then my hand went up to stop James saying any more. "No, no; it's not that. I... I simply need some time out. The time has come. I've hit the wall. We knew I would eventually. I need a break – a holiday – and I need to go soon." I smiled apologetically and fiddled with the stapler on the desk for a few moments while heavy silence filled the room.

Here goes, I thought as I fetched a couple of beers. "Let's deal with these out on the deck as we watch the sun set," I suggested, and waved the beers at James as I headed for the door. I just needed him to listen as I tried explaining things. We had worked together for a few years now, but my explanation went back to the beginning, to a time when I decided I was bored with my public service job. For something different to do, I enrolled in a Private Investigator's course. I needed somewhere to undertake the practical component. James took me on as an intern in his investigations agency. I worked some evenings and weekends for James, while maintaining my full time job as a public servant.

It was just an interest – a hobby – and things were going well. Then my husband, Paul, a mining engineer, died in a mine site accident. I threw myself into work. Working 24/7 helped to keep me sane and to

1

cope with the grief. We were due to leave for an overseas holiday a few weeks after his death. I cancelled. Threw myself into finishing the PI course and working part-time for James and got my PI's license. After that, James kept me on as a part-time assistant. That is, until I couldn't stand what was happening in the Public Service, particularly in our department. I quit. James took me on full-time.

The 24/7 regime continued. After about 18 months, James took me in as an equal partner in the agency. That's now all ancient history. I've been a widow for over five years, and I've hit the wall. It now feels safe for me to take a break without succumbing to grief. If I'm taking a break, I'm going to cross a couple of things off my 'bucket list'. I didn't allow myself time to weaken. I booked a flight to the UK and enrolled in a couple of archaeology subjects at York University. A real estate agent has two flats in York for me to inspect.

"Archaeology?" James queried. "What's the connection?"

"I did as much as I could in my undergrad degree, but I always enjoyed it and hoped to do more sometime. That time has arrived. Term commences in three weeks. I need to be there for that and will be gone for the whole term – unless they chuck me out earlier. James, are you okay with all of this? I don't have to go, or if I do go, I don't have to study. I could just take a short holiday."

James laughed. He was determined not to give me an excuse to cancel. He had wanted to discuss something with me, but decided it could wait until he had something definite to share… whatever that was all about.

Time passed quickly. James dropped me at the concourse. Another hug and I was trailing my case into the airport terminal. The unease I felt from the outset clung to me. We were so busy lately. The guilt I felt about leaving James to cope alone continued to dog me. He assured me he would be okay. Business had slowed down a bit and he had worked alone before I joined him. He would just go fishing a bit less often if things got busy.

The flight to England was long; not much else to say. It would have seemed worse if I wasn't flying Business Class. As usual, I fell asleep soon after take-off and slept for most of the flight. We landed in early morning darkness, the darkness a combination of time of day and rain. I peered out into the misty blackness. The rain was becoming heavier. I passed through the various checks, retrieved my baggage and headed for an exit indicating it provided access to trains.

By the time I disembarked at York, the day had truly come to life. I gave the cabbie the Lendal Street address of my hotel and, minutes later, he pulled up in front of the hotel. What a goose! Now I understand the driver's disgusted look when I gave him the address. The hotel, Judges Lodging, is only about five minutes' walk from the railway station. It took the taxi longer to negotiate morning traffic. Judges Lodging was a lovely Georgian townhouse overlooking York Minster and lived up to its advertisements.

I had two priority tasks: organising accommodation and purchasing a car. The second flat the real estate agent showed me, above a large store in Blake Street, was ideal and close to King's Manor where I would be studying. I signed the lease before lunchtime. Did I need a car? I decided I did and took myself off, map in hand and on foot, to a recommended car yard offering a repurchase scheme. A test drive of a second-hand blue automatic Ford Fiesta didn't produce any nasty surprises. I drove it away.

After rearranging the furniture and airing the flat overnight, next morning I purchased enough groceries to last several weeks. Lesson for the day: many bags of groceries mean many trips up and down the stairs. Moving in involved a few more trips up those stairs. Enrolment paperwork was my last task to complete and that was at King's Manor.

There were insufficient new students to warrant an orientation session, but a helpful staff member provided a tour of the campus. I stopped suddenly in front of a small museum. She explained it was volunteer run and the Archaeology School's pride and joy, its collection having been acquired from students' digs in England and overseas. Although closed, fantastic artefacts were visible through its glass doors – definitely a must-see priority. Another museum, the Yorkshire Museum, was located at the rear of the archaeology complex.

Monday, my first day as a new student, proved uneventful. There was time to explore the School's museum and ponder the question of becoming a volunteer. Did I want to commit to anything else? Geoff Featherstone, one of my lecturers, helped answer the question. He knew of my qualifications and past work history, and asked me to take over managing the museum and training its volunteers. After meeting the volunteers over morning tea, I agreed to look at what was involved, and spent the next week working out the requirements to bring it up to industry standard. I advised Geoff that I wouldn't have time to complete anything but would make a start.

As we discussed my future involvement with the museum, I remembered he was due to head off to a field school dig. He said he was leaving the next day but didn't seem too happy about it.

"It's not the dig we planned. The intended site became unavailable. So, we're off to sunny Crete for about seven weeks to excavate a fairly unexciting Minoan village."

"Crete! Oh yeah, I can see how the next seven weeks in the Aegean would be a drudge. I wish I could come and give you a hand to survive the ordeal." Note to self: be careful about wishes.

*****

My end of term exams were set down for the first two mornings of exam week. The Friday afternoon before my first exam, one of my lecturers raised an unexpected problem. "No doubt you're aware one of your subjects requires a written exam plus a practical component." No, I wasn't aware. That was news, but I nodded and tried not to look confused.

"Good. Normally, we expect to see some sort of fieldwork involved. I'm not sure what you've planned after your exams, but how would a couple of weeks on Crete fit in with your schedule? You'd be cataloguing and packing finds at Geoff Featherstone's dig site. No need to answer now, think about it over the weekend and give me your answer on Monday. If you do decide to go, you'll be leaving next Wednesday, straight after your final test."

Is he kidding? "Forget Monday. You can have your answer now. Yes, I will be ready to leave on Wednesday. Please provide travel details."

The weekend focused on emptying the fridge and arranging everything for the time I would be away. My exams over, Tuesday evening found me trying to cobble together the remaining meagre fridge contents to produce a meal. I decided packing was easier than culinary challenges, so I packed instead. My computer 'pinged', announcing an email from James. He queried when I might be coming home. Good question... and one I couldn't answer. After my return from Crete, I needed to establish what else I might have to complete before booking my return flight to Australia.

Wednesday morning arrived, and so did the University's car to collect me for the early morning drive to the airport. Then there was breakfast at a coffee shop, followed by an uneventful flight to Crete.

Once on Crete, the pace picked up. Finding the bus for the next leg of the journey proved more complicated than anticipated. I managed to locate it as it was about to depart. After the bus trip to the other side of the island, the last leg of the journey was by boat. There were few passengers. I was the only one destined for the bay where the field school was happening. After disembarking, I stood on the beach for a few moments just soaking up the sunshine and inhaling the smell of the ocean.

Although unaware at the time, this was the start of an adventure beyond my wildest dreams.

Chapter 1

Yawning and stretching, Troy Donaldson emerged from his tent to join the last of the stragglers on their way to the mess tent. It was late. Breakfast was almost over.

Geoff Featherstone, going in the opposite direction, commented as he passed, "Bit slow off the mark this morning are we?"

"Yeah, I worked on my report till the wee hours this morning."

"Someone commented that you were burning the midnight oil."

Soon, the mess tent became deserted. Troy sat alone nursing his rapidly cooling coffee. It cleared his fuzzy head – a bit. He planned his day: go up to the site and take the measurements needed for his report; catch up with Geoff to discuss finalising his project; take photos of the site when the sun was directly overhead, and work on the report this afternoon.

"Eh? ... Oh, sorry." Troy jumped, almost spilling his remaining coffee. Startled back to reality by the sound of a tray of dirty crockery slammed down on his table.

"Will you be much longer then?" demanded an amply bosomed caterer, standing hands on hips in front of his table.

"No. No, I'm just finishing. I didn't mean to hold you up." An apologetic smile as he added lamely, "My mind was elsewhere and time got away." Cold coffee skolled and cup added to the tray, Troy was out of the tent.

Students were already at work in their trenches as Troy made his way to the steep path snaking up the hillside to his excavation site. It was on a platform half way up a hillside that was part of the range separating their bay from the rest of the island. He marvelled at how travelling that path so many times over the last five weeks had improved his fitness. The memory of his first climb up the track to arrive at the top out of breath brought a chuckle. Today, he jogged the distance. "How did I miss taking those measurements?" He queried the universe. No one replied; he was alone on the track.

Once on the site, he told a non-existent audience, "Might as well check *all* the measurements while I'm here to see what else I've missed." Meticulous measuring and rechecking of every aspect of his site took longer than anticipated. Confident he had everything he needed, he took one last look around the site, and was off down the path back to camp.

As he approached the main dig site, a redheaded girl in the nearest trench stood up and stretched her back. "Hi Liz," Troy called out as he strode towards her, "Seen Geoff lately?"

She swivelled from the waist to face him. "He was here a while ago with the new girl from Oz. I think they were headed for the finds tent when they left."

"New girl from Oz...?" Troy repeated furrowing his brow. "What's that all about?"

Liz raised her eyebrows. "How long since you've read your emails? She's here to catalogue and pack artefacts."

"Thanks," he called over his shoulder, as he went striding off in the direction of the finds tent.

He pushed aside the flap and rushed into the tent. "Geoff? Geoff, are you in here?" It occurred to him that it was just as well someone had come to deal with the artefacts. There was stuff everywhere. Deciding he was alone in the tent, he turned to leave, but was halted by a quiet female voice coming from somewhere near the back of the tent.

"No Geoff; only me. He left a few minutes ago. Don't know where he was going." I answered.

He scanned the tent for the source of the voice, focusing on a mass of dark wavy hair and two big brown eyes now visible above the furthest bench.

"Oh, okay. Thanks. Uhmm ... you must be the new gir...ahh ...the new Aussie team member."

I slowly stood up. We shook hands across the bench.

"Welcome aboard. I'm Troy; Troy Donaldson."

"Sonoma, but Sonny preferably."

"It's none of my business I suppose, but what brings you to Crete when the field school is almost over?"

"Hmmm, well ...," I searched for the right answer. "It's a long story." I hesitated. "Troy Donaldson you said? Well, Troy Donaldson, you really should read your emails."

He grinned sheepishly. "So people keep suggesting. I'm beginning to think there could be some interesting stuff in my inbox."

I tried a reproachful look before changing the subject by asking, "How's the swimming around here?"

"Okay, I suppose. I don't think anyone has tried it."

7

I opened my mouth to ask why not but he continued before I could.

"Feel like a coffee? We could trade questions and answers in a more convivial environment."

He held the flap open and followed me out. As I exited ahead of him, I caught a glimpse of him shaking his head in apparent disbelief about something.

What is going on here, Troy asked himself. It usually takes me ages to get comfortable with strangers, but here I am inviting this woman for a coffee…and I've only just met her! For the next while, finding Geoff was no longer a high priority – and he thought he might have to review his plans for the rest of day.

The low hum of conversation greeted us as we entered the packed mess tent. Not a particularly big tent, students occupied just about every seat. Troy and I – both with coffee in one hand and plate with scones and appropriate dollops of jam and cream in the other – scanned the tent for vacant seats. Two students got up to leave. We made a beeline for their table. The noise level in the tent dropped considerably as the other diners trooped back to work.

"This is good coffee," I said as an icebreaker, adding an apprecia-tive nod, and then continued with, "How has the dig been going so far?"

"Good I think – yeah, good. Now it's my turn for a question, it's the same one I asked earlier: how come you've arrived here when it's nearly all over?"

I explained as succinctly as possible the situation leading to my arrival on Crete, interrupting the story only once to lick a spot of cream from a finger. "My specialty area is curatorship, so it was suggested I come to help out. I get to spend this last bit of the field school with the students and then stay on for another week or two to finish cataloguing and packing all the material in the finds tent. So here I am… and by the look of the finds tent, I will not be short of something to do. Now I think it's my turn again to ask a question."

"Er, yes, but I wonder if it might wait. I need to get some photos of my site while the sun is overhead. If I do not go now, it will be too late. You could come with me if you like. There's a good view of the campsite from up there. Might help you get a feel for the place." Without waiting for an answer, Troy, not relishing the prospect of another encounter with the buxom caterer, stood to move off.

We swung past Troy's tent to collect his bag before starting up the hillside path with Troy in the lead. About halfway up, he said over his shoulder. "I know it's a bit of a climb, but the view from up there on that platform is fantastic." I didn't bother to enlighten him, but my present view of the trim taut butt in front of me wasn't too bad either. That wasn't the only bit that was impressive. Tall, with dark blonde hair curling over his ears providing a sharp contrast with his brown eyes, Troy was an impressive specimen. His golden tan spoke of a love of the outdoors… perhaps not surprising for an archaeologist.

At the site, Troy explained the platform hewn out of the hillside was part of the village excavation on the beach. Recorded years ago but not considered significant enough to warrant investigation, Troy's site, thought to be a fort or lookout of some sort, now proved to be a high-class villa.

The sound of laughter floated up from the students below. I moved to the edge to peer down onto the main site on the beach below. "You're right. The view of the bay is breathtaking." I stood for a few moments gazing at the bay. "Is there much archaeology in the bay?"

"Dunno."

"What do you mean, 'dunno'? Hasn't anyone been out there to have a look? With the village so close to the beach, there is bound to be something out there. Don't you go swimming?"

"We've been busy. Nobody has time to go swimming. A couple of the students paddled in the shallows soon after we arrived. They said the water was too cold. Granted, they were not exactly the 'getting wet' kind. What's with you and swimming anyway?"

"Hey, I'm from the land of Oz. We are an island nation with a strong beach culture… you know, surf, sun, sand and all that." I remained at the edge, looking at the bay but seeing nothing. My mind wasn't there. It was revisiting my rather disappointing arrival at the camp. Troy's voice drifted through my thoughts, bringing me back to reality. "Sorry, did you say something?"

"Welcome back to earth. Why so glum? I thought you were impressed with the view."

"No… I mean, yes I am. I was thinking about something else."

"Can I help? It looked like whatever you were thinking about bothered you, or was a problem in some way."

I weighed up the situation for a few moments before carefully wording my reply. "No, it's not something I need help with, but thanks for the offer. It is just that I was a bit surprised by something today – disappointed, to be honest – and I was going over it in my mind."

"You were disappointed with the site? I wouldn't be surprised if you were. It isn't the most exciting site the field school's ever had. This wasn't the intended site, but it has worked out okay and produced a lot of good material, I believe."

"Aaww, look, I'm thrilled just to have the opportunity to be on a dig site. It hasn't anything to do with the site. It's more about the reception I received on my arrival. Geoff wasn't particularly welcoming. I got the distinct impression that he wasn't too happy about having me lobbed on him unexpectedly."

"I wouldn't read too much into it. It hasn't been a great time for him – a few problems, you know how it goes."

"No, I don't know – and, whatever the problems are, maybe I can help somehow. Maybe that is why I'm here, to help sort it out in some way. I understood he loved taking the undergrads on their field schools. Whatever the reason, he wasn't too pleased to see me today. I don't know whether it is something to do with me, or it's about what's going on here."

"Okay. Yes, he has been a bit prickly. It's not about you. It's about the site. Look, it's a long story. I don't really have the time right now to sit down and tell you about it."

"That's fine, but I need to know what I've walked into. How about at least giving me a clue? What does it matter that it wasn't the intended site"

"If the undergrads hadn't needed somewhere else to go, we wouldn't be here. Theo – Professor Theo Papakostas – suggested this location when asked if he could suggest an alternative site. It doesn't matter if the rookie students don't do a great job on a site if it's less significant. It wasn't a popular choice. Geoff, in particular, didn't want to come here."

"Why not? It seems like a great alternative."

"Ah, that's another long story… a myth, more like."

"You'll have to share that with me sometime. It's going to be hard to proceed effectively if I don't know what's going on." Curiosity aroused, but I accepted I would have to find another opportunity to learn more.

"Uh huh. Well, right now I have to climb further up this hill to find a good spot to take overhead shots of my site. If I don't do it now, while the sun is still directly overhead, it will be too late. I will talk to you about it later, but I have to take those photos now."

"…And I have to get to work. That finds tent is a bit overwhelming, and it's not going to get any better if I don't do something. You will tell me about it later… please?"

"Promise."

A brief reply, but I think I believe him. I headed back to the finds tent after watching Troy make the strenuous climb to a position high up and off to one side of the platform from which to take his photos.

The climb proved worthwhile for Troy. He managed some good shots, but the day was hot and sultry, and climbing across the rocks to his new position was exhausting. In the scant shade of a lone gnarled tree somehow managing to survive on the rocky hillside, he sat on a rock for a few minutes to recover.

Time to get back and write more report, he told himself, but looked for any possible procrastination available to delay returning to that task. Deciding to take one last look at the bay before returning to the beach, he climbed to a new vantage point that afforded a view of the entire bay. He stretched his back and, looking out to sea, slowly scanned the bay. His eyes swept past the small cove in the corner of the bay to his left. He caught his breath. Was something there? Had he seen something, or were his eyes playing tricks? Was it just the clouds creating shadows on the water?

"Binoculars!" he shouted to the deserted hillside, and scrambled back to where he had left his bag. It took a bit of scratching around, but eventually he found them – minus their protective lens covers. "Damn, I really must take better care of these in future."

After blowing the dust off the lenses, he picked his way back to his recent vantage point, adjusted the binoculars, and then attempted to steady his hands and control his breathing before using the binoculars. Only after a few deep breaths, did he again feel sufficiently composed to scan the cove.

"Yes! Yes," he yelped, and snatched the binoculars away from his eyes to rest them a moment before looking again.

No, he hadn't imagined it. He was quite sure he could see something. Although it was hard to tell from up there, its lines suggested that whatever that 'something' was, it was manmade. Convinced he was fully rational and had not imagined the object in the cove, he shouldered his bag, carefully picked his way back down to the platform, and then, ignoring caution, raced down the treacherous path back to the main site.

What to do first? Should he tell Geoff about it at this stage, or should he wait and investigate a bit further before mentioning it to anyone? He had to admit finding some previously unknown ruin was almost too good to be true. What if it were too good? …Better to investigate further before mentioning it to anyone. From up on the hillside, it was impossible to judge the depth of the water covering the structure, but regardless of the depth, exploring the structure was going to involve getting wet. With that thought in mind, he headed for the finds tent – and somebody who seemed a bit interested in swimming.

"You wanted to go swimming," he shouted as he rushed into the tent. "How soon do you want to go?"

I was standing in the middle of the tent holding a couple of trays of artefacts. A bit taken aback by the question, I was curious about what prompted it. "Er, preferably not right at this moment. I'm a bit busy. What's brought this on?"

"I think I found something – out there in the bay." He waved his arm in general direction of the sea. "We need to take a look."

"Okay, but a bit more explanation would be good. Sounds like it might require more than a bit of swimming. I suppose I should have thought and brought some gear with me."

"What sort of gear? What do you need? We just need to swim out and have a look. All you need are bathers – or something like that to swim in."

"Just bathers? I would think we might need more gear than that. You know: wet suit, mask, fins, tank – just the basics."

"Tank! … You scuba dive?"

"I'm a certified wrecked diver, if that's any use to you."

Troy's heart almost missed a beat. "You scuba dive!" he repeated. Mind in hyperdrive, he took a few paces across the tent, then turned and paced back again.

"We could go across to Timpaki on Friday. Are you interested in coming?" Without waiting for an answer, he ploughed on. "There's a small dive shop there. I've used it before. We could hire scuba gear."

"We probably could do that. Is the gear reliable… and what is Timpaki?"

"His stuff's reliable. He has links with the large dive company over at Rethymnon on the other side of the island. Timpaki is our nearest town, a boat ride away. It's where you caught the boat to come here. Only a small town – 'village' is probably a better description – of about 8000 people. It's a great place. Not so many tourists have discovered it yet. Every Friday there is a farmers' market in the town square. Some of the caterers take our boat across each week for fresh produce from the market. We could hitch a ride with them this Friday. In the meantime, I'll contact Niko and get him to organise all the gear beforehand and have it ready for us to collect."

"Sounds tempting, but when am I supposed to get all of this work done?" I indicated the contents of the finds tent with a sweep of my arm.

Troy's reply had a somewhat condescending note. "I'm not unfamiliar with cataloguing. I'll give you a hand with it. We could take some time during the day to dive, and then catalogue in the evenings after dinner to make up for lost time."

I produced my best pout. "Great, I've only been here five minutes and already you're expecting me to work overtime."

"Well, you wanted to go swimming. Anyway, someone always was going to have to give you a hand with this lot. There is no way you can get through all of this on your own in the time allocated. I don't know who, but they'll have to find someone to help."

"That would be you. I know you still have not read your emails, but here is a sneak preview of one of them. You are my supervisor for this practical project, which means you and I are going to be working very hard on cataloguing and packing, and that will continue well after all the students leave."

"What? Oh God, I wonder what else is in those emails I haven't read. Maybe we should make some time over dinner tonight to go through this whole thing. Dinner is available from 6:30." We agreed to meet at seven o'clock. I went back to work. He went to read his emails.

Troy had secured a table when I arrived at the mess tent. Over dinner, we agreed lists of diving gear required, and plans of how to deal with the artefacts in the finds tent in between all the diving. The rest of our conversation covered a wide range of topics but, towards the end, Troy's fantasising about what we might find out in the bay dominated. I intended to go back to the finds tent after dinner, but our discussions went late. I decided there was a lot to recommend an early night. I hadn't unpacked or set up my tent since arriving. By the time my tent was reasonably habitable, it was no longer an early night.

It was late, but I wrote myself a note. I need to talk to Geoff Featherstone about the artefacts. It seems some items were to go to

York University – no indication of which or how many. Nothing to indicate what happens to the rest of the finds. I imagine they stay here on Crete. I need that confirmed though, as it affects how it all gets packed.

It had been a long and full day. I slept very soundly that night.

Chapter 2

Thursday morning saw me in the finds tent well before breakfast. It was cool, the air fresh off the sea as I walked to the tent. There is something radically wrong with spending time in a tent when such a beautiful day is on offer outside. I managed a couple of hours' work before my stomach and fuzzy head alerted me to the fact that I needed food and coffee.

The rest of the day passed swiftly. Troy dropped in around mid-morning. Our dive gear and the trip to Timpaki were organised. We had coffee together before getting on with our own work. By the time lunch was available, I had made good progress but it was only a drop in the ocean compared to the overall task. Lunchtime provided what I thought would be an ideal opportunity to talk to Geoff Featherstone, but he had left the mess tent by the time I arrived. Mental note to self: catch up with Geoff somehow this afternoon and before I deal with too many more artefacts.

Troy came to work in the finds tent after lunch. Despite his mind being elsewhere on occasions, work flowed smoothly until late in the day. While some light remained, we decided it might be worthwhile taking a stroll down the long beach to investigate access to the cove where Troy's 'mystery structure' was located. At about six o'clock, we stopped work. The pile of completed work increased considerably with the two of us involved. The sand was quite firm underfoot as we made the longish walk to the cove.

There was an ideal spot close to our objective from which to enter the water. Nothing likely to cause us difficulties with that detected, and a quick look at the area, failed to find any inherent problems likely to cause difficulties once we were in the water. Satisfied with our findings, we strolled back and sat on the beach in front of the camp. The sand retained some of the sun's warmth, offsetting the cool breeze coming in from the bay. A pleasant interlude spent mainly in silence, it ended all too soon. If we remained there any longer, we ran the risk of missing dinner.

I caught up with Geoff Featherstone on his way out of the mess tent as we walked in. We found a table and Geoff waited at it while we got our meals – just in case they closed the kitchen before we finished speaking with Geoff. Our conversation wasn't fruitful. He had no information on the allocation of artefacts but would chase up the information I needed.

After he left, Troy and I discussed tomorrow's trip to Timpaki. It meant an early start. The caterers liked to be there for the first pick of the produce when the market opened. I was looking forward to spending a few hours there just looking around. All I remembered seeing as I arrived on the bus were a few orchards bordering the approaches to the town. Although feeling guilty about the trip, the opportunity to see a bit more of Crete was exciting.

We said goodnight and I went to my tent to prepare a backpack for tomorrow's trip: camera, bottled water, sunscreen and my purse. I thought I was too excited to sleep well. I was wrong. It was only thanks to my alarm that I was up and ready to go on time the next morning.

*****

Two catering staff and the pair of us were on board for the pleasant early morning boat ride to Timpaki. After agreeing to meet back at the boat at two o'clock, Troy and I set off to explore the town centre where local farmers were setting up their stalls in the *pazari,* the open-air market in the centre of town. First port of call on our way past was Niko's dive shop. Our gear was waiting for us. We arranged to collect it after lunch when we were on our way back to the boat. Then it was time for some serious sightseeing. Troy knew the place well, having visited a couple of times during the dig and from previously having holidayed here. He proved an excellent guide.

Orange trees dotted the length of the street and grape vines hung from houses. The town was a mix of buildings: some nice newer looking ones amongst very old ones. Sadly, there were also old concrete buildings, in ruins and covered in graffiti. We toured the town for a couple of hours before arriving back in the town centre. The main street was now chaos. Troy explained it was part of the main east-west route across the southern part of the island and subject to heavy traffic during the day.

We lingered as long as decorum allowed in a coffee shop and later treated ourselves to a long lunch at a tavern to fill in time before returning to the boat. While idling away time over lunch, I again brought up the subject of Geoff's less than warm welcome, and Troy's promise to tell me the story about the site, which he thought to be a contributing factor.

"Yes, I will tell you about it – when we get a moment alone. It is a bit of a long story, but it's not one to share in a public place. Don't let it concern you. It's not important, but it might help you understand Geoff's current frame of mind." It was clear I would get nothing more at that time and place.

As we made our way towards the dive shop, I spotted the two catering staff pushing a trolley loaded with boxes of produce. Everything in the market looked so fresh: tomatoes, cucumbers, lettuce, artichokes, melons, citrus fruit, olives, homemade cheeses and breads. We carried on past the dive shop and towards the boat where we caught up with the caterers as they finished loading their purchases onto the boat. After solemnly promising to return it to its owner, we relieved them of their trolley and used it to transport the dive gear to the boat. The trolley's owner gave us a curious look when we returned his property but didn't question its return.

Then, it was time to go. The long lunch, coupled with the wind in my hair and the briny smell of the ocean had me decidedly drowsy by the time we arrived back at camp. After stowing the dive gear, I clocked off for the day and took a nap.

I was amongst the first diners to arrive for dinner. Alone at a small table, I wasted no time despatching my meal. Afterwards, feeling invigorated and more motivated, I went to work in the finds tent. About half an hour later, Troy wandered in.

"Good minds thinking alike," he commented as he set himself up on the next bench. "If we get a bit done tonight and make an early start on it in the morning, we could go for a dive tomorrow afternoon."

I nodded in agreement. "My only concern with that proposal is the prospect of lugging the dive gear all the way along the beach to the dive site. It is a solid walk without being loaded up with the dive gear – not to mention a weight belt thrown in to add to the pain."

He replied smugly, tapping the side of his nose, "Leave it to me. I have it all under control," but didn't elaborate further. We worked until 9.00pm. Tomorrow would be another early morning start.

My clock woke me for the five o'clock start. I began sluggishly but persevered until about six o'clock, before abandoning work in favour of breakfast. The rest of the camp was barely stirring by the time I had eaten and was on my way back to the finds tent. Troy fronted up around seven o'clock. Mid-morning, Troy fetched coffees and we sat sipping them outside in the morning sunshine. As we enjoyed the coffee, a thought occurred to me. The pleasant mind-in-neutral break had allowed an exciting realisation to work its way to the fore. "Thank goodness the volume of new finds is diminishing. They should stop coming altogether by the middle of next week when the students start to depart. I believe the first contingent of students leaves for home early next week, and the remainder will be gone by the end of the week."

"Just as well, we've got more than enough to keep us busy, and I want to establish as soon as possible what is hiding in that cove. Once I can tell people what we've found, I'll be in a position to negotiate a longer stay on Crete to fully investigate whatever it is."

I understood why he wanted to extend his stay, but what lay out there could turn out to be nothing at all. However, I agreed there was merit in determining the nature of the object as soon as possible. If it turned out to be of no interest, we could get back to full-time cataloguing and packing without trying to fit in dives as well. The arrangement was to work until three o'clock, but I worked on alone after Troy disappeared around two o'clock. He reappeared about half an hour later, dragging a large trailer-like trolley loaded with our dive gear.

"Well, come on. You had better get changed if we are going diving," he commanded.

With my wet suit now packed on the trolley with the rest of our gear, I slipped a long shirt over my bathers before joining Troy and his trailer waiting outside the finds tent. "Where on earth did you find this thing?" I asked, indicating the trolley.

"Two of them came with all the camp gear. Designed for use on the beach, they transhipped all our equipment from boat to campsite and, eventually when we leave, they'll transport it – as well as all the crates of artefacts – back across the beach to the boat. They're easy to move."

I had some doubts about his last comment. Its oversized balloon tyres suggested the trailer shouldn't sink too far into the sand, but the wide handle on the end of the drawbar suggested moving it required 'two-men' power... and one of those 'men' was going to be me. I consoled myself with the thought that the trolley probably was better than having to carry everything ourselves. I was right. In spite of the big tyres, it was hard going. We both felt the effects of our exertions by the time we reached the end of the beach.

An ancient rock fall effectively separated our part of the beach from the cove on the other side. The jumble of large rocks gradually decreased in height as it neared the water, but stretched across the full width of the beach, halting the trolley's progress. I struggled into my wet suit.

"Hope you're feeling fit," Troy commented. "From here on we have to carry everything and that will be a challenge as we climb over those rocks."

"Eh? What are you on about? Who is going to be climbing over rocks?"

"Well, that would be us, if we're going to dive in the cove."

"You might, but I'm not."

"Oh, I see. With your superhuman powers you'll fly over the rocks.

"No, but I am going to put my gear on here and *swim* round the end of the rock fall and into the cove. All this stuff is much lighter to move if you are wearing it, and in the water."

Troy blinked at me a couple of times, and then laughed. "Okay, good thinking, Sherlock. Chalk one up to you."

The rock fall extended about four metres out into the bay. Its height decreased along its length until, at its extremity, there were only the tops of rocks poking through the sand. Our wet suits kept us comfortable in the cool water as we swam. We swam out around the end of the rock divide and up to a point on the cove's beach that Troy estimated was where the land end of his mysterious object should be. Only a slight undulation on the beach indicated where the mysterious object might be, any more definite trace of it obliterated by sand over the centuries. After agreeing a plan, we swam out, found the side of the 'thing' and swam along its length to get an idea of its size and composition.

It was a rock construction of considerable size now heavily encrusted with marine growth. Much longer than I imaged, it contin-ued well out into the bay. Towards its extremity, there was evidence of some cataclysmic event at some time in the distant past. A crack cleft the width of the object about four or five metres from its tip, leaving a gaping chasm at the top while the lower section remained intact – a bit like a green stick fracture. The bottom of the chasm had filled with marine growths over what must have been some considerable time. Similar growths also clustered in places along its sides.

I swam to the end of the structure and then across its width. Troy took a shortcut, swam through the break – somehow managing to avoid scraping himself on the coral – and waited for me on the other side. We surfaced, looked around, saw daylight was fading, and swam back to the beach. As our aim was to investigate the structure, I paid scant attention to the seabed, but a few lumps encrusted with marine growth managed to catch my eye as I swam over them.

We shed our gear and sat on the sand to review the dive. Troy's excitement level was almost off the chart. He could hardly contain himself as we discussed the find, his words running together to result in a collection of unfinished sentences. The size of the structure and the logistics of its construction amazed me.

"So you agree that it is definitely manmade?" Troy asked excitedly.

"I don't think there can be any doubt. I know you've had the camera working overtime, but maybe we need to make notes while everything is still fresh in our minds."

"You're right. We need to record our observations. I don't know about yours, but my wetsuit doesn't have a waterproof pocket for carrying a notebook and pencil."

"Funny that. Mine doesn't either. However, I do have one in my bag – which is on the trolley."

"…Which is on the other side of the rocks. I feel even less like climbing over those rocks now than I did before but, we have to go back to camp sometime, so I suppose we better get on with it."

"Off you go. Me? I'm going back the way I came: swimming. That way, I'll only carry the gear from the water to the trolley."

Troy gave me a sheepish grin. "I knew I brought you along for a reason. I like lateral thinkers."

As we sat amongst our gear on the trolley, we recorded details of the structure, starting with its estimated dimensions. Once he got started, Troy just stared out to sea and rattled off his observations while I wrote frantically to keep up. By the time he was finished, it was time to head back to camp for dinner. The prospect of dragging the laden trolley back up the beach was a bit daunting after expending so much energy on swimming. As we came down the beach earlier, I noticed a small cave, or grotto or some sort, a short distance back along the beach from the rock fall. I suggested we have a look at it and, if it was okay, we store our dive gear there instead of dragging it back to camp every day. Troy didn't take much persuading.

With our meagre remaining energy supply, we hauled the trolley about thirty metres back along the beach to the cave. It was larger than I imagined. We had to duck to enter it but, internally its roof was well above our heads. Inside, there was room for the two of us to move around freely, and space at the rear to store our gear safely.

The downside was that we couldn't rinse the gear in fresh water after our dive. We agreed it wouldn't hurt for a couple of days. After that, we would need a better way of transporting it up and down the beach.

We walked back to camp in comparative silence, each lost in our own thoughts. When we arrived at the mess tent, most of the students had eaten, so there were plenty of seats available. We settled at a large unoccupied table. Geoff Featherstone, on his way out, came over to join us and asked if we had dived today.

"I'm pleased to see some diving happening. While we've done all we can here on the beach, it would seem a bit remiss of us to leave without exploring the bay," Geoff explained.

"It's all her fault," Troy said jerking his thumb in my direction. "She's been on about going swimming, so I caved in and we hired some dive gear. Although, why she would want to go and find more artefacts out there beats me. We have more than enough cataloguing to do now."

We all laughed, and Geoff got up to leave. He took a few paces then turned and said, "Seriously, if you find anything of interest out there that adds to the story we've been building up of the village here on the beach, you will let me know won't you?" With feigned enthusiasm, we nodded our agreement. There was no way Troy would mention yet what we were investigating. Besides, it might not have anything to do with Geoff's village on this beach.

Somehow, the enthusiasm for spending time cataloguing after dinner seemed to have evaporated. Troy voiced the same feeling. "I don't think I can get my head around cataloguing this evening. I know it is important, but my mind is elsewhere at the moment. I think we need to talk about what we discovered this afternoon and work out a plan for how to proceed. Are you in a hurry to rush off, or are you available for a chat?"

It was getting late and most of the students already had turned for the night. Even so, the beach appealed as a quiet place to sit undisturbed for our chat. I agreed and grabbed my pocket recorder as we passed the finds tent on our way to the beach. It was a balmy night with a clear sky. The sea breeze was now quite cool and had strengthened, but the sand was warm. We sat at the base of one of the two scrubby-topped low dunes that hid and protected the campsite, and soaked up the ambience.

As we sat soaking up those first few moments of blissful silence, the wind lifted and tugged at my hair. When I turned to look in the direction of the cove, it blew a few wayward strands across my cheek.

21

I brushed them back into place and felt that my usual reasonably tamed hairdo had become completely unruly. My normally constrained waves that owed their obedience to a hairdresser's skill with scissors were now wild springy corkscrew curls sprouting at every angle from my scalp. I consoled myself with the thought that this was Crete. Perhaps I am to endure some wild Medusa-like curse… or maybe I simply need a haircut. I tried patting them into place, but they had a mind of their own, and the wind wasn't helping.

I realised Troy had been speaking. So preoccupied was I with my unruly mop, I hadn't heard a word he said. I turned to face him, catching only the last few words of his conversation. It was obvious he expected a response to whatever he had said. I prepared to launch into an apology for not listening until something out in the bay caught my eye.

"Troy, did you see that light out there?"

"What light – where? I don't see any light."

"Hang on a minute. I'm sure there is something out there. Look! There it is." I pointed out across the bay. "Must be a boat swinging at anchor. The light is only visible when it swings around to the right way to be seen from here."

"Yeah, I see it now. You're right; it is a boat. That's interesting. Nobody usually anchors here at night. Although, now that I think about it, when I was a bit out of sorts a couple of weeks ago, I came and sat here. I reckon there was a boat anchored out there then. I had other things on my mind and didn't take much notice of it at the time."

Dive planning abandoned, we watched the boat swinging at anchor for quite a while. At first glance, this was a relatively sheltered bay and seemingly a good place to anchor for the night. There were a couple of things wrong with that assumption. Firstly, we normally didn't see boats this close in, and certainly not at night, because it wasn't too much further to Timpaki, which offered boaties good facilities. Apart from that, the waters at the entrance to the bay become treacherous when tide and wind are opposed to one another.

Although it had been a long day and tomorrow would bring another early start on cataloguing, we continued to watch and speculate about the boat. Idle chat filled in time. I took the opportunity again to pursue Troy's promise to tell me about the site.

"It goes back to a few years ago. Two issues occupied the university hierarchy's thinking. There was growing concern over indications that some of our regular field school sites would become unavailable to us due to prevailing circumstances in their surrounding localities.

That included sites in our own country. The other issue was a new initiative that some professor dreamed up. He suggested that, almost as a special treat, the university could send an unsupervised post-graduate group to excavate some less significant site. The student group would have to plan the whole excavation from scratch."

"Some treat. I wouldn't have minded something like that when I was a student. What motivated this thinking?"

"The argument was that post-grad students about to finish their degrees would be tested on a real site without the benefit of a supervisor to guide them. It also provided an opportunity for the university to increase student's job-readiness before tossing them out into the real world. This 'treat' would become an annual event offered to only a select small group of exceptional students. After much deliberation, they came up with a single approach that would address both issues at the same time." I nodded and waited while Troy mentally composed the next bit of the story.

"A number of potential alternative dig sites were identified as suitable for either field schools and/or post-grad groups. The university had appointed a new Associate Professor. Giles Berwick, a new young academic recently engaged by the university, although already on staff, didn't have any teaching commitments until the following term. To give him something to do in the interim, they sent him out to investigate and report on the various potential sites, including this site on Crete. Everything went according to plan until he came here to this place. Normal protocol does not allow anyone to undertake fieldwork unaccompanied. Giles' assessment trips fell under the classification of fieldwork. At the time, he was the only one available to undertake the trips. It wasn't considered dangerous – he wasn't excavating – so he was sent out alone."

"I suspect the moral of this story is something like: if you break the rules, shit happens," I murmured.

"Yeah, you're not too far off the mark. Giles only had a couple of sites left to inspect. Everything had gone well. There hadn't been any problems... until his trip to Crete. His round trip (including travel) to inspect this site was supposed to take ten days. Alarm bells started ringing when he did not return to York after a fortnight. All sorts of searches failed to find any trace of him. His camp here remained intact and undisturbed. A few weeks later, his boat was located smashed up on a rocky beach not too far from here. Rumours were rife."

"That's rubbish! So, there was some sort of boating accident..."

"Possibly... All sorts of stories developed back home after his disappearance, some of them quite fanciful: a lost tribe resenting the intrusion of strangers for example. Not to mention the one involving some graphically imagined wild animal. Nobody actually mentioned a Minotaur, I don't think, but the inference was there. The university came in for considerable criticism for sending Giles out alone, and the circumstances of his disappearance remaining unresolved didn't help. Anyway, the upshot of the whole mystery was that, as far as the university was concerned, this site became taboo."

"I imagine that, ultimately, the university endeavoured to throw a blanket of silence over the whole incident in a bid to quash the rumours."

"That's pretty much what happened. It worked too until this year and the intended field school site suddenly became unavailable. They tried for other sites but, eventually, had to settle for this one. Geoff wasn't happy about it, but they had explored all other options without success. Then one of the students in the cohort for this year's field school somehow got hold of those earlier rumours about the site – and shared her newfound knowledge with the rest of the group. Not surprisingly, the whole group became extremely twitchy about coming here. Some parents pulled their kids out of the field school, even though it could impact on their grading."

"As you say, it was not a surprising reaction."

"Most people don't give the stories any credence. Geoff maintains he doesn't believe the stories, but wasn't happy or entirely comfortable about coming to this site. The students initially being very skittish made his life even more difficult. Most of the students remain nervous about being here, particularly at night. Geoff has run the undergrads' field schools for years and loves it. However, he does see the welfare of all students as his personal responsibility while they are on a dig site. It has been a particularly trying time for Geoff, having to deal with his own uncertainties – if they exist – as well as trying to keep the students calm and focused. To say he has been exceedingly cranky the whole time would be an understatement. The fact that his reception was a little unwelcoming is nothing to do with him or you personally; it's about the site."

We watched the boat in silence while I struggled to accept the gullibility of otherwise intelligent men.

Chapter 3

I was on my way to the finds tent by 5.00am this morning after a night plagued by uncomfortable dreams. I woke myself at a point when the first dream was coming to a situation my psyche couldn't handle. That was a relief but, when I drifted off again, the same dream – or at least the same man in the same boat – was back but in a slightly different scenario this time. Although I wasn't aware of any reaction to Troy's tale last night, apparently its memory lingered on, but without the benefit of any lost tribesmen or wild animals. Morning came as something of a relief.

I reflected on the previous night as I walked past the finds tent and continued down to the beach. No sign of last night's boat. The wind picked up overnight, creating a blanket of whitecaps on the bay. It was not surprising the boat upped anchor and moved on to somewhere more protected. With nothing interesting to delay me, I went back to the finds tent. By 6:30, I definitely needed coffee.

Not many students were about at that hour but, a few minutes after I arrived in the mess tent, Troy came in chatting to a tall, skinny dark haired lad. They went their separate ways: the lad to join other students, Troy to join me. I noticed he looked as bleary-eyed as I felt. "Good morning, and don't you look picture. How long did you stay on the beach last night?"

He groaned. "It was after midnight but I'm not sure exactly what time I left the beach."

"I see the boat is gone this morning. Was it still there when you left the beach last night?"

"Yes. What time did you check on it this morning?"

"Just before five o'clock. Somewhere in that four or five hour window, they moved on. They must've gotten up early; maybe when the swell came up."

"I don't know that they slept at all. There was still a lot of activity on board when I called it a night."

"Fishing, do you think?"

"Maybe, I doubt it though. Somehow it didn't look like they were indulging in any fishing type activity."

Conversation inevitably turned to yesterday's dive. He waffled on about how much more information he needed before he would feel confident enough about revealing his discovery to others. This resulted in more dive planning. A dive today was out of the question and I said so. "I don't think we'll be diving today. The way the wind was whipping up those seas, visibility will be down to zero. Anything else we might do instead of diving?"

"Possibly; I'll have a think about it." Then Troy suddenly harked back to last night's boat. "You know, I'm sure that's the same spot where I saw a boat anchored a couple of weeks ago."

I was surprised anything concerned him more than his underwater structure, but it appears boats anchoring in the bay were an exception. He retreated into his own thoughts – probably about the boats. I went back to work, leaving him sitting at the table with a half-cold cup of coffee. It was a good half hour later before he made an appearance in the finds tent.

Not confident about his commitment or that his mind would be on the job today, I offered him an out. "If you have something else you need to do for your new project or whatever, go and do it. I'll just work on here until three o'clock as originally planned when we had scheduled a dive for today. If there is something else we could do today instead of diving, let me know and I'll be ready."

He opted to stay for a while. "No, I'm fine to work here, but I might disappear sometime during the day for a while. I need to get my head around a few things and start a formal journal, but I'll do that later in the day when I'm more fully awake and a bit more intelligent."

"Oh, so you don't need to be intelligent for my cataloguing?"

"That's not what I meant. You need to think about what you are doing, but cataloguing is largely a routine type activity. It doesn't require creative thinking – which I'm not yet capable of this morning."

I understood. He was supposed to be my supervisor and not actually doing the job with me. I wanted to help with his new project, but I had to get my own work done. The only way that was possible was for us to work together on both tasks. About mid-morning, Troy announced he had other things to do and disappeared. I couldn't object. Not sure what his intentions were for the rest of the day, I was free to make my own arrangements, the first of which was to go for coffee. I stood up, rotated my shoulders and stretched my back. I was about to head to the mess tent when Troy reappeared carrying two mugs. Too windy to sit outside today, we sat at one of the benches in the finds tent.

After agreeing to have lunch together, Troy returned the mugs to the mess tent and went off to write up his project. Despite all the extra-curricular activities, progress on the cataloguing was good, and it was now reasonable to anticipate no further new finds this week.

Rough seas today delayed departure of the first batch of students who would now depart tomorrow, so the mess tent would be crowded again at lunchtime. The nature of our work had kept us separated. As I had been stuck in the finds tent, I had little interaction with the students. Within three or four days, all of them would be gone.

I couldn't help wondering what and who might remain after all the students departed. I mentioned it to Troy. He shrugged, and I could see the question hadn't aroused any interest for him. He was preoccupied again with the structure in the cove.

My stomach rumbled loudly announcing it was lunchtime. I was starving, but we hadn't set a time for lunch before Troy disappeared. I was debating whether to go for lunch or work a little longer, when Troy came into the tent. He announced he had worked out what we would do this afternoon and recommended we discuss it over lunch... now. No second invitation required, I downed tools and followed him out.

By the time we selected our food, the crowd was thinning out and the noise had abated. Eating initially took precedence over conversation until Troy had despatched most of his meal. Not surprisingly perhaps, his conversation focused on diving and his new discovery. He conceded diving was out of the question today, but he had an alternative suggestion. "How about undertaking an assessment of the beach? We could do some physical archaeology."

"Depends what you mean by 'physical archaeology', I want to know what I'm letting myself in for."

"We take a couple of tools over and dig around in the sand to locate the land end of that structure and anything else that we might uncover." Sorting out how we would approach the task and what we required for the job took some time.

Back in the finds tent, I swapped my lightweight runners for sturdy hiking boots and emptied out a backpack in readiness for climb over the rocks. The smaller hand tools went into the backpack. On the dot of 2:30pm, we set off for the cove. I carried the backpack and a shovel, while Troy carried a shovel, probe pole and the theodolite, which came apart and packed into its own duffel-like bag. By inserting an arm through each handle of the duffel, he wore it as a backpack. The climb to the top of the rock fall was moderately difficult, but the descent on the other side was a breeze and we soon found ourselves again on the beach in the cove.

Once on the other side of the rocks, Troy set about probing the depth of the sand and taking levels. I wandered off to inspect the cove side of the rock fall, starting at the water's edge and working my way back across the beach towards the base of the hill. At first, I found nothing of interest, just rocks. Then things got interesting. About halfway across the beach, I came to a mostly buried object that looked incongruous with its surroundings. Down on my haunches, I used my hand to scrape away some sand from around it – should have brought gloves! Not sure what I had found, I was reluctant to say anything until more of the object was uncovered. A few final seconds of vigorous brushing had my pulse racing and my suspicions confirmed. I yelped with excitement.

"Troy come and look at this." I continued removing sand until he arrived.

"What are you doing over here? The thing were looking for is over there. I don't know... What the hell have you got there?"

"Well, I'm not sure. You are the expert. To me, this looks like part of a column, maybe a stone stylobate. Is that what you call the base a column sits on?" Whatever it was, it looked manmade to me.

We agreed it was a stylobate. With the object photographed in situ and a GPS reading recorded, Troy went back to shifting sand at his site and I continued my investigation of the rock fall for anything else manmade-looking. My scrutiny of the rocks identified a couple more possibilities. Not wanting to interrupt Troy continually, I drew arrows in the sand to mark their locations before continuing. At a point that I thought to be the end of the rock fall and the start of the hillside proper, I took a few steps back and carefully scanned up the hillside from the beach to its summit. It proved not to be the actual hillside, but another accumulation of rocks against the base of the hill, probably caused by the same phenomenon as created the rock fall that divided the cove from the rest of the beach.

I hit the jackpot while inspecting the rock fall that formed the 'back wall' of the cove. This area produced a number of the same large cut sandstone blocks as were used in building Troy's mystery structure. Of more interest, was something barely visible under a pile of rubble. My pulse rate stepped up a notch after I trowelled away some sand and confirmed this as a set of steps. Another arrow in the sand. I chose not to call Troy over until after I had taken a closer look at the large blocks.

After scrambling up to one of the blocks, I used a trowel to scape accretion from one side of one of the blocks. Was it just my fanciful notion that there was a carving of some sort on the face of the block? Too excited to continue, I called Troy over to look at it. My voice must have conveyed some urgency. He dropped his shovel and ran to crouch beside me.

"Troy, take a look at what I found on the side of this cut block. It looks important to me."

"Wow, that's a symbol of some sort. I know symbols appear on some blocks in the palace at Knossos. I don't think they ever determined whether they were builder's marks, or whether they had other significance. Here, shoot some photographs while I get the GPS coordinates." I showed him the other cut blocks I hadn't yet looked at and the set of stairs.

We backtracked to anywhere else I had marked with an arrow in the sand to photograph and record the objects and their locations. Then Troy suggested I pick up a shovel and help him. His excavation had exposed the land end of what appeared to be part of the same structure as we swam around yesterday – only the marine encrustation was missing. We worked for only about another half hour after that. It was getting late, so we perched on rocks to review our progress.

"Well, it's been an interesting afternoon. What do we do next?" I asked as I cast my eyes over today's achievements.

"Yeah, it's amazing. If the visibility is okay, we will dive again tomorrow. I'm fairly convinced this is a significant site, and that our main excavation site further up the beach is part of a much bigger complex. We're a long way from being able to prove that yet. The first thing I need to do is contact Professor Theo Papakostas to check if they know anything about this site. The existence of our beach site and my hillside site is well known, but I've never seen anything recorded for this cove. I need to know whether anyone else knows about it. Strictly speaking, we have no authority to excavate here. If it is a completely new site, I'll need to do a number of things, including obtain permission to investigate further."

"Is Professor Theo the bloke to give us that authority?"

"I'm not sure how it works now. It used to be that the Republic of Greece owned the ruins and it would be managed by one of the Ephorates of Prehistoric and Classical Antiquities, and Theo was kind of their man on the ground."

With nothing more we could do at the cove today, we went back to camp and I managed to get in an hour of cataloguing before joining

Troy for dinner. Geoff Featherstone was sitting with students a few tables away. I needed to know how we would play it if he came over to enquire about what we did today.

"Good question; I will discuss it with Geoff before he goes, but I'm not sure when. I think we should see what happens. If he gets curious, I might share something with him... but not much until I know more about the site. If he doesn't ask the right questions, I won't mention it yet."

It became a non-issue. Geoff was still talking to students when we left to do more cataloguing. The strong wind that buffeted everything last night was now a gentle sea breeze accompanied by a beautiful starry sky. After about an hour of cataloguing, Troy stood up and stretched.

"I think I'd rather be outside than cooped up in here. How about we call it a night and sit on the beach for a while?"

There was no argument from me. As we stepped through the low brush windbreak separating the camp from the beach, I grabbed Troy's arm. "I saw a light out there in the bay again. I don't believe in coincidences. The arrival of two boats on two consecutive nights sounds a bit fishy to me," I whispered.

"Maybe boats anchor out there every night and we just aren't aware of them, but I don't believe that for one minute. Let's watch it for a while. I don't know that I can stay up until after midnight again though."

We sat on the sand in the shadow of the windbreak. As with the boat the previous evening, it was difficult to see what was happening on board, as there were no riding lights and only one dim light illuminated the cockpit area. After a few minutes of idly watching the boat swinging at anchor, I broke our easy silence.

"What will it mean for you career-wise, and what happens next, if whatever we find in that cove is confirmed as a new ruins site?"

"I guess it depends on how important the site is. If it is as significant as I think it might be, I'd hope to lead a dig to investigate it more fully. Truth is, I'm hoping that, as soon as I tell people about the site, I'll be approved to stay on here and not have to go back to York when we finish with the stuff in the finds tent. Even if it just gets me a couple of extra weeks to prove it *isn't* a significant site, I'll be happy. Career-wise, it could be just the thing I need." Troy spoke slowly considering each word, and then murmured, not necessarily to me, "Achieving that final goal..."

What final goal? That roused my curiosity, but Troy dismissed it as part of a long boring story of his career. We weren't exactly busy and needed something to keep us awake, so I pressed him further. He finally admitted that his 'final goal' was to rise from being an associate professor to a full-blown professor – and as soon as possible.

"You're still young to become a professor, but I detect a degree of frustration in what you said. I imagine there is a lot more to the story."

"Frustration, yes, you've nailed it there. It's just that this last hurdle is taking longer than anything else I've had to deal with. I guess the gods smiled on me from when I started university. I loved what I was doing, studies went well; I excelled at everything, and ended up leapfrogging quite a few people to make associate professor. Then everything came to a halt. I didn't seem able to progress any further towards achieving that final goal, and became mired down in academia."

"Back home in Oz, achieving what you call that 'final goal' requires completion of a significant body of new work which proves something hitherto unknown. Wouldn't discovery of a new site and uncovering its history constitute 'new work'? If so, I don't think you'll have to wait much longer… but, then what? What will you do after reaching that 'final goal'?"

"Some real archaeology. I need to get out from behind a desk and dig in the dirt somewhere, to get dirty and sweaty. To feel excited and disappointed, and every other emotion in between that goes with working on a dig."

We lapsed into silence again. I understood leaving academia as a professor enhanced his future re-entry to academia if he wanted it. With my gaze fixed on the boat, I mulled over his explanation and thought I detected some unspoken undercurrent. Before I could probe any further, it suddenly occurred to me that, back home, a boat behaving like this usually signified someone was squid fishing or there was a diver working below. I voiced my thought, startling Troy out of his reverie.

"Eh? What are you on about?"

"I'm just saying that, a boat anchored like that at night at home in Queensland, with a light over the side and close to the water like this one has, would be either fishing for squid or had a diver working."

"Squid fishing?"

"Yeah, you know what squid are?" Troy looked at me reproachfully. "Well, if you're fishing for squid at night from a boat, you turn off most of the lights on the boat and hang a single light down close to the water to attract the squid to the surface. However, you do have your riding lights on while you're about it. Then again, somehow I don't think that mob out there is fishing for squid."

"No, I don't think they're interested in squid either. However, I do like your alternative. A diver makes more sense than squid fishing and, if they have a diver over the side at night in these waters, it probably means they're up to no good."

"… And I wonder what sort of 'no good' that might be."

"Don't go there. We have enough on our plate at the moment – not to mention a finds tent full of artefacts to catalogue and crate." That brought us both back to reality, and Troy continued. "I still want to dive tomorrow afternoon but, maybe instead of skiving off to sit on the beach tomorrow night, we might do some cataloguing."

I groaned but it made sense. I was beginning to feel drowsy. A shower and sleep had more appeal than sitting on the beach any longer. Troy acknowledged there wasn't much happening in the bay and agreed I should go, but he would sit for a bit longer. I took my leave.

Chapter 4

I'd been cataloguing for about two hours when Troy joined me. I hadn't realised how late it was, and I was in danger of missing breakfast. I left Troy to it and headed to the mess tent. When I returned, he was making notes on a clipboard and explained that he was trying to calculate how much work there remained to complete.

The story wasn't as bad as I'd expected. Many of the remaining trays only contained a few items each, while some contained only one large item. The downside to it all was that some of the remaining artefacts still required cleaning and/or stabilising before anything else occurred. How much work they required would determine how much longer before we finished. It's not that I dislike cataloguing. It is just that there are so many other more interesting things for us to be doing. I queried his plans for today so I could work out how much time I would have in the tent.

"I'd like another dive this afternoon. I might have more to tell you later. I'm going to disappear a few minutes before ten o'clock. I have arranged a phone call with Professor Theo. It depends on what he has to say about the cove site, but I'm not sure I'll be any wiser after the call. He probably will need to look into it before he can give me any real answers. I think we should keep cataloguing and tentatively plan to slot in a dive at about three o'clock."

No surprises there, so we settled down to our standard routine until Troy left for his ten o'clock call. I was on my way for morning coffee when Troy reappeared. I scanned his face for indication of how the phone call went. No bad news evident there. I said he could give me details of the call over coffee, but it took a little more prodding than that before he shared.

"I'll try to give you the 'executive summary' of my conversation with Theo. As I expected, Professor Theo will do some research before getting back to me. However, he doesn't think there is any previous record of our cove site and that it's probably a new find. He got a bit excited about it, which was pleasing from my point of view, and he thinks whatever is at the cove might well be linked to the field school's excavations and also tie in with my villa up on the hillside."

"That sounds promising. I thought you'd be more excited. Is there something you're not telling me?"

"No, not at all. I'm trying not to get excited until I know if it is a new site. I don't want to get my hopes up, only to have the whole thing end up a massive disappointment."

"I know how important this is in terms of achieving your 'final goal' but, even if it isn't a previously unknown site, what we've uncovered so far must go some way towards helping achieve it. I can't help feeling there's more riding on this than you say. It may well be none of my business and you might not wish to discuss it, but I feel I could contribute better if I understood more of the whole story."

"Now is not the time. There is more, but it's for another time. We need to get on with this cataloguing if we're going diving this afternoon."

Okay, I get the message. While it had not relieved my curiosity at all, Troy left no doubt the conversation was over. While rounding up as much patience as possible to see me through until the next thrilling instalment of Troy's saga, there was nothing to do but to get on with things as planned.

We barely caught the last of the lunch session, and then catalogued until about 2.30pm, when Troy announced we had done enough for the day and it was time to go diving. Minus the trolley this time, we set off, stopping at the small cave on the way to collect our dive gear. Visibility was much improved. Troy focused on the structure, which we tentatively identified as a jetty, while I investigated some of the lumps on the seabed that I suspected might be pottery or other artefacts. We arranged to regroup after about half an hour.

My approach initially was to survey a defined area to establish the dispersal of debris over it. I swam a grid pattern over the area and was surprised at the volume of material on the seabed. Some of it appeared quite large, and I hoped they weren't just rocks. It was hard to tell because of the accretion built up on each 'lump'.

As I scraped sand and sediment away from my first object I chose, I realised it was a piece of pottery. A bit of a rub on the side of it that had been buried in the sand, and its black-and-white scroll patterned glazed surface emerged. However, my efforts stirred up sediment greatly reducing visibility. As the agreed half-hour was almost up, I swam back to the fractured end of the jetty where I was supposed to meet Troy, keeping a lookout for interesting artefacts as I swam.

Something grabbed my arm. I swung around in alarm to face it. It was Troy with his back to the jetty, his tank pressed hard up against its blocks. Maintaining his grip on my arm, he dragged me over beside him. He gestured for us to surface. We bobbed up together. He spat his mouthpiece as we broke the surface and, putting a finger to his lips, signalled me to keep quiet. I looked around frantically to see what might have precipitated this situation. There was nothing obvious. Troy leaned over to whisper in my ear.

"There's a boat back in the bay. I don't know what's going on or if it means anything, but they are a lot earlier than usual."

I opened my mouth to query the fuss. There was a boat in the bay, so what? I didn't get a word out. Troy shook his head at me, indicating I shouldn't speak. He resumed whispering.

"The boat's not the problem as much as the diver they've got working. I don't think it's good for us to be here. We should dive, swim through the fracture to the other side, and then swim towards the beach before surfacing. That way, we won't be seen."

It didn't take me long to realise there was a lot to recommend his suggestion. We dived and swam through to the other side of the jetty, and back towards the beach. When we were about half way back to the beach, we surfaced and hugged the side of the jetty. We remained silent. Couldn't hear anything, but we couldn't see anything either. We swam to the beach. Hidden from view by the rock fall, we shed our gear and, feeling somewhat exposed, made our way across the sand to the base of the rock fall. Tucked in against the rocks, we could see the boat, and hoped they couldn't see this far into the cove. In hushed tones, we discussed our options.

Troy stated the obvious. "I think we're both aware what's going on out there is not quite legal, and I think we're both aware that it's not in our best interest to be seen here right now."

I wasn't arguing, and didn't want to interrupt in case he had some bright ideas to share regarding improving our situation. When he didn't, I felt compelled to offer encouragement. "If that boat follows the usual pattern, we could be stuck here until the wee hours of the morning. I'm not sure I fancy that situation. Any ideas on how we might get back to camp unseen sometime this evening?"

"Not a clue, other than it's obvious any plan we come up with will involve waiting until dark. No ideas beyond that at the moment, but feel free to contribute."

"Totally devoid of inspiration I'm afraid. What I do know is that we're not going to lug all this gear over the rock fall tonight. If that boat looks like it's staying for the evening, we need to get across the rocks and back to camp as quickly – and as invisibly – as possible. We don't want gear slowing us down or clanging on rocks as we climb over this thing. I'm going to check for somewhere amongst the rocks to stash our gear for the night."

Somewhere to hide the gear; initially that seemed a hopeless idea. Then I noticed the size of some of the larger rocks prevented them from packing too tightly together. I was about to abandon my search as a futile endeavour when I noticed something encouraging in the corner where the rock fall turned to head across the rear of the cove. A large overhanging rock created a small gap close to the sand. It was only a small niche but, after judicious removal of sand, I was confident it would hold most of our gear. A short distance away and the little higher up, another crevice would hold our weight belts.

Troy maintained a vigil from the top of the rock fall while I dealt with the gear. It took me several trips and quite a while to move and stow all the dive gear. By the time it was hidden, light was fading fast. The surrounding hills meant nightfall came early to the bay, and it would soon be dark enough for us to risk making a run for camp. We still wore our dark wetsuits. I hoped these would make us less visible once we were out in the open.

While waiting for darkness, mind in neutral, I sat on a rock and stretched my legs, figuring I would need them to be cooperative when it came time to climb the rocks and make a dash up the beach. I didn't realise how dark it had become until Troy's soft call brought me back to reality. "I think it's time to make a run for it. If you're right to go, scramble up here beside me."

The rocks were warm and a couple of them were sharp. I joined Troy. After a quick check of the bay, we made our way down the other side of the rockfall. Something fast moving is likely to attract attention. We exercised maximum willpower and resisted temptation to rush. Once back on the sand on the other side, we tucked ourselves in close to the rocks and slowly made our way across the beach away from the water. The intention was to follow the rocks around, blending in with their shadows. Our slow progress was nerve wracking.

After we 'turned the corner' and started along the base of the hill back towards the campsite, we heard an engine roar into life. We froze, plastered ourselves hard against the rocks and waited. There seemed to be something happening on board the boat. They were messing about. Although the engine was running, the boat didn't move off. Then it swung towards the beach and began to move – towards us.

"The cave," I hissed at Troy. "Run!"

No further invitation required. The pair of us set off at a flat gallop while staying as close as possible to the rocky hillside. We threw ourselves headlong into the cave where we stored our gear after the first dive, and stood there, hearts hammering, waiting for whatever was going to happen next. Was the sound of the engine getting louder, or was I imagining it?

Then, in the blackness of the cave, I detected a movement. It was a shape crossing the cave opening. I drew a relieved breath as I recognised Troy silhouetted in the pale moonlight as he moved around near the mouth of the cave. After standing there for a moment, he beckoned me to join him. He leant in close and whispered, "It has turned out to sea. I think it's leaving."

"I thought it was coming this way."

"It was initially, but it didn't come in very far. I think it might have been picking up something – maybe a marker buoy or something. They didn't seem to have much idea of what they were doing."

Still unconvinced no further danger waited for us outside, we cautiously moved out of the cave. The boat had left and was now rounding the point to take it completely out of the bay. Troy checked his watch.

"You know, if we run, we might just get to camp in time to get changed and have something to eat before the kitchen closes."

No further incentive required. "Get a move on, I'm right behind you."

Back in my tent, I peeled off the wetsuit, threw on shirt and shorts over my bathers and slipped into a pair of sandals, before jogging to the mess tent. We just squeaked in before they closed down for the evening. There was little left for us to choose from, but it was food; it was hot, and we were hungry. Although we were alone in the tent, we ate in silence, both of us struggling to regain some semblance of normality after our earlier escapade. I eventually broke the silence. "What are your thoughts on today's efforts? I know we spent a lot of time on unintentional things, but did the dive prove worthwhile for you?"

"Oh yes, I confirmed a few things. I don't think we wasted time even though we didn't spend much time in the water. What about your survey of the seabed, is it worth following up?"

"Definitely; there's a lot strewn around that area. Some of it is quite small – probably pottery – but there are also some larger lumps. They could be rocks, but a couple of them seemed to have definite shape. I dug out a small piece close to the beach. It was pottery with a fair amount of accretion on it, except for the part buried in the sand. I'm no expert, but I think the decoration on the pot might be Minoan. It is made of reddish clay and has a black and white glaze in a continuous scroll pattern."

"It sounds Minoan. That sort of stuff is useful in dating activity at the site. We'll also compare it with pottery found at the school's site. It sounds like we might need to schedule a bit more diving."

"If we are going to do more diving, I will investigate a selection of that stuff on the seabed." We agreed: definitely more diving required.

My mind kept returning to the boats. "What's your take on those boats?" I asked. "We agree they are up to no good. The big question for me is, what sort of no good? I suppose it could be any of a number of things: drugs, artefacts, even arms in this part of the Aegean."

"It could be any of those things. I'm inclined to lean towards the illicit artefact trade. It's an ideal spot for smuggling artefacts from around this region. The bay normally is deserted and our camp isn't exactly conspicuous tucked away behind that dune and the natural scrubby windbreak. I'm still waiting to hear from Theo about our site. I was hoping he would give me a call, but he might send an email instead. If there's nothing from him by tomorrow lunchtime, I'll give him a call… and have a chat about the boats as well."

A bit low on energy, we lingered chatting over dinner. That is, until a stern faced female rudely interrupted us when she marched up to our table and demanded to know how much longer we thought we might be. "We really would like to get finished up for the night. It is now past our knockoff time," she informed us. "It's not a social centre you know. You can't just come in here late and then expect to spend half the night sitting here yapping. It's a mess tent – where you come to *eat.*"

We acknowledged she had a point, and was justified in feeling a bit put out. After piling everything onto our trays and carrying them across to the counter for her, we hurriedly exited tent. Troy chuckled. "That's two of the delicate petals in the catering corps I've upset in the last week. I'll have to up my game or I'll find myself banned from the tent and being given my meals in a paper bag."

It occurred to me that I didn't know what the caterers' contract covered, and I asked Troy whether they would disappear with the last of the students. He hesitated for a while before answering.

"That's an interesting question, particularly as we'll still be here for another couple of weeks after everyone else has gone. Maybe we better have a talk to Geoff about how 'independent' we're expected to be for that extra time we're here, and how that's all going to work."

I planned an early night but sleep eluded me. I knew I needed to write up notes on today's discoveries, so propped up in bed with my notebook, I started writing – and midnight snuck up on me. Despite being tired, there ensued a restless night dogged by vivid dreams. In a similar way to those of the previous night, they were not exactly nightmares, but bad enough again to leave me feeling unsettled next morning. As a result, the sun had well and truly made its way over the bay this morning by the time I felt sufficiently human to tackle breakfast.

It was some consolation to find Troy already in the mess tent and looking worse than I felt. I joined him at his table. He eyed off my tray as I set it down.

"Two cups of coffee... I see you're feeling bright and chirpy this morning as well," he commented. He too had been writing up his notes until early morning.

"So, what do we two impressive specimens have on our agenda for today? Did you get anything from Theo yet?"

"No, nothing yet. As soon as it gets to a civilised hour, I'll give him a call. Maybe after that, we'll have a better idea of what to do this afternoon. In the meantime, we'll carry on cataloguing."

"I'll head over to the tent now. The thought of overstaying my welcome and upsetting the catering staff again terrifies me."

It felt like swimming through treacle all morning as I plodded on with the cataloguing. Troy was missing for the best part of an hour after I left the mess tent. When he arrived, he was grinning broadly.

He tried calling Theo. He wasn't available, but his assistant said Theo wanted to talk to Troy, so Troy made an appointment to call Theo at ten o'clock. He certainly had perked up at the prospect of speaking with Theo. I guessed there might be disruption to the rest of the day after Troy made his phone call, so I suggested we apply ourselves vigorously to getting as much cataloguing done as possible beforehand.

In line with his arrangement, Troy left just before ten o'clock to make his call. Neither of us had any idea how long it was likely to take. After he left, I found it difficult to settle down to cataloguing.

I gave up and turned my attention to packing catalogued artefacts into crates ready for transport. The last crate sealed up, I checked my watch. Troy had been gone for the best part of an hour. Should I start cataloguing another tray's contents? To hell with it, I'm going to get coffee. Then, if Troy is still missing, I'm off to find him.

I couldn't stand it. Curiosity overcame patience, and I skolled the last of my coffee. Would Troy still be in his tent? I didn't know where else to look. On my way to his tent, I saw him entering the finds tent. I did an about-face and, with more than a little trepidation, followed him to the tent.

Chapter 5

"There you are. I was beginning wonder if the news was so bad you'd gone to thrown yourself off a cliff or something."

"Not today; I have been busy."

"Well, come on; Share!"

"Okay, okay; maybe I'll start with the most interesting bit of news. Professor Theo will be here late this afternoon. He's bringing someone with him – female I think. He wanted to make sure there would be beds available for both of them for one or two nights."

I looked at him eagerly, willing him to continue.

"I didn't think there'd be a problem as many of the students have gone and there are empty tents. As the bloke in charge of the camp, I had to square it with Geoff first, so I said I'd email Theo confirmation of the availability of accommodation. Then I went to find Geoff. He was busy with a couple of students and wasn't too happy about being interrupted, but I needed his okay so I could email Theo."

"Was he okay about it? It must have been difficult to do without actually telling him why Theo was coming."

"Yeah, I was a bit nervous about it, but Geoff was okay about Professor Theo coming. They're good mates and Theo, as the liaison person with the Ephorate of Prehistoric and Classical Antiquities, has every right to come and inspect what's been happening here. But he did want to know why I'd been talking to Theo and why Theo suddenly decided to visit."

"I suspect this does not bode well for our next meeting with Geoff."

"Nah, I think it'll be all right. I put him off by saying I could see he was busy and it was a long story. I arranged for us to meet at 12:30 in the mess tent so we could go over everything with him."

"Hey, what's this *we* business? This is your extra-curricular project. What could I possible say that you couldn't tell him?"

"Look, Theo's visit is about more than just the new site. I suspect we are going to get involved in more than we bargained for, and that this whole thing is going to take on *Ben Hur* proportions."

"That's very enigmatic of you. What did he say about the cove?"

"Didn't I say? Well yeah, it is a completely new site. It's previously unrecorded. He's a bit excited about what this might mean in terms of the whole bay, and wants the cove site investigated further."

"It looks like you better talk to your people quickly if you want to be a part of the next big thing… and before they hear about it from someone else."

"That's what the meeting with Geoff is about. It will start that process. Then, after we talk to Theo, I'll email my supervisor. It could turn into a busy afternoon. Maybe I'm in for another late night."

After a detailed account of his conversation with Theo, we spent the rest of the morning getting our facts straight in readiness for our lunchtime meeting with Geoff. We went for lunch at noon so we could eat before our meeting. Our thinking being that, depending on Geoff's mood, we might not feel much like eating after the meeting. As it was, nervous anticipation – or maybe dread – had set in and we barely picked at our meals.

Geoff arrived early too, but students bailed him up as he entered the tent, delaying our meeting a little. Troy and I whiled away the time planning our afternoon's agenda.

"We'll have to collect our dive gear. It probably would be good if we did that before Theo arrives," I suggested. "I don't much fancy lugging all that stuff back, but I don't particularly want to drag that trolley up there again either."

"I imagine Geoff will want to have a look before Theo gets here. If he does, we should go as soon as we finish lunch, show him round, and then bring the gear back. I thought that, instead of carrying it back, we could put it on and swim it all the way back to camp. That way, we would only have to carry it up the beach and into the camp. Geoff could walk back from the cove by himself."

I liked that idea. It wasn't a long swim, and much better than carrying the gear. It depended on what time Theo arrived, whether we took him to the cove this afternoon or left it until tomorrow. Geoff seemed in a reasonable mood when he joined us at the table. My apprehension lessened a bit. He got straight down to business and wanted to know about Troy's discovery right from his first sighting of the structure. Troy took a moment to marshal his thoughts. I spoke before he had a chance to begin.

"Geoff, do you want to have this meeting here in the mess tent?"

"Yes, there's nowhere else where we can sit and talk. Is there a problem?"

"No... well, yes, maybe. Look, Troy and I already have run afoul of the catering staff a couple of times for overstaying our welcome. We're a bit cautious about incurring another black mark. We could sit at one of the benches over in the finds tent. It's probably not as comfortable as here, but there is less likelihood of one of the catering staff wanting to throw us out."

"Ah, I see. That's not a problem. I'll fix it." With that, he went across to the food counter where the staff were busy cleaning up, and spoke briefly with one of them before returning to our table. "Problem fixed," he announced. "We can stay as long as we like. Now Troy, tell me the story."

Troy began his report, starting with having seen what we now believed to be a jetty from his excavation site up on the hillside. He chronicled everything that occurred up until last night, and concluded by stressing that there hadn't been much work done there yet, and the whole site remained largely a mystery. Geoff saved his questions until Troy finished. We had no answers for most of them, but Troy had his journal, including a rough sketch of the area, and these helped somewhat.

Then it was my turn. I didn't have much to add to what Troy said. The only information I had to offer was about my preliminary survey of the seabed in the area around the jetty. I explained about the variation in size of what I believed to be artefacts that littered the area, but couldn't offer much more than that.

As anticipated, Geoff wanted to see the cove before Theo arrived. No surprises there. He would want to appear as well informed as possible later when discussing the site with Theo. We explained about going to recover the dive gear, and he suggested we go straight away. Geoff left us for a few minutes to attend to something before we headed off, leaving Troy and I waiting for him outside the finds tent.

"Ahem, I notice we didn't mention anything about seeing boats in the bay. Are we going to maintain that stance?" I asked casually as we waited.

"Correct. When I spoke to Theo about the boats, he was emphatic about not mentioning it to anyone. I specifically asked about Geoff, knowing that we were going to be briefing him on the cove site. Theo was adamant 'not even Geoff', adding that he would explain later. I know it all sounds a bit cloak and dagger but, at this stage, I'm prepared to go along with Theo's request. Geoff only has a couple more days here anyway, so I don't see much point in getting him involved."

It occurred to us that, if we were going to swim the gear back, we needed to suit up. We jogged back to our respective tents and I struggled into my wet suit. I was a bit sweaty after jogging back to the tent and the suit proved predictably uncooperative when I tried to get it on in a hurry. I won out in the end, and walked briskly back to the finds tent to find Geoff and Troy waiting for me. There was little conversation either during the walk to the rock fall or as, in single file, we followed Troy over the rocks and onto the beach in the cove.

I sat on a rock and watched Troy wildly waving his arms about, reminiscent of an flight attendant going through inflight safety procedures, as he explained the jetty and site to Geoff. My eyes roamed over Troy as he went through his routine with Geoff. I couldn't help admire yet again my fit muscular supervisor who I suspected owed at least some of his looks to many hours in the gym. My mind was wandering into dangerous territory. I brought myself back to reality. I was not some giddy teenager looking for a holiday romance. I jumped down from my rock and wandered over to join the two men. Then, together we walked Geoff around the rocks, pointing out the identified manmade features and retrieving our dive gear as we went. After explaining to Geoff that we were going to swim back, I had a request of him. "I know we're being a bit inhospitable making you walk back on your own, but could I impose on you a little more?"

"Depends what it is." He was grinning so I felt game enough to ask.

"There's a piece pottery that I looked at yesterday. It's in close to shore, so it wouldn't take much to retrieve it. I was wondering if you'd carry it back for me."

"Y-e-s, but how big is it?"

"Not too big, sort of about Krater size." I waited for an objection, but he simply motioned for me to bring it to him. I snorkelled out and retrieved it. As I handed it to Geoff, I turned it so he could see the exposed glazed decoration.

"Oh, yes, definitely Minoan. It will take a bit of work to get it cleaned up, but it looks like a great example."

We watched Geoff disappear over the top of the rock fall before beginning our swim back to camp. I kept my eyes on the seabed as we swam through the shallow water close in to shore. Many potential artefacts slid past beneath me. Geoff was waiting in the finds tent when we arrived back. After we dumped our gear in a corner, I noticed Geoff examining the pot I gave him to bring back. As I walked over to investigate, he held the pot up to me like a winner brandishing aloft his trophy.

"This is a great find. I think it's close to being complete, but it is going to take a lot of careful cleaning to expose the whole thing."

"It would be miraculous if it were complete. Now that I get a better look at it, I'm thinking it might be one of those typically Minoan three-handled pots rather than a Krater. The accretion makes it hard to see, but it looks like it formed over some three-sided object." The other two agreed and I took it to the rear of the tent and submerged in a container of water.

After a shower, I felt more comfortable about our activities in the cove, and found I could settle down to work until Theo came. It was just after four o'clock when Troy led Geoff and two others into the finds tent. Geoff did the introductions. Professor Theo Papakostas and his colleague, Despina Tzavaros, had arrived.

Theo, short, with a square taut body and caramel coloured leathery looking skin, was much younger than I expected. His thick glossy black hair was greying at the temples, while his short well-trimmed goatee beard was grey with a liberal sprinkling of black. His eyes caught and held attention. They were dark, almost black, and so alert. There was a light in them that seemed to sparkle as they held your focus. His colleague was quite young. Although, all things being relative, lately I was beginning to think most of the world looked younger than I did.

As a bonus, they both spoke perfect English. We learned Despina was working on her doctorate, and we gained the impression that she was one of Theo's prize students. She provided a startling contrast to Theo.

Tall, slim and probably no more than in her mid-20s, she was an extremely attractive young woman. Her glossy black hair hung down her back in a thick single braid and she had the same coal black eyes as Theo, but hers were large and fringed with long curling black lashes. All this coupled with her flawless golden skin would make her hated on sight by every other female in the camp. This was exactly what I wanted to be when I grew up. Probably a bit late for that… but they say you should always set yourself worthwhile challenges.

Their attention focused on Troy. Not being one of the key players in their discussions, I moved to the back of the tent and got on with my own work. About half an hour later, they joined me and Troy asked if he could show Theo the pot I recovered from the cove. After examining it closely, both Theo and Despina concurred with our belief that it was Minoan. The two Cretans were keen to look at the cove but there was not much time left before the light started to fade. Rather than waste what little time there was by walking down the beach, we piled into their boat still anchored off the beach, and motored round to the cove.

Again, I was odd man out. I could have stayed back at camp. My only brief involvement was to explain the outcome of the area I surveyed and where I found the pot Troy had shown them. Full marks to Troy however, for making them clearly aware that I found the manmade remnants of a building amongst the rocks. After further brief discussion, we piled back into the boat, returned to camp, and Geoff took the visitors to their tents.

Later, Troy and the two visitors caught up with me in the mess tent, and the four of us dined together. Amidst all the clatter of trays and plates and while Despina was getting coffee, Troy leant over to speak quietly to me. "Theo wants to have a chat after dinner; just the three of us. I think he is going to send Despina off with Geoff to discuss the outcome of the field school. I suggested the three of us go to the finds tent as soon as we finish eating. Any problems with that? You haven't got a hot date or any other pressing commitments for this evening?"

"I think my appointment book is empty at the moment."

Geoff joined us about half way through our meal. Theo seized the opportunity to arrange for Geoff and Despina to discuss the field school dig after dinner. He excused himself from their discussions by saying he wanted to have a look at the finds we were working on. It seemed like we waited an eternity for Geoff and Despina to leave, but immediately they left the tent, Theo bounced up from the table and quipped, "As they say in the movies, the coast is clear. Shall we go to the finds tent now?"

Seated on stools at one of the workbenches, Troy and I turned our full attention to Theo, who began by explaining why he excluded Geoff from our meeting.

"Please don't read too much into my exclusion of Geoff from our discussions. I know he is due to leave in a couple of days, and I don't want anybody – any extraneous people, I mean – to know about something in which they won't be involved. I am going to ask you both for your upmost assurances you will not discuss what we talk about tonight with anyone else."

We both nodded and gave our assurances, but I needed to clarify a point. "Does that include Despina? I gained the impression you deliberately excluded her from any mention of the boats thus far."

"For the moment, yes. I know that seems strange – even difficult – but my reasons will become clear later. Now, I will explain why I particularly wanted to come here straight away, and the primary motivation for my visit."

Troy and I remained silent as Theo outlined what the authorities believed was a major artefact trafficking network operating through the Aegean and Mediterranean areas. They were unable to get a lead on the operation, but our sighting of boats in our bay was the first potential break they had in tracking down the network. When he finished speaking, Troy and I remained silent for some time as we digested Theo's information and its potential impact.

"Are the artefacts you're talking about just from Crete?" Troy asked as he considered the implications of the boats we saw anchored in the bay.

"No, but it might include some material from Crete. Artefacts are being pilfered – stolen – from many places, but mainly from key centres in the Middle East and northern Egypt. You might understand 'Middle East' as the Near East; places like Turkey, Iran, Iraq, Syria, Jordan, Palestine and even Cyprus. We believe Italy is involved somehow but it's unclear whether it is a clearinghouse for black-market trafficking or whether its artefacts also are a target. Of course, it's quite possible that both apply."

"I understand what you're saying, Theo, but not why you're restricting it to just us. Are others involved that we don't know about? In telling us, what are you expecting us to do?" Troy posed his questions cautiously. I was relieved to hear him ask them, as they were the same issues as troubled me.

Troy's questions brought another long spiel from Theo about the International Council of Museums (ICOM), their work and their role in fighting the illicit trafficking in cultural material. There was no point in telling Theo that, until about three years ago, I was a member of ICOM and am fully aware of their stance on illegal trafficking. Finally, he reached the interesting bit about why he was telling us the story.

"Troy, I understand you will be staying on after the others leave. How long is that likely to be?" he asked.

We explained that it would take an extra couple of weeks to finish cataloguing and packing the artefacts, and I took the opportunity to remind Theo of our request for details of the allocation of artefacts. Geoff did so earlier in the day as well, and Theo promised his office would send a copy of the document that York University already received but now appears to be lost. Then his attention returned to Troy's likely time on Crete.

"Now, about your extended period on Crete, it is obvious to me it will need to be longer than two weeks. How long, is difficult to determine. We might have to look at it in terms of temporary second-ment. Would you have a problem with that?"

"No problem at all. I'd be pretty miffed if I couldn't continue with investigating the cove, but I understand the politics involved and I'll have to cop whatever happens." Troy shot me a wry grin as he finished speaking.

Theo turned his attention to me. "Now Miss Whittington ..."

"Sonny please, Theo."

"Apologies. Now Sonny, what is your situation regarding leaving Crete?"

"I'm not University staff. My situation is a little different but, like Troy, I expect to be here an extra couple of weeks."

While I spoke, Theo consulted his phone. There was a brief pause, as he appeared to flick through emails. "Ah, yes, you're a part-time student completing a practical component for one of your subjects."

I blinked in surprise. That he could instantly access that sort of information about me was a bit unnerving. He didn't require a response, but I felt compelled to respond anyway. "I'm taking a sabbatical from my day job to indulge in some archaeology units purely out of interest. My qualifications aren't in archaeology, so I don't have anything to contribute to Troy's project."

Theo laughed loudly and proceeded to dumbfound me by reading off his phone not only my qualifications but also details of my work history and professional affiliations. Eventually, he stopped reading, returned the phone to his pocket and looked over the top of his glasses at me.

"So, not qualified to be any use to us? You are sadly mistaken Miss Worthington... oops, Sonny. I can't think of anyone better suited to what I have in mind for the pair of you in the near future. Troy, your next move is to alert your supervisors about your find and suggest a temporary secondment to my team for an undefined period. I believe Geoff will work with you on that, and he will be putting in a recommendation to that effect. My official documents to cover such an arrangement should be with your supervisors late tomorrow."

Troy absolutely beamed. "Thanks, Theo. Geoff and I have put together something that I'll send off this evening."

Theo then suggested that he would talk to the University about adding me to his team as a temporary postgraduate researcher – again for some undefined period – from the start of next week. It only required my agreement for me to go on to their payroll and receive cover under the University's insurance policy while I worked for them. I felt stunned but nodded my agreement without asking any questions. There were probably lots I should have asked and, no doubt, I would think of them later.

"Good, I'll have the agreement drawn up tomorrow. Once the paperwork is in place, you both will be working on investigating the cove. Despina will work with you as an archaeologist."

Troy interrupted, "Is Despina a diver? I'm trying to see how this whole set-up is supposed to work."

"No, not really; she tried diving but isn't certified or comfortable in that environment. She will confine herself to land-based archae-ology. However, Despina does know how to catalogue, and it is my intention that, when she returns in a couple of days' time, she will help catalogue the remaining artefacts so that this current job is completed and out of the way."

Troy looked pensive for a few moments before hesitantly voicing his concerns about the boats. He queried whether what we've observed was useful in any way. Theo allayed his concerns when he explained part of his reason for wanting us both to stay on was so we could keep a close watch on activities in the bay. He thought we might have to work split shifts: working at the cove part of the day and monitoring the bay at night. We queried Despina's involvement in monitoring the boats. Theo was emphatic that she would not be involved but would not elaborate other than to stress how we must not discuss our second-ary role with her and that she should remain completely unaware of anything to do with the boats or our monitoring activities.

Running a hand over his face, Troy looked up from his notes. "So-o-o, let's recap what happens if a boat appears in the bay again. My understanding is you want documented its arrival and departure times and the directions used to enter and leave the bay, and I presume anything else of interest."

Theo agreed, but added that he also wanted details of the boats. He brought two pairs of night vision binoculars with him for our use in this operation. He also wanted details of any boat relayed to him immediately on its departure from the bay. All of this was in a document he would give us with the binoculars tomorrow.

"A concern I have, Theo, is that working in the cove, we will be obvious to anyone coming into the bay and, your university's boat anchored off the beach as it is now, will be a deterrent to any would-be visitor." Troy studied the floor and paced across the tent as he spoke, his concern obvious on his face as well as in his manner.

Theo admitted to being aware of the issues, but believed he had measures in place that would eliminate those problems. Again, that was for tomorrow. Concerned that Geoff and Despina would become curious that we had been 'missing' for so long, we called it a night. I headed for my tent, wondering how difficult it would be to get to sleep tonight with so many questions starting to crowd my mind.

Foremost amongst the questions I needed to deal with were how much longer I would be on Crete and when I might return home. I had to think about the lease on the apartment in York and, more importantly, about not deserting James for too long.

Chapter 6

As anticipated, I spent a long time tossing and turning before falling asleep last night. I surfaced this morning feeling decidedly below par, but I took some comfort in the thought that Troy probably suffered a worse night than I did. Last night, we received so much information to ponder. I was definitely struggling with information overload, but a part of my problem was that the information was not complete. My feeling was that we received nothing more than an overview of what lay before us.

It wasn't so much Theo's plans that concerned me as much as their implications in other aspects of my life. I enjoyed being on Crete, and my sabbatical was all I'd hoped for and then some, but I was looking forward to going home to my real job and taking some of the workload off James. I opted to wait a day or two for things to crystallise before emailing James.

Nursing my breakfast cup of coffee and hoping it might clear my fuzzy head, I pondered Theo's intent to keep Despina ignorant of the boats, and wondered how the hell we were supposed to achieve it. She wasn't dumb – or blind – as we discovered last night. After leaving the tent, we ran into Geoff and Despina. Geoff's scowl clear indication he wasn't too pleased with the way the night panned out, but Despina was less subtle and promptly demanded to know what took us so long. Theo's glib reply silenced them both, but I was sure we were in for a solid interrogation from Geoff today.

Troy joined me in the mess tent and confirmed he had emailed details of his find to the University last night. I looked around the tent, "Have you seen our visitors this morning? I haven't seen them come in for breakfast."

"Haven't seen anyone yet, not even Geoff. Mind you, I'm not sure my eyes are functioning properly yet. By the look of us, I hope we have some fascinating objects to catalogue today or it is going to be one hell of a struggle to maintain focus. In my present state, I'm likely to drop headfirst into a tray of artefacts or computer keyboard."

I fetched another cup of coffee. After all, it wasn't sociable to leave Troy breakfasting alone. Besides, if I didn't sit here drinking coffee, I would need to start work; much better to be sociable for a bit

51

longer. I finally broke the silence by raising something that nagged at me last night.

"Theo's idea of a shift roster sounds good in theory, but I don't know how plausible it is. I'm not suggesting it can't be done, just wondering how we're supposed to do it without raising Despina's curiosity."

"Uh-huh, that and a couple of other things he mentioned seemed far removed from reality. It might all be hypothetical anyway. Once we start working in the cove – with or without the university's boat anchored out front – we will stand out like the proverbial. No boat intent on illegal activities will come anywhere near the bay. They might come into the bay but, once they see things happening here, they will take off again."

I shrugged. "Maybe that's what Theo is hoping will happen." I voiced my scepticism about that an a few other things. Troy echoed them and suggested that, if we didn't feel more confident about the plan by this afternoon, we should nail Theo to the floor – with or without Despina – until we get enough information to make informed decisions. The problem with that approach was that Theo might decide to leave at lunchtime. We revised out thinking and agreed to tackle him on our issues as soon as we saw him this morning.

I knew how important the secondment would be for Troy but, from my own perspective, I wasn't so sure how I felt about this new initiative. Under other circumstances, I'd probably be excited to be involved in investigating the cove, but somehow the plan had me feeling a bit unsettled.

Two parcels lay on the bench in the finds tent. I raised an eyebrow at Troy who just shrugged in reply. No point wondering, I opened one. Theo had been in earlier. The parcels contained the promised binoculars and documents, and their covert delivery suggested they should remain secret. We slid the contents of the parcels into my backpack that was in the corner with our dive gear.

To my relief, Geoff came to collect Troy. Together, they showed the visitors around both the field school's and Troy's excavation sites. This eliminated any interruptions and allowed me to work on undisturbed until coffee time. Their absence continued and I worked until my growling stomach announced it was lunchtime. I stood outside the tent for a moment soaking up the sunshine. The campsite had changed significantly during the morning. Where there had been many tents, there was now considerably fewer surrounded by an amount of open space. The sprawling campsite had decreased in size and compacted to one end. I recalled Geoff saying a barge was coming today to collect excess gear and take it to be loaded onto a ship for transport back to the UK.

After their absence all morning, I expected to see the gang in the mess tent. They weren't there. As I headed for a table towards the back of the tent, I noticed the tables all sported a sheet of white paper. I read the sheet on my table.

I had lost track of the days. Tomorrow, Geoff and the remaining students would depart for home. The flyer on the table announced an end-of-field-school party tonight. It was likely to last long and be noisy. Whether I went to the party or not, sleeping probably wouldn't be easy tonight. There was a twinge of regret. Everyone would be gone tomorrow and I hadn't gotten to know the students or been involved with them at all.

At three o'clock, amazed at how much I had achieved, I quit for the day. None of the missing academics had reappeared but, although my curiosity was nagging me, I decided to take my flagging energy for an afternoon nap. However, on leaving the tent, I decided a stroll down to the beach first might clear my head. The barge Geoff had mentioned was gently nosing its way up onto the beach.

I sat in the shade of the scrubby windbreak to watch its arrival. It barely made fast before a group of students pulling and pushing a heavily laden trolley came onto the beach. A second trolley followed a couple of seconds later and this time, Geoff and Troy formed part of the propulsion power. One of these trolleys was what we used to transport our dive gear for our first dive. There was still no sign of Theo and Despina, but their boat remained anchored off the beach.

I idled away quite a bit of time watching activities on the beach without feeling any compunction to assist. However, when it lost its appeal, I retreated to my tent and fell asleep the instant my head hit the pillow. I don't know how long I'd slept before someone calling my name brought me back to the land of the living. Groggily, I fumbled to open the tent flap to find a grinning Troy standing outside.

"Good morning... again. No, don't look so confused. It's still the same day as it was this morning. How long have you been asleep?"

"Dunno," I mumbled. "What's going on?"

"Theo and Despina are leaving. I thought you might want to say goodbye." My befuddled state continued to amuse him.

"Where are our guests? I do want to say goodbye. Oh, did we get any more information out of Theo about how his plan is going to operate?"

"Yeah, we managed to lose Despina for a while, giving us a chance to have a good chat and he's left whole lot of notes and stuff – a set for you too."

"Are you any more confident now that the whole thing is feasible?"

"I think so," he replied hesitantly. "One thing I picked up, although it wasn't spelled-out specifically, is that we might somehow get involved in tracking down some of the illegally trafficked artefacts. I don't have a handle on it yet, but the stuff that he left us might clarify things. We could see a bit of the Mediterranean area. How would that sit with you?"

I'd certainly need to give it thought before I could answer, and I didn't have the headspace to deal with it right now. I was almost coherent by the time we joined the others in the mess tent. We only spoke for a brief period but Theo was enthusiastic about all the work done in the bay so far, including at the cove. Then we said our goodbyes and headed for the beach, with me trailing the group. Theo dropped back beside me and, catching my arm, held me back for a moment until the group had moved a few metres ahead of us. He leant in close to speak quietly to me.

"I left documentation for you. There will be more stuff over the next few days. Try to read what you already have before the weekend. It will help you understand what lies ahead. Despina will be back on Monday to work with you and Troy. There's more about that in the notes. Come on, we better catch up to the others."

We quickened our pace and attached ourselves to the rear of the procession. Our guests' bags were already on their boat, so they were quickly underway. The three of us left behind stood waving as they roared off across the bay. On our way back to camp, Geoff encouraged us both to come to the breakup party tonight. We said we probably would, as we weren't going to get any sleep anyway.

I scratched through my meagre wardrobe for something a little festive for the party. The best I could come up with was a loose, thigh length Aztec print shirt over a pair of standard cargo shorts and sandals. As I stepped out of my tent on my way to the mess tent party, Troy called to me and I waited for him to catch up. He handed me Theo's folder commenting that there was a fair bit in it, and suggested we both read it and compare notes sometime over the weekend after everyone left.

The party was in full swing when we arrived. I couldn't help thinking the students who left early missed all of this. For them, going home must have been something of an anti-climax. Someone had attempted to decorate the tent for the occasion, even down to sprigs from the windbreak shrubs in glasses of water on each table. When we arrived, everyone seemed to be milling around a large bucket that served as a punchbowl. We joined the crowd.

It wasn't too bad for a limited resource party. There was food, limited alcohol – where did that come from? – and music, not to my taste, but it helped set the mood. Once the party got going and the food was under control, the caterers joined in, along with the barge captain and his deckhand who were spending the night. I chatted to students but, after about an hour and a half, my eardrums needed a reprieve from the music. At the first opportunity, I slipped quietly out of the tent. Troy disappeared from the party early and I assumed he'd gone to catch up on sleep.

I intended to go to my tent but it was a beautiful clear night and I wasn't sleepy after my afternoon nap. For want of anything better to do, I wandered aimlessly through the camp and onto the beach, planning to go for a walk along the sand. I kicked off my sandals and was about three paces down the beach when something in my peripheral vision brought me to an abrupt halt. I spun around and scanned the shadows along the windbreak. I caught my breath. Someone was sitting there. They had their knees drawn up to their chest, arms folded across their knees and their head resting on their arms. For a few moments, I stood rooted to the spot, not knowing what to do next. Geez, Sonny, this isn't any use, I counselled myself. Go and see who it is.

Taking my own advice, I picked my way over to the windbreak. He looked up startled by the sound of sand crunching underfoot. It was Troy. I was a bit wrong-footed. Did he want to be alone or was he in need of a friend? I was too close to turn and walk away, so I continued towards him.

"Hi, Sonny, looks like you escaped as well."

"Yeah, I took pity on my eardrums. I thought you'd gone to bed. Are you okay? Do want to be alone, or could you suffer some company?"

"No, I'm fine. There's nothing wrong, I just had enough party and decided to come and sit out here and to… I dunno… think about Theo and everything else I suppose. There's plenty of spare sand if you want to take a seat."

I sat beside him and let the silence envelop us for a while but, inevitably, Theo's visit caused conversation. Neither of us really knew what was ahead of us and, although I knew what it would mean for Troy to be involved, I needed to think about its impact on my other life. My intention was to go home by the end of the month, but I had the feeling this project could stretch beyond that. I felt guilty when I left for the UK, and the prospect of leaving James holding the fort for some time longer didn't improve matters. Troy commented that he knew nothing of what my 'other life' was really like; or much else about me for that matter. I laughed and admitted I was there almost under false pretences, and spent some time explaining my other life, my sabbatical and the extracurricular studies that brought me here.

"You sell yourself short. You've obviously worked with artefacts a lot in the past."

"Yeah, that's true. I worked in museums and galleries for a number of years, and it was through my museums work that I did a lot of wreck diving. Right now, that all seems a long time ago. By some unintended route, I went into the Public Service and spent a large slab of my working life there."

"So you're a public servant?"

"God, no, I escaped a few years ago; call it a conflict of ideologies. A few things that happened in my life probably contributed to the parting of the ways."

"Okay, so you're no longer a public servant, but a partner in a business. What line of business?"

"Promise not to laugh."

"Only if it's not funny…"

"Oh, what the hell, I'm a private investigator." I explained my path from public servant to a partner in a private investigations agency, including a token reference to the influence of my husband's death on all of that.

"You do come from a very different background from the rest of us in this camp. Perhaps now I understand what Theo meant when he said you brought other special skills to the project."

"Okay, now it's my turn. I understand that your 'final goal' to reach the top of the academic tree is about one last mountain to climb, so to speak, but what happens then? What's the next thing that drives you? Because I think you are driven – unbelievably driven."

"What happens after that? Well, then I do what I really want to do: go and be an archaeologist. I fought to come to Crete because I thought it would satisfy for a bit longer that need I have to get out and be a *real* archaeologist. I think it has made it worse. I'm dreading going back to the university; going back to my desk, to the lecture theatre. I'm struggling to continue to wait for the day when I can walk away from it all and do what I really want to do."

"If you're not happy, why wait? I understand it might seem like leaving something unfinished, but what's most important? You're a long time dead, so you might as well enjoy being alive. If you're so adverse to academia, get out."

He claimed it wasn't that simple and offered to elaborate. I promised to stop him if it got boring and Troy launched into his story. Apparently, he promised his dying mother he would always strive to reach the top; never settle for something that wasn't the best he could do. It was a long time ago at a traumatic time in a young lad's life. His parents were involved in a horrific pile up on the M1, which left his father dead at the scene.

In a critical condition after the accident, his mother lingered for about four days before succumbing to her injuries. "I was about 11 years old at the time and had just started at boarding school. They brought me home after the accident to spend time with my mother who it was obvious wasn't going to survive. It was during those last few days spent at my mother's bedside that she made me promise. After my mother's death, my only remaining relatives were the family of my mother's brother: my uncle, aunt and their only son."

He paused for a few moments and looked aimlessly out to sea. I kept quiet, anticipating there might be more to come. There was.

"My uncle and aunt, who always doted on me, took me in. At the time, their son was about nineteen and was an overindulged lad about town. When their son turned twenty-one, he went off on the modern day version of the 'grand tour': 12 months lolling about in Europe. He'd been gone about three months and was spending some time at an alpine resort when he was caught by an avalanche while out with a group of other young men. His body and those of a couple of his companions were found a while later. After that, I became the focus of my aunt and uncle's attention. I assume my mother had the same conversation with them as she had with me about reaching my full potential because, every time I achieved something, they reminded me how proud my mother would be that I had come top of the class, or got my degree, or whatever. They kept urging me to go forward as 'my mother would have wanted' me to".

"As you say, it was a long time ago. Have you considered that maybe you already have done as much as you want – reached as high as you wanted – in academia?"

"The only people I have left in the world would be extremely disappointed if I adopted that attitude. So, yes I am driven by a lot of things that don't make sense in the real world but, in my world, they are important." There wasn't much to argue against that.

We talked about how the cove project and the potential conference papers that would follow could clinch the final goal for him. It was getting late and I could feel the chill of the night air seeping into my bones. I called it a night and headed back to my tent. The party was still in full swing. I left Troy sitting on the beach. He gave me the impression he was a bit down after our conversation. I was concerned about leaving him alone like that and felt torn between going to bed and returning to the beach to keep him company. The need for sleep won out after I managed to convince myself he probably wanted to be alone. As I closed the flap on my tent for the night, I was relieved to see him making his way back to his own tent.

In the few minutes before sleep took over, I thought about tomorrow. For some reason I couldn't understand, I felt a strange excitement at the prospect of what the rest of my stay on Crete might bring. It was like anticipating a new beginning. Strange, because tomorrow I would be back in the finds tent, the same as I had been every day for the past two weeks.

Geoff, the students and caterers are to depart in the morning, leaving just Troy and I fending for ourselves until Despina arrives on Monday. Any concerns I had about the music keeping me awake proved to be ill founded.

Chapter 7

The campsite was humming when I ventured out of my tent this morning; only a few tents remained to come down. Finding myself superfluous to requirements, I opted to go straight to the finds tent and begin work. With no catering staff on duty any longer, we were fending for ourselves from today. I waited for Troy to appear before worrying about breakfast.

Cataloguing and packing artefacts was fast losing its attraction, or so it felt this morning. I could become a spectator of all the activity on the beach, but that would amount to procrastination, so I forced myself to work on until it was time to see everyone off. However, about half an hour after having convinced myself to work on, Troy arrived and suggested we go to the beach, as everyone was getting ready to leave.

We strolled down with the last of the students. Everything was loaded and the remaining students trotted on board to join those already on the barge. I expected a boat would collect personnel, but the students assured me it was going to be a hoot going back on the barge. The ramp was raised, the inboard diesel engine thumped into life, and students scrambled around hauling in both the anchors that held the barge fast overnight. Then, there was just Troy and I standing on the beach waving at the departing barge with its cargo of rowdy students.

As I made my way back to the finds tent with something of a heavy heart, I felt as though someone near and dear had departed. I suspect Troy shared my feelings. Neither of us spoke until we reached the tent and Troy brought us back to reality.

"I thought we were going to have breakfast once they'd all gone. Why have we come back here?" We both laughed. Our autopilots had brought us back to our usual place. A quick detour took us to the now deserted mess tent. "Do you think we'll be able to find a spare table?" Troy asked as he surveyed the empty seating area.

"My concern is that we're in danger of getting lost in the emptiness. Let's go and have a look at the kitchen so we can establish from the outset what terror it holds for us."

The whole setup now looked ridiculous for just two people: two enormous gas stoves and a separate gas hob, giant toaster, complicated looking coffee machine, and all the other paraphernalia. Until this morning, it provided sustenance for more than thirty people. We were going to have to tame at least some of the stuff if we wanted breakfast. Of more concern was what was there to eat for breakfast.

Deciding 'simple' was the way to go, we ferreted the necessary fixings out of fridges and cupboards. The coffee machine provided a challenge too daunting for first thing in the morning. Troy found a kettle tucked away in the back of a cupboard and we settled for instant instead. It wasn't the greatest coffee but it sustained us through our discussion on how to occupy the next three days. At least there was a plan for today: cataloguing all morning and reading Theo's notes this afternoon.

About mid-morning, Troy volunteered to make coffee while I worked on. He returned with coffee and feigned disappointment at finding the 'cupboard was bare'. "The lousy sods didn't leave us as much as a scone, a cake or even a biscuit; nothing."

"… And that's a good thing," I replied. "I didn't always indulge but the temptation was there every day. At least now I won't put on any more weight and, if we do enough diving, I might even lose what I've already gained, that is, unless you feel inclined to do some baking. Of course, if you did, I'd feel obliged to eat it."

"You're in no danger of gaining weight from any baking I do – even if I did feel inclined to do some."

It was a silent slog until lunchtime. "We seem to be making good progress," Troy commented as we walked across to the mess tent to face our next challenge: lunch.

He was right. We were sailing through the remaining trays. There were only one or two objects in each tray. I imagined they probably were from the early stages of the dig when there wasn't much coming from the upper layers of the site.

We rustled up salad and cold chicken, and more not so great coffee. It occurred to me that, while there was a supply of fresh fruit and vegetables in the fridges, when they ran out, we would need to go across to Timpaki for supplies. That only presented one initial problem: how to get there. "Do you know if the camp's boat is still here?" I asked Troy.

"Why? Are we going somewhere?" I explained about Timpaki and supplies.

"I hadn't thought of that. Now that you mention it, I don't know whether the boat is the caterers' or ours. They kept it in one of the big tents up the back. I don't know if it is still there – or how they got it from the tent to the water. I never saw them launch the thing."

After lunch, we investigated and found the boat on its trailer still in its tent and hooked up to a small tractor. A couple of drums at the back of the tent held fuel for the boat and the tractor.

"Apparently the boat belongs to the University and not the caterers," I observed. "It's a good thing that it is still here. I have the feeling it might be useful for other things besides keeping us fed."

"My thinking exactly, like maybe going out to where those boats seem keen to anchor, for a look around to see what the attraction is?"

"You read my mind. As it appears we are going to do a bit more diving over the next while, the boat will also make getting the dive gear and anything else around into the cove a lot easier."

Finding the boat led us to wondering what else remained now that everyone else had departed. We went to investigate the other two big tents behind the camp. The first one contained excavation tools, although much fewer than previously, and the big trailers we used previously for our dive gear remained in the second tent. Then, armed with Theo's folders, we spent the afternoon reading their considerable stack of paper.

It was amazing that Theo could produce such an amount of material in such a short time. However, Troy recalled Theo often went for three days without sleep if he was preoccupied with working on something big. Apparently, we were to become part of something 'big'. As I finished my folder, I took a deep breath and exhaled audibly. "Whew, it will take me a while to get my head around all this. In the absence of an executive summary, I'm going to need to make some notes."

We retrieved a whiteboard from behind the racks and got to work. Troy wrote while I dictated appropriate precis of the salient bits. Once we listed all the key points, it was clear the whole thing divided neatly into two distinct projects. The interesting aspect of it all was that somehow we were to juggle the two projects concurrently: investigating the cove site, and monitoring the visits of boats to the bay. In the end, with the board covered in Troy's scribble, we had produced a visual map of our tasks. Knowing we would have to clean the board before Despina arrived, we made our own copies of everything on the board. The camp didn't run to one of those electronic ones that print out everything written on it.

A key question continued to haunt us: what was it about Despina that Theo wasn't telling us? In spite of our prodding, the Despina situation remained a mystery. Theo steadfastly refused to elaborate further on the need for her exclusion from anything to do with the boats. We had sought explanation on more than one occasion, explaining how difficult operating in the dark would be, but he remained emphatic she shouldn't become aware of our interest in the boats. Perhaps we would have a better understanding after our Skype call with Theo planned for some time over the weekend.

I felt we should make the best of our time alone over the weekend and suggested a trip out into the bay for a look at the area where those boats anchored. We scheduled it for first thing the next morning, and spent the rest of the afternoon on critical planning to create a realistic timeline for the rest of the project. I reminded Troy that it all might be for nothing if York University refused the request for Troy's second-ment to work on the project and we both had to leave after completing work on the artefacts. He admitted to trying not thinking about it to avoid the risk of jinxing his chances.

As we strolled to the mess tent to see what culinary delight we might conjure up for our evening meal, we went over a list of questions we would put to Theo on the Skype call. The first question we would put point-blank: what's going on in regard to Despina? If we remained unaware of why her exclusion was necessary, the risk of something going pear-shaped due to our lack of understanding was too high and we might have to back out of at least the 'boats' part of the project.

There was an upside to being here alone: plenty of spare tables, no queues for showers, and plenty of hot water. We managed to produce a very nice pasta dish, which we washed down with a couple of glasses of the average quality wine left over from the previous night's party. After an exhaustive search of the Aladdin's Cave that was our kitchen, we decided there was enough food for us to survive for at least a couple of weeks, even with Despina joining us. That only raised another question: how to go about buying food when our larder needed replenishing. Paying for it out of our own pockets held no appeal whatsoever, but we conceded it would be better than starving.

*****

A check of Troy's emails this morning told us Theo scheduled the Skype meeting for eleven o'clock. We rescheduled our proposed trip out into the bay until the afternoon, and got on with cataloguing until it was time for our call. The call went well. Theo managed to answer some of our questions in his initial conversation without us having to ask them. Due to the way the call progressed, Theo dealt with everything else before we had opportunity to raise our questions, which primarily related to Despina.

"Okay, Theo, now for the really confusing part. What's going on with Despina? What's with all the cloak and dagger stuff?" Troy demanded. His frustration was evident in the demand and his tone left Theo little room to avoid answering.

I chimed in hoping to soften the atmosphere a bit. "We're sure you've got valid reasons for keeping Despina in the dark, but we're finding it confusing. More importantly, if we don't understand what's going on, we're likely – inadvertently of course – to do the wrong thing. So, as she is your postgrad student and someone who you appear to have high regard for, we don't understand why she is being sidelined."

A lengthy pause followed. Eyebrows raised, Troy and I swapped glances as we waited for Theo to respond. When Theo started to speak, his initial response was to apologise for the delay as he had been weighing up the 'need to know' aspects of the situation.

Troy abruptly cut across him. "Theo, let's be straight, if you don't think we can be trusted with information relative to what we're going to be involved in – what you're asking us to do – perhaps you've engaged the wrong people for the job. Some of what you're asking us to do is highly unusual, perhaps bordering on unprofessional, and might well compromise our effectiveness and/or our efficiency in other parts of the project. That might not bother you, but it certainly goes against my professional ethics."

When another long pause occurred, Troy forced the issue. "I don't know why it's taking so long, Theo. Either you trust us and tell us what's going on, or you find others who you do trust sufficiently to share the whole story with."

That jab did the trick. After some time spent placating Troy, Theo embarked on a long and sometimes rambling explanation. Once he started, we were reluctant to interrupt. He ended with one final question.

"Now, can you see how difficult this is for me and how delicately the whole situation needs to be handled?"

It was our turn to pause before replying. I spoke first as there were a couple of questions still in my mind, and I guessed Troy would have a couple as well. Quite a deal of discussion ensued before we had dealt with all the issues. By the end of the discussion, we had gained an understanding of various aspects of the project, including its management and inherent sensitivities. Almost as an afterthought, Troy raised the issue of his secondment.

"Theo, all this could just be hypothetical. There's no confirmation from York yet that I may work on this project, or of approval of my secondment – or that it might receive approval. Have you had any response from them?"

"If you don't already have an email, there will be one shortly. I received confirmation of the secondment just prior to this call, although they do want more details. Sonny, I believe you also will receive an email. They have no objection to your joining my team, but they will remind you about the report you need to write to finalise that last subject and, of course, completing the work with the artefacts. I have given assurances that work with the finds from the field school is a priority for you both until its completion."

As he flicked through his notes, Troy noticed Theo hadn't elaborated on the 'others', besides Despina, that he previously intimated he would send. In response to Troy's question, Theo said he would send four or five students – either in the last year of their degrees or beginning postgraduate studies – to undertake basic field excavation work. A barge would bring specialist equipment and its specialist operators.

"It seems our numbers could swell significantly," I mused. "Quite a few tents were left when the students departed, so I think accommodation will be okay. However, catering could prove a problem. The caterers have gone, and there probably is only sufficient food for three people for a maximum of two weeks."

"I thought of that," Theo confirmed. "I'll send caterers. There will not be as many as before. The provisioning arrangements will be similar to those previously in place and won't be your concern."

After the call ended, we agreed it was apparent that, although Despina was a bright rising star in his stable of students, Theo held some misgivings about her. He stopped short of stating those concerns specifically, but it didn't take too much to work out what they might be. My stomach rumbled loudly, interrupting our post-mortem of the Skype call

Rather than creating something to go on a plate, we resurrected some frozen bread rolls from the freezer and filled them with ham and salad before continuing our post-mortem as we ate. One thing that stood out was that we had a watching brief over Despina's activities.

This was more than intriguing. It was worrying, especially given the volume of artefacts presently stored in the finds tent.

"Yeah, very intriguing," Troy commented. "This watching brief will be an onerous undertaking. The gist of what Theo said was that when she is around a dig site, finds seem to go missing. He keeps stressing that it's all circumstantial and no evidence supports his suspicions, but he seems confident that's where the problem lies. It's hard to ignore that the sites she works on get looted soon after the dig is closed down for the season."

"He's formulated his theory over a fair amount of time. All her postgraduate work focused on various aspects of fieldwork techniques and approaches. This enabled her to spend most of her time on various dig sites, giving her intimate knowledge of the sites and the finds. If she's as bright as they make out, you'd expect whoever she works with to be a bit more circumspect, rather than following her around looting sites soon after she leaves."

I shared my worry about the safety of the field school artefacts for which I felt responsibility. "It sounds a bit parochial, but I am concerned now for everything in the finds tent. I might be more comfortable if we had everything crated before she arrived. I know it sounds like a hell of a job to have it all done by then, but I'm going to count the artefacts still to be catalogued, and keep a running total as we work through them."

"Hmm, yes, I think that's a good idea," Troy agreed. "We also need to consider those already crated. There's nothing preventing the removal of something from any of them. Cataloguing details eventually would lead to detection of any loss, but it could take a long time for that to happen. The finds from most dig sites go into storage when they arrive back at their ultimate repository and, depending on the need to do something with them, they could sit in storage for some time, even years, before they are looked at again."

"So-o-o, you're suggesting we count all the artefacts already crated as well? That will take a wee bit of time. "

"Yep, it probably will and, as your supervisor, I say it's a worthwhile exercise... and, if we don't get started, it won't get finished. We should get back to the finds tent and get stuck in."

Again, our boat ride out into the bay moved further down the priorities list. By the time we stopped for our afternoon coffee, we had counted all the uncatalogued artefacts. While Troy went for coffee, I entered details onto my computer. Then it dawned on me that this approach might defeat our purpose. I realised that anyone could access the computer and alter the data to suit their own purposes. In view of this, I transferred the data to a USB stick so it no longer resided on the computer. Over coffee, I shared with Troy my idea for a second safeguard for the crated objects.

"I'm thinking of sticking a hair across the two halves of each crate. It wouldn't provide any resistance if someone tried to open the crate and, therefore wouldn't attract any attention, but it would provide evidence that someone opened a crate. We could then check the crate to see if anything was missing. What do you think?"

"I think what you have in mind is a good idea, but one of us is going to end up awfully bald by the end of it all. There are stacks of crates. Anyway, it would have to be your hair; it's longer than mine."

"Such levity! I'll use one of those soft brushes with the long fine bristles. I only need to find something like craft glue to stick them on with – firmly, but not so firmly that they won't let go if someone tries to open the lid. A thorough search failed to uncover any glue. As a last resort, we hit the kitchen to see if we could manufacture something to do the trick.

Troy suggested egg white might work once it dried. We agreed to sacrifice an egg in the interest of testing the theory. I was more inclined to try making up a gelatine solution, so we produced a trial batch of that as well. Armed with our test solutions, we went back to the tent and applied them to separate crates. Then it was back to counting and recording artefacts for the rest of the afternoon while our trial adhesives dried.

By the time darkness enveloped the campsite, Troy had only a few more crates to complete, so I announced I would fix dinner while he worked on. A lazy sea breeze stirred my hair on the way back to the mess tent. There was a clear starry sky above and the smell of the ocean all round. We spent virtually no time outdoors today, and were likely to spend much of the evening indoors as well, as I was determined to go back to the finds tent after dinner.

What to prepare for dinner? This independent living lark was starting to wear a bit thin and it had only just begun. Not wanting to waste too much time on cooking or eating, I cooked a couple of nice looking steaks and jacket potatoes and made a salad. The thought of how nice it was outside lingered with me, so I carried one of the small tables out and set it up out front of the mess tent, and yelled for Troy to come to dinner. By the time he arrived, dinner was ready for alfresco dining. Eating outside was wonderful, and dinner wasn't bad either. The temptation was to slip into relaxed mode and remain at the table for longer, but I was keen to get back to work. After a quick clean up, Troy poured us both another glass of that mediocre wine and we took them back to the finds tent.

A check of the glue tests found that, although they both worked well, the gelatine solution was probably the better of the two. Equipped with that information, Troy began sticking hairs on the crates while I catalogued. Just before ten o'clock, we cleared the workspace, closed up and went back to our tents. I was particularly weary tonight. Sleep was not going to be difficult to come by.

Chapter 8

I woke early and dragged myself back to reality after a heavy sleep. Enthusiasm for another long stint in the finds tent was in short supply. Once outside, my spirits lifted. It was a glorious day. Today, we might get to investigate the bay.

Troy came into the mess tent whistling. "We should go diving today," he announced. "What time do you want to go?"

We agreed ten o'clock. Troy said he would work with me in the finds tent until about nine o'clock before going to get the boat and our gear ready. According to plan, Troy pulled up outside the finds tent to collect me just before ten o'clock. Once on the beach, he was hell-bent on doing the dominant male thing. He insisted on launching the boat himself and then skippering it across the bay. A glassy sea and almost no breeze made for a pleasant run out to the search site. GPS readings taken during the last boat's time in the bay gave us a good indication of where to search. We anchored, geared up and dropped a buoy over the side to indicate divers were working below.

Visibility was excellent, allowing me to see what were undoubt-edly artefacts on the seabed. Although without any real idea of what we were looking for, we believed there might be firmly embedded in the seabed some form of mooring to which to attach contraband. The water temperature was pleasant as Troy and I swam a grid pattern working outwards from our boat. To the starboard side of the boat, near the perimeter of our agreed search area, we found a concrete block on the seabed. From what we could see of it, its base was about a metre square.

Shaped like a four-sided pyramid with a truncated apex, about six hundred millimetres of its height was visible above the seabed. We had no way of knowing how much of it was below the sand. Cast into its flat top was a substantial stainless steel eyebolt. Troy photographed the mooring block from every imaginable angle until we were both satisfied we had achieved our objective. We surfaced, removed most of our gear and threw it up into the boat before, with great difficul-ty, scrambling back into the boat ourselves. Silence reigned as we stripped off our buoyancy vests. I hauled in the diver buoy and, as I did so, I became aware of how very conspicuous I felt anchored out here in this particular part of the bay.

"I'm not feeling all that comfortable parked out here like this. We are just a bit exposed. Could we head back to shore?"

Troy wasn't in a hurry, claiming he wanted to relax, check the images he had taken and stow the gear properly before heading off, but said he was prepared to leave now if I really wanted to.

"I think I do want to go now. You can stow the gear as we head back. Lift the anchor, please." Troy looked at me questioningly and I knew he was shaping up to argue the point. "Don't argue; I'm driving, just pull in the anchor, please."

With that, I started the motor and inched the boat forward to slacken the anchor chain, making it easier to haul in. When the motor sprung to life and we started to move, Troy threw his hands up in resignation and moved forward quickly to deal with the anchor. I let the boat idle until the anchor was safely on board and Troy regained his seat, then I slipped the motor into gear and we were flying across the bay leaving a wide frothy wake behind us. The wind quickly dried our wetsuits and, in spite of their protection, I felt a little chilled by the time we reached the beach.

Troy backed the trailer down to the water ready to load the boat. The prospect of hauling the heavy boat onto the trailer with the trailer's small hand winch was daunting. It looked like too much hard work to me. I asked Troy to back the trailer further into the water, and then gave him a practical demonstration of how to drive a boat onto a trailer. The thrust of the motor drove the boat onto the trailer for about three-quarters of its length. It only required a few cranks of that lethal looking winch to finish hauling it far enough onto the trailer to secure it to the trailer's front post.

Once the boat was securely loaded, Troy drove it back to its tent while I followed behind on foot. After unloading the gear and washing it, it was time for lunch. The dive had given us both an appetite but sapped our energy, so lunch was a quick cold chicken and salad again. Normal conversation didn't resume until after we partially demolished the meal.

"Where did you learn to handle a boat?" Troy asked with a hint of indignation in his voice.

"I had a boat license when I was fourteen. I grew up with boats, and I still own a beach place that only has boat access. I may be female, but I'm not useless." He burst out laughing and things were back to normal again.

Lunch over, I went back to work in the finds tent while Troy emailed this morning's photos to Theo. The end of the cataloguing was in sight. The pile of uncatalogued trays had diminished considerably. With us both working on them for the rest of the day, by tomorrow there should be work only for about a day or so left to complete. If Despina also helped, the three of us could finish the cataloguing and have everything crated by the end of Monday.

Something occurred to me as we worked on the artefacts. "I've been thinking about the artefacts seen on the seabed. I wonder if I shouldn't do a sweep of the beach directly in front of the school's excavation area to see what's there. There might be useful additions to what's come out of the excavations."

"Definitely, they would help tell the story of the site. We should try to collect some. As we can't spend too much time on it, we should look for things that suggest they might be particularly interesting."

"Depending on what time Despina arrives tomorrow, and how work in the finds tent progresses, a dive might be possible in the afternoon or, failing that, Tuesday morning."

With that in mind, we spent the rest of the afternoon in silence as we flew through the remaining cataloguing and crating. Five o'clock rolled around without us having taken a break. We agreed to work on and not come back to the finds tent after dinner tonight. The sun had disappeared over the hills and the descending darkness made it appear later than it was when we closed the tent, but it was too early yet for dinner.

On Troy's suggestion, we helped ourselves to a glass of leftover wine and wandered down to sit on the beach against the windbreak. It was a lovely time of day with just the last hint of twilight darkening into night. There were those birds again. I watched the straggly 'tail-end Charlie' group of birds glide across the sky on their way home for the night. There were only ever the same few untidy travellers. Their colours lost as they slid through the descending darkness; just black shapes against a darker sky. I watched for this migration every night if I was on the beach at the right time. Their passage through the night sky was regular. Constant and real, they were perhaps the one thing encountered so far on Crete that deserved that description.

We sat in silence for quite a while enjoying the ambience. Suddenly, Troy elbowed me in the ribs. "We have visitors. A boat came in a couple of minutes ago. I wasn't sure it was going to stop.

It came in very slowly, and looked as though it was just checking out the place, but it's dropped anchor now."

I looked out to sea. "Amazing, it seems to have found everyone's favourite anchorage. Will we check the coordinates, or just accept that it's anchored near that mooring?"

There was no need to check the coordinates. We knew its position. Troy pulled a notebook from his pocket and shuffled round 180 degrees on his backside so his back was to the beach. Then, using the light from his phone to see, he scribbled down details of the boat's arrival. I stood slowly and, remaining in the deep shadow of the windbreak, moved slowly over to the opening.

"I'm going to get the night vision binoculars," I whispered to Troy before disappearing through the opening. Once behind the windbreak, I jogged the short distance to the finds tent.

With binoculars in each hand, I returned to Troy and handed him his pair. We returned our attention to the boat. It presented a similar picture to our previous visitors. Again, there was one reasonably bright light low over the water that was only visible when the boat swung in the right direction in the light breeze. The dim glow from a low wattage light somewhere inside the cabin was barely visible, but there were no navigation or riding lights showing. Not surprisingly, there also was no sign of a diver's buoy. If I had a clandestine dive operation happening, I probably wouldn't advertise the fact either.

"This presents something of a problem, doesn't it?" I whispered. "Theo wants us to monitor the boat while it's in the bay, but we are a bit unprepared for this one. Neither of us had any sleep today, so we're not fit to go the distance of the midnight to dawn shift."

From experience we knew, now that the boat had arrived, there wouldn't be much happening for quite a while. It would just sit out there until well after midnight. On the assumption that we wouldn't miss anything during the short period we would be away, we decided to go for dinner immediately. Then one of us could sleep until midnight, while the other kept watch.

In the interests of 'quick and easy', we sacrificed a piece of rump steak and a mountain of vegetables in the creation of an excellent stirfry. Revitalised after despatching a wok full of food, we abandoned the original idea and decided to keep watch together, although it probably meant sitting on the sand until early morning. We surmised the boat was dropping off contraband for a second boat to recover tomorrow night. On this assumption, one of us would disappear after lunch tomorrow to sleep in readiness for the early morning shift the following day.

By eleven o'clock, I was a bit cold and stiff and told Troy I was going back to the campsite. I grabbed a sweatshirt from my tent and made coffee for both of us in the mess tent before returning to Troy. Around midnight, I saw Troy trying to do up the buttons on his shirt. It already was done up to the neck.

"You're cold," I hissed. "Go and get a jacket. The walk will get your circulation flowing again. I'll keep watch here but nothing is likely to happen for a while." The expected argument didn't happen and he disappeared into the campsite to return about ten minutes later.

We expected to be sitting on the beach until about 4.00am, which was when we assumed the boat would leave if it followed the previous pattern. I groaned inwardly at the thought, as that hour of the morning – just before the sun comes up – is the hardest time to stay awake. That's going to be when we really need to pay attention, as it is when our boat is likely to leave the bay. I was wrong. Just before two o'clock, there was increased activity. Someone opened a hatch allowing the pale cabin light to add some illumination to the cockpit area. I glanced across at Troy. He had his head propped up by an arm planted firmly on his knees. He wasn't watching the boat.

I carefully focused the binoculars on something happening at the stern of the boat. A person hauling in the light that hung over the side caught my eye. Suddenly, the stern cockpit area lit up. The brighter light hauled in from over the side now augmented the low wattage cabin light. After a few seconds, the brighter light disappeared. Although the cabin light provided some illumination, it wasn't bright at the stern where there was some activity. However, it did provide a better view of that area of the boat than without it. Until it lit up the area, I hadn't been able to determine whether there was a structure attached to the stern or not. Now, in the faint glow from that cabin light, a dive platform extending out beyond the transom became visible.

After carefully adjusting the binoculars, I maintained focus on the dive platform. My arms were beginning to feel they might fall off from holding up the binoculars. It took about ten minutes, but I received my reward for the constant monitoring. A diver surfaced and, removing his tank and weight belt, threw them up onto the platform.

"Diver!" I yelped, waking Troy.

"Huh … what? What's happening?"

Keeping my eyes on the boat, I told him about the dive platform and the diver who had surfaced. As I spoke, the diver shed mask and snorkel before clambering up to sit on the platform to remove his fins. Then, leaving all his gear for someone else to deal with, he disappeared below decks. Almost immediately, the throb of a diesel engine coming to life drifted across the bay. The sound of the engine briefly mingled with the rattle of the anchor chain as the boat sat idling for a few minutes before heading off in a westerly direction. We watched it disappear behind the western headland. There were two options open to us: sit here and wait to see if anything else happens, or go to bed.

"Assuming that boat deposited contraband out there, is it likely another boat will come this morning to collect it?" I asked.

"I don't think so. More likely, a second boat will collect it tomorrow night. That seems to be the pattern so far: two boats, one on each of two consecutive nights."

It was intriguing that it had taken the diver so long to attach whatever it was to the mooring block – if that's what happened out there. Troy agreed, but claimed he was more interested in sleep and that he would think about it after ringing Theo first thing in the morning. I was in need of a shower, and knew I wouldn't get to sleep without one so, by the time my head hit the pillow, it was three o'clock. I don't remember another thing until 7.00am rolled around.

*****

Troy came out of the finds tent and fell into step beside me as I made my way to the mess tent for breakfast. He had an email from Theo saying Despina now was unlikely to arrive before late this afternoon. That left us to our own devices for most of the day. Over breakfast, Troy flipped through his notes to prepare for his phone call to Theo. On his way to make the call, he stopped to share an idea with me.

"As we've got the morning to ourselves, I think we should take a look at the mooring block again to see what's out there before anyone else arrives."

There was a pause while I struggled with the idea. "That's tempting. Curiosity about what might be hanging off that mooring is nagging me, but I'm not sure it's a good idea."

"Why not? I'm dying to find out if there is something out there. I thought you would be up for taking a look at what they were up to last night."

"We think a second boat will come through tonight. What if that boat is hanging about somewhere close by; just waiting for nightfall? With just the two of us here, I don't think it would be safe for us to be out there poking about."

Aware there might not be another opportunity, we discussed all options without achieving any resolution. Finally, we agreed Troy should seek Theo's advice when he spoke to him. We went back to the finds tent and, although it was early, Troy tried calling Theo. He was in his office and the call was long. As the call progressed, Troy paced the tent, before eventually wandering outside with the call still in progress.

After quite some time, Troy reappeared looking pensive. He pulled a chair over to sit opposite me. This was not looking good, so I opened the conversation. "Did Theo have anything interesting to say? Did he get the photos?"

"Yeah, he seemed a bit excited by them, but I got the feeling there was something else going on as well. I gave him details of last night's boat and asked him about going out for a look at the mooring this morning. He shares our view that the second boat will probably come tonight."

"What did he think about us having a look at the mooring this morning?"

"Nah, he was dead set against it; seems to share your thinking about the second boat maybe hanging around not too far away. He doesn't want us going out there again for a while."

The day followed the monotonous routine of so many days before it. We worked on solidly until three o'clock when the sound of an approaching boat halted operations. We jogged to the windbreak and cautiously peered through the branches. A barge slowly made its way to the beach. There were a number of people on board and some large equipment occupied the main cargo space. It didn't look too threatening, so we went to meet it.

Despina ran down the ramp and jumped onto the beach. She explained it was the university's barge and on board were the team and the equipment Theo had promised. As we spoke, unloading the gear began. A four-wheeled vehicle a bit like a quad bike on steroids came down the ramp, followed by something that looked like a front-end loader but with a grab instead of a bucket. Last of the load to come off the barge was its human cargo: three males and a female carefully picked their way down the ramp.

As we made introductions all round and inspected the equipment, another three people came down the ramp. Despina introduced them as the catering staff. They asked if we had something that they could use to bring their stuff ashore. Of course we did. We still had those two huge trailer things in the tent behind the camp. We headed back to camp and the rest of the procession fell in behind us.

Despina reclaimed the tent she so recently occupied. We left the others to sort out their tents. The operators brought their equipment up onto the vacant area so recently occupied by students' tents. One of the operators was concerned about leaving sensitive electronic gear out in the open. He commandeered an extra tent for storage. Troy took the three caterers through to the tents so recently home to the previous caterers. After they dumped their gear, Troy showed them the mess tent and took them to get the trailers.

While that was happening, I took the rest of the new arrivals on a tour of the site. We met Troy and the caterers as they left the mess tent on their way to the trailers.

"You know how those trailers are a bitch to move, particularly once they're loaded. I was wondering if it were possible to couple them to that little tractor we used to tow the boat," I ventured. "I never checked to see if the trailers were fitted with hitches."

"That would make life a lot simpler. I'll check it out. We're on our way over there now."

The tour of inspection over, after arranging to meet in the mess tent for dinner at seven o'clock, I left them to settle in. I hoped the caterers could rustle up something for dinner by that time and that I hadn't set them an impossible task. At a loose end, I went back to the finds tent to check we had left nothing lying around that Despina shouldn't see. There was. I cleaned the whiteboard again – to ensure the ghosts of Troy's earlier scribble disappeared completely. Then I picked up Theo's folders and my laptop and took them back to my tent.

The sound of the tractor brought a smile. Good for you, Troy. A few moments later it went past on its way to the beach, pulling a trailer with the three caterers perched on top. No workplace health and safety officer present, so it probably didn't matter as long as no one fell off and was hurt. On its return journey the caterers trailed behind on foot. There was no room on board for anything extra and, judging by the amount of stuff to be unloaded, I voiced my doubts about whether dinner was going to be a possibility by seven o'clock. They assured me it would be, particularly as Troy was going to help them unload the trailer. The surprised look on Troy's face at that revelation was worth seeing. I departed quickly before they had any bright ideas that I also might like to help.

I started to walk off, then doubled back to speak to Troy. It occurred to me that the second boat was likely to come into the bay tonight and neither of us had managed to stock up on sleep in preparation for the late night vigil. I had some doubt as to whether the boat would actually stop in the bay once they saw the barge on the beach, but Troy informed me that the barge departed as soon as it was unloaded. Dinner was ready on time and, as there are only nine of us, we rearranged the furniture and all sat together. It gave us a chance to plan the agenda for tomorrow.

Not surprisingly, the first thing on the agenda was for all of us to visit the cove straight after breakfast to get a feel for the job ahead. Despina advised that Theo had ideas of coming to the site sometime tomorrow, although there wasn't anything definite about that. I spoke to Despina about finishing the cataloguing, and the possibility of completing everything in the finds tent by the end of the tomorrow. Then, at Troy's request, the two operators gave us a rundown on their equipment and its intended use on our project.

Keen to get everyone back in their tents so we could plan the rest of our night, at about eight o'clock, I made some lame excuse about wanting an early night and stood up to leave. It had the desired effect. Everyone else said they were going to follow my example and all traipsed out of the tent. Troy and I went to our tents but, after a few minutes, quietly took circuitous routes around the rear of the campsite to regroup in the finds tent. As neither of us had any sleep during the day, we would both monitor the bay tonight, and hoped our vigil wouldn't go any later than the previous night's did.

To avoid our exodus to the beach being detected, we went back to our tents, turned out the lights and, to any interested observers, went to bed for the night. After about half an hour, I stealthily made my way to the windbreak. My route again took me behind the darkened tents of the campsite. The place was deathly quiet and still. The only lights still on were in the operators' tents. I checked over my shoulder that no one followed me, and quickly slipped through onto the beach. Troy joined me a couple of minutes later and we took up our now customary position on the sand in the shadows of the windbreak. It was already close to ten o'clock but no boat had arrived. It suddenly occurred to us we would not be able to go for coffee tonight.

"I can hardly go and rummage in someone else's kitchen to make coffee as I did last night. Looks like we're in for a long night," I whispered.

As I finished speaking Troy pointed to where a boat slowly made its way past the western promontory. Similar to previous boats, it showed no navigation lights and only had one dim internal light visible. Tonight, I remembered to bring a sweatshirt bottled water and the binoculars. It was after one o'clock by Troy's watch when he spotted some activity. We watched a repeat performance of the previous evening of a diver shedding his gear on the dive platform, then scrambling into the boat and disappearing below decks. The only variance was that it took the boat a little longer to get underway after the diver was on board. It idled for about ten minutes before hauling in the anchor and then for a further five minutes before moving off.

Last night the boat's passage was from east to west. Tonight, it came in from the west and, after describing a wide arc, left the bay in the same direction. Again, we sat and watched the boat until it disappeared behind the bay's western headland. Common sense kicked in after staring at the empty bay for a further ten or fifteen minutes, and the need for sleep prevailed. As we re-entered the campsite, Troy whispered in my ear.

"Are we going to take the covert route back to our tents, or are we going to march straight through the campsite to our beds?"

"I'm tired. I'm taking the direct route. If I encounter anyone, I'll say I had a nightmare and went to walk it off."

I expected to go straight to sleep, but it took an eternity to happen, and the precious few hours before my alarm sounded did not produce deep sleep. The others were already moving around the camp as I trudged to the mess tent. According to plan, straight after breakfast we all went and scrambled over the rocky divide and into the cove. This was a familiarisation visit, so we brought no equipment. On our way to the cove, Con, the ground penetrating radar equipment operator, identified sites along the beach close to the hill for testing. Troy was the guide in the cove, showing and explaining everything that happened at the site to date. A strenuous question and answer session commenced after the tour. It looked like going on for some time. I escaped. Getting everything in the finds tent finished had become a fixation with me.

Back at camp, my first port of call was the mess tent for coffee. Bliss! It was real coffee. The caterers had the monstrous coffee machine operational again. So, armed with my caffeine fix, I retreated to the finds tent and got busy. The others returned at about eleven o'clock and, following my example, went directly in search of coffee. No one came near the finds tent so I worked on in blissful solitude until lunchtime.

Chapter 9

By the time I stopped for lunch, there were only a couple of trays left to deal with. While the temptation was to push on to get them finished, the lack of sleep was catching up with me and I needed to take a break.

I walked to the mess tent with a couple of other latecomers and found everyone else already there. Conversation flowed freely, mostly focusing on devising a work plan for the cove site. Troy tried to steady discussion by reminding them that, if Theo arrived today or tomorrow, he might already have a plan he wanted followed. There was no mistaking the excitement at the prospect of beginning what had the potential to become a major excavation.

In an effort to get some direction happening, Troy suggested that, after lunch, the students get together to develop a list of the equipment they needed taken to the cove. He reminded them to include bottled water, as it was too far to walk back every time someone wanted a drink. Con and Chris, the equipment operators, would work out their own plan of attack. The group split up. Students occupying one large table, while the operators moved to a small table against the side of the tent. That left Troy and I sitting alone. I jerked my head towards the finds tent to indicate we should adjourn to there.

Perched at my workbench, Troy cast his eyes around the tent. "Have you finished the artefacts?"

"No, there are two trays left, but only about half a dozen artefacts in them. Unless something happens, I should get them finished this afternoon. Have you heard from Theo?"

"Not yet. I planned to ring him once lunch was over, so I might do that now."

"The sooner he comes, the better. We still need something that tells us which artefacts are supposed to go where. Once I get these last couple of trays finished, everything will be ready to ship out. As I understand what typically happens, most of it then becomes Theo's, with only a small portion of it to go back to York."

Troy made the call, checking first that no one was around to overhear when he gave Theo details of last night's boat. However, Theo's office advised that Theo was already on his way and would probably arrive here within the hour. I made a start on the last of the artefacts. There would be a certain satisfaction in being able to tell him we had completed work on the field school stuff. I was just finishing when Despina came in to tell us there was a boat heading towards the beach. It was a safe bet it was Theo. She and Troy left the tent and headed for the beach. I quickly closed the last crate and followed them down to meet the boat.

Theo brought the boat around by himself. We helped anchor it front and back off the beach, and carried his bag and a box of other stuff up to one of the spare tents. He wanted to check around the camp to see how everything had been set up and to have a chat with the caterers. We left him to get on with it while Troy and I went back to the finds tent. I wanted to discuss a couple of things with Troy before we spoke with Theo.

"What are we supposed to do after this? Are we supposed to monitor the bay every night – all night – or is one of us just to take a look after eleven o'clock each night to see if anything's happening?"

"Good question. When we had that last conversation with Theo about all this, I thought he suggested that we were supposed to monitor the bay every night. However, from what we have observed so far, I think we're almost convinced that the boats don't come every night. There's always a period of a few days between activities, although that period of time is not consistent."

"That's the problem with trying to monitor them. We haven't been able to determine a regular pattern yet – or maybe they don't work to a regular pattern."

"The mess tent is a lot more pleasant for sitting and chatting. How about we relocate to there?" Troy suggested, casting his eyes around the finds tent.

The mess tent, deserted apart from caterers clattering around in the kitchen, offered an additional bonus. We discovered the refrigerated cabinet near the food counter now held other cold drinks besides bottled water. We both selected a fruit juice. The table we selected provided a good view of the area immediately outside the tent. It would allow us plenty of warning if any of the others came towards the tent.

I reminded Troy I still had to write a report on the cataloguing project to complete my subject's practical component. My inclination was to delay starting it until after speaking to Theo about the division of artefacts. However, I thought having to write the report would make a good excuse for me to disappear for slabs of time – like going missing for an afternoon to get some sleep in preparation for a night's vigil over the bay. Troy agreed it was a good ploy, but we couldn't work out how to split up the monitoring duties. As we usually knew before midnight of the arrival of a boat that night, the vigil only needed to extend past midnight if one arrived.

With the issue still unresolved, the sound of laughter close to the tent ended the discussion. A couple of the others were making their way to the tent for coffee. The rest of the crew trailed some distance behind. It's amazing how so few extra people can totally annihilate the peace and tranquillity of a space. Excited chatter and laughter rendered any further serious conversation impossible. When Theo arrived with the last of the crew, Troy beckoned to him over to our table.

"Theo, we were wondering if you had developed a work plan for the team already. I started one before I realised you might already have one you want followed."

"No, Troy, I haven't done anything. You should work with the students to create a plan. The only thing you should keep mind is that Con might need an assistant from time to time."

"That could be me," I volunteered. "It's probably better that those who are real archaeologists stay with the excavation. I have less value in that regard and might be better employed in other ways, like helping Con."

"You sell yourself short. You have an important role in the project, but your reasoning makes sense just the same. I'll leave that to you two to work out." Then, lowering his voice to a whisper, Theo continued, "I need private discussions with you both. Perhaps we could give everyone else something to do, so we can sneak off somewhere private. I have your contracts with me, so perhaps we can use those as an excuse to go off to peruse them and get them signed."

I triumphantly announced, "We finished the work on the field school material in the finds tent today, but still haven't any indication of who gets what. If we sort that out, we'll be in a position to send it all off to wherever it's has to go."

He smacked his forehead. "I keep meaning to send that information. I'll bring my laptop to the meeting and email it to both of you. We will discuss it at our meeting even though you won't have your copy yet."

We noticed the crew was getting ready to leave the mess tent, so Troy went over to ask them for the equipment list they drew up. A list triumphantly appeared from someone's pocket. Troy scanned it before taking the students to the stores tent to acquire the tools on the list. "We have a meeting with Theo shortly which may take some time. While we're tied up, perhaps you could take your tools down to the cove ready to start work first thing in the morning." There was another burst of excited chatter as Troy led them like the Pied Piper to sort out their tools. Theo went to his tent for his laptop and, with nothing better to do or anywhere else to go, I strolled to the finds tent to await our meeting.

We had given the place something of a token clean when we heard Theo was arriving today. Now that work on the finds was finished, it was obvious the place could do with a lot more attention. I devoted my time to additional housekeeping while I waited for the others to return. After expending considerable energy and 'elbow grease', I cast my eyes around the tent, and admired my handiwork. As my eyes slid around stacks of crates, something struck a discord. That's not right, I told myself. It wasn't like that before. I stood, leaning back against the workbench for a while, mulling over what was wrong with the situation for it to attract my attention. Theo and Troy came into the finds tent together. I tried giving Troy a meaningful look but it was lost on him, so I resorted to a more direct approach.

"Guys, could you both stand on the other side of this workbench, please. I want you to have a look at something." They did as I asked and stood looking at me, curiosity written all over their faces. "Theo, just bear with me for a moment please, as what I am about say won't mean anything to you – but I want you to observe. Troy, have a look at the stacks of crates. What do you see?"

Troy moved his head from side to side like a tennis match spectator as he scanned the stacks of crates. His reply a few seconds later was hesitant. "I can't see anything major. The only thing might be that crate at the end over there has been bumped or something, and now isn't quite lined up properly."

"Give the lad a prize. Well spotted, my friend." I pulled out my phone and showed him the photo I had taken of the crates before going down to the beach to meet Theo earlier today. "See, they were all very neatly lined up. Neither of us has been anywhere near the stacks since then. I came back here a few minutes ago to find that one had been moved."

We both turned to look at Theo. I bit my lip while I thought about it but, at that moment, a significant question hung in the air. "Uhmm, Theo, I'm a bit hesitant to ask this question but I think it has to be asked. During the time you spent with the crew, was Despina with you the whole time?"

He studied the bench as he considered the question. While I had my phone out, I took a photo of all of the crates, and zoomed in closer for a second photo of just the end row where the crate was out of alignment. Theo cleared his throat before speaking. I put my phone back in my pocket and focused my attention on him.

"I can't be sure. We were all over the place and there was so much going on. However, I think that, just before we came back to the mess tent for coffee, Despina wasn't with us. I don't know how long she was missing, but she caught up with the last of us as we entered the mess tent. I know what you're suggesting, but one crate a bit askew doesn't prove anything in itself."

"We are aware of that," Troy replied. "That's why we're bit hesitant to even mention it."

"Troy, maybe we should check the crate... check if the tell-tales are intact," I suggested. "It's a bit odd that it's a third crate down in the stack that is out of alignment. If it had been the top one, I might not have given it a second thought. It does look a bit odd however, when the top two are perfectly aligned and the next one isn't."

Troy removed the top two crates from the stack. Then, picking up the third crate, he carefully carried it across to the workbench. We both peered at the tell-tales hairs. The lower ends of the hairs were detached, while the upper ends remained attached to the lid. We shared a look before I spoke again.

"Hang on, don't touch anything. I want to photograph those tell-tales." I took a couple of photos with my phone. "Okay, let's lift the lid."

Troy carefully lifted the lid while I located the list identifying which objects were in each crate. I read from the list, "Four small pottery shards with glazed decoration..."

"Shit!" Troy slapped his hand down on the workbench. "There's only three in the crate. Give me details of what they were so we can work out which one is missing."

I read the description of each piece from the cataloguing sheets. It was the biggest of the four pieces that was missing: a piece of fine red clay about a hundred millimetres across. The black glazed background featured a white line drawing of a male figure holding a spear aloft. Theo came around the bench to read the cataloguing details over my shoulder.

I went back and looked at each sheet for the other three objects that remained in the crate. They were smaller, irregular shaped pieces and, while they also featured glazed decoration, only fragments of the decorative images appeared on each shard. The photograph of each object taken at the time of cataloguing was attached to its cataloguing sheet. I brought up the image of the missing piece. There was nothing to suggest it came from the same pot as any of the other pieces in that crate.

"You don't think it might have gotten into another crate – somehow?" Theo asked hopefully.

"No, it could not," Troy answered. "I packed these last three crates today and entered them on the spreadsheet. I'll check the other two crates I did today, but I'm sure there is no error."

Troy fetched the two crates he had put to one side. We opened them, showing Theo how the tell-tales detached when the lid is lifted. Their contents agreed with their records.

I looked meaningfully at Troy. "We should re-attach the tell tales on those two crates. I want to put a note in the crate from which the piece went missing. Then we can re-attach the tell-tales to that one as well. They might come in handy again. You never know…"

"This is most unfortunate," Theo began. "We need this material moved from here as soon as possible. Of course, all we've proved so far is that one small artefact has gone missing. We don't know for sure when it disappeared or how. It could have been anyone of the crew, but I think we all share the same suspicion. I'll arrange for the barge to return as soon as possible to collect the crates. In the meantime, we will say nothing to the others about the finds or their impending relocation. Are we agreed?"

We both nodded our agreement. Keeping quiet about the barge coming for the finds was not going to be difficult. The difficult part was going to be making sure that nothing from the cove site disappeared into a pocket instead of into a finds tray. Troy was thinking ahead.

"Do you have a plan for managing finds from our new project?" he asked Theo. "This little exercise only confirms that anything found on the cove site is fair game. Finds will need close scrutiny and careful management if they are not to get 'lost' along the way."

"I acknowledge it's a concern," Theo replied gravely. "It was my intention that Sonny should manage all the finds. I know that won't stop things disappearing before they get to the finds tent, but I don't have any ideas on how to deal with the problem."

"I can't stand over people watching what they might uncover. I wonder if teaming everybody up with a partner might help... some sort of buddy system," I suggested. "I know it puts the onus on everyone to keep an eye on their partner, but I can't see how else to monitor that stage of the process."

Hands thrust deep into his pockets, Theo stood staring off into the distance for a few seconds before commenting. "Your idea could form the basis of a security procedure, but I just can't visualise how it might work. There's no denying this is a major concern, and I'm damned if I want to let people make off with our cultural heritage."

"Okay, that was a major distraction, but can we give security some thought and discuss it again later?" We nodded and Troy continued. "Good, now can we talk about those boats that come in the night before anyone else might happen to be around to overhear?"

Troy briefed Theo on the boat that visited the previous night. "It's too early to be certain but it looks like the pattern is for two boats to come – for whatever the reason – one on each consecutive night. During these last two visits, thanks to your night vision binoculars, we've confirmed that whatever they're doing involves a diver. If we want to find out what's going on out there, somehow we're going to have to inspect the mooring block after the first boat departs and before the second one arrives."

"I agree that is what's required," Theo concurred. "However, such a move could be fraught with danger – not only to the diver but to the whole exercise. If the second boat is close by and observes someone checking out the mooring, it is likely to make a run for it rather than come to collect whatever it is supposed to pick up. The ultimate aim is to cripple the trafficking network to the extent that it can no longer operate or, preferably, to eliminate it altogether."

We outlined our plan for monitoring the bay and expressed our concern about doing it covertly so that the rest of the crew were unaware of our activities. He didn't have any ideas to contribute and, the sound of footsteps crunching across the sand towards the tent ended the conversation. Theo opened a folder he placed on the bench earlier and removed a stack of paper. "Okay if there are no real issues with them, perhaps you could take your contracts and study them in detail," he said as naturally as if we'd been discussing the contracts the whole time.

"Ah, yes, we better go through these for all the fine print you've got hidden in them," Troy responded tongue in cheek.

As we spoke, the footsteps stopped somewhere close to the tent. We kept up the babble about contracts and terms of employment. After a couple of minutes, with a jerk of his head towards outside the tent, Troy drew our attention to the sound of retreating footsteps. I was closest to the entrance so, while Troy and Theo kept discussing Troy's contract, I tiptoed to a spot near the doorway. My vantage point provided a view of a wide expanse of the campsite. The only moving thing in sight was Despina's retreating rear end. As she was sufficiently far away not to be able to hear, I held up my hand signalling to the other two that it was safe to stop babbling now.

"She's gone. There wasn't anyone else moving about out there. Of course, she might have come here quite innocently to ask something relevant about the dig... or not. If we were generous, we might suppose she heard us discussing private matters and decided not to interrupt. Should we perhaps really deal with the contracts now?"

We discussed and signed our contracts. Mine was sufficiently general, and broad enough not to help clarifying my role in the project. My initial interpretation of it was that my duties were whatever anyone asked me to do at any time. Duration of the contract was 'indefinite' with the added qualifier that that 'a review of the end date should occur prior to the end of the year or sooner as determined by progress on the project'. I definitely wouldn't be here until the end of the year and had decided that, if asked to do something that went against the grain, I would be going home immediately – contract or no contract. Anyway, I had squared it with my conscience already that I could probably stay a month without feeling too guilty or upsetting James too much.

Troy, as overall project manager, would oversee all aspects of the dig. Theo and Troy discussed his position until Troy was satisfied he fully understood its scope. Then it was my turn to clarify a few things. I was to manage all aspects of the finds, as well is being the dive-buddy for Troy. I also was to try to find some time to explore the seabed between the cove and our existing campsite. There was no guidance on how far out from the high water mark I should explore. The question and answer period did finally end, but not until both of us had exhausted questions regarding our contracts... and received some clarification of a number of points.

The two men began discussing a work plan. I elected to check my emails and found the promised document relating to the division of the artefacts.

"What's up? What disaster has befallen us now?" Troy asked anxiously. "You could plant potatoes in the furrows in your forehead as you read whatever that is."

"I was reading the document on the division of artefacts. It is going to mean more work for us before these crates are ready for shipping. We'll have to separate the stuff for York, so the rest of it can go to Crete University, and we'll have to adjust our other lists accordingly."

"Argh, I had forgotten about that. I was feeling relaxed about having finished with all this lot. When do you want to do that?"

After briefly pondering the question, I replied, "Maybe not for a couple of days. We should get the dig underway first and then work out a good time to do it. Perhaps we could schedule it over a couple of evenings so as not to be absent from the dig site during the day."

The two men agreed and Theo said he'd postpone the barge until we completed separating the material. This development put the artefacts at risk for a bit longer by rendering them now not ready to leave straight away. I decided to wait until Troy and I were alone to discuss my concerns, and to work out what we might do to expedite their removal.

Dinner that evening was rowdy. Everyone was excited about starting excavations the next day. The students were exhausted after having spent the afternoon moving equipment to the site, which involved walking between the campsite and the cove many times. They were all keen for an early night. As they left the tent in ones and twos, I signalled Troy to stay. My original intent, once the students left, was for Troy and I to go to the finds tent to discuss sorting the artefacts. However, I decided it would be safer to stay where we were. With the caterers making so much noise cleaning up and in the kitchen, eavesdropping from outside the tent would be impossible.

"I'm anxious to get those artefacts out of here. I've yet to write my report. It gives me an excuse to sit in the tent while I'm doing that, but I can't be in the tent and keeping an eye on whatever they dig up at the cove. I'll send Geoff Featherstone an email tonight asking if there are any particular artefacts he wants for the York collection. I imagine Theo has right of veto over anything York wants but, if Geoff identifies specific items, it's worth a try. The problem with that is that we'll have to wait for a reply from Geoff before we can start sorting artefacts."

"Uhmm, not necessarily so," Troy mused. "We could ring Geoff now."

"What, at this hour of the night?"

"It's still early; not even eight o'clock. It's worth a try. We'll tell him it's urgent – without saying why – and ask him to email something or call us sometime tomorrow." Troy pulled out his phone and flicked through his contacts.

Troy's phone was on speaker, and Geoff answered almost immediately. We outlined what we wanted and explained the urgency as something to do with scheduling the barge. Geoff didn't argue or question anything. He described a couple of pieces he would like for York University's collection, but would give it some thought overnight and email a list first thing in the morning. I promised to email my report to him by the end of the week. We ended the call without any mention of the missing artefact.

"If I get that email tomorrow, we could start sorting those objects tomorrow night," I suggested to Troy.

"That could work in our favour. After dinner, we come across to the finds tent and work on sorting those objects until it's time to go down to the beach. If we work those students hard enough during the day, they should all be in bed by the time we go to look for boats."

Things looked like they were moving quickly, so I decided to make a start on my report immediately while Troy went back to his tent to check his emails. Once I made a start, the report flowed pretty well. After about an hour, the first draft was almost complete, but I couldn't do any more until we sorted the objects. I stretched and walked around the bench a couple of times to clear my head and maintain circulation. Troy came into the tent as I was about to perch on my stool again.

"All's quiet in the camp," he announced as he drew a stool up to the bench and sat down to face me. "What time do you want to go to the beach?"

We agreed on ten o'clock, which gave us a half-hour to fill in before we left. I had something to discuss with Troy and this seemed a good time for it.

"I had a good look at the tent flap arrangement when I opened up tonight. Apart from the flap with the long zip closure that we use all the time, there's also a storm flap, currently rolled up and held back out of the way by a couple of straps. There are a few eyes on the opposite side of the entrance that allow the storm flap to be tied securely in place across the zippered flap in the event of bad weather."

"I knew there was an extra flap but I've never looked at it. What are you thinking?"

"A couple of padlocks would be handy. I have one small luggage padlock. We need at least one more to prevent anyone opening the tent. I suppose we could ask Theo to get something for us but it might be a while before anything arrived." I took Troy out to show him how the storm flap secured across the entrance. "It goes across the entrance in the opposite direction to the zippered flap which, from our point of view, is a bonus. Once the storm flap is securely closed, it is very difficult – if not impossible – to get to the slider on the zip of the flap underneath to open it."

"I think I might have a couple of luggage locks. I used them on my bag when I came over here. That would give us three we can use."

"Thanks. I'm mindful that we don't want the place to end up looking like Fort Knox. I'll test it with just one lock initially to see how easy – or otherwise – it is to get to the zip. One might be enough, but two certainly would be all we need. Having to unlock it every time we want to come in will annoy us, but I think it's necessary. If someone tried to gain entry, they'd run the risk of standing out here in full view while they fiddled with locks and flaps.

By the time we finished examining the tent flaps, it was time to go down to the beach. I simplified the exercise by stashing my sweatshirt and the binoculars in my backpack, which I left in the finds tent. I grabbed the backpack and, after scanning the campsite for any sign of activity, we closed up the finds tent and started for the beach. The small moon that night provided enough light for us to walk freely without being too obvious. We took up what was becoming our regular position by the windbreak.

It was unlikely a boat would come tonight, or maybe even for the next few nights, as we believed it was too soon after the previous visit. In case we were wrong, we sat on the sand until almost midnight.

Chapter 10

As anticipated, no boats came last night and both Troy and I were up early this morning. My first priority was to check the finds tent and the stacks of crates. My immediate assessment was that no crates appeared out of alignment. Nevertheless, something didn't seem quite right. I stood for a few moments scanning the crates trying to work out what bothered me. Again, I was almost convinced something was not right, but whatever it was eluded me.

Maybe, if I had a better view, what was bothering me would become clear. I moved around to the far side of the first bench and, resting my hands on the bench, focused on the stacks of crates, trying to picture them as they were last night. Troy came in while I was doing this.

"Are you okay? What's up; what are you doing?"

"At the risk of looking really stupid, I think there is something different about the stacks of crates this morning."

"Not again... and so soon!"

"Oh God, I'm slow!" I reached into my pocket and retrieved my phone, remembering I'd taken a photo of the crates after we'd straightened them up and dealt with the missing artefact yesterday.

I compared the picture on the screen with the stacks as they were now. Troy stood beside me to view the screen as well. He spoke first. "See there, in the middle." He pointed to a section of the stacks. "That column of crates on the right has been moved; not much, but moved. The whole column is not quite square to the front properly – as it was last night. The fronts of those crates are now on a very slight angle; enough to make the gap between them and their neighbours look a little strange."

The moment he pointed it out, it became glaringly obvious. I photographed the stacks and returned my phone to my pocket. Troy jumped as I slammed my hand down on the bench top.

"Sorry, didn't mean to startle you. I'm just so angry. Can you stay here for a while? We need to check that stack, although I know we're supposed to go to the cove this morning. I'll get coffees before we make a start. It will also give me a chance to calm down a bit." I strode over to the mess tent for coffees.

Back in the finds tent, I handed Troy his coffee, checked the numbers on the crates in question and found their cataloguing sheets on the desktop computer. I opened my laptop, plugged in the memory stick and went to the spreadsheet listing which objects were supposed to be in each crate. Each stack consisted of eight crates on top of one another. It would take some time to check all the crates in this stack.

Troy lifted each object out of its crate, checked it, called its details to me, and I checked them against the cataloguing sheet and the spreadsheet. We had opened the third crate and finished checking five objects when Theo joined us. He scanned the scenario in front of him, and then faced us with raised his eyebrows in silent question. We didn't answer Theo's question until we finished that crate.

Troy called, "That's the last one. Five objects, but…"

"… But there should be six." I completed the statement for him.

"Yeah, you can see the empty recess where the sixth one is supposed to be. Looks like it is a fair sized artefact; I can't tell what it was, but it looks a bit like…"

"O-o-h, yes, they've hit the jackpot this time. There's supposed to be a bronze double axe in there," I snarled.

Theo wiped his hand across his face. When he looked up his face was grave. He shook his head. "I assume we have another incident like last night."

"Yes, it seems so. We still have the remaining five crates in the stack to check. It would be good if you could stay and watch," I suggested.

A search of the remaining five crates in the stack revealed two other small objects had disappeared. Though not as significant as the axe, their loss was still disturbing. Theo let fly with a string of Greek that neither Troy nor I understood, but didn't need translated. I think I said something similar – in English – when we first confirmed the crates had been disturbed. Theo's tirade probably was as unsuitable for polite company as mine was.

We told Theo our thoughts on using padlocks on the storm flap. He agreed and expressed his concern and disappointment at the losses. I wondered if we had any graphite powder. I thought there should be some amongst the conservation materials, and went to search under all the benches. None found. Disappointed, I leant on the last bench and thought about an alternative. An idea came to me – definitely left field but worth a try. "I'll be back in a minute," I called to the others as I was on my way out of the tent – and on my way to the mess tent. I examined my wild idea for flaws as I went, but didn't identify any.

The person from the catering crew I spoke to looked taken aback by my request. I wasn't sure whether she had a problem with English or if it was because the request was so way out. She uhmmed and ahhed and consulted with a colleague before the pair of them disappeared into the mysterious world that was their storage area. They reappeared shortly, triumphantly brandishing aloft a packet. They had found me a packet of cocoa powder from somewhere in their Aladdin's cave.

Back in the finds tent, I placed the packet of cocoa powder on a bench and went in search of a soft brush while the other two stood around looking bemused. With my necessary materials set out up on the first workbench, I helped Troy spread out the crates from the stack over several benches. We left a good space between each of the crates to facilitate easy access without undue handling. Although the brush I found wasn't a mop, I hoped it would do the job.

Troy and I wore latex gloves when handling any of the crates. I prayed whoever helped themselves to the artefacts wasn't so careful. Then the fun began. I carefully dusted all over each of the crates with cocoa powder. As I finished dusting the first one, I yelped with delight. "Yes, it works!"

There were unmistakable fingerprints. The shiny surface of the polypropylene crates had recorded someone's identity. Troy cut short lengths of clear adhesive tape and handed them to me. I managed to lift reasonably clear prints with it. To preserve the prints, I stuck each piece of tape onto an overhead transparency sheet using one sheet per crate. Then we recorded crate identification details on each sheet before sealing the sheets in clear plastic sleeves. All the evidence went into a small cardboard box.

Troy recorded the whole procedure on his phone. I don't know if the graphite would have been any better to work with, but the cocoa left an awful mess to clean up. We cleaned the cocoa off the benches, crates and ourselves with copious amounts of soapy water, dried the crates and attached new tell-tales. With all evidence of our inspection now removed, we restacked the crates. There was just one more thing to do. Throughout all our work with the artefacts, we followed best practice and wore white cotton or latex gloves. However, gluing the tell-tales onto the crates needed bare hands. Our fingerprints also would be on the crates. For the prints I had lifted to be useful, copies of our prints would be needed for elimination purposes. Theo confirmed he hadn't touched any of the crates.

"Good, it's just us. Okay, Troy, I need your fingerprints. The cocoa won't work; we'll need to use a stamp pad."

After rummaging in a drawer for a stamp pad and retrieving a few sheets of paper from the printer, I was ready for a practice run. It worked well once we knew how much ink to have on a finger. I recorded Troy's fingerprints on one sheet of paper and then he did the same for me. When they were dry, the labelled sheets in their sleeves went into the box with the others. As Troy and I stood scrubbing our fingers with ethanol, I started to think beyond losing the objects and looked at the bigger picture. An idea was beginning to germinate and discussing it with the others might help it along.

"Whoever filched the objects from the crates was somebody in this camp. That's a no-brainer. There is no one else around. Nobody has left since the new crew arrived. Given those facts, the missing artefacts are still here somewhere. I accept they might be secreted somewhere for later collection but, as they are small objects and not many have been gathered at this stage, I don't think that's the likely situation. To me, it is more likely that person has them tucked away amongst their personal possessions."

Theo and Troy nodded as I spoke and, as I finished, Troy picked up the conversation.

"The missing objects are somewhere in this closed environment we're living and working in. It doesn't matter where the culprit as secreted them. If the intention is to gather more and possibly larger objects, it will create a problem. There is only so much room in a bag along with one's personal belongings. In which case, a safe hiding place would be needed for the loot."

Theo appeared to ponder the facts before commenting. "It's true, nobody has been in or out of the place – except the barge skipper and that was before things started disappearing – so everything should be here somewhere, and so should the person who took them."

I continued to share the rest of my thoughts. "We could try putting in place various preventative measures, but we'll just make life more difficult for ourselves without any guarantee that the artefacts will be any safer. We talked about putting padlocks on the storm flap. It might be a deterrent, but it's also ridiculous to do that – or to *have to* do that. Wouldn't it be more productive – or effective and efficient – if the authorities simply arrived and conducted a search?"

Troy agreed. Theo was reluctant to involve the authorities and risk scaring off the culprit. He focused on the bigger picture of the boats and the trafficking network, and was keen to confirm if there was a connection with our culprit. His point about 'bigger fish to fry' made us pause to consider the complexity of the situation. Troy voiced his disagreement, and pushed to conduct a local search.

I agreed with Troy, "There is nothing to link the present problem beyond this location but, if we let it go on unchecked, the situation could develop sinister complications. At some time, the culprit needs to remove the loot from this bay. Depending on what was in the stash, they may need assistance with doing that."

Both men nodded and Troy said, "You're suggesting that, by nipping it in the bud now, we avoid any suggestion that this is nothing more than an individual collecting souvenirs." I confirmed his summation, and felt a bit reassured when neither of the men argued or disputed my reasoning.

Just as I was feeling smug, Theo unexpectedly changed tack. "Has anyone had breakfast? I haven't had anything yet. If we don't go shortly, they will have closed the kitchen. Troy, you gave the students their tasks for today. I suggest you send them off to the cove – all of them. Then you come and join Sonny and me in the mess tent for breakfast. That will give me a little time to think this over and we will be able to discuss it further in private in an empty mess tent if we need to."

Troy went to deal with the students. Before Theo and I headed for breakfast, I took the box containing the fingerprints to the far end of the tent and stashed it in a deep drawer, scattering the drawer's original contents over the top. A straggly group of students passed us as we strolled to the mess tent. Troy trailed behind them.

Theo waved to them and called out, "I'll see you at the dig shortly."

Our late arrival didn't impress the caterers, but they didn't make an issue of it. Only the dregs of the food remained but, when one of the caterers noticed Theo was with us, they offered to make whatever we felt like. Theo ordered an enormous breakfast, while I exercised restraint on behalf of Troy and myself and asked for scrambled eggs and bacon for both of us. Troy joined us while we waited for our breakfasts to arrive. Seated at a table some way from the kitchen, we ate in silence. Troy and I realised Theo was pondering our situation and we were keen to facilitate the process by remaining quiet. Discussions didn't resume until after we had coffee.

Theo led off. "I think you are correct. We do need to take action now and not let the situation escalate. Apart from anything else, the thought that this might continue, will be a distraction in itself. I need you at your best. I think this may well be a very important site – a very big site. If I am right, there will be a lot of work required to unravel its story. What we do at this early stage will be important in securing funding later for the rest of the work to be done."

Troy would join the students straight after breakfast. Theo would join them as soon as he made some phone calls. Although it was unlikely anyone would sneak back to help themselves further, I was told to stay in the finds tent – just in case. They would let the crew know subtly that I was working on the allocation of artefacts before shipping them out. We now had a plan for the morning. I had mixed feelings about remaining at the campsite. Part of me wanted to stay and protect the finds in the tent, but part of me wanted to keep an eye on what was happening at the cove.

On returning to the finds tent, I checked my emails to see if there was anything from Geoff Featherstone. There were quite a few new emails including the important one from Geoff as well as one from James. I looked at Geoff's, leaving James' until I had some 'my' time to read it. While I was enjoying Crete and it was a great opportunity for me, I have to admit that, in quiet moments, I do miss my 'real' job and James.

Geoff's list was brief; only two objects. Unfortunately, one of the objects he wanted was the double axe, which was now missing. I didn't like his chances of getting it anyway as it was the only one found so far. Unless another one turns up, I can't see Theo relinquishing the only one of these iconic Minoan artefacts to a foreign university. The other object Geoff had designs on was a piece of jewellery – probably a pendant – that featured another Minoan icon. This silver piece was similar to the famous Malia bees pendant in the Heraklion Museum. We found several similar pieces and I felt Theo might be more accommodating about this piece going to York.

I brought up the documentation for the piece and located its crate. It was a relief when the pendant was where it was supposed to be. I removed the pendant and placed it in a new crate of objects to go to York and adjusted documentation accordingly. That was easy. The next task required decisions about what else to send to York. I wasn't confident about doing that. Theo's document showed York was entitled to some larger pieces as well as four small pieces of pottery. I thought about my favourite pieces among those I had catalogued. That created another snag. One of the pieces I would have selected was the first piece of pottery that went missing.

Nevertheless, I made a start on the slow process of selecting pieces, but soon reached the end of my capabilities. The rest would have to wait until Troy was available. It was closer to lunch than morning tea, but I went for coffee anyway. It occurred to me that I hadn't heard the crew come back for coffee. I spoke to one of the caterers about it. "They must've been very quiet. How long ago were they here?"

"No … No come for coffee today," she replied hesitantly as she practised her English.

"That's strange. Do you know why they didn't come for coffee?"

There was a delay of a few seconds while she mentally composed her response before speaking. "They take… uhmm… they take coffee with them to work."

So, the kitchen had thermos flasks of some sort. That was worth remembering the next time we were stuck on the beach in the middle of the night monitoring boats. I took my coffee back to the finds tent, but didn't want to sit inside, so I dragged a stool outside and sat in the shadow of the tent. I must have wasted a reasonable amount of time sitting pondering the mysteries of life or whatever because just as I decided to go back to work, I heard the crew making their way back for lunch. I remained on my outdoor perch and Theo and Troy joined me while the rest of the crew streamed over to the ablution block.

They checked the finds I'd selected for York and Troy gave me a rundown on work in the cove that morning. Theo reported there weren't many finds so far. They would take more trays back with them this afternoon in case anything else turned up. I still hadn't worked out how to manage the finds tent once new artefacts started arriving while the earlier ones remained here. We closed the tent and padlocked the storm flap in position using two of Troy's padlocks, and went to investigate the lunch menu.

Everyone appeared exhausted and lunch started out quietly. They recovered quickly and the tent soon buzzed with excited discussion of the morning's work. Nobody appeared to be rushing back to work after lunch. I discovered Theo decided they should have 'European-style' lunch breaks involving a siesta of about two hours. Not a bad idea as today was hot. By the time they returned to work, the sun would have lost some of its sting. The tent emptied as students went for their post-prandial nap, leaving just the three of us in the dining area. I asked Troy about helping select artefacts for York. He suggested making a start on it now and finishing off tonight if needs be.

The three of us strolled to the finds tent. I went through the tedious process of unlocking the storm flap and opening up. Theo pulled up a stool, obviously intended to stay and watch. I seized the opportunity and quizzed him about the phone calls he was going to make.

"I did talk to the authorities this morning. They were very interested in my information. They agree with your reasoning, Sonny, that this is the right time to act rather than let it go on. I am waiting for confirmation, but they tentatively set tomorrow to come and make things happen. I mentioned the fingerprints you lifted and that got them excited. They will bring a number of officers and it is likely they will fingerprint everyone in camp as a routine procedure. I will update you when I get confirmation."

While Theo brought us up to date, Troy fussed with the artefacts. I realised Troy had stopped what he was doing and now stood leaning on the bench. Glancing in his direction, I immediately became concerned. He looked deeply troubled.

"Troy, are you okay? Is something wrong?"

"Argh, I'm not sure. I can't say at this stage."

"Maybe you should," I encouraged him. "Come on, share it. What's bothering you? You're starting to worry me because it looks serious, whatever it is."

"Okay, okay. Look, I wasn't going to say anything because I'm not sure. I think we might already have a problem on the new dig."

Theo jumped in, "What sort of…"

Troy cut him short. "Whoa, Theo; like I said, I'm not sure. I didn't want to stir everyone up until I was sure."

I was losing patience. "Don't worry about 'definite'. Just tell us what you think might be the problem."

"Right; a few things from near the surface ended up in a tray this morning. Where is the tray anyway? Never mind, we'll get back to that. I was helping grid up along the eastern end of the cove, so I wasn't really watching what was uncovered. On one occasion, I walked back to get extra pegs and took a quick look at the finds tray as I walked past. I didn't think any more about it until we were ready to come back for lunch. I looked in the finds tray again. There hadn't been much, if anything added since I looked previously. That wasn't surprising, but one piece which caught my eye before no longer appeared to be in the tray."

"Good God! In broad daylight; under everyone's noses …" Theo exclaimed.

"Let's not go off half cocked. I haven't checked the tray. It might be that some pieces thrown in on top made it seem like there were fewer than before. The one I'm talking about might have become buried under other pieces." Troy's attempted explanation didn't wash.

"You might be right, Troy," I murmured. "There might be nothing amiss at all. However, confirmed or not, all of us in this tent are close to believing something else has gone missing. I hope those officers do arrive tomorrow. This business is leaving a very bad taste. We'll all find our focus affected if it goes on for much longer."

Theo looked at us and nodded. "I will make another phone call to see if I can hurry things along." He went off to make his phone call, leaving Troy and I sorting artefacts for York.

By the time Theo returned, we had filled another crate, and were reasonably confident we would finish the task this evening, in plenty of time to undertake our boat monitoring duties. Theo agreed that, if we finished it tonight, he would check our selections for us in the morning. The sound of chatter drifted into the finds tent as the camp came back to life and students regrouped ready for the trek back to the cove. Troy and Theo went to join them. Then they were gone and I was alone – in both the finds tent and the camp.

I didn't have much to do. After adding a couple more paragraphs to the report I was to send to Geoff, I remembered the email from James. He didn't have any problems; mainly spoke about his current investigation. There was nothing at all heavy about the email. It was just chatty, but I thought I detected some undercurrent, an unasked question perhaps. It was some time since I last contacted him and he might be getting concerned about my return... or perhaps I imagined it because I was feeling a bit guilty about delaying my return to Australia.

My reply apologised for the delay in confirming my return and explained the date was unclear at this stage, but that I anticipated being back home within the next month. As I pressed 'send', I hoped it was the truth. I wondered about the accuracy of it afterwards. The more I thought about it, the more certain I was that there would be nothing to hold me here beyond another couple of weeks at the most.

As I couldn't think of anything else that needed doing that afternoon, I rolled up the sweatshirt from my backpack to use as a pillow and climbed up on a bench for a snooze. That's where I was when Troy came in just before six o'clock. Fortunately, he came back to camp a few minutes ahead of the rest of them and saved me the embarrassment of Theo finding me asleep. However, he made sure he got good mileage out of the moment.

"Oh good, now that you're well rested, you should have no problem staying up until all hours of the morning if a boat comes to visit tonight. I probably could even organise a night off to catch up on some sleep."

My response is better left unrecorded but in all honesty, it wasn't such a bad idea. However, I wasn't going to share that assessment with him. Our light-hearted banter ended as Theo made his appearance. Sensing he had interrupted something, he looked from one to the other of us before speaking.

"We will have *unexpected* visitors early tomorrow morning. The plan is for them to arrive before everyone goes to the cove. Troy, if they haven't arrived by the time you normally start work, maybe you should call a meeting. Discuss the plan for the day, have a post mortem on today, whatever. Just keep them in camp for as long as it takes for the others to arrive."

It was the news I had been waiting for. Why didn't I feel relieved – even overjoyed? After briefly thinking it over, I realised what I was feeling was doubtful. I stood, hands on hips, staring out of the tent at nothing in particular as half-formed scenarios flitted through my mind. Something brought me back to my surroundings, and I found Troy and Theo studying me intently. Theo asked the question that I'm sure Troy shared.

"Something is troubling you? Do you have concerns about tomorrow?"

"I'm just a bit sceptical about what the outcome will be. I can't help thinking how idiotic we're going to look when our 'visitors' do their thing and come up empty-handed."

Theo pursued it further. "You do not think it will go well tomorrow? You think the missing material will not be found?"

"Yeah, I do. It's just a gut feeling. Argh, look, I'm an investigator. Sure, there are things you need to learn, but a lot of the job is about instinct; intuition. It's about listening to and going with what your gut tells you. In this case, I may as well tell you, my reaction is a mixture of what my gut tells me and what I know from my experience and training." I looked from one to the other hoping to see something that indicated they understood what I was saying.

"At the risk of sounding really thick, I'm not sure I follow you," Troy confessed. "Can you share what you think will happen tomorrow, and why you have such negative vibes about the whole exercise?"

"It's a bit hard to explain. I'll try, but not here. I don't feel comfortable discussing anything confidential in here. The mess tent might be better when everyone has left after dinner tonight. That also gives me time to organise my thoughts so I can explain things more rationally for you." They agreed and our discussion ended.

The three of us went off to our own tents to clean up for dinner. I felt dopey after my afternoon nap and needed to get my head around what was really bothering me about tomorrow's raid. Was I just having something of a negative reaction? The kind of feeling you get when you're trying not to raise your hopes too high. I didn't think so. What I felt or thought probably had no bearing on what might happen tomorrow, but I wanted to be able to explain to the others what underpinned my concern. If I could do that – lay it out logically for them – it might let me see opportunities to remedy what I felt was going to be a disaster.

My thinking until I joined the others for dinner totally focused on tomorrow's raid. The more I thought about it the more sceptical of its success I became. No inspirational ideas emerged on how to turn a potential disaster into something positive. I went to dinner even more troubled by the prospect of tomorrow's operation than I was before.

Chapter 11

The good thing about working students hard in the heat all day was that dinner was less rowdy and they all looked to escape to their tents as soon as they had eaten. That was particularly useful tonight. I knew that, having lifted the lid on this particular issue, Theo and Troy would pursue with some determination my misgivings about tomorrow's exercise. I suspected my 'gut instinct' might be one of those 'special skills' Theo thought I brought to the project.

How to explaining my misgivings with any degree of clarity still bothered me. Somewhere along the line, I decided the simplest approach was to remove the situation from its real context and approach it as though it was any other theft needing investigation. Once I worked that out, it simplified the challenge. The last students had barely left the tent when Theo pressed me for my promised explanation. I hesitantly began.

"Don't see this as someone in an isolated bay pilfering priceless cultural artefacts. Instead, let's think of it as being in the real world around where we live. There has been a theft of some minor property. Someone who has stolen something and we need to discover the stolen goods in order to prove their guilt – or maybe their innocence. If I stole a few small objects, I wouldn't hide them in my locker, my bag, under my bed, or anywhere else, that might reasonably tie their theft to me. I don't think our culprit did either. It's possible they did take the first piece back to their tent. That was an opportunistic moment rather than a planned event. Their collection of ill-gotten gains that we know of remains not huge, but it now comprises too many pieces to explain easily."

"I follow your reasoning," Troy conceded, "But, if the pieces are not in someone's tent, where are they stashed?"

"Dunno, but any thoughts or suggestions are welcome at this point in time. If this were just a standard theft investigation, I would look for somewhere reasonably close. Somewhere the person could visit easily and frequently – if they intend to keep adding to their collection, without raising suspicion. At first glance, an isolated campsite like this suggests it has limited places like that. In fact, that's not the case. Think about places that any of us could go to legitimately. Places that don't belong to any of us individually. Of course, there is the option to secrete the objects anywhere and not necessarily within the camp. They could be in a rock crevice somewhere… or *a cave!*"

As I added my last comment, I spun round and looked hard at Troy. Excitement was evident all over his face. I knew we were thinking the same thought. Theo looked confused. We didn't bother enlightening him. Apart from that which immediately came to mind, we needed to identify other places to suggest to the officers when nothing materialised in any tent. I took out a notebook.

"Okay guys, now it's your turn," I said. "Where might objects safely remain undetected for some time?" The discussion started slowly but gained momentum.

Suggestions of a wide range of places received discussion, rejection or recording. It was nine o'clock when discussion began to wane. I ended discussions by reminding Troy we had plans for tonight: finishing sorting artefacts for York and then our nightly vigil. As I opened the finds tent, Theo asked if there had been any curiosity about the padlocks.

"No, but we did some ground work that might have reduced the level of curiosity." Troy replied.

"How so? What do you mean by 'ground work'?" Theo asked.

"We used your visit as the excuse," I said and Troy laughed. "In the mess tent after we put the locks on, Troy and I openly discussed how, now that you were in camp, we had to go by the book to ensure proper security for the finds."

Theo didn't object to any of the material we selected for York, and didn't stay long. Before heading for his tent, he promised to talk to us in the morning. Troy and I worked on until Troy announced he had completed the list for York. Just as well, it was time for a stroll down to the beach. We soon found ourselves seated on our usual bit of sand. Alone at last, our first topic of conversation was THAT suggestion which had arisen back in the mess tent.

"Should we be proactive and explore that cave where we stored our dive gear after the first dive and before the boat arriving during daylight upset things?" Troy asked.

"I think it's worth a look, but I don't think we'll find anything there."

"You don't think it's ideal for hiding things? We hid our dive gear there."

"Nah, it was okay for dive gear; too big and too open for artefacts. A cave is an obvious place to search. Any smaller, less obvious cave – close by and easily accessible – might be worth a look."

Troy queried what I thought to be the most likely hiding place. I didn't have anywhere in mind and suggested that, if they didn't find anything in the tents tomorrow, I would follow whatever my gut suggested. Still keen to have a look at 'our' cave, Troy suggested that, if we stayed in the shadows, we could walk there now.

"No, if you're really keen to have a look, we could slip away to check it out in the morning while everyone else is being held at the campsite."

Silence reigned for a while, with each of us engrossed in his own thoughts. Troy checked the luminous dial on his watch.

"It's after eleven o'clock. Either no one is coming tonight or they're running late."

A few moments after he spoke, a pale light moved past the eastern promontory. Our boat had arrived. Another drop-off occurring so soon was surprising. With our arms resting on our knees to steady the binoculars, we watched the boat searching for the requisite anchorage. Tonight's activity didn't deviate from the usual script. We were in for a long night. It was unlikely the boat would leave before 2.00am at the earliest. With no need for close monitoring of every moment of the boat's presence, I took the opportunity to ask Troy how he came to be on Crete.

"You've got me curious. You said you thought coming to Crete with the field school would help ease your desire to be out in the field again. How did you manage to swing it to get time off? Ignoring the potential of this new project, was it worthwhile?" I wasn't sure he had heard me as he took a while to respond.

"It wasn't easy. There was no need for me to come at all. Geoff has done it for years and manages it very well on his own. In fact, I didn't have much to do with the field school. My supervisors weren't keen on letting me come and took some persuading. However, it's a recognised fact that academics need to work in their appropriate disciplines periodically to maintain their industry currency – to understand new trends and what issues students completing their degrees, and the industry in general, are facing. I hadn't been out in the field for quite a while, so I used that to strengthen my argument to do some fieldwork. Geoff was about to leave for Crete, so they let me accompany the field school on the proviso I found my own project here to work on.

"That was a long shot: finding some separate project of acceptable substance to work on."

"Yes, initially, but I knew about those ruins on the hillside. If all else failed, I could base something on them."

We both watched the boat anchored in the bay. "Judging by the way that boat is swinging around, it must be windier out there than it is here," I commented. "I imagine they'll still put a diver down even if visibility is poor." Not long after I'd spoken, we watched the diver step off the stern dive platform.

There would be nothing else happening until the diver resurfaced. We lapsed into silence. The binoculars are heavy, so I resorted to only the occasional look. Troy kept his glued to his eyes. He was watching the boat, but the firm set of his jaw suggested his mind was elsewhere – not necessarily a happy place. I tried lightening the mood by chatting some more.

"So how did it all work out? You said the field school didn't need you. Did your being here create any problems?"

"It was awkward. I felt superfluous to the whole exercise. I don't think Geoff was particularly happy about my presence which didn't help, but he ended up just accepting me as something that was thrust upon him."

"It seems to have worked out okay. How did you sort it out?" Troy fell silent. I let him be until he was ready to speak again.

"It didn't take long to get the camp set up and started on the dig. There was an allocation of responsibilities at a planning meeting on the second night. I realised I was surplus to requirements. After the students disbursed, I took Geoff aside to see what I might contribute. We agreed that, for the first couple of days, I would assist with getting the dig underway. Geoff assured me he was happy for my assistance. The first few days of starting a new school always are absolute chaos until youthful exuberance and confusion are brought under control, and students started remembering all the stuff they have been taught. I took Geoff's assurances as polite platitudes but played along. It took until about the fifth day for everything to settle down. However, once that occurred, I again felt sidelined."

As he finished speaking, Troy lowered his binoculars and glanced across at me, but quickly returned to watching the boat. He continued to tell me about his own project.

"With nothing to do with the field school, I sought to base a project on the ruins on the site on the hillside platform. It had the potential for a worthwhile project, and Geoff assigned two postgraduate students who accompanied the field school to assist with my site."

"That was good of Geoff, but I suppose it made things less awkward for him. Anyway, your site ultimately proved worthwhile."

"Yeah, it kept the three of us occupied for the duration of the school. It was exciting proving that it wasn't a makeshift fort, but the remnants of a high status villa and it justified my time on Crete."

I looked through my binoculars before posing another question. There was activity. The diver was surfacing. He followed the routine of the previous divers. Within moments of his disappearance below decks, the sound of the inboard diesel coming to life and the rattle of the anchor chain drifted across the bay. All controlled and precise, within what seemed like only moments, the boat was heading westward out of the bay. Tonight's operation was quick. It was just after one o'clock when the boat disappeared from sight behind the headland. We watched for a further twenty minutes, although we knew it unlikely anything else would happen.

If Theo's information was correct, our 'surprise visitors' would arrive very early tomorrow morning. I set my alarm a little earlier than usual, as I wanted to be up before the action started. I was not particularly sleepy thanks to my afternoon nap, so tossed and turned for ages before finally falling asleep.

*****

Somewhere in that twilight zone prior to deep sleep, a disturbing thought occurred to me, and it revisited me in those few drowsy moments before I awoke properly this morning. It had me out of bed in a flash. No doubt, it stemmed from the discussion we had about likely hiding places for the missing artefacts. What better place was there to hide something than where it could do the most damage to the person who reported its disappearance? Translated, that meant, hide it somewhere that would incriminate me. The only way that might occur was for the missing objects to be in my tent.

My tent is small fortunately, and I currently am experiencing a minimalist existence. Nevertheless, it took me more than half an hour to go through everything in my tent and, just for good measure, I checked under the thin mattress on my bed. The backpack I used to take gear down to the beach every night came in for scrutiny as well. My search turned up nothing. I was relieved but felt foolish.

I sat on my bed and thought about how my day might pan out. With no reason to hang around in the finds tent, logically, I would join the others at the cove. It was a few days since Troy and I had dived.

Maybe once things settle down today, we can spend some time in the water. I was looking forward to investigating artefacts on the seabed and maybe bringing some back to work on. The best thing to do at this stage was get breakfast out of the way. I took my backpack to the mess tent with me with the intention of putting it back in the finds tent after breakfast.

Troy and Theo sat at a small table off to one side of the tent; I joined them. "Are you planning on going somewhere?" Theo asked as he eyed off my backpack.

I dismissed the question by simply saying it contained some gear that I used. I needed to have a word to Troy but it shouldn't look too contrived. I pulled out a notebook and flipped to a page covered with writing. Placing it in front of Troy, but in the middle of the table, I pointed to something on the page, causing Troy to lean in to look at it. I leaned in towards him as well and, seeing the confusion spreading across his face, spoke quickly.

"Pretend you're reading something interesting and don't look so confused. As soon as you can, I suggest you go back to your tent and search every possible nook and cranny before our visitors arrive. It's just a precaution, but it's one I think worth taking."

He played the game well, nodding and looking interested as I pointed and spoke quietly to him. When I finished speaking, we both sat back. I put my notebook away and Troy looked hard at me across the table.

"I think that's a good idea," he said nodding. "It might be worthwhile doing that."

Theo had played along with the charade, tilting his head to look at the notebook as if following our conversation. Now he sat back as well and echoed Troy's comment about it being a good idea. He concluded by giving Troy a knowing look and a slight nod. Troy bolted his breakfast down and left. As he walked away, he turned and spoke loudly so that everyone in the tent could hear. "Don't go away you two, I'll be back shortly. I just want to get something."

Troy returned after about half an hour, stopping to talk to the rest of the crew as he made his way to our table. He asked the crew to hang around the camp for a meeting with him in about an hour's time. Then, smiling he sat down at our table, but I could see the concern behind the smile. While pantomiming reading something from his notebook, he gave us results of his search.

"Nothing found. More worrying though was that I discovered somebody had been in there at some point in time."

I pursed my lips and nodded as though I was agreeing with something he was saying and hoped it hid my shock. I glanced at Theo. He was in deep consideration of a spot on the tabletop. Troy's information was tantalising; I wanted to know more. Most of the students had left or were leaving the mess tent and the caterers were cleaning up. With the clattering and banging coming from the kitchen, I felt it safe to question Troy.

"Are you sure? Was anything taken?"

Stretching and making a show of laughing, he leaned slightly forward to answer. "No, nothing taken; a couple of things have been ever so slightly disturbed; hardly noticeable at all if you're not looking for something."

He scratched his chin and thought about it. "Not today or yesterday, but a couple of days ago I threw some stuff on top of the things that have been disturbed. Before you ask, I wouldn't have disturbed them accidentally when I threw the stuff on top."

"Anything sensitive in there they might have accessed? What about the notebook with the details of the boats coming into the bay?"

"No, there's nothing contrary to our best interest in my tent. That notebook is in my backpack which, apart from last night, was in the finds tent."

Theo shook his head in disgust. "I can't believe all this. What in hell's name is going on? I hope to God this morning sorts it all out. This is no good for my blood pressure. I might take a stroll down to the beach to help me calm down a bit...," and added in a stage whisper, "And hang around in case we get some visitors."

That left Troy and I wondering how to fill in the hour before Troy's meeting with the crew. When all else fails go back to the finds tent, and that's what we did. After we stashed our backpacks under a bench at the far end of the tent, we didn't have anything to do, but it was a good place to look as though we were busy. So, we sat at a bench chatting until the faint drone of a motor drifted into earshot. We belted out of the tent, hesitating long enough for the padlocks to be put in place, and then jogged to the windbreak. We saw a boat had already nosed up onto the sand. With more decorum, we walked across the beach for anticipated introductions to the boat's occupants. It didn't happen that way. Intent on wasting no time standing around chatting, the visitors headed for the camp site, with the rest of the gaggle of bodies – we were a total gaggle of eight in number – following along behind.

Troy left us to return to the mess tent and his meeting with the crew. Theo and the visitors accompanied me to the finds tent. The visitors' leader explained their planned search. Theo handed over the box containing the fingerprints we had lifted earlier, and explained that all our crew were now with Troy in the mess tent. After pointedly suggesting that Theo and I remain in the finds tent and that they would send Troy to join us, the visitors strode off to the mess tent.

We questioned Troy when he arrived about our crew's reaction to the visitors and whether any one displayed a particular reaction.

"I watched for that. I made sure I could see everyone when the officers introduced themselves and explained their presence. I think our suspicions were right on the money. For a moment or two, I thought one of our crewmembers was going to make a run for it. I definitely saw panic in her reaction. It only lasted a fleeting moment. I suspect that, after a rapid assessment of her situation, she decided she was safe. Besides, there was nowhere to go to get away. I guess all we can do now is wait to see what eventuates. As I was leaving, I suggested to the visitors that they need to consider the catering staff as well."

I mulled Troy's report over for a few moments before commenting. "Her momentary reaction suggests they won't find the stuff in her tent. It probably took her a moment to realise she would be okay as they wouldn't find anything to incriminate her. That brings us back to the question of where might the stuff be hidden. Troy, to eliminate the possibility, maybe you and I should slip away now to have a look at that cave." My last comment caught Theo's attention.

"What's this cave you're talking about? I'll come with you."

We explained about the cave where we had stored our dive gear. It didn't seem relevant but we probably should check it anyway. Troy suddenly cut across the conversation. "Oh hell, I just remembered that before *that* cave, there is a smaller one. I noticed it the other day when I was with Con. It might be a better bet than the one we were going to look at."

"Good," Theo exclaimed clapping his hands together. "We should look at both caves to make the walk worthwhile."

The cave Troy led us to was small and almost invisible unless you were walking up close along the base of the hill. The opening, with a maximum of about 200 millimetres in any direction, was about the same distance above the sand. Troy shone his torch in to the cave. It appeared quite shallow but wide, stretching away some distance from either side of the opening. Theo stopped Troy as he was about to put his hand in to check the interior.

"Better not touch anything. There might be nothing there, but it is better that the officers check it out."

We reluctantly agreed and continued down to the larger cave. Having moved around quite freely in there, we knew that the cave was spacious enough to hold a number of large objects easily. Internal walls were craggy with many crevices and niches. Troy and I entered the cave and Theo followed us in, making it a very friendly gathering.

The sand inside the entrance to the cave showed significant disturbance. We couldn't tell if it was our legacy or someone else's contribution. Our torches picked up nothing as we shone them around the walls. Troy and I went to opposite sides of the cave and began systematically examining walls. I came across a small niche that looked as though a small rock had rolled out of its resting place leaving a bit of a gap similar to one left after removal of a brick from a wall. I shone my torch into it. There was something loose in there.

"Troy, Theo, come over here and observe, please. I think there is something in this hollow."

I retrieved a latex glove from my pocket but didn't put it on. I used it as you might an oven cloth to grab something hot. With my two observers peering over my shoulders, I reached in carefully with the glove and withdrew one of the loose objects. Troy and I shone our torches on it. I raised my eyebrows questioningly at Troy as we stared at the glazed pottery shard.

"Ah hah, I saw something like this recovered from the cove site on the first day."

"Put it back," Theo directed. "We will draw the officer's attention to these two caves and leave him to organise his men to investigate."

After carefully replacing the object, we scuffled up the sand as we exited the cave so it wouldn't be so apparent we had been stomping around in there. As we approached the campsite, Troy suggested we wander down and check the anchors of the visitors' boat.

"They're fine. They only arrived a few minutes ago," Theo objected.

"I'm not sure we're supposed to be out roaming around. I suspect we're supposed to stay in the finds tent. It was a polite way of confining us to camp. I thought that, if we had a particular reason for being on the beach, we're less likely to raise the ire of that bloke in charge."

"Good thinking, Troy. Anchors should always be checked shortly after they're placed to make sure they're holding properly," I added. "Come on, Theo."

To strengthen the subterfuge, after checking the anchors, we wandered along the beach a bit before returning to the campsite. Nobody appeared to have missed us.

Back in the finds tent, as Theo hadn't objected to our selection of objects for York, we packed them and asked Theo to organise the barge as soon as possible. After that, we settled down to speculate on what was happening in the rest of the camp. I asked Theo to clarify something.

"I have never heard you use the word 'Police' to describe our current visitors. Therefore, I assume they are Interpol. That makes sense, as it is Interpol that's been working with ICOM on the trafficking of cultural objects. Am I correct?"

"Ah, yes, they are from Interpol. Over the last few years I have been working closely with them and the ICOM directorate on trafficking matters."

It was only just over two hours ago that the officers arrived, but it felt like an eternity, and we had run out of things to talk about. As I retrieved a bottle of water from my backpack, I realised we hadn't spoken to Theo about last night's boat.

"Troy, we haven't reported on last night's vigil on the beach. While our esteemed visitors are here, might it be a good time to investigate what is hanging off that mooring block?"

Theo looked apprehensive as Troy began his report, and considered the information for some time before commenting. Troy and I both urged him to organise with the Interpol officers for us to conduct the dive. Eventually he acquiesced, agreeing to speak to the officer in charge.

I fussed around cleaning down benches but it only filled in a few minutes. Troy announced he was desperate for coffee. I agreed. It wasn't that I needed more caffeine. It was just that getting coffee might alleviate the ever-increasing boredom. After a few more minutes, desperation won out and, locking up behind us, we went to the mess tent, fully expecting to run into a hostile barrage of visitors. By now, Interpol had been in camp about three hours.

There was nobody in the tent but us. Even the kitchen was deathly quiet. Why question good luck. We got coffees and sat at a table where we decided to stay until someone came looking for us.

Chapter 12

While the mess tent was a pleasant environment, there still wasn't much to talk about, so we sat and sipped our coffees in silence. The best part of an hour elapsed before anyone came looking for us.

The officer in charge strode in looking none too pleased to find us there. After some pointed comments about us not doing as instructed – which we ignored – he informed us they were nearly finished with the crew. Almost on cue, the caterers returned looking none too impressed with the morning's events. They were silent and went directly to the kitchen. Theo asked if there was anything to report. The officer confirmed he wanted to discuss the outcome of their search. However, he kept glancing at Troy and I as he spoke, clearly suggesting we should disappear. Theo got the message and clarified that anything said would be to the three of us. The officer shrugged and drew up a chair. As he did so, Troy stood up.

"Now you're finished with our crew, they're likely to head straight here. They'll be desperate for coffee by now. It might be better if we went to the finds tent," Troy suggested.

We followed Troy to the finds tent and all took up our perches around one of the benches. As encouragement, we all looked expectantly at the officer, but he remained silent. After a few moments of no response, Theo offered a vocal encouragement.

"Are you able to share any information regarding the results of this morning's search, or are we sitting here waiting for something else to happen?"

After clearing his throat and referring to his notebook, the officer began to recite what he considered appropriate for our ears. It was disappointing but not surprising. They searched everybody's tent but found no sign of the missing objects. They took everybody's fingerprints for comparison with those from the crates. He asked for suggestions about where else to look. Troy and Theo hesitated, but I had several ideas of my own and didn't hesitate to put them forward.

"Without knowing the scope of this morning's search, my comments might be irrelevant. I believe there are other sites besides staff tents that merit searching. Principal among those is the tent that stores the excavation tools, and the tent that houses the boat is probably worth a look too. Apart from that, there are a couple of sites outside the camp which might be critical to your investigation."

He looked me up and down with open scepticism for a moment or two before responding. "What makes you think these tents might be important?"

"There are a number of shelves, racks, containers and other items in the store tent which are ready-made hiding places for small objects. The same is true but to a lesser extent for the boat tent."

"I see." His scepticism didn't disappear. "Have you investigated these places yourself? I have no desire to waste time searching places where it has already been established there is nothing to find."

"No we haven't checked those places. They only occurred to me this morning while we were hanging around in here, so I don't think searching those tents would be a waste of time. Whether you find something or not is another matter." This pompous ass was not going on my Christmas card list, and he was succeeding in bringing out my worst side.

Theo intervened before the relationship could deteriorate further. "If you wish to take a look, I could show you those two tents," he volunteered.

The officer grunted his approval and gestured for Theo to lead the way. As he exited the tent, he turned to Troy and I, and asked us if we would mind very much waiting here until he returned. We didn't bother to reply. He was already on his way to the stores tent with Theo.

"Pleasant chap, wouldn't you agree?" Troy commented. "I suppose we should feel sorry for the poor bloke: riding into camp with his cavalry all gung-ho only to come up empty-handed after several hours' work."

"Of course we should feel sorry for him for that, and for having to put up with the unhappy staff, but somehow I don't."

By the time Theo and his 'companion' returned, it was lunchtime. I detected an improvement in the officer's demeanour, and Theo was positively beaming as they entered the tent. Theo stole the officer's thunder.

"We found them! No, we found *some of them.*"

The officer held out a bucket. The missing field school objects lay in the bottom. Troy and I donned gloves and checked the objects for damage – none detected. After checking the identity of the objects against our records, I posed another question.

"Okay, these are the missing field school objects, but what about the things we believe have disappeared from the cove site?"

The officer look confused. "Are you telling me there are more objects missing? I was not aware of this."

Theo explained how we had just started the new dig site, and that some things already appeared to have not come back to the finds tent. The assumption was that, at some time and somehow, they had joined the other missing artefacts. He told of our conclusion that, if they were not found with the other missing objects, it was likely they were hidden somewhere between the cove and the campsite. We could think of a couple of likely hiding places along the base of the hill.

Oh dear, there was that sceptical look plastered all over the officer's face again. I explained this too had only occurred to us this morning and, like the tents, there wasn't an opportunity to check it out or tell him about it. I smiled ever so nicely as I offered that we would show him the places we mentioned if he was interested in having a look. Rather more forcefully than was required, he assured us he was interested in having a look. I suspect that, while we didn't think much of him, his exasperation with us also had increased... although we were ever so obliging and very polite.

We fell into step behind Troy who led the way to the first small niche we looked at this morning. I stepped up my pace to walk beside him, leaving the others some distance behind us. As we approached the niche, we dragged our feet a little, knowing it would mess up any footprints we left earlier. With us all assembled outside the niche, Troy took charge.

"This is the first of the places. You will need a torch to be able to see in there." he offered the officer his torch, and I offered Theo mine.

The officer came up with a handful of loose material from inside the cave. We assured him it was rubble and not artefacts. Then we strode off to the larger cave further along the hillside.

Halted a few feet in front of the entrance, Troy suggested the other two investigate the cave while we waited outside. The officer led the way in. Troy gave Theo an exaggerated wink as he walked past in the officer's wake. We hoped that, if the search became a protracted exercise, Theo might 'miraculously' find the objects we discovered this morning. The officer could do with some cheering up. I couldn't help but think it was better if he was in a good mood when we got round to discussing the boats that come in the night... and the possibility of a dive on the mooring block.

It seemed to be taking an eternity for anything to happen in the cave. Finally, a commotion from inside made us rush to the entrance. We feigned excitement and surprise as the officer held out his hands to display the artefacts they found. Of course, no one brought anything appropriate for carrying the pieces back to camp. A rummage in my pocket produced a wildly coloured bandanna. I spread it on the sand. The officer placed the artefacts in the centre of it. I tied all four corners of the bandanna together, making it an easy bundle for Theo to carry back.

By the time we deposited the objects in the finds tent, lunch was over for the crew and the mess tent was empty. The officer and his men joined us for lunch. It turned out much friendlier than the rest of the day had been so far. When lunch was almost finished, Theo whispered quietly to the officer in charge that there was a further serious issue for discussion. The officer's smile seemed to evaporate at the very mention of another issue.

Leaving his men to relax in the mess tent, the officer in charge followed the three of us back to the finds tent. Troy was curious about whether to send the crew back to work or not. The officer suggested they have the afternoon off to laze about in camp. We supported the idea in the hope that it might lessen the hostility that prevailed since the raid. While Troy went to talk to the crew, the officer in charge rostered his men to take turns on the beach to direct anyone venturing beyond the windbreak back to camp. Another officer would ensure anyone (to our thinking that meant Despina) who showed an interest in what was going on in the bay was directed back to their tent.

Once we were back in the finds tent, Theo detailed our observation of the boats coming into the bay at night. Troy provided dates and times reading directly from his notebook. We brought up on the computer images of the mooring block to help illustrate what we believed was the reason for the visits. Having reached the point where there were no more questions to ask and no more information to give, the officer stood and paced about the tent. After a couple of minutes he stood drumming his fingers on the bench for a few moments before breaking the heavy silence that had settled over us.

"This is troubling news. From what you tell me, a boat came last night and it is likely that a second boat will arrive tonight. Is this correct?"

We nodded silently but I needed to explain something further. "We do anticipate a boat will come tonight. However, my concern is that, with your boat sitting out there in full view on the beach, it might

114

not stop, electing to travel on past the bay rather than risk drawing attention to itself."

"Hmm, you make a valid point. If they were used to seeing nothing on the beach, something different – like a boat – would be enough to scare them away. I need to give this situation some thought."

Feeling I might be on a bit of a roll, I plucked up courage to continue. "Of course, this could all be speculation. We don't know what's going on out there other than they always have a diver working during the time they anchor out there. We have never risked taking a look at what that mooring block is being used for."

He looked genuinely surprised. "Why not? I would have thought you wouldn't be able to contain your curiosity. Have I misjudged all of you."

"We were tempted," I admitted, "But were concerned that the second boat might be hanging around somewhere close by – out of sight but with visuals on the bay. We didn't want to risk what might be a nasty experience if they observed us showing too much interest in their enterprise. We are very isolated and have no way of protecting ourselves here in this camp."

He was off pacing again, so once more silence descended on the tent. After a few moments, he returned to the bench. "I need to discuss this with my men." At the entrance to the tent, he turned and gestured to Troy and I. "You took those images of the mooring? Does this mean one of you is a diver?"

"No, it means both of us are divers," Troy corrected him.

"Oh, I see. Do you have dive equipment here in camp? If we wanted to look out there now, would you be able to dive?"

"When do we go?" Troy and I chorused together.

"Good. I will talk to my men now and come back soon. In the meantime, you should get ready for a dive."

We were grinning widely and then we remembered Theo was there. We needed his approval to do this. We turned to face him, but his stony face suggested he was going to veto the whole thing.

"Well, are we going to do this, Theo?" Troy demanded, exasperation creeping into his voice.

"I believe we need to know what is going on out there and that means investigating that mooring block. However, you are not going out there..." I groaned audibly, "... without me," he continued with a twinkle in his eye. "I am also a diver and brought equipment with me." What a tease! Then, we were all laughing and there were high fives all round.

We wasted no time. The three of us went back to our tents and climbed into our wetsuits before congregating back in the finds tent. The officer was waiting when we returned and struggled to hide a smile as we marched in.

"We didn't want to waste time, so we got ready while you were talking to your men," Theo explained.

"So, Theo, you think you are going to dive as well?"

"But of course. My role on ICOM demands that I know what is going on. The only way to accurately report on our findings is to see for myself."

"What if I had decided it was too risky and we weren't going to investigate?" the officer asked.

I answered for Theo. "We'd have gone anyway. It's too much trouble getting into these suits not to get them wet. If things got unpleasant, hopefully you'd come to our aid."

"Humf," he snorted, "This is how it is going to work: a couple of my men will take our boat around the western end of the bay. I believe you said that the second boat arrives from that direction. Another man and I will take you three out in your boat to the mooring block and put you over the side. Then we will take a quick trip around the eastern end of the bay to check for any boats that might be hanging around. Are there any questions?"

"Er, only one," Theo responded. "After we check the mooring block, are we expected to swim to shore while you lot run around in boats?"

"No, of course not. My colleague and I will take a very quick run around the eastern end and then come back to collect you when you complete your dive. Is it too far for you to swim to shore, old man?" He finished sarcastically.

"No, that isn't a problem for any of us. However, we don't want to find ourselves waiting out there for you to come back when you do not intend to return to collect us. I am merely checking what the plan is."

It looked like the slanging match could go on for a while so I took the initiative to intervene. "Look guys, you can continue swapping insults if you like but, if we don't go shortly, it will be too late. So, are we all going now, or are Troy and I going to get our boat while you pair stay here arguing?" That did the trick.

Everyone went to organise the respective boats. We stowed our gear on board and, with the officer at the helm, set off for the mooring block. A bit of delicate manoeuvring ensued before we dropped anchor at the correct GPS coordinates. After the usual equipment checks, the three of us rolled backwards off the gunwales and into the water. Visibility was excellent and we were only about three metres away from the block. Troy surfaced and signalled the boat that we were in the right spot. After only a few strokes, we heard the anchor hauled in. For a split second, I experienced an eerie feeling of abandonment – perhaps even panic. It disappeared when I saw the large object tethered to the mooring block.

We approached carefully. Shackled to the eyebolt was a large capsule-like fibreglass container. It appeared to have built-in buoyancy. Tethered to the mooring block by short ropes, it floated only a few centimetres above the mooring but remained well below the surface. Troy clicked off a number of photos of the container and its attachment before we examined it closely.

It had some fancy stainless steel clamp arrangement locking the shallow lid onto the deeper body of the container. After inspecting it from every angle, Theo signalled us to surface. On the surface, Troy asked the question.

"Our assumptions were right. I think it's safe to assume last night's boat attached that container to the mooring block for tonight's boat to recover. The question is, what happens next. Do we leave it there and do nothing, or do we try to open it to see what's inside?"

"We need to know what's inside that thing," Theo replied, "But I don't know how we're going to open it. Those clamps don't look like they will be easy to open underwater. Besides, opening it underwater, if we could manage it, would destroy anything delicate inside it. We need to haul it onto a boat and open there. It would be handy to have a boat around right now."

As Theo finished speaking, we became aware of an approaching boat. We prepared to dive again – just in case – but it slowed and we recognised our boat and our 'crew man' waving to us. He cut the motor and let it drift up to us.

"What has happened? Why are you up here and not down there?" he demanded, and pointed towards the seabed in case we hadn't heard or understood him.

Troy pulled himself up onto the gunwale to show the men the images of the container. While everyone was otherwise engaged, I moved close to Theo to speak without the others overhearing.

"Theo, I think we should look at those shackles on the eye bolt to determine how easy or otherwise they will be to undo if we decide to raise it."

Theo simply nodded. We checked our air supply and dived again. Not surprisingly, they were done up tightly. We surfaced and spoke to Troy.

"We are going to need a wrench to undo those shackles. Is there anything in the boat we might use?"

The crewman ducked into the boat and emerged a few seconds later with exactly the tool I wanted. I took receipt of the tool as tacit approval to lift the container, and suggested Troy join us at the mooring block, as I wasn't sure how difficult or heavy the exercise would be. It proved complicated. The shackles were extremely tight, and there was nowhere for the person using the wrench to brace themselves. By a process of trial and error, we devised a method that required the involvement of all three of us. I wondered how a diver working alone could manage the task. With the container finally free of the block, we towed it to the surface.

It proved equally difficult to lift it into the boat. With a lot of heaving and shoving, we finally dragged it over the side and onto the floor of the boat. The next challenge was for Troy and I to haul Theo into the boat. While we did that, the Interpol men examined the container in an effort to work out how to open it. It didn't take much to work out that the clamps had to be unscrewed. Like everything else so far, that was no easy task. The clamps, screwed tightly, had a good dollop of sealant applied around the screws to prevent any leakage into the container.

With barely enough room for the three men to work around the container, Theo and I took up relaxed positions in the bow. From our vantage points, we had a view of all that was going on in the bay. After a period of heavy labour, they were ready to lift the lid. Even that presented a challenge. A thick layer of the same sealant glued the lid to the body of the capsule. The three men sat back to contemplate the problem. I moved over to the capsule and examined the seal before motioning Troy to join me. As a last ditch effort, Troy and I pounded the blades of our dive knives in as far as they would go between the lid and the box, and worked the blades. Eventually, the lid popped free.

Theo, his excitement at fever pitch, moved to stand by the container. As the lid came free, I heard him gasp. Troy and I rose to our knees to peer into the container. The only thing stopping me gasping the way Theo had was the fact that I had neither breath nor energy left after struggling with the lid. The contents stunned me.

Cocooned in lashings of modern day packing material, was an exquisitely carved statue. Surprisingly small for its weight, it was about 400 millimetres high and carved from what I thought to be a single block of marble. The most breathtaking thing about the statue, apart from the delicate detailed carving, was its adornment. Lavish gold and gemstones decorations accentuated its beauty. I could make out lapis and other stones, which I guessed were either rubies or garnets. An embedded weapon – or sceptre – protruded from one of the statue's hands. It looked bronze, as was the stylised animal head on which the figure rested one foot.

From the moment the lid came off, Troy photographed the statue and all that happened. Then, with our dive gloves still on, we carefully lifted the statue out of its resting place and stood it upright on the floor of the boat so he could get images of it from all sides. Like a protective mother, Theo hovered ready to grab it at the slightest indication that it might topple over.

It was getting late; the sun was beginning to weaken. I was concerned that, if we were putting the container back, we needed to go over the side again soon or we would be working in the dark, and we hadn't come prepared for that. "This is a fantastic moment, but it's going to be dark before we know it," I reminded them. "What happens next? Are we going to put this back where we found it, or are we taking it ashore? We need to decide now."

The statue went back into the container and we replaced the lid. This went against Theo's training, and he argued strenuously that we should take it, not put it back on the mooring. I was half inclined to agree, but only half. The other half of me knew that, if we were going to get anywhere with halting this operation, it had to look like it hadn't been disturbed – well, as undisturbed as possible. We couldn't replace the sealant. The moment someone at its destination attempted to open the capsule, it would be obvious someone had tampered with it.

With the lid secured, Theo supervised the four of us as we lifted it back over the side. The Interpol men held the ropes until we were back in the water, then the fun began. The capsule's built-in buoyancy made it more difficult to swim it back down than bringing it to the surface had been. The three of us ended up lying on top of it as we swam it down, and then two of us straddled it while Troy loosely fitted the shackles to reattach it to the mooring block.

By the time we were confident the container was securely tethered, visibility had deteriorated. The bottom of the boat wasn't visible until we were a couple of metres from the surface. There was the usual protracted and somewhat undignified performance of shedding gear and scrambling back aboard. The officer in charge was speaking on the radio and, within seconds, the Interpol boat came round the western headland, and both boats headed back to shore.

While the others took care of the boats, Theo and I went for showers. One of the Interpol men was despatched in their boat to spend the night in Timpaki. I was the first of our mob to arrive in the mess tent and claimed a four-seater table to the rear of the dining area. Over the next few minutes, the other three men joined me. I was famished and, by the speed at which food disappeared off plates, I wasn't the only one. No conversation interrupted the despatch of food, but the silence couldn't last forever. Theo saw to that.

"I looked up that statue before I came to dinner. I wanted to see if it was on ICOM's list of stolen artefacts. It is. It disappeared from a museum in Persepolis about two years ago, although nobody checked on it for a number of years before that. It was in storage awaiting restoration work. Somehow, it managed to escape from an otherwise secure storage area at a major museum."

"It would need a lot of help to escape," Troy suggested.

"The whole thing reeks of insider assistance," I observed. "I wonder how many other things in long-term storage have escaped without anyone noticing."

Theo nodded excitedly. "Exactly; I rang the director of that museum. We were students together a long time ago and have remained good friends. Of course, I couldn't tell him much, like where his missing statue was for instance. However, I did suggest that he initiate an immediate full-scale audit of his storage facility. He is savvy enough to know that, when I say something to that effect, he should comply without asking too many questions."

"Speaking of a certain artefact," I began, "What happens next?"

Tito – I had discovered that was the name of the officer in charge – looked a bit confused by the question. "What are you asking?"

"If it follows the usual pattern, another boat will come tonight to collect the container from the mooring block. Every night Troy and

I monitor the bay. So, what I'm asking is: are we to monitor the bay tonight and do we do anything if a boat arrives?"

"Ah, I understand. We – my men – will monitor it tonight. You may join us if you wish. However, we will do nothing to interfere with whatever happens out there."

I glanced at Theo who seemed relaxed about Tito's reply. I didn't feel the same. "If we do nothing, the statue will disappear and be lost again. Do we let that happen?" The whole concept of something recently found knowingly being lost again was beyond my acceptance.

"It will not be lost again," Tito said very pointedly. "We are focused on the job we have to do. There is more at stake than grabbing one boat and its illegal cargo. We want the whole network. We may not get it, but we want as much of it as we can get, hopefully to smash the network's operation." I was properly contrite and apologised.

Tito left the tent to organise the night's surveillance. Theo chuckled. "You manage to stir him up very nicely every time. Don't worry about it. He's a bit – how do you say… *pompous*, but completely dedicated to what he does. What he won't tell you, because he believes the fewer who know the better, is that we placed a very small tracking device amongst the packing in that container."

"Good, I'm pleased, but what happens when they unpack the container and the device is found? Any chance of tracking the artefact then disappears, and the network will move their operation somewhere else away from this bay." Again, I was uncomfortable with the way things were going.

Theo tried reassuring me nobody would discover the device but he wouldn't elaborate. I'm not big on blind acceptance of something not backed up by either fact or hard evidence. In this instance, I had no choice other than to trust others knew what they were doing.

We didn't linger over dinner that evening, only chatting for a few minutes after Tito left. On our way out, we stopped by the table where our crew sat. To make the first move towards restoring cordial relations, Troy tried a few well-chosen words in an effort to placate the rising dissension stemming from today's fuss.

"I understand how you feel. I'm not overjoyed at having lost a whole day's excavation either. I will try to persuade people to let us go back to the dig site in the morning. I'm sure none of us wants to spend another boring and unpleasant day in camp. I will let you know the outcome at breakfast." Troy's words didn't meet with outright rejection, but they did encounter varying levels of scepticism.

With nowhere else to go so early in the evening, we three once more found ourselves perched on stools in the finds tent until it was time to go and watch for a boat to arrive. I couldn't help but see tonight's surveillance activities as nothing more than an exercise in futility but, who knows, maybe something exciting will happen and I wouldn't want to miss it.

Chapter 13

After dinner, Tito bought the Interpol men to the finds tent so we could explain our surveillance procedure. Tito reiterated that we could observe but not be involved tonight. It's fair to say we felt a bit put out by his attitude. Nevertheless, in spite of Tito's position on the matter, we were not about to abandon something we started. Troy and I followed our normal routine and, around ten o'clock, went to the beach and took up our usual position. Tito and his 'watchers' were already in position on the opposite side of the walkway through the windbreak from where we normally sat.

Troy checked his watch; it was close to midnight. We exchanged glances. Was it possible tonight was a fizzer with no boat? Tito went down on his haunches beside us. He was concerned that, after two hours, nothing had happened. We shrugged and agreed it differed from previous visits. He stood up to leave, but stood perfectly still when Troy hissed, "Boat!"

Tito joined his men and, from our separate positions, we all watched the boat come in slowly. Larger than usual, after considerable manoeuvring, the boat finally dropped anchor. Troy and I assessed it as a new player unfamiliar with the procedure.

"It will be interesting to see which way it goes when it leaves," Troy commented. "It should follow the same route as the others unless there's a buyer somewhere around here. Due to their unfamiliarity, it's likely they'll leave later than usual." Troy's prediction proved accurate.

It was well after three o'clock before the diver scrambled back onto the drive platform. With relief, we heard the motor start and the boat moved off. Like its predecessors, it came in from the west and now described a wide arc to leave in the same direction. As we watched it, Troy nudged me.

"Every night we've sat here watching the boats, what have we *not* seen?"

The question was a bit left field and I shrugged in bewilderment. "Dunno. If this were a crime scene, the question would be not about what was there, but what was missing. So, you're suggesting we've missed something?"

"No, more like *something* was missing."

It came to me in a flash. "No containers!" We've watched three pairs of boats go through the same ritual, but on none of those nights did we see a container handled on or off a boat. We didn't know about the containers, so we didn't miss them. Only the diver caught our attention." We both thought for a moment before Troy spoke again.

"Why didn't we see a container? Granted, a container could be hauled over the seaward gunwale – away from us – but it would be visible as it passed over the top of the gunwale."

"We didn't see it because it didn't happen... well, not like that anyway," I replied. "That leaves only one way it might have happened. The containers were in the water – below the surface somehow – when they were transported."

Troy pondered it a few moments before commenting. "That would be no mean feat. The built-in buoyancy in the one we looked at would make it difficult to keep it submerged. The tendency would be for it to float up and be towed along on the surface."

"Anything being towed along underwater would tend to act as a sea anchor, making for slow going and reduced manoeuvrability," I added.

By the time we arrived at that realisation, the boat had long since disappeared around the headland. Should we share our thoughts with Tito? We debated the issue briefly before agreeing we had to. Theo elected not to break with his on-site tradition and went to bed as usual tonight. Right now, I wished he were here on the beach to be a part of those discussions.

Tito and his men were still in position when we decided to call it a night. We went over to them. After telling Tito we were going back to camp, we told him we had something we thought worth discussing – even though it was late. If he were interested, we would meet him in the mess tent after he dismissed his men. He agreed, saying he would only be a few minutes. These days, the mess tent remained open all night. At this hour, the caterers already would be in the kitchen preparing for breakfast and the day ahead. I led the way back to camp with Troy trailing in my wake. Somewhere between beach and mess tent I lost my tail, and I found myself alone in the mess tent for a couple of minutes before he reappeared.

"Where did you get to? I thought you must've piked and sloped off to bed."

"Nice to know you missed me. Theo will join us in a few moments. I agree he needs to be a part of the discussion with Tito, so I woke him."

We got coffee and waited. A few minutes later, Theo arrived closely followed by Tito. One of the caterers was at the servery when the two men arrived. I saw alarm spread across her face before she disappeared into the kitchen. That brought the bloke in charge out at breakneck speed. He demanded to know why we thought we could have breakfast at this hour. Once reassured we were not interested in anything but coffee, he retreated to the kitchen again.

Troy led the conversation; after all, it was he who had spotted that something was missing. Theo and Tito listened intently as Troy outlined the mystery of the invisible containers. His presentation ended with the pair of us apologising for not having worked it out sooner. Tito surprised us by becoming very agitated by Troy's information.

"How did we miss this? I never took my eyes off the boat, but I never thought about not seeing the container. Maybe my men are right. Maybe I am getting too old."

We laughed at his discomfort, but Theo remained serious. "This is a significant breakthrough. We guessed transportation of the objects was by boat but, despite all the time and effort expended, until you two observed boats behaving strangely in the bay, we didn't know how it happened. We still don't know where the material goes after it leaves this bay. We had no doubts that what was happening was going on and you confirmed that aspect but, beyond that, it was a dead end."

My frustration was getting the better of me. I was unhappy about the whole situation but it wasn't Theo's fault. "I don't see how we've helped in that regard, Theo. Yes, we confirmed that boats were moving the stolen material around, but that's all we have done. The boat left the bay, sailing off to the west the same as the others did, but we still don't know its destination. What's the effective range of your tracking device? It would need to be very long range to be effective now that the boat is gone." Tito was getting coffee and I'd forgotten he was there until he spoke.

"Relax; we will not lose the boat. At a couple of points along the coast, between here and the end of Crete, people will track its movement. In addition, the man I sent to Timpaki this evening is working with the local police and the Coast Guard to track a vessel whose coordinates we phoned through to them while we were watching the bay. They're using some sophisticated satellite tracking technology to follow the boat. We will know which way it goes and where it stops."

Troy asked Tito about work on the dig. "It's almost breakfast time. I told the students I would let them know whether we were going to the cove today or not. It's not worth going to bed at this hour, so I'll hang around until after breakfast and then I might try to catch some sleep. So, Tito, what am I going to tell my crew?"

"They can't resume work immediately. The officer from Timpaki will arrive back shortly after breakfast. It depends on his news what happens next and how soon work can resume. I know everyone is fed up, but I believe they will be back at work by morning tea time." Troy looked at Theo, imploring him to intervene, but Theo shrugged and shook his head.

"Okay, if that's how you want it to be. Fine, that's how it will be. I understand you two are in charge and everything is your way or not at all. However, when a mutiny breaks out after they get the news at breakfast, you two can deal with it," and he gestured towards Theo and Tito.

The two men look stunned. I wished for the ground to open up and swallow me. It didn't oblige. Having said his piece, Troy stormed out of the tent. I went after him but my slight delay meant I didn't see which way he went. I'd had enough of other people's company anyway, so I had a shower and opted for a walk along the beach instead. I'd gone about a hundred metres towards the western end of the bay when I heard the faint sound of the boat. It was Tito's man coming back from Timpaki much earlier than expected. I met him as he nosed the boat up onto the sand and helped him anchor it. I suggested he might find Tito still in the mess tent and left him to his own devices as I went off in search of Troy.

If this man's news was going to impact on our day, Troy needed to know what that news was. I was just plain curious about it. My first guess was right. Troy was in his tent updating his journal. We hurried over to the mess tent together, but the officer was into his report to Tito and Theo by the time we arrived. Theo looked up as we approached their table, and I raised my eyebrows questioningly at him. Apparently, they hadn't gotten to the bit we were interested in yet. The officer was updating them on progress with tracking the boat. He also provided a rundown on what happened in Timpaki last night. Finally, discussion got round to the topic that affected what we could do today.

The officer pushed a small box across to Tito. I recognised it as the one in which I placed the fingerprints lifted from the crates. The officer said something to Tito. I didn't catch what he said, but I saw Theo tense in response to it. Tito just nodded and hesitated for a couple of heartbeats before tearing off the tape and opening the box. He ran his eyes around the assembled gathering like someone creating a dramatic moment before announcing the prize winner's name. Reassured we were paying attention, as he withdrew a thick envelope from the box, he asked us to give him a moment. That envelope was new, not one that we placed in the box before handing it over. With the multipage document from the envelope in hand, Tito took himself off to another table.

I watched him scan through to the end of the document before returning to the first page. He read it again carefully and slowly this time while we sat and waited. Then, still holding the document, he sat for a few minutes. The tension mounted around out table. About ten minutes elapsed before Tito returned to our table.

"After searching the camp yesterday, everyone was fingerprint-ed. Not you three, as you had already given me yours. We did some preliminary comparisons between those from the crates and those collected in the camp. This officer took everything to Timpaki last night where an expert did a more thorough comparison. This is his report." He brandished the multipage document in the air. Fine, get on with it, I thought but refrained from voicing it.

"Does it tell us what we want to know?" Theo asked cautiously.

Tito, looking uncomfortable, nodded. "Yes. Action taken now will eliminate any further occurrences of the problem."

"You are sure? There's no room for error – or doubt?" Theo asked.

After a deep breath, Tito looked at Theo. "The report clearly identifies whose fingerprints were on the crates. Obviously, Troy's and Sonny's were identified, but those of one another from this camp were identified as a match for the others on the crates."

I glance from Troy to Theo; both looked grim. "Do you intend to share the identity of that person, or has it been declared top secret?" I asked in frustration.

"I understand your impatience," Tito said quietly. "For reasons that might be clearer later, there is a protocol to follow here. Troy and Sonny, if you will excuse us please, I need to speak to Theo alone. What Theo chooses to share with you later is a matter for him to decide. Unfortunately, identifying the owner of those fingerprints is not the end of the story. Due process, including interrogation, must now occur."

Troy and I turned to leave but, after a couple of steps, I turned to asked one final question. "Was the same person involved with all the artefacts?"

Tito was looking at me when I asked the question, but he turned to Theo. "I'm sorry, Theo, but yes it was."

Outside the tent, I sensed Troy was seething about his exclusion from the discussion. The whole business was disconcerting, so I suggested a walk along the beach. We sat on the sand and watched the sunrise make its way slowly across the bay. There was that straggly bunch of birds again, crossing the sky in the opposite direction this time. I carefully voiced a thought that had bothered me since yesterday. "I've been thinking about the pilfered artefacts. I know they are no longer missing, but my thinking was more about what might have happened if we hadn't discovered the thefts and taken action to stop them."

"That's obvious: things would continue to disappear. Where's this going?"

"If things continued to disappear, it could have resulted in a fairly substantial collection over even just a few weeks. They might have been small items, but there could have been a lot of them. We know how much went missing over only a couple of days."

"Yes, so…?" Troy's frustration hadn't diminished at all.

"How would 'whoever' get their amassed collection away from here? We said before, there is only so much you can stash in your bag amongst your undies. How else do you move an amount of stuff? My thinking is that, one way is to make many trips over the course of the dig to Timpaki or somewhere else, taking a few things away each time – maybe in a handbag or backpack. The other way that occurs to me is to gather it all up at the end of the dig and pack it in something, other than you bag… something that would be loaded with the rest of the gear but wouldn't be suspected or inspected."

"Hmmm, I like both options, but I'm inclined to think the second one might be the one planned for use on this occasion. It would be hard for someone such as Despina to justify tripping off with any regularity and there doesn't seem to be any evidence of her operating that way when she was on previous sites."

"If it were packed in with some other gear, it would need to be in something that only limited people accessed, maybe only the culprit and one other for instance."

"Yeah, I think you're right. Do you have something or someone in mind, or is this simply wild speculation?"

"A bit of both perhaps. Think about the gear that the two operators, Con and Chris, brought over. Nobody but the two men themselves touches that stuff. Some of their 'technical equipment' comes in large cases. Is there any spare room in those cases to stow extra material? …Or does someone bring a spare empty case specifically for this purpose?"

"I think we should give this more thought when other issues are sorted out. In the meantime, such speculation achieves nothing. To hell with it, I'm not sitting here all morning. Let's have breakfast," Troy suggested wearily.

In the mess tent, Theo sat alone holding his head in his hands. Neither of us was sure what to do, but we opted to go and check on him rather than leave him alone. He looked haggard and seemed to have aged considerably in the time we were gone. We probably didn't look too flash ourselves. As we approached the table, he waved us to the chairs facing him. Troy asked how he was holding up and whether it was okay for us to join him.

Theo gazed at us for a few moments before answering. "I don't know how I feel – apart from angry. The news comes as a shock. I would not have believed it. If nothing else, it proves I am not a good judge of people. Troy, I know you want to talk to your crew about what is going to happen today. As soon as I receive word from Tito – probably in a few minutes – you can tell them they are going back to work today. It will be for the best. Once they are busy again, all yesterday's upset will start to disappear. Unfortunately, you will have to expend some energy on rebuilding the comradery that previously existed."

"Are you able to tell us the identity of the person in question?" I asked.

"We will discuss it in detail as soon as I get word from Tito." I saw Troy's jaw clench at the continued frustration.

With nothing more to be gained from further questions, and the smell of breakfast becoming irresistible, I suggested, "I don't know about anybody else, but I'm going to get some breakfast. Is anyone else hungry?" Troy accompanied me to the servery but Theo remained at the table and declined our offer to bring him food or coffee. As we were about to head back to the table, Tito came in and went straight to Theo. We chose a table some distance out of earshot and watched the conversation between the two men become agitated on several occasions. Just as we finished our coffee, the two men stood up and shook hands. Tito left the tent and Theo came to our table.

"If you wouldn't mind waiting," Theo began, "I will just get a coffee and then I'll join you." Back at the table, Theo worried his coffee with a spoon for a few moments before opening up to us. "First things first I think. Troy, work can resume at the cove this morning, but maybe wait an hour or so after breakfast before heading up there. Once the workers settle down for the day, I suggest you come back here to catch up on some sleep for an hour or two. There is no further need to worry about artefacts disappearing."

Troy nodded to indicate his understanding. Silently willing Theo to carry on, neither of us wanted to speak.

"Good, that was easy part. Now for the part I find most difficult. Firstly, I have to admit to being an old man who believed his judgement infallible. I did not listen to your suspicions, but it appears they were well founded. Tito confirmed Despina misappropriated the missing artefacts. She was my star post-graduate student, someone with a brilliant career ahead of her. She had almost completed her doctorate. She will quietly disappear from the camp with the Interpol people, presumably while the rest of the crew are having breakfast. I will think of some reason why she had to go back to the University. We will not mention the real reason, but it will probably come out when she is formally charged."

We were stunned. Although we suspected it might be Despina, having it confirmed wasn't gratifying. Theo assured us there was nothing we could do to help. He had administrative matters to attend to and would catch up with us later. Troy went off to round up his crew, leaving me at a loose end. Where else would I go, except the finds tent? With a considerable degree of satisfaction, and relief, I removed the padlocks for what I hoped would be the last time.

My heart went out to Theo. Although I hadn't known him long, I admired and respected the man. It was heart wrenching to see him so devastated, so torn between so many different emotions. He was right; we could do nothing that would help. I looked for something to do until we caught up with Theo later. I rinsed off my dive gear and checked it before stowing it again. I was tidying up the benches when Troy came bounding into the tent.

"Now that things are back to normal, how about we catch up on a couple of hours sleep and then go for a dive? Doesn't look like Theo's in any hurry to leave. He can hold the fort while we dive."

"A dive sounds good. I've been dying to have a good look at those things on the seabed. Maybe I'll bring some back and start the conservation process. When are you heading up to the cove?"

"I told them we'd head up in about ten minutes. I don't know where Theo is but I suppose he'll turn up when he's ready."

"He said he had administrative tasks to attend to. I don't know what that means, but I suspect it has something to do with Despina. The whole business has really rocked him."

Troy left to round-up his crew and head to the cove. I watched them go past the tent like Brown's cows. I decided to join them and, as I was closing the tent – without the padlocks – I saw the Interpol mob escort Despina off the campsite. I discreetly followed them to the beach, watched them pile into the boat and get underway. One lone figure remained at the water's edge. Theo was a despondent figure as he stood there hands on hips, watching the boat depart. As I was unsure what to do for the best, I hesitated briefly before joining him. He gave me a wan smile, and we walked down the beach to the cove together.

The top of the rock divide provided a bird's eye view of the whole cove. We paused briefly to take it all in. Troy stood in front of his crew waving his arms around like a policeman directing traffic, and I heard him allocating tasks to various members. Then Theo and I made our way down onto the sand. Once the group settled into their allocated tasks, Theo insisted Troy and I go back to camp for some sleep.

We asked if he could keep an eye on the dig this afternoon while we dived. He was available. With that settled, we headed back to camp. I slept, but my dream yet again was troubling. In the dream, the traffickers discovered we tampered with the container and the punishments meted out were horribly brutal. I woke suddenly, coiled up tightly in the foetal position and hyperventilating. I was a lather of sweat. My clock indicated lunch would be well and truly underway by now, but I elected to take a shower before heading to the mess tent. The shower revived me somewhat but I was still dopey from the deep sleep.

Troy and Theo were there when I arrived. Most of the crew had already left the tent. I selected food and joined the two men. Theo reported that, as he was coming for lunch, Tito had called advising that he had formally charged Despina. She would appear in court tomorrow. The news brought me out of my fog.

"Will you be required at the hearing?" I asked

"Yes, I am needed to give evidence. The university will send the boat for me this afternoon. How long I will be gone depends on the hearing. My thinking is that I will be back here the day after tomorrow."

"We can manage here, Theo, if you have things to take care of back at the university. Take time to do that… and to catch up on sleep and relax a bit. Is there any need for you to rush back here?" Troy asked.

His enigmatic reply had us wondering what else this place could possibly have in store for us. "There is likely to be a need for me to come back here quickly. We will see," was his response.

Immediately after lunch, we unhitched the boat from small tractor, loaded our dive gear onto the carrier attached to the rear of the tractor and chugged off towards the cove. We worked in our own areas during the dive. Troy cleaned an area of the jetty to check its construction, while I targeted what I hoped was a group of artefacts and not a pile of boulders. We both had success. Construction of Troy's jetty was from massive cut stone blocks laid in a brick pattern, while my lumpy object proved to be a large amphora. When our dive time expired, we swam ashore and shared news of our finds with Theo. He wanted to see for himself, and said he would join us in a dive on his return from the hearing.

We headed back to camp and were rinsing off our gear when Troy stopped suddenly. "Wasn't a boat supposed to collect Theo this afternoon? It's getting late. It will need to hurry up if it's to get back before dark."

"We should have thought earlier and taken him back in our boat." I had just finished speaking when Theo wandered into camp, his phone clamped firmly to his ear.

He finished the call and threw his hands in the air as he walked over to us. "An earlier phone call said there was only one boat available and it had a problem, but they would be here to collect me later this afternoon. I realised it was getting late and I should come back to get ready to leave. Then, as I was walking back, I get another phone call saying the problem is major and the boat will be out of action for some days. I am supposed to be at the hearing tomorrow."

"We'll take you back in our boat," Troy reassured him. "What time do you have to be there tomorrow?"

"I was told to be there by eleven o'clock at the latest."

"Not a problem; we'll leave at seven o'clock. That will allow plenty of time to get to… where is the hearing anyway?"

"Heraklion."

"We'll be back in Timpaki in plenty of time for you to drive to Heraklion, put on your collar and tie and be at the hearing on time." After dropping Theo at Timpaki, Troy would spend the day there, and Theo would let him know by three o'clock whether he was returning that evening or on Friday with the catering staff. I was acquainted with the fact that I'd be supervising the dig in Troy's absence.

"What? You're leaving the least experienced person in charge of the zoo?"

"It will be okay," Theo reassured me. "Everybody knows what they have to do. If something you're not sure about happens, give Troy a call."

The men went off to make phone calls: Theo to the university, and Troy to Niko at the dive shop to organise replacement tanks. Troy and I spent some time getting the boat ready and loading the empty tanks.

Dinner that night was not as rowdy as in the past, but it was a lot less subdued than it had been last night. Spirits were improving. I hope I don't do anything tomorrow to upset their complete return to normal.

Chapter 14

As planned, Troy and Theo left early for Timpaki. I breakfasted with the crew and shared with them that I was their supervisor for the day. That brought plenty of suggestions about what they'd be able to get away with. The laughter accompanying it was a good sign that things were close to normal again.

Theo was right; everyone knew their job and just got on with it. The day produced more finds than I expected and, by lunchtime, there was high excitement about the way the dig was progressing. I helped with the excavations until about four o'clock when I saw Troy coming back across the bay. There were two people on board, and I guessed Theo returned rather than staying overnight at Heraklion. I took the trailer down to the beach ready to load the boat. As we secured the boat on the trailer, Troy spoke quietly to me.

"Theo's a bit tense. I don't know why. I asked. I was concerned something had gone wrong at the hearing, but he didn't want to talk about it. He now says he wants to meet with us as soon as we put the boat away. ...No, I don't know what it's about."

Troy and I dealt with the boat while Theo took his bag to his tent. We went to the finds tent and waited for Theo to arrive. We returned to our earlier conversation about how Despina might move the stolen artefacts from the bay. It seems we both gave it more thought in the interim. Troy voiced his conclusions. "The more I thought about it, the more convinced I became that there had to be someone else involved, and the most likely candidate is one or the other of the operators."

"Yes, I'm fairly convinced of it as well. However, I don't think this is a good time to share our suspicions with Theo. He looks a bit too fragile to deal with another shock right now, but I think we do have to talk to him about it at some point."

We barely had ended our discussion when Theo reappeared. Perched on a stool at a workbench, I could feel my stomach tightening. The look on Theo's face did nothing to relax me. We waited expectantly as Theo appeared to be composing what he was going to say. After a few moments of silence, he started speaking.

"Firstly, I imagine you want to know about the hearing. It was difficult to sit through. I had so much hope for that young woman. I simply had to outline what had happened that led to her final downfall. There was a predictable outcome: they found her guilty. Sentencing is tomorrow. I did not want to hang around for that. Whatever they hand down won't make up for my disappointment." He lapsed into silence again while we nodded sagely at his revelations.

"Tito caught up with me prior to the hearing to organise a meeting as soon as I was free. He wanted to bring me up to date with where they are at with tracking the boat. They tracked it until it docked at Favignana."

With no idea what or where Favignana was, I asked Theo to clarify before he went any further. "Thanks for asking," Troy commented. "It saves me having to question if my memory serves me right."

"Oh, sorry, you probably have never heard of Favignana. It's part of the Egadi Archipelago: one of the three small islands a few kilometres off the west coast of Sicily. Its history goes back to the Phoenicians. These days it's a popular tourist destination with hydrofoil connection to the mainland."

"So, our boat was tracked to this island?" I queried.

"Yes, the boat docked there and the tracking device indicates it is still there," Theo confirmed.

"Why Favignana? There's nothing there. I once vaguely thought of holidaying in the area, but there was nothing to do so I didn't go," Troy recalled.

At Theo's mention of the place, I pulled out my phone and searched. Gotta luv Google! "Tuna fishing and caves," I responded to Troy.

"Eh? What are you on about?"

"I'm telling you what there is for a tourist to do there. You're supposed to loll about enjoying a break. The fact that there is nothing much else going on probably makes it an ideal place to take their illegally acquired artefacts."

Theo chuckled and held up his hand to stop us. "You make a good point, Sonny. Anyway, that's where the boat went and its cargo is still there."

As Theo spoke, I was thinking about the statue. "That's not quite true, Theo. What we *know* is that the cargo went onto a boat here – a different boat from the one that brought it into the bay –and that a second boat that took it away from here remains at Favignana. We don't know if the *statue* is still there." Troy looked puzzled and my comment offended Theo judging by the tone of his voice when he spoke.

"What do you mean 'we don't know where the statue is'?" he demanded. "That's what I've been explaining. It arrived at Favignana and hasn't gone anywhere since."

Okay, slowly and gently might be best now that I appear to have ruffled feathers. "We know a tracking device was slipped into 'the cargo'. The statue was a solid block, with no obvious openings where a device could be hidden, no matter how small."

"That's true," Troy conceded. "They probably reuse the containers. They look expensive. Perhaps, they open the containers, and the contents move on to another destination after the boat arrives at Favignana. The boat and the container probably remain at the place where they docked. In this case, the tracking device might still be in the container and not have moved on, but its contents might now be somewhere else."

"Christ, that hadn't occurred to me." Theo smacked his forehead. "I don't know how that will impact on what I was going to talk to you about tonight."

"Well, the sooner you tell us what it is you want to talk about the sooner we'll know," Troy responded.

"Yes, I suppose so. I had meetings with Interpol and ICOM while I was in Timpaki, about what happened here and how it fitted into the bigger picture. This bay is the best lead we've had so far. The suggestion – by Tito of all people – is to ask you to go to Favignana to follow up on what we know up to this point. We would provide you with all the information gathered so far. You would fly to the nearest airport at Trapani. Then, you make like a couple of tourists going to the island for a few days holiday. Your task is to try to locate the statue, as a primary objective, but equally important is anything you find out on what happens to artefacts after they reach the island."

"That sounds like something someone should do," Troy conceded. "What makes you think we're the right people for the job? And, while we're off swanning around on a Mediterranean island, who is looking after the project here?"

"You might not think you're suitable but, together, you're ideal for what we need. Sonny is a private investigator with the deduction skills – the thinking processes – useful for unravelling this crime. You have the archaeology knowledge and skills that might prove vital to a successful outcome."

"Hmm, I see how that might work, but what about the dig site here?"

"That is not a problem," Theo reassured him. "This is the university's long break, so I don't have to be there, but I can be here supervising work at the cove. I don't know that the students will be excited about that, so we might keep it from them until the last minute."

I wasn't sure how I felt about our 'mission'. I needed more information, but definitely felt a spark of excitement. "We need a lot more information before we can give you an answer. What you think, Troy?"

"I'm not sure more information will do it, but it would help."

"Relax; I have all the information in these folders. I just need to know if you will at least consider what we are asking. Will you think about it?" Theo asked.

We agreed to read the folders, and discuss it before getting back to him.

"One other thing," Theo added, "This needs to happen as soon as possible. We don't want to lose track of anything. The more time we lose, the less chance there is of a successful outcome. And after what you have just alerted me to, I am even more worried about wasting time than before."

What could we say? We assured him we understood the urgency and would get back to him as soon as possible. Then he dropped the real bombshell.

"We hoped that, if you agreed to do this, you could leave for Sicily tomorrow."

I stared at him for a moment before grabbing my folder and heading to my tent. The folder contained a lot of information, mainly copies of reports, and it was heavy going to understand it all. Nevertheless, I stuck with it through to the end of the folder. My head was pounding and my stomach was rumbling. Time for dinner. Still cautious from previous experience, I pushed the folder under my mattress before going for food. I joined Theo and Troy at their table.

Theo announced that Troy said he did not wish to discuss the proposed trip yet, needing more time to think about it. I echoed Troy, adding that I thought Troy and I needed to discuss it privately before we spoke to Theo again. Conversation was sparse and stilted during the meal. As soon as he finished eating, Theo excused himself and left, probably intentionally leaving Troy and I alone. Troy confirmed he read the folder from start to finish, but he was doubtful about how much he managed to absorb.

I understood. It took some getting through. I explained to Troy that I needed a mind mapping exercise to distil the facts and to see where linkages existed. He agreed but admitted he didn't have a clue what that involved. We collected our folders and regrouped in the finds tent. I arrived first and trundled out the whiteboard in readiness. Troy arrived a few minutes later with a large glass of wine in each hand.

"Where did that come from?"

"If you remember, we talked about buying alcohol for ourselves the next time we went to Timpaki. I was in Timpaki today and – surprise, surprise – I remembered. We now have a limited private wine supply here in camp."

It was red and it was good – and didn't need to be chilled. We sacrificed a few moments to do justice to the wine before beginning work. Then the night developed into a long hard slog as we worked on mapping our task. By eleven o'clock, we were finished and our assumptions covered the white board. We sat back, interrogated and discussed the information. My eyes were getting heavy, so I was relieved when, just before midnight, Troy announced he thought the operation worthwhile and that it should happen. He stopped short of saying he wanted to 'give it a go'. I agreed our efforts to date would be for nothing if the proposed second phase didn't happen.

Troy took our glasses and refilled them. While he was gone, I considered all the implications that we hadn't yet discussed that might be associated with such an exercise. I felt sure Troy was not aware of the risks that might be involved. By the time he returned with the wine, I had worked out what I needed to talk through with him. After a couple of sips, I opened the conversation.

"I don't know if you realise there could be significant risk involved in undertaking this task."

"Are you suggesting I'm a naïve wimp or something?" he demanded a little indignantly.

"No, not at all. It occurred to me that, if there was a special someone in your life – or even your aunt and uncle – perhaps you should seek their thoughts on the matter before committing yourself."

"Someone special...? You mean like a partner, or a girlfriend or something?

"Yes, I suppose that is what I had in mind, but it means anyone who would be concerned about the risk involved and the danger you might be putting yourself in – and who maybe should have a say in your final decision."

"There is no special person," he snarled in reply.

Oops, looks like I touched a nerve. "I'm sorry if I upset you. I wasn't prying. I just wanted you to think about all aspects of what we are being asked to do before you make a decision."

Silence reigned for a couple of minutes. We drank more of our wine. Then, normal communications resumed. After revisiting some of the points we raised earlier, there was agreement that we would tell Theo we were interested, but a number of things needed clarification before we would finally commit to the task. Nevertheless, we decided we shouldn't wake Theo at this hour. We'd tell him in the morning.

*****

My mind continued to race long after I fell into bed. After a period of tossing and turning, sleep finally came. It wasn't restful, and I crawled out of bed this morning decidedly below par. I went in search of coffee, hoping it would reconnect me with the living. Troy and Theo were already devouring their breakfasts in the mess tent. It was little consolation that Troy didn't look much better than I felt. The other two dawdled over their coffee while they waited for me to finish eating. Then, there was no reason to delay matters any further. It was time for *that* talk with Theo that could result in our flying out of Crete today.

Troy began speaking, but I cut across him before he said too much. There were things we needed to know which could affect what we are about to agree to.

"Theo, did Despina reveal the names of her associates?"

"What? No, she didn't give us names. Do you think she had associates?"

"She had to dispose of the things she pilfered somehow. It might be she had a bent dealer who sold them for her, but I don't think that was the whole story. She took only small things she could manage herself, and the dealer would be okay to get rid of those. You said looting of many of the sites students worked on occurred at the end of the season. Somebody had to provide the looters with information. You indicated some suspicion surrounded Despina before this dig. Explain the process – the sequence – of moving objects from an excavation site to the university."

"Uhmm, similar to York's system; small objects are packed into small crates. Then it depends on how far and how they have to travel. Normally, we pack the small crates into larger crates, not as big as a container – more like big boxes. Those boxes often accompany the

139

students when they leave the site. Larger objects require the provision of discrete crates to suit each individual item. If there are sufficient bigger pieces, their crates go into a container or something similar to keep them together. Is this what you wanted to know?"

"Yes, can I assume that those bigger pieces are amongst the last things to leave the site?"

"Usually, but it depends on how they are to be transported. Sometimes a container goes by road to the port for loading onto a ship. Sometimes we collect them with our barge or a small vessel. At least one person remains in charge of them at all times until they are loaded onto the ship or barge."

"Was that person sometimes Despina?"

"Yes, sometimes – perhaps often."

"You should check your records for any correlation between the looting and the occasions when Despina was left in charge. Your previous comments indicate you have suspicions about that, but we need evidence of definite connections between the two."

Deep furrows creased Troy's forehead as he listened. "Sonny, is this relevant to what Theo asked us to do?"

"Definitely; the task would be a lot easier if we knew names or contacts. It could mean the difference between a waste of time or coming up trumps. Apart from that, we need to know what we might be dealing with."

Silence reigned until another thought came to me. "Theo, Despina is likely to be unwilling to give up the information we want. I'd expected her to be downright uncooperative. It might be worthwhile if Tito searched her communications: emails, phone calls the works… and looked for a second phone and/or email address that we don't know about, maybe in a different name. Someone needs to check her financials, not just the bank accounts we know about, but other 'hidden' accounts."

"Are bank accounts going to be relevant?" Troy queried.

"Yes, the money she gets from flogging off small pieces has to go somewhere. Those transactions are evidence of the duration and significance of her pilfering. They could provide the identity of her dealer, but I think this is just a small operation on the side. If she has been part of a trafficking network, she probably receives payment for her 'services'. Once we locate those payments, it should be possible to track them back to their source."

"Right," Theo replied, "I'll call Tito now to get something moving."

Without looking at me, Troy started speaking slowly. "Sonny, I am starting to feel a little concerned about what we might be getting into. Are you sure all this is necessary, and you're not being just a bit too cloak and dagger about the whole thing? I have to ask – even at the risk of sounding a wimp – are we likely to be in danger? I mean *real* danger and not just that we'll need to be careful? I know you brought all this up last night – about the possible danger, I mean – but I am now starting to see things a little differently."

"You're not a wimp for asking that. It's good you're starting to see the magnitude of our task. Yes, I believe there will be a high level of danger attached to the task. Actually, I'm cursing the fact that I will be going in unarmed. If I was involved in something of this magnitude at home, I would definitely be carrying a weapon."

Theo's return cut short any further discussion. "Tito will put some of their technical people onto it straight away. However, he suggests we take no further action – or decisions – until I hear from him again. That gives you a bit longer to think about whether you want to do this or not. I'm starting to wish I never agreed to ask you to get involved. It might just be an old man getting nervous but, to me, this is starting to look a lot more dangerous than I realised."

"About that, Theo," Troy began, "What are the chances of getting a weapon for Sonny? Obviously, she couldn't bring her own from Australia, but I think one might be handy if things go pear-shaped after we leave here."

Theo looked at me, clearly alarmed by Troy's request. "You think a weapon necessary? I need to talk to Tito of course, but I hadn't considered there might be such a need."

"There are two things that I think: one is that Despina will not give up any names. She will be too afraid to do so. Those involved in such a network have a lot at stake if she talks. They might take steps to prevent any possibility of that happening – if you understand what I mean. They would simply apply an ancient solution to eliminate that possibility. The other thing is much the same. This is likely to be a highly organised network raking in big money from illicit trafficking. If something threatens their continued operation, I don't doubt they would not hesitate to do whatever is necessary to eliminate such risk… and that could be us. As an archaeologist, Theo, you would know that over the centuries there have been instances where something or someone has proved to be a problem for some reason. The solution has always been to eliminate the problem so that whatever it is your doing can continue unhindered. Death has long been an ancient solution to such problems."

"That's a bleak picture you're painting," Troy mused.

"I see why a weapon might be useful," Theo conceded. "I should go, you've given me things to think about and do. It occurs to me that we had this discussion but you haven't actually agreed to undertake the operation."

"That's true, we haven't. So, we better say yes now if we are going to, before Troy's feet get any colder." I looked questioningly at Troy.

"It's not about getting cold feet. There are a lot of things to consider," Troy retaliated.

"Like what: your career and how you getting yourself killed probably won't progress it at all – and how such an outcome probably isn't in your grand plan for the future?"

"No, that's not what it's about. Of course I'm in."

"Right then, Theo, that's a 'yes' from Captain Cautious here, and from me also. Okay?"

"Thank you, yes. Now I must take care of a few things – and you have a dig site to supervise," he added nodding at Troy.

Troy and Theo headed off to their respective tasks. I had things to do and I needed peace and quiet to do them. I went over the operation again and, when I had come to grips with it, prioritised the tasks involved. Then it was time to become organised. I fetched a notebook and, perched in front of the whiteboard, made copious notes, and went into crystal ball gazing mode. I noted all the scenarios that might occur, ways of dealing with them, any special equipment needed, and what our escape plan might be if it came to that. By the time I finished, everyone had returned for morning tea. Troy and Theo came looking for me.

We went for coffee together and sat apart from the others in the mess tent. Theo filled us in on progress with all that he had asked Tito to look into. Not surprisingly, Despina was not forthcoming with names or connections. They found an email address that traced back to Despina, as well as a prepaid phone. The technicians were still working on those but there might be more information by this afternoon. There was nothing yet to report on her financials.

I asked how Tito had reacted to the request for a weapon. Theo laughed, "I thought he was going to have a fit at first, but he settled down. He can't authorise it, but said he would talk to people who could. However, he wasn't sure that they would approve such a thing."

Troy queried how much time we would have to get ready if they decided to go ahead with the operation. "I asked him about that as well," Theo began slowly. "It is difficult to know when everything will be ready for it to begin. However, Tito indicated they might have done enough by tonight for it to start. He will call this afternoon but, if everything is right, you might fly out tomorrow. Depending on what time he calls, you could go across to Timpaki this afternoon and overnight there. One of Tito's men would drive you to the airport tomorrow morning. Ideally, you should spend some time with Tito and maybe the technical men before you fly out."

Troy studied his boots while Theo spoke. Now, he looked up and nodded, "Okay, it sounds like we should pack now and be ready to go in case we do have to overnight in Timpaki."

Everyone agreed. We went off to get ready and Theo went to look after the dig. Packing didn't take long; I have so little here on Crete. I packed my computer and everything else I needed to take went into a small bag. I went back to the finds tent and Troy joined me a few minutes later. We spent time discussing various aspects of the operation until we heard the crew returning for lunch. A rush to the mess tent, allowed us to select our lunch at leisure before the hungry horde arrived.

Theo was finishing a phone call when he wandered in after everyone else. He came directly to the table and checked that we would be there for a bit longer as he had something to talk through with us. This left Troy and I hanging while Theo decided what he wanted to eat and returned to our table. As he sat down, Troy couldn't contain himself any longer.

"I suppose you're going to leave us hanging in suspense while you devour all that food before sharing your news."

Theo chuckled, "I wouldn't want this to get cold," he said, jabbing at his food with his fork. "Maybe you will have to suffer for a few minutes more. You wouldn't want me to pass out from hunger before I could tell you the news."

We all laughed. Ours was a bit brittle. Theo began demolishing the pile of food on his plate. It was all a ruse. After only a few mouthfuls, he looked at Troy with a twinkle in his eyes and announced, "I think that bit will sustain me until after I have finished telling you the news." He pulled out a notebook and began reciting Tito's information. "Firstly, the thing probably most important for you is that you will leave for Timpaki this afternoon. Tito will send a boat to collect you. You are booked into a hotel there for tonight and will have a working dinner with Tito and maybe one or two others. Any problems with that?"

We shook our heads. It was a relief for things to get moving. We were ready to go. Theo continued with the rest of Tito's information.

"Tito is emailing information about how things are likely to proceed once you leave Crete, and also details of what they have found so far on the other things we asked him to look at. If the email has arrived after lunch, I will print it for you so you can study it before you leave for Timpaki."

The rest of the information Theo shared was sketchy at best. I assumed the details were in the emails expected from Tito. When he finished lunch, he went back to his tent and Troy and I went to the finds tent. There was nothing to do but wait, so that's what we did, and speculated about the impending operation and what tonight's dinner might bring. On his way to the cove, Theo hurried into the tent and handed us both a sheaf of papers, suggesting we add them to the other material in our folders. Then he was gone again.

This was the information emailed by Tito. It included details of our travel arrangements. Our hotel accommodation was booked at Favignana, and our contact there was somebody called Dominic. The flight from Crete to Trapani would leave at the civilised time of nine o'clock next morning. This allowed for a leisurely drive across the island to catch it.

Theo came back into camp about three o'clock and announced the boat would be collecting us in about half an hour. We gathered up our gear and waited restlessly for what seemed an exceptionally long half-hour. Theo and the crew heard the boat coming and came down the beach to see us off. Turnaround time was minimal; we stood at the water's edge with our gear as the boat nosed onto the sand. Our gear went aboard quickly and we followed it. The motor roared to life again and we were reversing out into the bay, with those on the beach waving and cheering.

It was pleasant on the water. The sting had gone out of the sun and the gentle afternoon breeze was refreshing. As we turned and headed for Timpaki, my stomach tightened a little. It was game on. Our operation had begun and, at this stage, neither of us knew what adventure lay ahead of us. Perhaps, had we known, we might not have gotten aboard this boat.

Chapter 15

A car waited at Timpaki to take us to our hotel. The driver told us Tito would join us at seven o'clock. My room was spacious and came with copious supplies of toiletries. After freshening up, I met Troy under the hotel's vine covered pergola.

As the evening closed in around us, Tito arrived and announced two others would join us for dinner. The others, two of Interpol's technical staff, arrived just after seven o'clock and we adjourned to the restaurant for what proved an excellent meal in a somewhat tense atmosphere. This probably was due to our state of mind rather than anything else. At the end of our meal, Tito took us through to a small private room adjacent to the restaurant. There we found maps, paper and folders piled on a table, and a laptop connected to a projector. Tito had been busy. We sat and Tito wasted no time in getting down to business.

He projected a map of Favignana Island onto a screen, which one of the others pulled down from its recess in the ceiling. A detailed study of the map occupied some time. Our hotel, Hotel Il Portico, was close to the town's main piazza, and close to the harbour where the ferries and hydrofoil docked. Amongst the other paper Tito provided to help us get a feel for the place were a few tourist type pamphlets including one on our hotel.

Of more interest, was news that they had uncovered a throwaway phone, and a couple of bank accounts connected to Despina. One account was offshore, registered in the Caymans. Unravelling the transactions in both accounts remained ongoing. They believed there was another email account somewhere, but so far hadn't been able to locate it. Tito still had no names that might help with our mission. Despina maintained her silence although she was aware they were unravelling her life piece by piece.

Our meeting lasted much longer than I anticipated. Tito did most of the talking, with the boffins providing information about bank accounts and the phone but appeared to have little else to contribute. As the end of the session approached, we both received new phones and new credit cards, along with the usual lecture about restricting spending to 'essential' items and our requirement to account for all spending. Oh good, we're on an operation and have to worry about keeping receipts for everything. That's probably not going to happen – well, not very well anyway. When his part of the evening ended, I asked Tito if there was any progress on my request for a weapon. He made sure the others couldn't hear him tell me that 'something' would be available. I assumed that meant something would miraculously appear after we arrived at Favignana. It certainly couldn't be on the plane with me when we left Crete.

The technical chaps left a bit before the end of the meeting. After arranging to collect us at seven o'clock next morning for the drive to the airport, Tito also left. The meeting had been intense, and involved considerable mental effort to take in everything thrown at us. Troy and I sat in silence for a few moments digesting what we had learned, and wondering yet again, what we had let ourselves in for. We added the new bits of paper to the ever-increasing stack in our folders and retreated to the bar for a drink before turning in for the night.

*****

Old habits persist. I was up early this morning. It took about all of ten seconds to be packed and ready to go. We indulged in a long leisurely breakfast before waiting in the lobby for Tito to collect us. The drive across the island was a definite improvement on my previous bus trip. Tito dropped us at the airport, indicated the check-in area, and departed without further ceremony. Following check-in, we waited about half an hour in the lounge before hearing our flight called.

After the short uneventful flight to Trapani, we took the airport shuttle to its terminus on Torre di Ligny. As it was some distance from the ferry terminal on Viale Regina Elena, we caught a taxi and arrived just in time to board a hydrofoil leaving for Favignana. Normally about a 30-minute trip, ours took a little longer as this trip scheduled a stop at Levanzo on the way.

We knew our hotel was not far from where we disembarked from the hydrofoil, but we opted for a taxi rather than risk getting lost and having to drag our luggage all over town. The hotel is newish, built in 2005, and small with only 18 rooms. It is comfortable, and its fittings and furniture reflect its comparative newness. While it provided everything one expects in such accommodation, there was no restaurant as such. There is a bar/lounge and a complimentary breakfast is included in the tariff, but no options for dining in-house. We discovered we had adjoining rooms connected by a lockable door. A few minutes after I unpacked, Troy knocked on the interconnecting door and I let him in.

We were planning the next day's agenda when a knock on my door interrupted us. We froze, our only movement being to exchange glances. We weren't expecting visitors. I hesitated a few moments while deciding whether to answer the door or not. The knock came again. I opened the door carefully. A tall good-looking man smiled at me. His coal black eyes matched the thick thatch of black hair that curled over his collar, ears and forehead, and he sported a deep tan.

"*Buon giorno. Mi chiamo Dominic,*" he introduced himself. "*Permesso?*"

Opening the door wide, I waved him in. "*Si,si. Avanti. Mi chiamo Sonny,*" and flicking my thumb in Troy's direction, "*Il suo nome è Troy.*" The basic introductions over, the man who was to be our contact entered the room.

Dominic nodded to me and shook hands with Troy before dragging a chair over to join us at the coffee table where we had been working. If this bloke didn't speak English, this was not going to be a long and beautiful relationship. My Italian is lousy and Troy doesn't know any, or so he confessed on the hydrofoil on the way over. I was about to pose the question in Italian but changed my mind and asked in English, "Do you speak English?"

"Yes, of course. Would you prefer we use English?"

Seriously, he needed to ask? "Well, that might be a good idea. I don't have much Italian – and he has none," I said as I nodded at Troy. "Besides, we'll look more like tourists if we speak English."

Dominic brought yet more bits of paper to add to our folders. Then he opened his backpack, which sported the name of a well-known travel agency emblazoned in big fluoro coloured letters across the front of it, and withdrew two similar but smaller backpacks that he handed to Troy and I.

"Your hotel bookings were arranged by this travel agency," he said as he indicated the name on all the bags.

That caused a twinge of alarm. Why would Tito use a commercial operator for our bookings when this was supposed to be a covert operation? My face apparently displayed my concern.

"Don't be alarmed," Dominic reassured us. "That agency did not make the bookings, but everything will appear as if they did." Grinning broadly, he dived into his backpack again. "I believe this is for you?" He said, raising his eyebrows questioningly at me as he handed over a small heavy package.

Not sure what to expect, I open the box carefully. Yes! I feel better about this operation already. The box contained a Glock, holster, box of ammunition and basic cleaning material. The latter tended to indicated they expected me to use the weapon, or why else would I need to clean it. "Thank you. Yes, this is for me. I don't know what your gun laws are over here, but I know I don't have a license to carry anything in this country."

"Things are a little more relaxed in this part of the world. Don't worry; records show the weapon registered to you. The registration will disappear when you no longer need it."

He and Troy swapped pleasantries while I checked and loaded the weapon. Then it was time for more important stuff: food.

"What have you arranged for dinner?" Dominic asked.

"Nothing," we choroused in reply. We hadn't gotten around to thinking about it yet and, as we didn't know what was close by, hadn't made any plans. Dominic queried whether we wanted something with lots of Michelin stars or somewhere that had good food. We voted for good food.

"There's a trattoria not far from here that has good food that is not expensive."

"Sounds good; is it too early for dinner yet?" Troy asked.

"No; we can walk and have a drink before we eat. After, we can do what the locals do after dinner."

"That sounds ominous. What's that?" Troy asked.

"*Passeggiata,*" I replied. "In the evenings, the locals stroll around a piazza or some such place. They do it as a family or with a group of friends, talking, taking in the night air, relaxing before bed – and walking off their meal."

"We've been known to do that on Crete before today, only there it's called strolling along the beach," he responded.

We were early and had the pavement to ourselves. I checked no one was within earshot before asking Dominic about something that was bothering me. "I know you are supposed to be our contact, but I'm not sure exactly what that entails. Is it safe for us to be seen together, and where is it safe for us to talk?"

He laughed. "I am your guide who you hired through the travel agency. It is safe for us to be together. At this stage, it is safe to talk just about anywhere. That we will be speaking English is a bonus. Most of the locals will not understand us, but some will, particularly some in the hospitality industry. We just have to be careful not to talk about anything sensitive when people are around. If there are people close by, you make like tourists with your guide."

Dominic led us into the trattoria, ordered drinks at the bar and we carried them outside. I heard him tell the barman we would come back to order food later. Now that we were sitting rather than walking, I noticed that the night air was a bit fresh, but refreshing rather than uncomfortable. For something 'tourist-focused' to talk about as we sipped our drinks, Dominic explained the local tuna fishing industry, saying how this was one of the few *tonnare*, traditional tuna fisheries, that remained, but we had come too late for the *mattanza* that occurs in May or June. If I had been here then, I would not have watched the *mattanza* – the 'chamber of death' – where tuna are bludgeoned to death after being driven into a net enclosure.

He explained that the tuna fishermen hire their boats out for fishing excursions and cruises around the island. This way, the boats are busy for most of the year, but they are not always out catching fish. This is especially true during the tourist season. Okay, we are doing the touristy thing but is he giving us information about the potential use of the boats to help maintain the tourist guide image, or for some other reason?

Troy checked there was no one too close and then quietly confirmed his interpretation of Dominic's information, "So, the boats we monitored were able to slip in and out of here without anyone paying too much attention, and nobody wanting to see their catch when they returned."

"Well, nobody would ask to see the fish they caught," Dominic corrected him, "But *someone* would be *very* interested in their 'catch'. We have determined from the satellite tracking data that the boats do not call in anywhere else on their way back to Favignana harbour. Therefore, this suggests that somehow what they bring back is dealt with here. It means that Favignana harbour is likely to be a vital cog in the trafficking network."

"We need to see what happens when those boats arrive back. We still have the mystery of the transportation of those containers to sort out," Troy reminded me.

"Yes, but we need to know which boat and when. We could spend time watching every boat coming back into the harbour without being any the wiser for it. Ideally, if we knew a particular boat had collected a container at Crete, we could be waiting in our dive gear somewhere in the harbour ready to take a close look at how they managed to transport the containers invisibly." I explained my thinking to Troy.

Dominic smiled knowingly. "But we will know. Tito has stationed a couple of his men in your camp. They have taken over your monitoring duties. We will be given details when such a boat is returning here and receive its satellite tracking information in plenty of time to prepare for its arrival."

"Is there somewhere here where we can hire diving equipment?" I asked. "It might also be useful if we were able to hire a boat, not one with the owner as skipper, just the boat. Whether we need one or not will depend on what we find when we have a look around."

"There is a dive shop here. They run dive courses and hire out gear. I can organise that when you need it. It depends on what sort of boat you want, but there are some available for hire. Talking about hiring things, what are your plans for tomorrow?"

"We were thinking of hiring a couple of bikes and cycling around the place to get a feel for the layout of the area and to act like real tourists," Troy replied.

"That is good. You should know the place in case we have to do something tricky in a hurry. Will you want me to come cycling with you? I can come with you to hire the cycles if you need my help."

The mention of 'something tricky' wasn't likely to make Troy feel any better about this operation. I suspect he is still a bit nervous about it. I thought about Dom's offer regarding hiring the cycles. "I don't think we need you to come with us when we go pedalling around the place, but it would be good if you came with us to hire the bikes. I could manage that much Italian but, if you are there, I won't have to speak anything but English. It could be a good thing if nobody knew that I can speak the language a bit – and am able to understand a lot more."

As promised, the food was good and not expensive, and it was pleasant strolling around the piazza afterwards. At about ten o'clock, we walked back to the hotel together and, once Dom saw us safely to our rooms, he said good night and left. Troy and I spent some time poring over a map of the town, planning the route for our cycling sightseeing tour the next day.

*****

The complimentary breakfast this morning saw us spoiled for choice. I decided to play it safe and stick with simple rather than lash out on a huge breakfast. We had arranged for Dom to meet us at eight o'clock and then walk us to the nearest place to hire a couple of bicycles. He arrived shortly after the appointed hour and, equipped with our new backpacks, hats and sunglasses, we set off. Hiring the bikes wasn't a drama. We knew we would need identification and had brought our passports. This added further credibility to our role as foreign tourists. Dom did a very good impression of a tour guide helping his clients get what they wanted and interpreting for me. When the man asked for my credit card, Dom interpreted and I declined, giving him cash instead. The hire was very cheap. For the two bikes, it was less than five euros for the day.

Overall, I rated our performance as tourists with their guide quite credible. With Dom and our bikes out on the street, there was lots of gesturing and flapping of maps as we continued our charade of tourists getting directions. Troy and I set off and Dom walked off in the opposite direction. After a couple of hours riding around the town, we rode some distance along the coast. The town area is very flat with hardly any traffic. Most of the locals walk or ride bikes.

Our return to the town centre coincided with lunchtime. Troy claimed he was starving and was happy to eat at the first place that served food. I explained that I wanted to find a cafeteria where we wouldn't have to ask for what we wanted. It didn't take us long to find a suitable cafeteria where we pointed to what we wanted and didn't have to ask for anything. We only just managed to finish lunch before the place closed down for the usual siesta. We bought a couple of bottles of water as we were about to leave and got back on our bikes again. This time, we set off in the opposite direction, towards the harbour and beyond. With no one much around during siesta, it allowed us to look around the harbour without attracting attention.

Then, for a better view of the place, we decided to climb the hill that had at its summit the derelict building, Forte di Santa Caterina. I knew there was no entry allowed to the building – locally known as 'the castle' – but visiting it would help maintain our tourist image. We left the bikes at the base of the hill and started up the path to the summit on foot.

About halfway up the winding path, we met two American tourists coming down the hill. They advised us not to go any further as there was nothing to see up there and there is no entry permitted to the old building. Although we did not intend to continue to the top anyway, we thanked them for their advice and agreed it wasn't worth going further. As if acting on their recommendation, we sat down where we were to take in the sights, and continue our role as tourists. The tuna fishing industry building stood out across from the town on the western side of the harbour.

We collected our bikes from where we left them and rode back into town. After returning the bicycles to their owner when he reappeared after siesta, we strolled back to our hotel with the intention of taking a nap. As we entered the lobby, a figure emerged from behind a newspaper and fell into step with us. Dom had waited for our return. I unlocked my door and the other two followed me in. After handing out bottles of water, I joined the men in the small lounge area at one end of my room. Dom looked grim and seemed anxious for us to settle so he could talk to us.

"After you left, I received word that a boat visited your bay last night. Its visit followed exactly the standard pattern. They tracked the boat westward along Crete and then out into the Mediterranean. It came directly to Favignana and docked at the port this afternoon."

"That's not possible," Troy interrupted. "We were down at the harbour earlier this afternoon, and then we climbed up the hill and were watching from up there. No boat came in during all that time."

"It arrived about half an hour ago. You missed it. That's unimportant anyway. What's important is what happens tonight. If they follow the usual pattern, a second boat should make the pick-up from your bay tonight. We need to be ready for it tomorrow."

We spent the next hour going over the likely scenario for the boat's arrival the next day. Today's boat arrived just after siesta ended. Dom explained that probably was a bit later than usual. "It seems likely last night's crew were new to the operation. They arrived in the bay a bit later than expected. Then they seemed to take much longer than usual to anchor and complete their mission. Because of this, they didn't leave the bay until just after 3.00a.m."

I thought aloud. "If their timing had mirrored the previous boats', it's likely they would have arrived back here during siesta, when there was nobody much about when they docked."

"That is what we believe is supposed to happen," Dom agreed. "It wasn't a problem today because it wasn't carrying anything illicit."

"If the second boat visits the bay tonight as we expect, we will need to be ready and in place by the start of siesta tomorrow." I looked at Troy to see if he had any thoughts to the contrary. He didn't.

He nodded his agreement, but furrows formed across his brow. "You're right; we need to be in our dive gear and in the water out of sight somewhere in that port area. The question is: how do we do that?"

Dom didn't have any suggestions to contribute, so I continued. "I've been giving it some thought all day. I haven't come up with a plan yet. Dom, where does the dive shop runs its dive courses?"

"It depends but, for beginners, they usually are in that little bay on this side of the harbour. They dive in that small area between the eastern side of the harbour and the Coast Guard headquarters."

"Okay. That gives me something to consider. The two arms of the harbour look like they are manmade."

"Yes and no. The eastern arm is manmade. The western arm is partly natural but has a lot of construction added to it. That is the same for the causeway arrangement joining the harbour construction to the island. There is a natural rocky strip extending out to form part of the western arm. The harbour development, in more modern times, required the provision of better access. Construction of the section that supports the Via Molo San Leonardo was necessary to provide for heavy vehicle traffic that now comes down to the docks. Is that helpful at all?"

"I don't know," I had to admit. "I thought we could enter the water in that bay where they run the diving courses and remain there until the boat arrives. Then we need somehow to get around into the harbour to inspect under the hull of the boat. My problem is, I don't know about those constructed areas. If they are solid rock filled construction, it means we have to swim all the way around the eastern arm to get into the harbour. It's not a massively long swim, but the longer we're in the water, the greater the risk and the more time we have to allow for completion of our operation."

The two men listened intently. Then Troy dropped his head and studied his feet. I knew he was mulling over my idea. Dom took to staring out the window as he thought about it and, after a few moments, he spoke first.

"I will see if there are plans of that area but I don't think my chances are good in the time available. I know an old man who might have been involved in some of the construction work. I will try to talk to him. He might know something useful, or he may be able to point me in the direction of someone who does know. I will go now to see if I can catch up with him. Later, I will collect you so we can go to dinner together."

I didn't feel like company. I wasn't going to take a nap, but I needed to be alone to give some thought to our plan of attack for tomorrow. To this end, I suggested none too tactfully that Troy bugger off to his room. He was looking weary and I felt sure he'd be out like a light within minutes. I sat doodling aimlessly on a notepad as I let my mind drift over our task for tomorrow.

At some point, I must've dozed off. I woke with a start, with my head on the desk and someone pounding on my door. I massaged my face to get it to wake up too as I groggily made my way to answer the door. It was Dom. My appearance obviously belied the fact that I had been asleep. He apologised for waking me, but it was well after seven o'clock. I showed Dom into my room, unlocked the connecting door and sent him in to wake Troy while I splashed water on the face and combed my hair. We didn't waste time on dressing for dinner and, within about ten minutes, were on our way down to Dom's car.

He drove us to the Nautilus restaurant –*Ristorante Nautilus* –along the coast a short distance from the town centre, and probably well within reasonable walking distance from our hotel. The menu was good; the food was even better. We sat in small alcove off to one side of the main dining area. It provided a reasonable degree of privacy and, as we would be speaking English, allowed us to feel reasonably confident that no one would be eavesdropping on our conversation. Dom led off with news of his meeting this afternoon.

"As promised, I went to talk to the old man, Francesco, who I thought might be able to give me some information about the construction of the harbour. He knew quite a bit about it but said his friend, Giovanni, knew even more. So, Francesco and I drove over to Giovanni's house and I spent the rest of the afternoon with the two old men."

"Was it a worthwhile meeting?" I asked.

"I think so, yes. I have some hand drawn sketches. They are not plans. They are ... how do you say ...?"

"Sketches maybe, or mud maps?" I suggested.

"Ah, si... mud maps that might be useful. I will give them to you when we get back to the hotel. The main thing they told me was that there is a short section constructed differently from a breakwater. A breakwater has all of the rocks piled up on top of one another. This section they talked about is built more like a bridge."

"Okay, some of it is solid rock filled, with a small part of it constructed on pylons – like a bridge. Have I got that right?"

"Yes, that is correct. The part that is on the pylons, as you call them, allows the sea to move freely between the harbour and the small bay where they run the diving courses. That piece of the construction is at the beginning of the eastern arm, where it branches off from the connection to the island."

"This is good news. You've done a great job, Dom. I hope the two old men don't get suspicious and start asking questions around the place."

"Don't worry, Sonny. I told them that one of my tourists – Troy – was a civil engineer and had asked questions about the construction that I couldn't answer. I said it made me feel very inadequate as a guide, so I came to them for information to redeem myself when next I spoke with Troy. They laughed and gave me top marks for doing my job properly." He was beaming with pride when he finished his story.

"Right, tomorrow morning we should hire dive gear and go down to that little bay to check things out. We could say we were planning to go diving the next day and wanted to check the gear beforehand to make sure it was okay. Then, somehow, we need to get back into the water – or be in the water – when our boat arrives. How does that sound to you, Troy? Maybe we should even make arrangements to hire a boat for the following day to maintain the pretence of a dive trip."

"About the timing," Troy began thoughtfully, "If we hire a boat for the day after tomorrow and then hire some dive gear, we could be down at the bay just a bit before siesta. We could check out our options for getting into the harbour and then, if needs be, mess about on the beach for a while until the boat comes in and then go for another dive. However, if anyone is watching, that process will attract attention. A better option would be to enter the water just before the boat comes into the harbour."

"If we get good info on the boat's likely arrival, we could enter the water as the boat approaches the harbour entrance. That would give us time to check out our access to the harbour and maybe even be in the harbour when the boat finally docks." Troy's idea made sense, and Dom was nodding his agreement as well. "We'll look at Dom's mud maps when we get back to the hotel to see if our plan is feasible," I continued. "If we go with this plan, even if we can't swim into the harbour through the pylons, we still should have enough time to swim out and around the end of the eastern arm to access the harbour that way."

"I'm thinking," Troy began, "We need someone keeping watch up top when we're busy underwater. We need to know what happens when the boat ties up: if someone comes down to meet it, or what happens on the dock."

"I don't know what Dom's brief is, but maybe he can be the observer," I suggested.

"I can do that," Dom volunteered. "When we go down to the bay, I will look for a good vantage point from which to observe all that happens once the boat docks."

"I think that's all we can plan at this stage. We'll look at those mud maps when we get back to the hotel to check if the plan is at least feasible in theory. There's plenty of time before tomorrow to think about it and come up with improvements." I didn't think any improvements would occur to us over night, and I didn't want to over-engineer the plan. My philosophy is that the more detail in your plan, the more there is to go wrong.

Dom drove us back to the hotel. I was ready for a sleep and, fortunately, Dom didn't want to hang around. He gave us the mud maps, arranged a time to meet up in the morning, and left. Troy didn't hang around either. I went to bed convinced that, with tomorrow's plans occupying my mind, sleep would be difficult. How wrong can you be? I fell asleep almost immediately.

Chapter 16

Dom is expected around ten o'clock, so today allows us a leisurely start. I studied all the paper we accumulated and then concentrated on the mud map Dom provided. Even if the map was only partly accurate, it promised us easy access to the harbour from the bay. Confident there was no more to do to prepare for the day ahead, I went for breakfast.

A few minutes after ten o'clock, Dom pounded on my door. Troy was already in my room, and we had everything we needed in our backpacks and our bathers on under our clothes. The morning went according to plan. Hiring a boat for tomorrow took longer than antici-pated as we made a fuss about finding one that suited us for diving. That done, we went through the rigmarole of selecting and hiring our dive gear for two days – and none too subtly let it be known we would test it before our dive trip tomorrow. As it was twelve o'clock, lunch was our next priority.

Dom drove us to the bay where we would dive and surprised us with a picnic hamper. Sitting on a rug in the shade of the trees, we ate while surveying the bay. We discussed our plans, and Dom checked his phone for an update on the boat's arrival. Troy and I had received a cryptic text message from Theo saying nothing more than a boat had arrived the previous night. Initially, Dom told us the anticipated arrival of the boat at the harbour was about two o'clock. His latest update indicated the boat would be at the entrance by 1.30 p.m. That suggested we should be in the water by one o'clock at the latest.

We sorted our gear and wriggled into our wetsuits. I checked that Dom was still okay to observe the dock area while we dived. He assured us he had found a good vantage point this morning. As soon as we dived, he would walk the short distance to his observation point, leaving the car parked where it was now at the bay. Everything appeared to be in place, so we lugged our gear down to the water and got wet.

The old men's mud map proved to be remarkably accurate. The area with the pylons offered good access to the harbour. It was a reasonably long swim through the pylons, but there were no obstacles apart from the good coating of marine life on the pylons that looked like it would tear to pieces anything coming in contact with it. We surfaced cautiously to check on the harbour before clearing the last of the pylons. With only part of our heads above water and treading water gently, we scanned the harbour. What we assumed was our boat was just coming through the entrance. We maintained our position until it was clear the boat was heading for the western side of the harbour. Then we dived and swam towards it.

It tied up in front of the tuna fisheries building. As we swam closer, I began to have some doubts about this whole exercise. Although we were deep, I could see the hull clearly. Our ideas about how they transported the containers looked way off the mark. There was nothing visible below the hull where we had expected to see the container attached somehow. Maybe they had some other ingenious method that hadn't occurred to us. There was some sort of activity happening topside. The boat bobbed about at its mooring. After about five minutes, everything went quiet. We waited about another 15 minutes but with no further sign of anything happening on the boat, we abandoned the exercise and swam back towards the pylons.

At about half the distance through the pylons, Troy signalled to me to surface. I bobbed up beside him and he spat his mouthpiece. "What just happened over there? Could we have gotten it so wrong?" His level of exasperation equalled my level of confusion. "I can think of three possibilities," he continued. "Either our expectations were the stuff of fantasy, or they have some ingenious way of transporting stuff that we still don't know anything about… or, could it be, that it was the wrong boat?"

"I don't have an answer, Troy, only a sneaking suspicion trying to develop into something more – and it doesn't align with any of your possibilities. I need to think on it a bit more. I think I can safely say now that it wasn't the wrong boat. We expected our boat at that time, and the boat we looked at is the only one that entered the harbour during our dive. Let's end this dive the way we planned to and then see what Dom can tell us about what went on once the boat docked."

We dived, cleared the pylons and swam about half way across the small bay before surfacing and swimming to shore. After lugging our gear across to Dom's car, we shed our wetsuits and climbed back into our clothes. As we spread our gear out to dry, Dom joined us. He looked as confused as the rest of us. We spread the rug out again and sat down to hold a post mortem – one that I hoped would give rise to sound clues as to why we saw no container.

Dom's report on what took place on the pier was not enlightening. "As the boat tied up, a man came out of the fisheries building, got into a blue van parked alongside the building and drove onto the pier to park beside the boat. Three men were on the boat. A brief conversation went on between the crew and the man on the pier. The man seemed agitated; waved his arms around a lot..."

"He was Italian. They do that when they talk." Troy was still light on for humour, but Dom didn't seem to notice the jibe.

I tried to get Dom's report underway again. "What happened after that? It seemed like activity on the boat ceased after only a few minutes."

"Yes, that first conversation was brief. The man was still waving his arms about when the three crewmembers simply climbed off the boat and joined him on the pier. I thought things might get rough. It didn't, but what looked like a very heated conversation took place for a couple of minutes. Then, the crew simply walked off the pier, leaving the man still talking to their backs. He must have realised it was pointless, and pulled out his phone to call someone. After a few moments of messing about with the phone – it looked like the person he rang didn't answer – he returned to the blue van. The man threw the phone into the van, climbed in after it and drove off. He returned about 20 minutes later, parked the van back in the same place and went into the fisheries building again."

"So, nothing was loaded or unloaded but, the fact that the man took the van to meet the boat, suggests he was expecting to collect something," I thought aloud. That fitted with the suspicion I had been toying with since our dive. No point in sharing it yet, it's still only a half-baked idea. I realised Dom had started speaking again.

"... not much use but I photographed everything that happened, including the van's route when it left the harbour."

"We did the same," Troy said, "Took a lot of images of n-o-t-h-i-n-g."

There's not much more we can do sitting here. Let's go back to the hotel and have a look at the photos, maybe it will trigger some bright ideas for us," I suggested.

I was wrong. The photos told us nothing, maybe with the exception of the direction the van took when it left the harbour. With nothing else to go on, I thought it might be worthwhile exploring something about the van and its driver. "Do we know anything about that van or the driver? Is there any way we could obtain details?"

Dom shrugged. "I have requested registration information. If it was the owner driving the van, it will give us a bit more information on what might be going on."

Something niggled. Something about the photos was trying to speak to me. I couldn't think with the other two chattering in the background. "Geez, it seems like forever since I last had coffee. A cup would go down really well about now." I remained seated at the computer picking through the images and hoped the other two would get the message and do something about coffee for us all. It worked. Both of them moved to the bench and a period of rattling and banging associated with coffee making followed.

It hadn't achieved anything other than coffee. Removing the chatter from around me hadn't allowed anything to jump out at me from the images. I abandoned the computer and joined the other two in the lounge area. They were conducting their own speculative post-mortems on what went wrong today. It seemed like a good time to suggest that perhaps nothing had gone wrong. Perhaps, as far as other people were concerned, today was exactly as it should have been. Only we three expected to find a container suspended under that boat, so only we three were disappointed. There was much shaking of heads from the other two. They were not buying that explanation for one moment. I desperately wanted some time alone.

"Time is getting away. I have a few things I want to do – and maybe even fit in a nap – before dinner. How about we give it a rest for now and regroup later for dinner, say, at seven o'clock?" Hooray, there was agreement and, within moments, I was alone.

My return to the images still refused to produce anything enlight-ening, but the departure of the other two gave me the opportunity to do something I'd been itching to do since the end of the dive. I dug my phone out of my backpack and called Theo. He answered on the second ring and I launched straight into my explanation for the call.

"Today's boat was a fizzer. There was no container anywhere about that boat. Nothing was unloaded or went onto the boat. The only curious thing that happened was that a van drove onto the pier to meet the boat and something of an agitated discussion followed between the driver of the van and the boat crew. I know any one of a number of scenarios could be at play here." There were plenty of possible reasons put forward by the other two and discussed at length. I outlined them for Theo before adding my own thoughts. "Any of those reasons could apply, Theo, but I have a feeling it was a different story. Do we know if the first boat left the container at the mooring block?"

"Yes, one of Tito's men who is a trained diver and I checked the block the next morning. Attached to it was a container the same as we found there previously. That's a strange question, why do you ask?"

"Has anyone checked the mooring block since the second boat's visit?"

"N-o-o, why would we? The second boat would have removed the container. There would be nothing to see out there."

"That's just the point, Theo. I think the container is still on the mooring block. For whatever reason, that second boat didn't pick up the container."

"Perhaps you should tell me what you think has happened."

"I was just getting to that. My understanding of what happened is that the boat arrived a little late and took a long time at the mooring. I think it might have been a new boat – a new crew – and for whatever reason, they were unable to retrieve the container. Maybe they were unable to release it from the mooring block. I don't really know what might have gone on out there, but I think it was a failed retrieval attempt and not a case of the wrong boat being tracked back here to the harbour."

"This is disturbing news. We did not know the container had not left this bay. You are correct, it could be that something went wrong and it was simply a failed retrieval. My thinking – unfortunately – is that something more sinister occurred. What if the traffickers received a tip off about the boat being tracked and, of more concern, what if they also were told that divers would be checking the hull when it arrived at Favignana?"

"Perhaps, but it would be worth knowing if the container is still on the mooring block and whether another retrieval attempt happens tonight."

"There is probably just enough light left for a quick dive. I will go now to organise it."

It was interesting that news of the failed retrieval, if that's what it was, hadn't reached Crete… or perhaps it had, but just not Theo. One thing was obvious. There was nothing more I could do until I heard back from Theo. It would be useful if that happened before we went to dinner tonight, but in the meantime, a nap seemed like the best option.

His call came through not much before seven o'clock, and delivered more information than I expected. They managed a very quick dive before the light faded. Yes, the container remained attached to the mooring block. He hadn't been able to call me earlier as Tito called the meeting with Theo as soon as he returned from the dive and, although Tito waffled on for ages, there were no issues for discussion. Theo stopped short of making any accusations, but some disturbing thoughts occurred to me. His call turned into a whole world of bad news when he changed the subject to tell me something else that had happened. With the call ended, I resolved not to mention speaking to Theo or any of his information.

Dinner was a low-key affair at a trattoria close to the hotel. At the outset, conversation was light on. The other two were still glum after today's dismal outcome. They had already discussed it from every possible angle, and I had nothing new to contribute, or was prepared to contribute yet. As I sensed we were all getting ready to leave, Troy sat bolt upright and slapped his forehead. "What about the boat?" he demanded.

"What boat?" Dom and I chorused together.

"The boat we hired for our dive tomorrow. We were never going diving anyway. So, what are we going to do about it? We won't need it, but it will look a bit odd if we don't take it out after all the fuss we went through to hire it."

Dom said he would call and cancel the hire for us, and then he asked about returning the dive gear. Dependent on what happened at Crete tonight, we might need to dive again tomorrow. I didn't want to share too much with the others at this stage, so suggested we get the tanks refilled first thing tomorrow and then dive for a bit somewhere so it looked in keeping with our original plans.

After returning to the hotel and saying good night to Dom, Troy went to his room. It was still early. I spent a few moments thinking about what we might do this evening that could help our cause rather than wasting the night. I knocked on the interconnecting door and Troy invited me in.

"How does a bit of a stroll in the night air appeal to you?" I asked. He looked hard at me and considered the question through the time span of a couple of heartbeats before replying.

"I don't have any other plans and I'm not sleepy, so I could be interested. What did you have in mind?"

"Come and have a look at my computer with me. I think there might be something we can follow up on instead of sitting around doing nothing tonight."

"Should I call Dom?"

"Nah, I don't think that's necessary. We are just going for a bit of a stroll around the neighbourhood," I replied with a wink.

I brought up Dom's images from earlier today and showed Troy how in some of them he had managed to capture street signposts as his camera followed the van away from the harbour. My suggestion was to trace the van's route on a map and then walk it. I didn't share the rest of my thinking with Troy but, I wanted to be prepared if another boat retrieved the container tonight. If a boat brought it back here tomorrow and the same van collected it, we might have an idea of the route of its delivery to the next stage of its journey.

It took longer than I anticipated to locate the streets and plot the van's supposed course on a map. With the route marked out on the map, we decided it wouldn't be too difficult to walk it, even at this time of night. My only concern was the female receptionist who seemed to rule the foyer from early morning until about eight o'clock every evening. I shared my concern with Troy. "I think that receptionist should be finished work for the day by now. I'm not sure why, but I would prefer she didn't know we went out tonight. She and Dom seem... familiar. I feel that, if she saw us leaving, Dom would know and be waiting for us before we were out the front door."

"What does it matter if Dom knows we have gone out for a stroll? He doesn't have to be glued to us every time we move."

"Can't answer that yet; let's just put it down to gut instinct telling me it's best if he doesn't know."

Troy made no secret of his uncertainty about what I proposed and posed every possible argument against what my instinct was telling me. We were wasting time and I wanted to get away. "If you're uncomfortable about doing this, stay here. I'm perfectly capable and happy to go on my own. In fact, I think it might be better if I do go alone if you're going to be jumping at shadows all night."

Of course he wanted to come and have a look at things, he assured me. We carried nothing obvious, not wanting to look like anything other than two people out for an evening stroll, but my pockets contained my keycard, credit card, a pocket torch, a bit of cash and the folded map with our route marked on it.

The receptionist was working late tonight. Well, I assumed she was still on duty. She wasn't at her desk, but I saw her talking to a couple of men at a table in the bar area. We waited at the bottom of the stairs and watched her briefly before risking crossing the foyer. As we hesitated, a couple walked in off the street and made their way into the bar area without generating as much as a glance in their direction from the receptionist. If they hadn't caught her attention, I doubted we would either. I decided we should risk it. Without rushing, Troy and I walked through the foyer and out onto the street.

Once out on the street, we kept our heads down and walked quickly to the corner of the building. A laneway ran down the side of the hotel, separating it from the neighbouring building. The only light in the lane was in an area around the hotel's side door, which opened into the lane. Soft light from inside spilled out through the open door and mounted on the external wall above the doorway was a low wattage fancy looking light. No one was around, but the cigarette butts littering the ground around the doorway suggested smokers – probably staff and patrons alike – used the area when in need of a smoke.

We hurried down the lane, across the hotel's small rear carpark and the adjoining nature strip and onto the major street that ran parallel to the rear of the hotel. The street was deathly silent. No vehicles came or went and no sound of TVs reached us. We noted that the good residents of this street went to bed early as we watched houses the length of the street gradually plunged into darkness. That was the easy bit done.

What seemed straightforward on the map became more complicated on the ground. Somehow, the real world wasn't as clear or tidily laid out as the map was. It took a good deal longer than I imagined locating and exploring the streets in question. More frustrating perhaps was the fact that ultimately we were no wiser for our efforts. All we had gained was an idea of the direction the van took towards the outskirts of town. We still didn't know its destination. By the time we reached the end of what we knew of the route, it was after 11 o'clock and returning to the hotel seemed not only a good idea but also the only option available to us.

The return journey was quicker than the outward one and we soon found ourselves back in the hotel's carpark. A gaggle of what I assumed to be guests' vehicles occupied the space. We stood in their shadows for a few moments, checking for any sign of movement. No one came out, so we quickly crossed the narrow open space to the hotel's rear wall. I led the way and peered around the corner of the building. The lane seemed darker than earlier when we set out. It took me a moment to realise that someone turned off the light over the side door during our absence. It was kind of them to oblige us that way, I thought as I quickly entered the lane and headed for the front of the building. The sounds of patrons lingering in the bar drifted out through the open door as I hurried past.

Damn! The receptionist was back at her station. She half rose from behind her desk and reached for her phone in the one movement as I came through the front door. The shocked look on her face caught my attention. Why would our returning to the hotel cause such a shock? Taken aback by her reaction, I looked over my shoulder, intending to alert Troy to her presence and our reception. He wasn't there. He was right behind me when we started down the lane. I spun on my heel and felt my stomach tighten as I ran back to the entrance to the lane.

I had a fleeting glimpse of a shape on the ground part way down the lane before I found myself slammed against the wall. Instinct told me the crumpled shape was Troy. The side of my face scraped against the rough surface. A shoulder in the middle of my back pinned me to the wall, preventing me from moving my arms. My attacker wrapped a trunk-like arm tightly around my throat. With his other hand, he grabbed a handful of hair and reefed my head back further than I thought possible without breaking my neck. I couldn't breathe.

I dredged up some of my training: don't struggle, try to relax and conserve oxygen. It didn't help. His rough face was next to my ear. His breath stank of garlic and wine. He softly growled something in Italian in my ear. I didn't catch what he said, either because my Italian wasn't good enough or because I was starting to lose consciousness.

My lungs were burning, my eyes were becoming heavy and I could feel a blackness descending. In what probably would be one of my last conscious moments, out of the corner of my eye I caught a movement. I forced myself to move the only bit of me I could move – my eyes – in that direction. The idea that I might be hallucinating passed through my mind. Troy, blood streaming down his face and head and shoulders bent low like a rugby back barging into a ruck, charged at my assailant.

The arm disappeared from around my neck as my attacker, aware of troy at the last moment before impact, turned to face Troy. He let go of my neck to free up his arm to fend off the impending assault. Troy bounced off the man and landed a few feet away. He lay crumpled and motionless. I started gulping in air as soon as the arm around my throat loosened. My attacker had not let go of my hair and I felt my head dragged back even further. Then, needing both his hands to break his fall, the attacker let go of my hair.

I spun around to face the man. He went down on one knee, but used both his arms to push himself up and be back on his feet in an instant. He was quick, but I was faster. When he was only halfway back up, I kicked out with everything I had, even lifting myself off the ground in the process. The toe of my sturdy hiking boot for an instance buried itself in something soft and squishy. He grunted and bent over clutching his groin area. I pivoted to one side, extended my arms and, with hands clasped, swung my arms upwards firmly in beach volleyball style. I didn't hit him quite as squarely under the chin as intended, but it was close enough. The impact sent him flying backwards off his feet. As I raced to Troy, I heard a sickening crack as the man's skull connected with the pavement.

Troy had managed to sit up but didn't have much idea what was happening around him. A severe blow above and to the front of his left ear resulted in a nasty wound that matted his hair and face with blood. Had the impact been a fraction lower, it would have struck the temple area and might have resulted in a different outcome. I draped his arm over my shoulders and helped Troy to his feet. Then, with my other arm around his waist, I managed to drag and carry him to the hotel's front door. The receptionist was no longer at her desk. I struggled on through the foyer to the lift and up to our floor. We staggered through my room to the interconnecting door, and through into Troy's room where I dumped him on the bed.

After soaking one of the hotel's lovely white towels in the hand basin, I used it to clean Troy's wound and face. I was in the process of doing this when loud pounding on my door threatened to knock it down. My gun was in my bag. If only I took it with me, things might have been different tonight. I grabbed it and tucked into the small of my back as I went to answer the door. A distressed looking Dom burst into the room the moment the door started to open. A flood of questions greeted me as he rushed through my room to the interconnecting door and into Troy's room.

"How is he? Tell me how this happened. What were you doing out tonight? I thought you were having an early night."

"Whoa, Dom; maybe you should tell us what you're doing here, and how you got here so quickly. Our side of the story is simple. As neither of us was sleepy, we decided to go for a walk before turning in for the night. We were on our way back up to bed when I realised Troy wasn't with me. I went back to look for him and was attacked as I entered the alley. I didn't see what happened to Troy. I saw him on the ground injured when I returned to the alley. What happened is all a fog to him at present; the head wound, you see."

Dom paced the room and appeared to be considering what I told him, but didn't do anything about explaining his sudden appearance. If at first you don't succeed, ask the question again. "Well, Dom, how come you arrived so quickly?"

"I have a friend... a colleague... working close by. He noticed something going on in the lane and went to investigate. He arrived in time to see you deal with your attacker and help Troy into the hotel. He rang me and was then going to help you with Troy but, by the time he had spoken to me, you were already up here."

"Your friend doesn't happen to be that brassy looking receptionist you are s-o-o friendly with?"

"What? No, we are not friends. I have been... trying to get close to her... no, that's not right. I have been trying to cultivate her. Yes, that's the correct English, I think. At first, I thought I might be able to persuade her to help me by keeping an eye on what goes on here, but then I realised that there is something going on with her. I think she cannot be trusted and I became worried about your safety. That is why a colleague was keeping an eye open on this place while he was working on something else."

"So we need to be wary of her in the future?"

"No, you will not have to worry about her again. Look out of your window."

When we first arrived, I was disappointed my window didn't have a view and only overlooked a section of the lane where all the action tonight happened. I changed my mind about what it offered as I looked down on the alley. Although I couldn't see the vehicles, blue flashing lights lit up the alley. Torchlight skittered across the scene and men were setting up bright work lights, but what they focused on was out of my field of vision.

An interesting scene played out in the section of the lane I could see. Our receptionist, still in her stiletto heels and tight short black skirt, was being bundled into the back of what I took to be the local version of a paddy wagon. A police officer on either side of her was trying to lift her into the wagon. She was not being cooperative. Even from this distance, I could see her once crisp white shirt streaked with blood. A couple of paramedic-type personnel rolled a gurney through my field of vision. That brought me back to reality with a thump.

"What is happening down there?" I asked cautiously. "I'm not sure I understand – and I think I need to know."

"There was a fight... you understand? Two lovers fight and it is not good..."

"A lovers' tiff that turned sour?"

"*Si,* that is how you say it: a lovers' tiff that turned violent. She was holding her lover when police arrived and will be charged with his murder."

"Christ, he is dead then?" My question almost pleaded with Dom to refute it.

"*Si,* but it is not a problem. No one saw what happened and circumstantial evidence says she is guilty. Maybe, in the future, there will not be enough evidence to convict her." He shrugged and turned to Troy who spent the last few minutes lying quietly taking in our conversation. "Troy, a friend of mine who is a doctor will be here soon to take a look at your injury."

Troy became agitated and attempted to get up. "It is okay. Relax. He is safe, one of us. It will not be a problem for him to come," Dom reassured us both.

After dealing with Troy's injuries and giving him some pills for his headache, the doctor and Dom left. The doctor did not want Troy to go to sleep because of possible concussion, and I didn't think I could sleep anyway. However, I think we both dozed off just before dawn.

Chapter 17

Neither of us was up too early this morning. Dom's friend, the doctor, visited again at some barely civilised hour – well, if you have only just struggled out of bed, it's barely civilised. He pronounced Troy 'okay' and not concussed. Troy was more alert than I thought. He asked whether it would be all right for him to dive today. The doctor hesitated but, after issuing a myriad of cautions, conceded it probably would be okay for him to dive – but, not too deep and not for too long.

Over breakfast, I asked Troy why he wanted a clearance to go diving. While, as far as the dive shop was concerned, we were going diving today, there was nothing to say we had to, and there was nothing to indicate we should. Halfway through breakfast my phone rang. It was Theo. A very short and hurried call to tell me another boat came last night and they were tracking it. There was something decidedly off about the call. I almost was convinced he had made it covertly. Although I knew Troy was waiting expectantly for me to share what the call was about, I took a moment to weigh up a few things first. I suggested we return to our rooms where we could talk privately.

We decided to forego coffee with our breakfast in the interest of getting back upstairs for our discussion. Neither of us does well without an early morning coffee, so I made us coffee and we settled in for what I felt might be a difficult discussion. After a deep breath, I plunged in. "I'm starting to feel a little concerned as a result of a few things that have happened, and doubts are starting to flutter about in the recesses of my mind. I'm developing a list of questions that need answers. Your thoughts on some of those might help me decide whether I'm being paranoid or not."

"I'm not sure what you're on about, but roll them out and we'll have a look at them."

"Okay, but I'm not going to talk about our dive to day being a fizzer. There are other issues." Troy nodded his understanding and I continued. "Although there wasn't anything worth photographing today, I'm a bit curious about the location from where Dom took his shots. He must have found a fantastic site to be able to take those shots that captured the street names. The first one or two might have been possible with a long lens and a high vantage point, but I can't see

169

how he could possibly take those later ones. They were too far away and probably hidden from Dom by buildings."

Troy took a moment to consider my comments before replying. "I see what you're saying. I hadn't thought about it but, now that we have walked the route, I have to admit I can't believe he took those last few from anywhere down near the harbour."

"Moving on to the next issue; what's all this stuff he is feeding us about just happening to have a colleague 'working on something else' in the vicinity who alerted him to our fun and games in the lane last night? That 'coincidence' stretches belief a bit too far. There were a number of things about last night that I'm having trouble swallowing: his story about 'cultivating' the receptionist doesn't ring true, or fit with what we've seen going on in the reception area between those two. It seems he wants us to believe the whole incident from last night just disappeared and the woman's arrest – for something she didn't do – is okay because it eliminates a potential risk."

"Maybe we don't know the whole story. If we knew all the facts, how it all hangs together might be perfectly clear."

"Why hasn't he told us all of the facts? Your encounter could have been fatal... and it appears I did kill someone. I think that entitles us to know a whole lot more than we are being told."

"Good point. I'd like to know if there are going to be repercussions; am I going to have to appear in court or make a formal statement? It is going to be difficult to get on with things if we keep half expecting something to come along and bite us... like you being accused of murder."

"So, you don't think I'm being paranoid. That's encouraging. The other thing I wanted to mention is about that call I took during breakfast. It was a hurried call from Theo telling me another boat came into the bay last night. My thinking about yesterday's failure to locate a container on that boat was that it was the 'right' boat but, for whatever the reason, it hadn't managed to retrieve the container. When I was alone yesterday afternoon, I rang Theo and asked if he could organise a dive to inspect the mooring block. He rang back just before we went to dinner to say the container remained tethered to the block."

"Does that mean another boat is likely to dock here today?"

"Yes, they are tracking it and it is headed for Favignana. Let's say that, because of my other escalating doubts, I don't want to say anything to Dom about this second boat. I want to see if he tells us about it... or, for that matter, if Tito tells Dom about it." Our discussion ended with Troy nodding his agreement as Dom knocked on my door.

Dom had cancelled the hire of the boat for today and our tanks were back at the dive shop for refilling. He scrutinised us both. "You two do not look too good today. Your appearance will raise questions, especially your face and the bruises on your neck, Sonny."

I combed my hair without looking in the mirror this morning, perhaps I should inspect last night's damage. It wasn't pretty, but it wasn't serious. Now that Troy was clean and his wound covered with a plaster, he didn't look too frightening. However, I could see Dom's point. "You make a valid point, Dom. Perhaps it would be wise for you to collect the tanks for us when they are ready."

He received a call as I finished speaking. After checking the caller ID, he moved to the other end of the room to take it. The call didn't last long, but he stood there with his back to us for a few moments after he put his phone away. He slowly made his way back to us and announced, "We are expecting another boat to arrive this afternoon. You should prepare to dive again."

No other details of the call were forthcoming although both Troy and I asked questions. I might be wrong, but Dom didn't seem too pleased with the call. He didn't hang around too long. After saying he had things to take care of and would be back at about noon to collect us to take us to the bay, he disappeared.

As arranged, he returned at noon, and we all rode the lift down together. I stopped dead in my tracks as I stepped out of the lift. That woman was back behind the desk today. A hand in the small of my back eased me forward again. I fell into step with the two men all the way to Dom's car. As soon as we got in, I demanded answers. "What is that woman doing behind the reception desk? How can she be back here again today when they arrested her for murder last night?"

"It is not the same woman, Sonny. It is her sister. They are identical twins and they share the receptionist's job between them. There is a slight difference between them but, if you don't know what to look for, you don't notice it."

"Is it safe for us to continue to stay in this hotel? It would not be safe if the other sister came back, but does a different sister make our situation any safer?"

"It is safe. Gia, this sister, does not know the details of last night's incident. The man that died was her sister's lover. Gia believes the two of them had a bad fight and her sister accidentally killed the man. I chatted to Gia earlier today to see what she knew." Okay, for now,

I will accept Dom's story, but I remain unconvinced about the truth of it.

Today followed along much the same lines as yesterday. After we left the hotel, Dom parked at the small bay again. There was an antipasto lunch accompanied by crumbed chicken pieces and juice, followed by some time spent checking our dive gear. Our information indicated today's boat was on time and would arrive at about 1.30pm. That left us little time to waste again today before entering the water. We wanted to swim around in the bay for a few minutes before making for the pylons. Our cover story was that Troy was teaching me to dive. As with yesterday, as soon as we entered the water, Dom picked up his camera bag and headed for his mysterious vantage point.

We stuck to our plan. After messing about in the small bay for about five minutes, we dived and swam to the pylons. When we surfaced before heading out into the harbour, the boat already was in the harbour and nearing the end of its trip.

The boat tied up in front of the tuna fisheries building the same as yesterday's boat did. Something strange below its hull was visible to us even from halfway across the harbour. As we closed in on the boat, any doubts I had about what we were seeing disappeared. Suspended on a form of bridle arrangement below the hull was a familiar-looking fibreglass container. The short ropes and shackles previously used to tether it to the mooring block now suspended it from the bridle. We maintained some distance between us and the boat. Our position meant we were sufficiently close to see what was happening, but far enough away to give us a head start if we needed to escape. Nothing happened for what felt like a long time but, in reality, was only about five minutes.

We detected noises coming from on board the boat, and it began bobbing about in response to some activity happening topside. The container began to move. Something or someone began hauling up the bridle. This dragged the container to the rear of the boat. Its movement stopped for a short period when it was just below the surface. The boat, tied too tightly against dock, necessitated a brief pause in retrieval operations. After loosening the stern line, the rear of the boat swung a short distance clear of the pier, leaving a gap of a few feet between the boat and the pier. Then, the container began moving again and, hauled up quickly, it disappeared from view.

I signalled to Troy to stay where he was while I swam under the boat to check if I could see what happened to the container. I stayed deep, only edging closer to the surface when I was directly under the hull. There was no sign of the container, but sudden movement above startled me. I dived quickly and swam back to Troy at full speed. I realised later, the movement I'd seen was the bridle dropping back into place. Troy and I cleared the harbour at a fair depth, only reducing our depth as we swam through the shelter of the pylons.

To avoid any impression we had come from the harbour, once back in the bay, we again swam a fair distance across it before surfacing. We swam back to shore and shed our wetsuits. There was no sign of Dom. We dressed and spread our gear out on the grass beside the car to dry. Troy explored the picnic hamper for leftovers and discovered some cold chicken and juice. He spread the rug out again and despatched the leftovers while waiting for Dom to return.

After his snack, Troy stretched out on the rug and had dozed off by the time Dom arrived. Our guide would have passed for a tourist himself. He had a big floppy hat, large sunglasses and carried a mega sized camera bag. After dumping the bag and helping himself to some juice, he joined us on the rug.

"How was the dive? Did you get through to the harbour okay?"

"Your mud map was spot on and we swam through the pylons as planned," I replied. "The dive was enlightening. We have confirmed why the containers were never visible. We took photos and we'll explain later." I couldn't help think it was funny that Dom didn't ask those questions yesterday. If I were generous, I might put it down to the confusion resulting from yesterday's outcome. I continued the debrief session. "Did anything happen on the dock after the boat arrived?"

"Oh, yes. One man, the same one from yesterday I think, was very interested in the boat. His van was already alongside the fishery building, so I am convinced he must be an employee or have something to do with that place. He helped the boat tie up before bringing his van alongside. That man and two men from the boat raised a container like the one you described. They loaded the container into his van. He drove to an address on the edge of town and, about half an hour later was back on the pier beside the boat. The boat crew lifted what I think were the floorboards of the rear deck area. The container went back onto the boat. I couldn't see what they did with it, but I think it went into the hold. Once it was back on the boat, the floorboards were replaced."

"Good work, Dom," Troy said enthusiastically. "What happened to the bloke in the van after the container went back on board?"

"He parked the van back where it was before the boat's arrival and then disappeared into the fishery building. I watched for a few minutes after that, but he didn't come out again."

I was thinking about our next move while Dom spoke. "We should go back to the hotel and go over every detail. However, there is one thing I want to know more about, and I think we need to look into that now. We need to know the address of where the van took the container after it was unloaded, and then keep an eye on it. It seems that the contents of the container were unloaded at that address and then the empty container returned to the boat. We need to know what happens next to the contents, and whether somebody else is involved in moving them on."

"It's being taken care of," Don assured us. "A colleague is watching the house. He will contact me if there is any activity. Two men between them will maintain twenty-four hour surveillance of the place until something happens or we call it off. You're right; we should go back to the hotel. I need to report to my superiors."

Back at the hotel, we showed Dom the photos we took of the container suspended under the boat. Then he surprised us with the collection of photos taken from his vantage position. Taken with a top-quality long lens again, they clearly showed the man on the pier, the van – including its registration – the house where we believe the container was unpacked, and the return of the container. He hadn't spent his time sitting there only clicking off photos.

While there were no details of the owners of the van or the boat, or the name and address of the house now under surveillance, he had sought information on the identities of the four men involved with handling the container. That information hadn't come through yet. After studying the photos, we discussed what our next moves might be.

"God, we shouldn't have come back here," I exclaimed part way through our discussions. "We should have hung around somewhere near the harbour so we could watch what happened to the boat after the container went back on board. Do you think it would be too late to go back for a look?"

"Don't worry about it," Dom said calmly as he selected a number on his speed dial. He stood up and walked over to the window. The call ended, he returned to his seat. "The boat remains tied up at the pier," he announced. "Apparently the usual practice for these boats is to remain tied up overnight before going out to sea again early the next morning. They will continue to track this one when it leaves."

Dom barely finished speaking when his phone rang. This time, after checking the caller's ID, he excused himself and left the room to take the call. Fine, if that's how it's going to be, but we have things to do as well.

"Troy, we need to send our photos to Tito. We might as well do that while Dom is busy with what is obviously 'need to know' stuff. Apparently, we aren't on the list of those who need to know. Do you want me to send your photos off with mine?"

Troy handed over his memory card and I sent off both sets of photos. I was tempted to send Dom's as well, but thought better of it at the last minute. However, I would ask him about their likely distribution when he returned. Just as I finished sending the photos, Troy suddenly jumped out of his chair.

"I'll be back shortly," he said quietly as he was on his way to connecting door to our rooms. "If Dom comes back before I do, tell him I've just gone back to my room for something." He was flicking through the contacts on his phone as he disappeared into his room.

I had started making coffee when Dom knocked on the door. I let him in and went back to the coffee. Troy re-entered the room via the connecting door. He made a great show of doing up his belt and rearranging his shirt. Definitely an Oscar-winning performance, no one would doubt he had been to the bathroom. He gave me a look I couldn't interpret, but it was enough to get my antennae twitching, and I think I heard the faint clanging of alarm bells.

"You still want your coffee?" I asked innocently.

"Yes, thanks. I'll make it." He joined me and we stood jammed up side by side in front of the small bench – and with our backs to Dom.

Troy and I continued with our coffee making doing the 'after you – no, you go ahead, after you' stuff that invariably takes place when two people try to do something in a small space and using the same things. As we were going through this process, Troy slipped into my hand a narrow strip of paper torn off the bottom of a note pad. I needed to read it but, from Troy's antics, I knew I needed to do that without attracting attention. I struggled to resist the temptation, and Troy kept signalling with his eyes for me to read it. Finally, I paused for a moment, read the note, and then looked over my shoulder at Dom. "I'm sorry. Two sugars was it, Dom?" I asked innocently. Dom, checking something on his phone, was not interested in the coffee making activities and mumbled 'two please' without looking up.

175

The note was more confusing than helpful. *Be careful. Say nothing.* That's all it said, but that was enough. Troy was giving me a heads up that something was not kosher. As I made a show of wiping my hands on the front of my shorts, I slipped the note into my pocket before carrying the two cups of coffee over to where we were sitting. Troy joined us and, as he sat down, questioned Dom.

"Everything all right then? Anything happening we should know about?" Troy asked.

"Er, no, nothing is happening. Why do you ask?"

"The phone call; I thought there might have been something happening."

"Ah, I see: the phone call. No that was about something else; nothing for you to worry about."

"Right, so it looks like nothing will happen until tomorrow. Good. I have quite a bit of students' work to mark. I need all their results completed within the next few days. I think I'll go back to my room and make a start on it." Nobody said anything to the contrary, so Troy rinsed his coffee mug and started back to his room.

No you don't, I thought. You're not leaving me alone with Dom after that note you gave me. "Troy, I wish you hadn't mentioned that. I still have to do that report on the field school stuff to complete my subject. I must submit it in the next couple of days or I'll fail that subject. Looks like I should work on it tonight."

"Yeah, it's that time of the year we academics hate: nothing but marking piled up to our ears," Troy replied. He was getting good at playing along.

"Well, Dom, looks like you've got an early night," I said as I collected the mugs. "We'll think of you having a leisurely night off while we're slaving away up here."

"Oh, of course; is nine o'clock tomorrow morning okay to collect you for our dive trip?" Poor bloke did look a bit confused. It seems this wasn't how he planned to spend the evening, but he accepted it and stood to leave while waiting for an answer.

"N-o-o-o," Troy began thoughtfully. "Let's leave it until later – say, eleven o'clock. I think we need to be here in case there is some action in the morning. If anything is going to happen, it probably will happen before lunch."

I nodded my agreement and Dom, looking less than pleased, started towards the door. I called after him. "Dom, hang on. The memory card with your photos; don't forget it."

He thanked me, took the card and left. Troy was standing with his hand on the knob of the connecting door. He called 'goodnight' after Dom, but remained where he was until Dom left my room. Then he winked at me and returned to his room, leaving the connecting door marginally ajar. I made a production of washing and drying the coffee stuff and cleaning the table. Next door, I heard Troy drag a chair across the floor and thump about for a few seconds before silence settled in.

I went back to my computer and looked at the photos we took this afternoon. I was so engrossed in studying the images that, about five minutes later, Troy startled me when he slipped into my room again.

"Elvis has left the area," he announced. I raised my eyebrows at him. "Dom has driven off. I can see down onto the main parking lot from my window. It took him a while to get to his car, and I was concerned he was lurking in the hallway somewhere."

"You want to tell me what this is all about?"

"I must tell you, I could have killed you when you gave him that memory card back. We needed to get a better look at some of that stuff."

"And we shall. While he was taking his phone call and I was sending our photos off to Tito, I copied his memory card to my computer. Now, suppose you tell me what this is all about."

"I can't explain it, but something didn't ring true. As we agreed earlier, we aren't getting all the information. It was as though he was holding back on something. Anyway, as I said, I can't say why but somehow I thought something was not right. When I went back to my room, I rang Tito. I didn't really think I'd get him, but I did. I outlined what happened today and asked him about the two blokes who were monitoring the house where the van took the container. Tito has no one monitoring anything. My phone call wasn't long, but I mentioned to Tito a couple of things that bothered me. Bottom line: Tito is concerned about Dom. He suggested we needed to be careful and not share anything more with Dom. Tito is going to contact someone else and put something in place, but he didn't explain that."

"It looks like our radar is finally in sync. I too smelled something a bit off without being able to put my finger on it. That's why I copied those photos of his. I think we should initiate an independent agenda and see where that takes us."

"I have no argument with that, but how do we disengage ourselves from Dom? I know we've put him off until eleven o'clock tomorrow, but I'm not sure that he won't check on us anyway."

"That was my thinking too. One thing I am certain about: we are not going diving tomorrow under any circumstances. I have a bit of an idea, maybe the beginnings of a plan, in the back of my mind. I think we should work on it now for a while. Our first priority is to leave this hotel."

"How do we do that? I suspect if we set foot outside the door, Dom would be hot on our heels."

"Agreed; I detect something almost imperceptible between Dom and that woman who is on the reception desk every day – which ever sister it is and in spite of his denials. They both tried to be very 'businesslike' this morning, but there was a hint of something – some familiarity – that I picked up. Maybe it is this sister he's been chatting up all along and not the one under arrest. However, you're right. I think if we checked out, Dom would be here by the time we were out the door. That leaves us with two options. Normal practice is that at about 8.00p.m., the receptionist goes off duty and some sort of night porter takes over. He stays on duty until she comes back again at about eight o'clock the next morning. We could either leave later tonight, after she has left, or we could duck out very early tomorrow morning."

We discussed checking out tonight and finding somewhere else to stay, or waiting until the morning and working out what to do after that. My main concern was the lack of a vehicle. I wanted to look at the house to which the van took the container. Maybe he didn't know it, but Dom was careful not to give us the address other than it was on the outskirts of town. However, his photos today of the van on its way to the house showed a couple more street signs – and the house.

I opened my copies of Dom's photos and we spent some time scrutinising each one and noting any identifying features. Those that inadvertently captured a street sign helped us plot the van's course after it left the harbour and, this time led all the way to a house. After about 20 minutes of hard slog, we were reasonably confident we knew where to go and would be able to identify the place when we got there.

"That's fine, Sonny, but we need transport if we are going to take a look. It's a fair trip to the area where we think that house is."

"Yes, if we follow the same route as the van took. Last night we followed the van, but I think there is a quicker way. Look at the map. If the map is accurate, I think we could cut across the park. It's only a short distance from this hotel along Via Marconi and across the park to Via Vespucci. We now think the house is along the short street that comes off Via Vespucci. What do you reckon, worth a bit of a night hike?"

Troy studied the map, tracing a possible route and shortcuts. "We wouldn't need a vehicle. Actually, we don't have to go down Via Marconi. That looks like parkland between the two big roads. Maybe we could leave from the rear of the hotel and cut across the park to come out on the other side where that short road joins Vespucci."

"Well spotted! That's not far at all. We're less conspicuous on foot than in a vehicle. How about we get a couple of pizzas delivered, seeing as how we are supposed to be working in our rooms this evening. Then, after dark – well, after eight o'clock I mean – we go for a stroll?"

I advised reception we had ordered pizzas. She would send them up to our rooms when they arrived and we could pay the delivery person directly. That was easy. I wasn't so sure leaving the hotel was going to be as simple. My preference was for nobody to see us leave – or return.

The pizzas arrived and were excellent. At about 8.30pm, I ventured downstairs to check out the reception area. If someone occupied the reception desk, I would go to the brochure stand to look for something. There was no need for the pretence. The desk was unmanned. A noisy crowd occupied the bar/lounge area and I could see the night porter assisting behind the bar. I went back for Troy. With our backpacks, we went down to the ground floor, pausing at the bottom of the stairs to check nobody was watching, before heading out onto the street.

We kept our heads down as we walked the short distance along the street from the hotel's entrance to the corner of the building. Still a bit rattled after last night events in the lane, we took a long hard look down the lane before turning the corner and hurrying through the lane. Tonight's scenario was much the same as last night. There was a pool of light at the hotel's side doorway. We approached it cautiously; the door was open but no one was about.

Troy drew my attention to the generous littering of butts around the door. It looked as though the collection had grown since last night. Maybe this area doesn't get much attention in terms of housekeeping by hotel staff.

I risked a quick look through the open door. It opened into a short passage that ended in a tee junction with another passage. Good, it didn't open directly into a room. Tiptoeing down the short passage, I peered right and left along the intersected hallway. To the right, it led to the bar and reception end of the building. At the far end to the left, next to a set of lift doors, I saw the start of a staircase. This might be the best way to get back in unseen.

From behind the hotel, we crossed the hotel's rear carpark, and then Via Antonio Meucci diagonally to bring us onto Via Marconi. A short distance up Marconi, there was another lane between buildings. We used it to access the park, striking out at a wide angle to cross the parkland. An idea came to me when I realised our path was taking us quite close to Piazza Matrice. I stopped and spoke quietly to Troy. "If my memory serves me correctly, there is a hire place in the Piazza. It won't take us long to detour through the Piazza to see if it is still open at this hour." I strode off for the Piazza.

Troy caught up with me. "What are you going to hire?"

"Anything, but I think they have scooters." When we arrived, the man was preparing to close for the night. It took a bit longer and more fussing about than I had expected, but we managed to hire two Vespa scooters. He took us through the shop to collect the scooters from a storage area in the rear of the premises, before letting us out the back door with our machines. A short path led from the rear of the store onto Via Vespucci.

We travelled Via Vespucci to its junction with Via Colombo. The short street we wanted actually branched off the latter. Having found what we were looking for, we rode back across the park to a clump of trees opposite the street and hid the scooters from any passing traffic. Then we retraced our route on foot to end up at the large camping ground beyond the end of the short street.

The house we wanted was the last one on the dead-ended short street. Hidden amongst some shrubs directly across the road from the house, we settled down to watch the place. Nothing happened for about half an hour except Troy became fidgety.

"Sonny, what exactly are we looking for? I'm not enjoying sitting out here like this. What do you think is going to happen, that is, apart from the possibility of our being discovered by some nosy neighbour?" he asked.

"Not sure; maybe nothing. I thought we might watch for an hour or so and then go back to the hotel if nothing happens. ...And you can relax; we are not going to get sprung by any neighbour."

After almost an hour, the blue van from Dominic's photos parked in the driveway opposite us. The garage door opened and the van driver went inside. No one switched on a light until after the garage door closed behind the van driver, but the moonlight was bright enough for us to see a white van parked inside the garage.

The driver's visit was short. About 15 minutes later, the garage lights went out and the van driver emerged and drove off. The garage door closed immediately behind the van driver, and the whole scene across the road went back to being exactly the way it was when we arrived. Nothing happened during the following 20 minutes, so we returned to our scooters.

After a short distance through the park, we travelled back to the hotel in comfort on the sealed road. We parked the scooters at the rear of the hotel. I peered around the corner of the building to check the side door. One of the staff was outside smoking and two others, on their way home, exited the hotel's side door and made their way down the lane to the street running past the front of the hotel. After extinguishing his butt with his shoe, the smoker went back inside. I waited a couple of minutes, before moving quietly to the side door. Although I could hear patrons in the bar, there was no one in sight.

I beckoned Troy to follow me and we slipped inside. I checked the door. Inside, the handle opened it easily, but opening it from the outside required a key. We hurried to the stairs I had seen earlier at the left end of the passage, and climbed silently to our floor level.

At our floor, after a few moments of listening for any sounds on the other side of the door, Troy slowly opened the door and checked. The hallway on this floor was deserted. I examined the lock on this door. It was not as obliging as the one downstairs. From the hallway on our floor, it required a key to open the door to access the stairs. I wanted to leave via these stairs in the morning.

In desperation, I tore the cover off my notebook, folded it over and jammed it between the lock tongue and the lock plate set in the doorjamb. We hurried back to my room and I scratched around in my computer bag for the remains of my roll of duct tape. Armed with my manicure scissors, I went back to the door, carefully opened it and removed the piece of cardboard. Using several short pieces of tape, I taped the lock tongue back in the lock housing to prevent the door from locking. It was almost midnight by the time we regrouped in my room.

"We're going to need to sleep fast," I told Troy. "I want to leave here about 4.00a.m."

"Where are we going at that hour of the day?"

"I want to go back to watch that house again. I have a feeling things will happen early tomorrow morning. The boats leave the harbour early, and I think that the next stage of the journey for whatever was in that container will be by boat, a different boat from the one it arrived on."

"Thank goodness for the scooters."

"Pack everything tonight. If I'm right, we won't be coming back here. We'll be catching the early morning hydrofoil to the mainland."

"What about our accounts? We can't just disappear into the night without paying for our rooms."

"They'll use the credit card imprints they took when we arrived. It's not as if they can't recoup the money owed. I also don't want to draw any more attention to ourselves by leaving without paying our accounts, but it is important no one knows of our impending disappearance in advance."

Although not yet convinced this would work, Troy went to pack. It took me little time to get to bed, but I slept lightly and not very restfully.

Chapter 18

I was awake a few minutes before the alarm sounded. After splashing water on my face and pulling on clothes, I slipped the room's keycard into my pocket, picked up my two bags and was ready to go. Troy knocked gently on the connecting door and came in carrying his gear.

"Have you got your keycard?"

"I didn't think we were coming back, so I left it in my room."

"If my assumptions aren't right, we'll have to come back here. Take your keycard so you can get back in without having to asked reception for another one."

"Isn't there some rule – or law or something – about making off with the cards?"

"We'll post them back later if it makes you feel better. Just get it so we can get moving."

The duct tape I placed across the tongue of the door lock remained in place and doing its job. I ripped it off as soon as we were through the door. The place was deathly quiet; too early even for kitchen staff. We wasted no time descending the stairs and quietly let ourselves out the side door. A bit more confident once we were outside, we jogged down the lane and around to our scooters – not an elegant sight when you are loaded up with even small bags like ours. Fortunately, the good citizens of Favignana are a trustworthy lot. The scooters were where we left them. They were fitted with carriers and came complete with a couple of luggage straps. We strapped on our small amount of luggage and set off.

The quickest and shortest route to our destination involved a one-way street – going the wrong way for us. I counted on no traffic at this hour, and told Troy to follow me. We entered Vespucci from the wrong direction. I opened the throttle, wanting to reach our destination as quickly as possible to avoid any vehicle that might be about. Our destination was the clump of trees where we hid the scooters earlier last night.

We turned our headlights off when we left Vespucci. As we were coming from a different direction this time – and without lights – it took a bit of messing around in the dark to find our clump of trees. We invested a bit more time in making sure we hid the scooters well.

After all, all our gear was now on board them, including my computer. I hoped the good citizens would behave and our gear would still be there when we returned.

We set off on foot, heading for the same position we occupied earlier in the night and settled down as comfortably as we could behind the shrubbery. Just after five o'clock, the sound of an approaching vehicle caught our attention. Its headlights swung into view, lighting up the length of the short street as it approached. I quietly whispered to Troy to try *carefully* flexing his legs and ankles in case we had to make a dash for the scooters. The cool breeze was sufficiently strong to whip strands of my hair around to sting my cheek. I didn't mind; it also rustled the shrubs, which would hide any movement of the plants we might create by flexing our limbs.

The same blue van drove up and parked in the driveway. The resident apparently shared our conviction that there would be no one around at this hour, and left the garage lights on when he opened the door. The two men disappeared inside and emerged a few moments later carrying a box. The rectangular box looked to be about 400 millimetres deep. Initially, I thought it was cardboard, but careful scrutiny with Theo's binoculars proved its fabrication involved some form of plastic material. The dark blue lettering stencilled on its side announced it contained tuna.

Although it didn't appear too heavy, it took a man at each end to carry it. Once loaded, the van doors closed with barely a sound. The resident stood, illuminated by the garage light, watching the van drive off. As soon as the resident went back into the house, Troy and I took off at a flat gallop back to the scooters. We halted near the Colombo/Vespucci Junction. The road was wide at this point and we didn't want to find ourselves spotlighted by the van's headlights as it turned onto Vespucci. After a few moments, the van sped past and entered Vespucci. We continued running across the roadway and into the park.

We were running flat out when I stepped in a hole of some sort. I stifled a yelp as pain shot through my ankle. After a few seconds spent vigorously rubbing the affected part to ease the pain, I gingerly tried a couple of steps. The ankle protested but was okay. I hobbled the last couple of metres to my scooter. Instead of following the van along Vespucci, we cut across the park onto Marconi. The van could not legally turn into Marconi and I didn't think it would want to draw attention by doing the wrong thing, even at this hour of the morning.

If it were going to the harbour, it would take Via Roma and Via Florio. I hoped my hunch was right. We turned onto Via Meucci and stopped just prior to its junction with Via Roma. Concealed in deep shadows, we watched the van go past a few moments later. I was right; it was heading for the harbour.

We waited until the van's taillights disappeared as it turned off into Florio before we followed it along Florio to an area near the ferry terminal. The parking area at the ferry terminal seemed like the best place close by for us to park our scooters. I left Troy with the scooters and luggage and strolled towards the harbour. There were two boats alongside the fishery's pier... and the blue van arrived as well. No surprises so far, everything happening in line with what I thought might occur. The driver parked alongside the fishery building and went inside. I casually sauntered down to the pier, hoping I passed for a tourist out for an early morning stroll.

As I entered the pier, I was concentrating on the van and didn't see where the bloke that appeared in front of me came from. He was polite and curious and assumed I was lost. I spoke in English, making a show of trying to find the occasional appropriate Italian word to explain my presence. He spoke little English but we managed a good – if exhausting – conversation.

I explained that fishing – but not for tuna – was big business in my hometown, and that my family had messed about in boats since before I was born. At least, I think that was the message I managed to impart. I was interested in how these fishermen worked. He told me the furthest of the two boats was about to leave to work 'somewhere in the Mediterranean' for two days before returning. A group of businessmen had hired it for a fishing trip. The nearer of the two boats wasn't going fishing. As soon as it was loaded, it would take frozen fish to Agrigento on the island of Sicily. I was interested in this one. As we chatted, I watched the van driver and another man load boxes onto the boat... similar boxes to the one I saw loaded into the van earlier this morning.

There was nothing else I needed to know. I made a show of checking my watch and told him my partner back at the hotel would be looking for me. Lame excuse that it was, it got me off the pier. After a short brisk walk, I was back with Troy and the scooters. All the way back to the scooters, something about his mention of Agrigento rummaged in the deep recesses of my mind without bringing anything to the fore. No point in mentioning something so vague to Troy as we discussed what I had discovered and I outlined my thoughts on our next move. It was a few minutes after six o'clock and there already was movement at the ferry terminal.

"I think we should buy our tickets, put our luggage in a locker, and then return the scooters to the hire place. Nobody will be there at this hour but it should be okay if we just leave the scooters. Once we ditch the scooters, we'll need to hurry back to the terminal. It's not too far away, but we'll need to look lively about it. What do you think?"

Troy was a bit concerned about abandoning the scooters like that, but we bought our tickets for the first hydrofoil trip of the morning and I checked its departure time. The young man behind the counter apologised profusely. It running about ten minutes late today. I was pleased to hear that. Our luggage in a locker, we set off for the piazza. At the hire place, we parked the scooters out front and dropped the keys through the letter slot in the front door. Then we jogged to the ferry terminal. My ankle let me know it would prefer not to do this, but it wasn't too bad and there weren't too many other options.

We arrived at the terminal to discover we still had half an hour before the hydrofoil departed. After retrieving our luggage, we bought coffees and croissants and settled down to watch other passengers arriving. I wasn't expecting any surprises but couldn't be sure we wouldn't run into trouble. I was anxious that Dom didn't know what was happening. We knew it would only need someone at the hotel to alert him to the fact that we had done a flit in the night to bring Dom looking for us. We were first on board and selected seats that allowed us to keep an eye on everyone boarding the hydrofoil. They seemed keen to make up lost time. As soon as there appeared to be no one else waiting to board, it cast off and headed for the mainland.

The half-hour trip was uneventful. It was still too early for anything much to be open in Trapani. We filled in time with coffee in the small cafe attached to the terminal. The waitress informed me a nearby vehicle hire place usually opened at 8.30a.m. Troy found a tourist map amongst the brochures and we discovered the hire place was only about a block away. At 8.45a.m., we strolled to the hire place.

A young woman was opening up for the day when we arrived. Troy hesitated before entering. "What's next in our plan?"

"We hire a vehicle and drive to Agrigento, hopefully before the boat arrives. Then we shall see what we see."

"Do we have to drive?"

"Well, we could fly, but we'd have to hang around and wait for the next flight, and it wouldn't necessarily take us to where we want to go, and we'd still have to find some other means of transport after the flight."

"Okay. I wasn't too worried about driving. I just wasn't sure it was going to be the quickest way of getting there."

We hired a small Peugeot on Tito's credit card after I had flashed my international driver's license. Troy gathered a selection of touring maps from a rack. We drove our not so new – but cheap – vehicle along to a shady area where we parked and studied our maps. I drove – well, I had the international license – while Troy calculated distances to our destination so we could work out how long the trip might take. This became easier once we stopped and could spread the maps out properly.

From Trapani, we drove to Alcamo before heading south to Castelvetrano where we picked up the coast road. What had bothered me about Agrigento suddenly became clear. Agrigento isn't on the coast. Everything coming in by boat comes in through Porto Empedocle. This was likely to be our boat's destination. The distance from Trapani to Empedocle was about 180 kilometres. This allowed us plenty of time to be in Empedocle and checking out the port area before lunchtime. As we approached the port area, Troy checked his watch and chuckled.

"About now all hell will break loose in Favignana." I glanced sideways at him and sought explanation. "Dom is supposed to be picking us up from Hotel Il Porto about now. He is not going to be impressed by our disappearance."

Up ahead I could see a scenic lookout area with an undercover picnic table and parking area. I pulled in. Troy looked surprised.

"What's up? Why are we pulling in here? It's not too much further to the port."

"I want to make a quick call to Tito. Something has bothered me since yesterday and I want to check it out."

My chances of reaching Tito were minimal, but I keyed in the number and let it ring. I was about to give up when Tito answered.

"Where are you? Dominic rang from the hotel. They are concerned you left without checking out."

"Hear me out, Tito. The contents of that container we've been tracking are on their way to Sicily, supposedly to Agrigento. As Agrigento isn't a port, it is likely they will head for Empedocle. I think the boat will unload at Empedocle and return to Favignana. I don't think those contents will remain in Empedocle. They will continue on their journey somehow, possibly to the mainland of Italy. Now, more importantly, are you still on Crete?" Something suggested to me that he would not hang around on Crete when the action is here.

"I am in the air on my way to Trapani. I'll be meeting Dominic who is coming over on a late ferry."

"I don't trust Dom. Make what you like of that, but I no longer feel safe around him. We have seen much to confirm he is a liar. I feel he has another agenda, and I don't think that agenda is in the best interests of Troy and I… or a successful outcome to the project. I can't tell you what to do, but be aware that, if Dom comes anywhere near me, I am out of here and off the project. I was due back in Australia last week and would be happy to leave for home right now. Is that clear?"

"Perfectly clear; perhaps your concerns have some substance. I subscribe to the philosophy of keeping your friends close and your enemies closer. A couple of my men are with me. I didn't ask Dom to join us but he insisted. It makes me suspicious about his motives. We have worked out a story that will allow one of us to be with him at all times. I assume you are on Sicily. Keep me informed… and take great care." I shared the gist of the phone call with Troy before heading off again for the port.

At the first opportunity, I pulled off the Via Empedocle, which ran past the entire breadth of the port. Via Molo branched off Empedocle and ran down the left arm of the harbour. Molo Levante ran down the right arm. The seaward end of that arm appeared to be for boats to tie up and unload. There was no sign of our boat, so we went for food from one of the many outlets within a short distance of the harbour. Spreading our beach towels out under a couple of trees overlooking the harbour, we ate lunch and took turns to doze for a while. Our boat came in at the end of siesta and tied up.

Troy watched through his binoculars. A white van met the boat, and transhipped boxes from boat to van. Then the van left the port area. A silver grey van arrived shortly after the white van's departure. More boxes from the boat were loaded into this van. Troy suddenly sat upright. "Take a look – quick!"

I grabbed my binoculars and focused on the boat. Two men were loading the van. One lifted a box from the hold and rested it on the gunwale while the other man carried the previous box to the van and returned. The present box resting on the gunwale sported a large red X next to the blue lettering on its side. "You think that's our box?" I asked.

"It's the only one that was marked like that."

"Looks like we won't be staying here tonight; we better get moving if we're to follow that van."

We threw our stuff into the car. As I slid into the passenger's seat, Troy took the wheel and drove off sedately watching the traffic while I focused on the van and provided a running commentary. I was wondering if I'd come to the wrong conclusion about what had happened. I knew I was right when the van turned off onto a lesser road that passed through the Valley of the Temples. According to the map, there was a lookout area located part way along this road. Without warning, as we came round a bend I caught sight of what looked like a safety fence off to one side and not too far ahead.

"Troy there's a lookout just up ahead. Slow down. Stop! Stop, pull in." We came to a halt in a shower of gravel and dust at the lookout area.

"What are we stopping for? We'll lose that van."

"We're going to make like tourists. Bring your camera and let's look at the ruins. I'll explain as we go."

I grabbed a brochure and bounded over to the safety fence. Troy, not looking too enthusiastic, followed me.

"We're archaeologists, Troy, marvelling at the wonder of those ancient temple ruins. Start taking photos and I'll explain while I do my 'excited-by-the-view' performance."

"My studies failed to include drama subjects. Maybe I should have gone to some school of dramatic art instead," he grumbled. "… And that brochure's got nothing to do with these ruins."

"I know that, but it's a useful prop. From a distance, nobody would know that." I gestured at a particular ruin with the brochure and then pretended to read from it. "I think we have a tail. I want to waste a few minutes here to give it time to get away from us… or to see if it picks us up again after we leave here." I punctuated my explanation with lots of pointing at various ruins, and kept the charade going for about ten minutes before returning to the car.

"Turn your phone off, please Troy." He started to argue about the possibility of Tito wanting to contact us. "It doesn't matter. Turn it off. Shut it right down and don't turn it on again," I commanded as I did the same with my mine. A heated 'debate' about the intelligence of such action ensued. After a couple of minutes, my patience ran out. That doesn't often happen but, when it does, it doesn't leave the other party any room to manoeuvre. Troy complied.

After another five minutes of sitting in silence – and one of us sulking – while ostensibly admiring the view, we set off towards

Agrigento. The atmosphere in the car remained a little tense. Troy was making no secret of the fact that he was unhappy about the phones... and about my attitude as well, I suspect. As soon as we were underway, I explained my motive again and more coolly this time.

"I believe we picked up a tail soon after I spoke to Tito. If I'm right, it means someone is tracking our phones. Let's see if we pick up the tail again. If we do, I have some ideas on how to lose it. Don't worry about the van. This road only leads to Agrigento, so it will be heading that far at least."

"Yes, but we don't know where it will go in Agrigento. We will lose track of what it's carrying."

"Hmm, yes, that's true but I don't think Agrigento is its final destination. I think it's heading for a port somewhere – maybe Catania or even Messina. I know our prime interest is in the contents of that container but, at the moment, I'm more interested in our safety."

Silence reigned. A couple of minutes later, I checked my wing mirror. Our tail was back. "Troy, check your rear vision mirror."

"Bloke on a big red motor bike following us, but he is a fair way back."

"That's our tail back again. I think he came out of the driveway of a farm back there. He probably waited behind the trees along its fence line until we went past. It's the same one that's been hanging around since before Empedocle."

I told Troy to continue into Agrigento and explained what I would look for when we got there. By the time we got to Agrigento, there had been no sign of the van for quite some time. It wasn't an ideal situation. We would have to rely on hunches for a bit and hope we would find it again. I was mulling this situation over in my mind when I saw the sort of place I wanted.

"Up ahead, Troy, that department store. See if you can find a parking space close by." He nosed into the curb in front of a gift shop one up from the store.

"I'm going shopping in the department store. You should look exasperated as you watch me go. Then lock the car and wander into that gift shop. Buy some bottled water if they have any but, whatever you do, don't take your eyes off the car. Try to stay invisible from the street while you're about it. Watch for anyone going anywhere near the car. If someone does, watch closely what happens. Then, wait until whoever leaves, and wander over to that bench under the trees and wait for me there. If nobody goes near the car, wait till you see me in the street again and then come out to meet me."

He agreed unenthusiastically and threw himself into his role as I disappeared into the department store. I found the escalators and went up to the next floor. An area dedicated to selling mobile phones was towards the rear of that floor. I found a model that would suffice and the sales assistant retrieved two units from stock. I asked him to substitute the display unit for one of the units from stock. I needed one already charged and registered on the network, as it would take hours to charge the ones from stock. He finally agreed. I added a cheap car charger to the purchase and paid for it all with Tito's credit card.

I had what I wanted, but the carry bag screamed 'telefonino' and sported various well-known mobile phone brand names in bright colours all over it. Not wanting to advertise that I bought new mobile phones, I returned to the women's apparel section on the ground floor. This section had its own carrier bags: fluorescent pink with a black line drawing of a female silhouette.

I found what I wanted: a large garish sunhat. The female sales assistant looked astonished that I should want to buy such a thing. I consoled myself with the thought that it might not be the most chic hat, but it had two things going for it. It was cheap, and it was large enough to warrant one of those supersized pink carrier bags. Out of sight of the sales assistant, I shoved the bag with the two mobile phones into the pink carrier bag, burying them under that hat. I left the store jauntily swinging my bright pink carrier bag.

Ah-hah, so the ploy had worked. Troy was sitting on the bench under the trees, alerting me to the fact that someone had visited our car. Ever the happy shopper, I skipped towards him, shaking my bag at him and laughing. He shuffled along the bench and I sat beside him. I offered to show him my purchases and he put on a creditable performance of not wanting to see what was in the bag. Troy described what he had observed from the gift shop.

"A large bloke in black garb approached the car. After looking around, he ran his hand along part of the hood and down over the rear passenger-side wheel arch. He tried to make it look like he was admiring the car. He was a big bloke and had to bend over slightly to run his hand over the wheel arch. Then he stepped back and admired the car some more before sauntering off."

"I don't suppose he had a motorcycle helmet tucked under his arm."

"No, and he wasn't wearing leathers, but his black outfit could have been what that motorbike rider was wearing. I couldn't get a good look at him, so I wouldn't be able to recognise him again."

"Okay, I don't think it's an explosive device; he probably planted a tracking bug." I thought for a moment before continuing. "I'm sure we need more fuel. We should pull into the first service station we see and fill up. It's unlikely the bug will pick up sound from in the cabin but, once we get back in the car, we don't talk about anything except getting fuel and finding our hotel – and we do it in a very chatty way as though we are just deciding what to do next."

"Definitely should've gone to drama school. Okay! Okay!" He held his hands up in surrender.

There was a service station a few blocks from where we parked. As Troy did battle with the intricacies of a type of bowser neither of us had used before, I made a show of suggesting the tyres needed checking. The air hose was a close relative of a boa constrictor. However, after a struggle, I managed to wrangle it out of its storage cabinet and worked my way around the four wheels. I left the rear wheel on the passenger side until last – and until Troy finished fuelling up.

I suggested he check what I was doing. He stood so our two bodies completely masked the wheel. I slipped my hand under the wheel arch and yanked the magnetic bug free. Troy paid for the fuel. I waited in the car with the tiny bug concealed under the brochures on the back seat. As we drove off, I launched into a conversation about finding a hotel. No hotel that suited my needs appeared for some time. I was beginning to think I'd have to change the plan.

Then, some distance up ahead, I saw a large modern looking hotel. Just the sort of place that might have what we needed. I pointed it out to Troy. As we drew nearer, I could see the entrance to the basement carpark. I turned the stereo off and spoke hurriedly. "That one, Troy; see over there." I indicated he should drive down into the basement carpark.

As we drove slowly through the carpark, I noticed a short ramp leading up to a rear exit. Parking bays bordered both sides of the driveway through the parking area. Its capacity wasn't large but held enough vehicles for our needs. Then I spotted exactly what I wanted.

"Stop! Stop, Troy. Just wait a minute." I dived out of the car and over to the nearest parking bay occupied by a shiny new-looking Mercedes Benz. After forcing the bug down behind the Merc's number plate, I was back in our car within seconds. "Okay, Troy, there's a rear exit over there. I don't know if it's meant for vehicles or people, but I think – hope – we're small enough to fit through it." We pulled our side mirrors in flush with the side of the car just in case.

It wasn't intended for vehicles. The doorway was a tight fit but we passed through it without scraping paint – just! We shot through the opening, over a narrow concrete path and across about 50 metres of manicured grass before finding ourselves on a narrow laneway. It was unsealed and rutted, but Troy maintained as much speed as possible to get away from the hotel. "I hope that wasn't their best putting green we just ploughed furrows through," he commented through gritted teeth as he fought the steering wheel and we bounced along the lane.

The lane ran parallel with the road we travelled before detouring through the hotel carpark. It wasn't on any of our maps. I hoped that somewhere soon it would join a major road. After about 500 metres of spine-jarring ride, the lane remained the same width but gained a sealed surface. There was no outcry after us, so Troy adopted a sedate speed befitting this quiet back lane and we continued to head north along it.

"Well, we might have lost our tail, but we have also lost the van. What are we supposed to do now?" Troy grumbled.

I undid my seatbelt and reached over into the back of the car to retrieve my pink carrier bag. Seat belt back on, I replied. "I don't know if we will find the van. While I waited in that department store for the sales assistant to get the phones, I watched through those huge glass panels on the front of the building. I could see the traffic travelling past along the main highway. I saw our van pull onto the highway and head north."

"I wonder where it went," Troy mused. "I expected it to be long gone by then."

"Maybe, but it had real boxes of tuna on board. Perhaps it had to deliver some in Agrigento. Presumably they would want the van's journey to be above suspicion, so they probably deliver tuna along the way to maintain the pretence and avoid suspicion."

"It will be a long way ahead of us by now. We spent a fair bit of time getting rid of our tail. We might never find it again."

"True," I conceded, "But it will be crawling along, snarled up in inner city traffic, while we are flying along this back lane. I think I see a major junction up ahead."

Once on the sealed part of the lane, Troy gradually increased speed until we were probably exceeding the speed limit for this area. There was a delay at the junction of the lane with the SS640, the main highway, until a short break in traffic allowed us to enter the highway safely. Traffic thinned out relatively quickly and, by the time we reached the outskirts of town, it was flowing nicely with considerably fewer vehicles. Neither of us knew what the legal speed limit was once we left the urban area. Troy decided the safest approach was to keep pace with other vehicles around us.

I unpacked the new phones and checked the battery level on the display unit; fully charged. I unpacked the ex-stock unit, plugged in the car charger and attached the phone. We would be in Messina long before this phone was charged but at least we had one phone fit for immediate use.

While I was engrossed in getting our communication systems organised, more of the traffic dropped off. I sat back and stared aimlessly up ahead. All I could see were the three or four cars between the dark blue container carrier up ahead and us. I sat up in my seat suddenly alert and paying attention. The stretch of road leading up to Caltanissetta included a short sharp bend. From my position in the passenger seat, I could see the vehicles well ahead of the container carrier as they followed the bend in the road. Could that be our van? It certainly looked like it.

More vehicles, including the container carrier, turned off at the junction with SS643, opening up my field of vision. The exit of the carrier container allowed me frequent glimpses of the top of the van as it continued towards Catania. Somehow, the Peugeot was still holding together. Troy moved up the convoy to position us about three cars behind what we believed was our van. I fished out my binoculars and kept them trained on the van. The wriggly stretch of road after Catenanuova provided an unexpected bonus. On one of the bends, I managed to get a fleeting glimpse of the van's plate. It was too quick for me to read the whole plate, but the bit of it I saw was enough.

"That's our van," I announced. "Now, the big question is, will it stop at Catania or go on to Messina?"

"How much further from Catania is Messina?"

I did a quick calculation. "Judging by the map, a bit over an hour's drive."

"Do you think he will drive straight through, or is he likely to spend some time in Catania as he did in Agrigento?"

"Dunno, but I'm guessing he might make deliveries there before heading off to Messina – if that's where he is going."

"So, what's our plan? We can hardly follow him around the streets of Catania without him noticing."

I didn't have an answer – or a plan. We tossed a few ideas around before agreeing to drive through Catania to somewhere on the outskirts of the other side of town where we could keep watch for the van if it continued on to Messina. Based on gut instinct, I believed Messina to be its destination. Troy's concerns that we might lose the van at Catania were justified, but I was just about over this whole exercise of tailing a van across Sicily. I was more interested in going home to my real life than tearing across this island.

My thoughts were such that, if we lost the van, we would hand the whole thing back to Tito to work out how he could deal with it. Somehow, it seemed best to refrain from sharing those thoughts with Troy for the moment.

Chapter 19

At Catania, the van turned off before the city centre. I noted the street. We drove to the other side of Catania, got fuel and coffee at a service station, and pulled into a layby a bit further on. There was nothing else to do but wait and watch. So, we sat in comparative silence, each of us lost in our own thoughts as we waited. The wait dragged on. It was getting late, and I'd lost all interest in the exercise at least half an hour ago. We took turns watching the highway. I was nodding off when Troy nudged me in the ribs.

"There's our van."

"You're sure?"

"Yeah, I got a good look at the number plate."

"So we're off to Messina. Let's head off; just keep a few cars between us."

My thoughts became preoccupied with what might happen at the Messina end of the journey. I began thinking aloud, "Messina is a port city. Only a short stretch of water separates it from the mainland of Italy. It would be a good place for moving the contents of that container to the mainland. So, how might it occur? My thinking is that the van probably will deliver the box with the red X on it to somewhere in Messina this evening ready for it to be shipped out tomorrow."

"Are we going to trail the van around Messina to see where it's delivered and then stakeout the place overnight?" Troy asked.

"No, I don't think so. He probably still has boxes of tuna to deliver, and we would stand out like the proverbial if we followed him around while he was about it. I think I'd like to take a look at the port arrangement to get a feel for which boats leave for where, so we can try to work out what's likely to happen next."

As in Catania, the van turned into a side street close into the city centre and disappeared. We continued through the city to the port area and parked to study its layout. It appeared to cater for commercial operators of ferries and hydrofoils, as well as smaller independent vessels like fishing boats. A couple of men worked on a small boat tied up at one of the wharves. I wandered down to ask a few questions. Troy wasn't happy about having to keep watch from the car for anyone or any other vehicles that might show an interest in our being there.

196

There was a vehicle parked near the fishing boat. As I approached it, a young lad walked up to the vehicle, unloaded a stack of pots of some sort, and turned to return to the boat. I called out to him. He stopped and faced me. Again calling on my best rendition of a tourist, I asked in stumbling broken Italian if there was another hydrofoil leaving for the mainland this evening, although I knew there wasn't. According to the timetable, I had collected from among the brochures at the service station, the last one for the day left the harbour as we arrived. The lad confirmed it.

I tried looking upset, and then shrugging, asked if they were about to go fishing. Maintaining the tourist image, I asked what they fished for, where they went and how long they would be out. His answers included the information that they would be calling into Reggio Calabria. I pretended excitement and asked if they took paying passengers, adding that we needed to get to Reggio Calabria by early tomorrow morning.

He shook his head. "No, but the first hydrofoil tomorrow leaves at about 6:30a.m."

I asked if any other small boats would go out tonight. Another negative response. He assured me there were no others going out tonight; they had left already. Other boats would go out in the morning, but at about the same time as the first hydrofoil. There was nothing else to gain from the lad. I was about to take my leave when an older man on the boat brusquely called the lad back to the boat.

The tone and words were a bit disconcerting, so I made my way smartly back to the car. Troy had nothing to report other than that the man on the boat stood with his hands on his hips scowling at me the whole time I was speaking to the lad. Uh-oh, my antennae are twitching. "I think we should move off from here. Let's go a bit further up the road to see if there is somewhere else offering a good view of the harbour."

After driving a while without finding a suitable place, we slowly made our way back towards the harbour. As we drove, I broke out the new (display) phone and keyed in Tito's number. He answered immediately and his surprise at hearing me was unmistakable.

"Sonny, where are you? Whose phone are you using? Did you lose the phones we gave you?" He was surprised, but also there was unmistakable hostility in his voice as he spat out the questions.

"We had a bit of a problem and turned the phones off. We followed the van with the contents of the container to Messina."

"Do you know where the van is now?"

"No-o-o, we lost it in Messina." Something was not right. Tito should display at least some pleasure at hearing what I just told him.

"You heard about Despina?"

"Yes, Theo let us know. He didn't give too many details but I don't suppose that matters… dead is dead."

"There have been other deaths as well – on Favignana. You need to take care. Where exactly are you now?"

"We're travelling. I really rang to tell you we lost the van in Messina and that we think they might try to move 'the cargo' to the mainland through Reggio Calabria. Troy and I are pulling out at this point. *We are not following it any further.* I assume you will have people on the mainland who can take over tracking it when it arrives."

"I see. I'm disappointed. I wasn't expecting that. I thought you would want to see it through to the end."

O-o-oh, he was not happy. "No, we have done as much as we can. Now you need to get the professionals to take over."

"Okay, I hear what you are saying. You have made your decision. I will need someone to collect our gear that you have. Where will you be tonight?"

Hmmm, no concern about how we were getting back to Crete or anywhere else for that matter. If he took the credit cards off us now, we would have to pay our own way off Sicily… and pay for our own accommodation tonight. Think, Sonny, think! Something smells decidedly rotten right now.

"Oh, boats leave here overnight and early in the morning. We found a good vantage point that overlooks the harbour. We thought we would spend the night there keeping watch for you. That way we could give you information about the boat and its departure. That's if my hunch about it being shipped to the mainland is correct of course." Troy gave me a startled look as I outlined our plans for the night. "Tito, I've got to go. It's probably not safe to stay on the phone too long anyway." He agreed and I ended the call.

As soon as the call ended, Troy demanded, "What do you mean 'we're going to keep watch all night'?"

We approached the place where we parked earlier in the evening. "Troy, don't park where we did before, park on the opposite side of the road. See, over there; reverse into the clearing at the base of that hill. I'll explain when we're parked."

As soon as we parked, I went over my conversation with Tito for him. "Something is not right, Troy. I think we are in danger. Tito didn't say the 'right' things – didn't ask the right questions – and was very interested in exactly where we would be tonight. I think this is a good place if any unexpected visitors come calling during the night. We won't stay in the car. We'll climb up there among the rocks where we can hide but keep watch at the same time."

"So, we are going to keep watch for the van?"

"No, I told Tito we were finished and it was now his responsibility to pick up the trail. When I told him we were finished, and that we'd lost the van in Messina, he didn't ask for any details of the van or anything else. How is he going to put others on the job without those details from us?"

"Ah hah, maybe he didn't need to because he already knew all about the van and what was going on? Who the hell can we trust in all of this?"

"Exactly; that's my thinking: Tito already knows all there is to know. I don't know who we can trust, but I'm beginning to think we might have thrown our lot in with the wrong side. Come on; let's get moving. I don't know how soon we might receive visitors. There's just one little job we need to do before we abandon the car."

There were two balloons advertising an expensive brand of women's fashion in the bottom of the carrier bag from the Agrigento store. I gave them to troy to inflate. Blowing up balloons always makes me light headed. While he was busy with the balloons, I reclined my seat, rolled up the loose floor mat and placed it on the seat and leant it up against the backrest. I now had a 'body', albeit a very slim one. By the time I had retrieved the large beach towel from my bag and spread it over the rolled up mat, Troy had inflated one of the balloons. I placed it on the top of the end of the rolled up mat and against the headrest of my seat. My body now had a head. Then, with a final flourish, I flopped that sunhat over the balloon. Now my snoozing 'passenger' was complete.

It didn't look all that convincing in the fading light, but it might do the trick once night fell and it became dark. Then it was time to attack Troy's side of the vehicle. One of us was supposed to be on watch, so I reclined the driver's seat only about halfway back and appropriately positioned the rolled up mat from the driver's side floor and the second balloon. Troy gave me his floppy rag hat to complete the scenario. I cast an eye over my handiwork. No, it wasn't great but it would have to do. We left brochures, maps and any other unneces-sary junk spread over the back seat to ensure the car wouldn't look too abandoned, grabbed our bags and headed for the rocks.

The backpacks containing all our important stuff we kept with us. The small cases and our computers we hid among the lower rocks. We climbed a short distance up the hillside to a jumble of larger rocks. Bunkered down behind them, we found the small gaps between the rocks provided a clear view of the clearing and car below, a fair stretch of the road, and a small section of the harbour. With much wriggling and fidgeting, we each found our most comfortable position. This could be a long night – especially if I had misjudged things.

There was no moon to speak of, and the pale glow from the lights on the various harbour structures didn't quite extend to our parked car. Spasmodic traffic along the road cast transient shadows across the area. It was a cool night. The smell of the sea wafted over us on the soft night air. Rugged up against the evening chill, we were comfortable enough, but limbs started to stiffen as we remained huddled behind the rocks... and the weapon in the waistband against my back grew uncomfortably cold.

I blinked myself alert. Did I see movement, or were my eyes playing tricks as they grew tired? No, there was movement. A figure moved along the base of the hillside. Dark, silent and moving fast, it hugged the hillside as it swept around the edge of the clearing toward our car. I gently touched Troy's arm and gestured with my head in the intruder's direction. When level with the rear of the car, the figure increased speed and ran across the open space to the passenger's side of the car. It stood just aft of the rear wheel arch and with its back to the car. After a moment's hesitation, it slid sideways along to a point just behind the passenger's door. We had left the windows half open on both sides of the car.

I removed the Glock from the waistband of my jeans and silently worked the slider. Slightly to my left was a gap in the rocks I could shoot from if I needed to. I shuffled silently to it and stood up behind the large rock. To get circulation flowing again, I flexed arms and legs as much as possible without creating a disturbance, and rubbed my hands together to warm them ready for action. With my hand resting on the edge of the gap in the rock, I steadied my aim on the dark figure.

Flattened against the side of the car, the figure hesitated again. It twisted sideways for a quick look in through the window, presenting the wide expanse of his back to me as he did so. In a spilt second, he turned to face the car and fired three shots in quick succession through the open window. I was so engrossed in the tableau playing out beside the car, I hadn't notice a motorbike appear. It entered the area from the same direction as the shooter had come.

Three shots from the motorbike rider's weapon struck the dark figure, spinning him around and slamming his back against the car. The impact threw the dark figure off balance and he stumbled. He didn't go down. Supported by the car, he managed to raise his weapon. The motorbike rider was off balance. He was battling to keep the large bike upright and aim his weapon at the same time. If he managed to get a shot off, it was more likely to hit us than the intended target.

"Vest!" I hissed, and took the head shot. The dark figure left a dark streak down the side of the car as he slid down to lie in a crumpled heap on the ground.

"What do you mean... what about a vest?" Troy whispered. He looked stunned and confused by what had just happened.

"The bloke who shot up my seat was wearing a bulletproof vest. That's why he wasn't killed when the motorbike rider shot him."

"Now what?"

Before I could answer, a familiar voice called softly. "Sonny, are you okay?"

"Dom? Dominic, is that you?"

"Yes. It is safe. I am one of the good guys... and thanks. Nice shooting. Please come down."

We picked up our backpacks and climbed down to the car. With my backpack over my left shoulder, I let the Glock dangle from my right hand. Nothing to do with lacking trust, just being cautious. Dom's weapon was nowhere in sight, so I felt a little easier about our meeting.

Dom nodded in greeting. "We need to get away from here," he said. "It will not be safe to stay here too long." I didn't need any persuasion.

Troy was already on his way to collect our cases from where we stashed them among the rocks. I went round to the driver's side and dismantled my earlier handiwork. Then I went to the passenger's side. Dom rolled the body a few feet away from the car and opened the door for me. There wasn't a lot left to dismantle. The shots pulverised the backrest of the seat and everything on it. I brought the seat upright and arranged the other floor mat and beach towel across the now gaping hole in the backrest to prevent my falling through it as we travelled. Then, I leant up against the side of the car.

"Sonny, are you okay?" Dom sounded genuinely concerned.

"Just a bit weak-kneed at the moment; I don't often go around shooting people."

"Of course, I'm sorry. I didn't think. However, I am pleased you have maintained your skill. I didn't realise the shooter was wearing a bulletproof vest. I'm pleased you worked it out so quickly. Will you be okay to go now?"

"I'm driving," Troy cut in. "Where are we going?"

"Follow me. We are going to go a few kilometres further up the highway. We can talk later."

With that, Dom mounted the Ducati and it roared to life. Troy ran around and dived into the driver's seat as I gingerly tried out my makeshift passenger's seating arrangement. We sped along the highway away from Messina. The situation had reversed, now we followed the big red bike.

After a few minutes of silence, Troy stole a quick look in my direction before asking the question that he had held onto for a while. "When you spoke to Tito back there... you know, when you told him we were pulling out... you said something like 'dead is dead'. What was that all about? Who is dead?"

Bugger; I hoped he hadn't noticed that, but no point in avoiding the question now. "Despina; I'll tell you as much as I know as soon as things settle down a bit." In hindsight, that was a bit rough, but this was not the time to be discussing disturbing news.

After about 15 kilometres, Dom signalled and turned off the highway onto a track running through what appeared to be a hilly private estate that, in the pale moonlight, looked like grassy acres dotted with stands of pine trees. Only a short distance along the track, the land dropped away in a gentle slope to the sea. A huge house – a villa I suppose – stood in a clearing not far from the water. Dom continued around to the back of the house and we followed. He gestured to a place for us to park as he kicked out the stand and dismounted.

"Bring everything you need. We will not come back here again." He took my case and called over his shoulder, "Follow me, there is a boat waiting."

Troy hesitated. I immediately picked up the rest of my gear. Spending time in a Sicilian jail for killing a Sicilian held no appeal. Anything that took me away from here probably was a good thing. I would deal with whatever came next after we got there. My hurry seemed to provide Troy with enough incentive to comply, and we followed Dom down a pathway that involved many steps and ended at a small jetty. A sleek looking speedboat lay alongside.

"This is Francesco. Pass him your luggage and climb aboard."

We obeyed in silence and Francesco helped us on. While we were still settling ourselves, the boat throbbed as it came to life. Dom cast off and jumped aboard as Francesco reversed from the jetty. Francesco turned the boat around and we were flying at high speed across the dark sea on an almost moonless night.

"Where are we going?" Troy demanded.

"Reggio Calabria. There is a place similar to the one we just left over there," Dom shouted above the roar of the engine. "We will spend the rest of the night there. It will be safe. It takes about thirty minutes to get there, and then we will be able to talk without shouting."

The trip was quicker than he said. We idled into some sort of boathouse and tied up. Dom helped Troy and I out of the boat, and then he and Francesco unloaded our gear. The four of us climbed another steep path, again containing many steps, to another big house. Dom pushed open the huge carved timber door and marched in. We traipsed in after him. I wondered who owned the house and why the door was unlocked, but other more important questions needed answers first.

As Dom led us into a dining room, the wonderful aroma of cooking wafted through the place. A young woman came in and spoke quietly to Dom. As she turned to leave, Dom introduced her.

"Sonny, Troy, this is Angelique. She tells me we will eat in about five minutes. Would you like a drink while we wait?"

We all settled for a glass of white wine, and it turned out to be an excellent choice. Soon, steaming bowls of exquisite seafood pasta arrived on the table. Angelique and Francesco ate with us but disappeared as soon as the meal was over. Dom probably orchestrated this so the three of us could talk freely. The tale he told as he updated us on all that had happened almost defied belief.

"We will spend what's left of the night here. Early tomorrow morning, we will drive to the airport, to a private jet waiting for us there on a private runway. We will be in the air at first light."

"Where will we be going? Troy asked.

"I believe you still have belongings on Crete. We will fly to Crete and then go to the dig site. Once you have collected your things and done anything else you need to do, the plan is to fly you to London. Do you have any problems with that?"

We both shook our heads. I, for one, would be pleased to be getting closer to heading home. Nevertheless, we still had many blanks to fill in about what had happened after we left Crete.

"We need to know about everything that happened after we left the dig site, Dom, not only on Crete but everywhere we have been as well. Are you able to tell us?"

"You know about Despina ..." he began.

"Assume we know nothing and start from the beginning, please," I suggested, particularly as I still hadn't shared with Troy what little I knew about Despina's death.

"Okay, on Crete, it was found Despina had a case to answer and she was to be transported to the Greece mainland for trial. On the way to the airport, the vehicle she and her guards travelled in was ambushed. The guards died immediately at the scene. Despina received critical wounds. The attackers probably thought she was dead and left her. She died a few hours later in hospital without regaining conscious-ness. Theo was devastated. It was hard enough for him that his star student had been up to no good, but then to have her killed..." He left the rest unsaid but it didn't need saying. We sat in silence for a moment, all too aware of how her death would affect Theo.

"What happened on Favignana?" Troy pressed. "It seems things went pear-shaped there as well."

"Favignana was very sad... even more so than Despina." I raised my eyebrows in question but said nothing and he continued. "Despina's death was tragic but, in a way, she simply paid a high price for what she had done. Favignana was much worse. Remember the two old men I went to talk to about the pier. They are both dead; tortured first."

Dom shook his head as if to clear the horror of it from his memory. No doubt, he felt responsible for getting them involved. He continued with the tragic Favignana story. "Another man that I worked with – you never met him – was also found washed up on a beach; shot. He was supposed to watch the house they took the container to, but they captured him. They were after me as well."

"Oh, Dom, I'm so sorry. I might have triggered that when I spoke to Tito after we arrived on Sicily."

"No, it was happening already before you left Favignana. Tito knew you left the island shortly after you got on the hydrofoil, but he needed to keep the pretence of chasing down artefact traffickers going for a bit longer. That's what kept the pair of you alive for so long."

"You knew Tito was rotten?" Troy asked aghast at the danger we had been in.

"No, not at first. We knew there was some problem with the task force. That's why they weren't getting the results they should. There were a number of situations where it was obvious who to arrest, but they managed to get away. A few things started to fall into place while I was on Favignana, narrowing the suspects down to a possible three."

"What alerted you to Tito as the culprit?"

"There were a number of little things. In my line of work, you develop finely honed instincts. Those instincts told me I should disappear – become a ghost."

I wondered exactly what his line of work was, but I knew what he meant about instinct. I decided not to interrupt the flow of information by asking the question.

Dom continued. "We had people monitoring the three possible suspects. When I heard about the deaths on Favignana, I knew it could only be Tito. I checked with the person who was monitoring him and a few things fell into place. The same source also told me that you escaped to Sicily. I knew that sooner rather than later you would also be in the firing line, so I decided to follow and try to keep you safe."

"If you were busy monitoring Tito, you did well to find us once we got to Sicily," Troy marvelled.

"You forget; I gave you those phones. It wasn't only Tito tracking you. My team was tracking you as well. Fortunately, I had enough time to pick you up and follow you before you turned them off. By the way, where are those phones now?"

"I hope the fishes are keeping Tito entertained," I laughed. "I dropped them over the side as we came across in the speedboat."

Dom laughed. "Good thinking. I was going to tell you we needed to destroy their SIM cards."

"So what happens now, are we still targets?" Troy asked, his continuing anxiety clear. "And what happens when we get back to London, are we still in danger or does it just go away?"

"I would not be honest if I said there would be no further danger. For the next couple of days, we need to be very cautious. After that, there will be no more cause for concern. Certainly, by the time you get back to England, there will be no further danger for either of you."

Dom's assessment of our future safety was only partly reassuring. It was intriguing that the danger would just disappear, and within such a short timeframe.

"A lot of things are happening away from here. A number of major things will happen tomorrow which will eliminate the most serious risks and, by the end of the following day, the last mopping up of the problem will be completed."

All of that was 'need-to-know' and, apparently, we didn't need to know the details. I knew I would not relax my guard until we were back in England – and possibly not even until I was back in Australia. However, the inferences drawn from Dom's comments made me feel a bit reassured about the likelihood of our survival.

It was obvious our discussions were almost exhausted, but there was still a nagging doubt in my mind. It was the doubt that earlier led me to question where Dom's loyalties lay. Perhaps that needed dealing with now. I asked the question. "Tell me about the vantage point you used to observe the harbour." Dom's brow furrowed, so I rephrased the request. "Where was your observation post? Your photos covered a lot of territory, right down to the house where the container was stored overnight. I am amazed that any vantage point would allow vision of anything so far from the harbour, let alone allow for such clear photographs."

"Ah, yes, I see what you are saying. I did have a good place slightly up the hill but, no, it did not allow me to take all those photos I showed you. My colleague picked up the blue van on its way from the harbour and followed it to the house. He sent me his photos, which I then included on the memory card for you to see. This man was the one I sent to monitor the house for us. He was the one who was shot and washed up on the beach."

The pain at the mention of that unhappy episode was clear on Dom's face as he spoke. Both Troy and I managed a slight uncomfortable shuffle in response. Then Troy found his voice.

"That ancient solution applied again." Dom looked confused by the comment. Troy explained. "Throughout history, there was a sure-fire solution to rid you of a problem. It worked to clear your way of rivals, enemies – anyone who was making life difficult. Death was an ancient solution to many problems."

With downcast eyes, Dom simply nodded and said, "*Si*, for them it made at least some of the problem go away. That still left you two and me to get in their way; to be problems. We were problems they needed to get rid of and – perhaps – still need to do this." That shot rather a large hole in my reassurance about our future survival, and it probably wouldn't let Troy sleep any easier either.

Dom checked his watch. "We have about four hours before we need to leave for the airport. I suggest you try to get some sleep. I'll show you to your rooms."

Chapter 20

We followed him up the beautiful curved staircase to our rooms. Both rooms were ensuite, and our luggage was waiting for us in our rooms. I took a quick shower, dressed in the clothes I would wear on the flight to Crete – there wasn't much else clean – and set my alarm. I was surprised at how soundly I slept. I expected the vision of the shooting, and everything else we had learned tonight, would haunt me all night. Nevertheless, my inbuilt alarm system woke me just before the alarm was about to do its job.

I went and knocked on Troy's door. It was a few moments before he answered. We packed our luggage again and descended that staircase together. Downstairs, Dom and Francesco were already in the dining room. In our honour, Angelique laid on a full English breakfast. Neither Troy nor I are that way inclined at the best of times, and we certainly didn't feel like that this morning but, loathe to disappoint her, we tucked in.

None too subtle glances at watches encouraged us not to dawdle over breakfast. We ate quickly. Dom and Francesco led us to a shed some distance to the rear of the house. It contained, among other paraphernalia, a large white van with distinctive signage along its sides.

"It won't be the most comfortable ride of your life, but it will get us to the airport quickly and safely," Dom assured us. "Sonny, I hope you haven't packed your weapon. You should keep it close at hand… just in case." There goes my confidence again about our likely chances of survival.

Dom, Troy and I scrambled in through the rear doors of the van, and Francesco and Angelique rode up front. Once we were underway, I realised what Dom meant by getting us there quickly. This was no ordinary delivery van. A very powerful motor throbbed under the bonnet. We three in the rear, perched on the not too comfortable makeshift seating, found ourselves sliding all over the place as the vehicle cornered at speed.

To my relief, the Glock proved unnecessary. No incidents marred our trip to the airport. We couldn't see where we were going from inside the van. After we felt the vehicle bounce over a couple of speed bumps, Dom announced that we were now on a side road leading to the where our plane was waiting. A couple of minutes later, the van came to a halt and Francesco threw open the rear doors.

Angelique stood guard with a semi-automatic weapon tucked under her arm as she continually scanned the area. Dom jumped out of the van and helped Troy and I out with our luggage. A Gulfstream jet was warming up on the private runway. Francesco locked the van, and then the other three escorted us to the plane. When we were on board, the plane taxied and suddenly we were in the air. I silently bid farewell to Italy.

Troy seemed to relax, but our three companions remained alert and tense. That was good enough indication for me that we were a long way yet from being safe. I didn't feel any need to relax just yet. The Gulfstream was fast, much quicker than a commercial flight. Soon we were starting our descent to land on Crete. I heard Troy breathe a contented sigh and whisper, "Aaah, Crete."

Dom's next words effectively banished any relief Troy might have experienced. "When we land, I want you two to sit on the floor in the aisle. You must stay away from the windows. There must be nothing to suggest you are still on the aircraft. We will leave, but you must stay on the floor until told to leave. Do you understand?"

We both nodded, but I sought more information. "What's the game plan? What happens when you three leave the plane?"

"There will be three of us disembarking: two men and one woman. One of the men quite obviously will be me. We are hoping the other two will pass, at a distance, for you two. We will walk quickly across the tarmac to a waiting car. The plane will taxi into a private hangar where you will disembark. There is a whole lot more to the story after that, but we will deal with it when we come to it."

Things went according to plan. The plane touched down and taxied to a halt. Dom got up and stood beside me as I sat on the floor. "It is best if you keep your weapon ready."

He went forward, opened the cabin door and extended the stairs. Standing at the cabin door, he scanned the area before beckoning Francesco and Angelique to follow him down the stairs. The pilot came out, retracted the stairs and closed the cabin door. We stayed on the floor as instructed, but felt a bit foolish about our situation. The plane began taxiing towards the hangar and, after a minute or two, came to a standstill again. I guessed we were now in the hangar.

We remained on the floor. I thought I heard the sound of a motor approaching – possibly a car. Then the unmistakable 'thunk' of car doors closing. It seemed ages but, in reality, it probably was only a minute or so before the pilot reappeared to open the cabin door and extend the stairs. He gestured for us to leave. We grabbed our backpacks, which had travelled with us in the cabin, and disembarked.

A car had reversed into the hangar and parked with its boot open at the rear of the plane. I noticed the partially closed hangar doors. They remained open only wide enough to allow the car through. Dom stood at the bottom of the stairs and signalled to us to descend quickly. He pointed to where a door stood open in the far corner of the building and told us to wait in there. Our instructions were to walk directly across to the side of the building and then make our way along the wall to that door, rather than taking the more direct route diagonally across the hangar to the door.

The door opened into a storeroom with a small office setup at one end. Three other people were in the room: again two men and a woman. I removed the Glock from my waistband where I had shoved it as we came down the stairs. One of the men gave me a 'calm down' signal and told me to relax as the three of them exited the room. Troy and I exchanged shrugs. We had no idea what was going on. However, I figured that, for some reason, the three people who just left were going to pose as us. With nothing to do but wait for the next instruction, I perched on the edge of the desk and Troy made himself comfortable on a fuel drum. After a while, we heard the car drive off, followed by the rumble and clang of the hangar doors closing.

A few moments later Dom appeared and announced, "Now we wait some more… but not for too long."

We could hear Francesco and Angelique chatting to the pilot out in the hangar. Dom left the room and returned with the other two and the pilot carrying large flasks of coffee and 'snacks'. The snacks could have fed an army for a day, but we were strangely hungry in spite of the big breakfast. They joined us for coffee before the three of them disappeared into the hangar once more. Dom remained with us and eventually noticed us looking at him expectantly.

"Oh, yes, you want to know what is happening," he laughed. "In a few minutes our transport will arrive for the next leg of our journey. We will leave your luggage here. If there is anything you need to take back to the dig site, you should put it in your backpacks. We will not be at the camp long, just long enough for you to collect your things and say goodbye to Theo. Then we will come back here."

"Theo is already at the dig site?" I asked.

"Yes, he has run the project in your absence."

"We have dive gear at the camp which needs to be returned to Niko at the dive shop," Troy said.

"Theo has taken care of that. If there is anything you need to get from your luggage, you should do that now." We both shook our heads. "Good. Then everything can stay on the plane as it is now."

A new sound filled the space and things began to vibrate and rattle. "Our transport has arrived," Dom announced. "Come on; quickly."

We followed him to a door in the hangar's rear wall. A shower of fine sand met us as we exited the building. A smallish helicopter, its rotor still slowly revolving stood a short distance from the rear of the hangar. Dom led the way and the three of us climbed aboard. It took off immediately, heading off across the island. Once we were airborne and cruising, I pursued more answers. "What happened to that car we arrived in and those other three people we saw briefly?"

"They are in the car on their way to Timpaki. At the harbour, they will load their gear onto a boat, but they will spend the night in Timpaki. In the morning, if needed, the boat will set off in the general direction of the dig site but it won't actually go there."

"What do you mean by 'if needed'?" Troy queried.

"By tonight, if everything goes according to plan, their role playing should be over, and they will return from Timpaki without going anywhere in a boat."

"So they are decoys," I said.

"Yes, if that is the word you wish to use. If anyone was interested in your arrival on Crete, the car would lure them away from the airport so we could leave without being observed."

The helicopter set down on the sand between the camp and the cove. The moment it was safe, we were out of the chopper with our backpacks and jogging back along the beach to the camp. Theo was waiting, and hugged us as we came into camp.

"You must collect your things first and then meet me in the finds tent," he directed us.

There was little enough to collect, but we didn't want to leave anything behind. It took only minutes to collect our gear and return to the tent where we spent so much time over the previous couple of weeks and where Theo now was waiting. Entering the finds tent again created a strange emotion. In a short time, I would be leaving this tent, leaving Crete and these people forever. I had spent so much time in the finds tent. It almost felt like a part of me. In spite of my being anxious to leave and go home, leaving created an emotional tug that briefly brought a lump to my throat.

Our time with Theo was brief, as we needed to get back to the airport as soon as possible. We gave him back the night vision binoculars and his folders that were now massive, and spent a couple of minutes bringing him up to date on what had gone on after we left Crete. What had happened to Despina deeply distressed him, and he was mortified that Tito so comprehensively deceived him. There was agreement that anything else could be finalised by email.

There was one other thing we wanted to do before we left, and we invited Theo to participate. Troy and I had discussed the cave where we stored our dive gear after that first dive. There was something about a jumble of rocks at the base of one of the cave walls. It didn't look natural. Both of us had suspicions, but neither of us voiced them at the time. We took Theo back to the cave, took photos, and started shifting the rocks in question. We had moved about half of the rocks when we found it difficult to get a secure grip on one slightly larger rock.

Troy walked over the area already cleared of rocks to enable him to get a better grip on the large rock from around the opposite side. It required the two of us to shift it. He took a couple of steps across the cleared area. We heard a loud crack. His foot sunk into some sort of cavity in the sand. He stepped away, and we both dropped to our knees. Theo produced a trowel and brush from his pocket and we removed sand from around where Troy's foot had left a deep impression.

We removed only a few centimetres of sand. I gasped. A rib cage appeared. Using hands and the trowel, the three of us quickly removed more sand. A grinning skull appeared. Unnerved I stepped back. Troy and Theo continued removing sand from the skeleton. We could make out a hand carelessly thrown across its chest. Then, through the thin veil of remaining sand, we glimpsed a ring on that hand. Troy frantically brushed away the last of the sand from the hand. It sported a distinctive ring. Shaking his head in disbelief, Troy stood up and took a step back from the remains.

"A myth is laid to rest today. Say hello to Giles Berwick," Troy said with a catch in his voice.

"This is York's young academic who disappeared?" Theo asked.

"Yes," Troy responded. "Knowing what we know now, I suspect he ran afoul of the illegal traffickers who have been using this bay."

"But to kill him?" Theo said in disbelief.

"Death is an ancient solution," I murmured. Theo continued to look confused, so Troy explained.

"Well, when something constitutes a serious threat of some sort, like Sonny once said, death is an ancient solution to the problem. As archaeologists, we often encounter instances throughout history of application of such a solution. Think of all the skulls that have been unearthed over just the last few decades. How many of them show clear evidence of its owner felled by sword or club. The victim might have created a problem within his own group or for some opposing group. Regardless, the price paid in both cases was the same: death."

Theo nodded, "Yes, we see evidence of that 'solution' many times in our line of work."

Troy continued, "I think that was the solution applied to Giles when he became a problem for the traffickers. The attempted attack on our lives on Sicily was an attempt to apply the same solution to the problem we posed. The same outcome might have resulted if not for Dominic's intervention." We stood for a few moments silently absorbing Troy's comments.

We had a helicopter waiting and we had delayed its take-off longer than we intended. Theo undertook to deal with formalities in relation to Berwick's remains. I made the hard decision. There was one other thing we hadn't discussed with Theo that I felt he needed to know. He seemed stronger and more 'together' now than immediately following all of the Despina stuff. I steeled myself and plunged in.

"Theo, we speculated about how Despina moved all the small objects she undoubtedly collected from the various sites she worked on. We don't know how often it occurred or how much she took, but we suspect there might have been quite a bit. The question in our minds was how she got the objects away from the site and safely back home without anyone noticing. We don't have the answer, but suspect she used an accomplice. Again, we don't know who that might be, but something for you to think about when you have a moment: who was part of your team on this dig who might have been on the other digs with Despina."

"This is an interesting concept. I understand you don't know the answers but, perhaps, you might share you suspicions with me."

"I'm not sure they are even suspicions, Theo," Troy said.

I continued. "As Troy says, not exactly suspicions, but maybe you could start by looking at the two operators of that special equipment. If they don't fit the picture, then you have the rest of the team to think about." We apologised for leaving on something of a sour note. I hated having to burden him with more bad news and doubts about his handpicked team.

Dom was waving at us from the helicopter, encouraging us to hurry. The three of us trotted to where it waited. Then, after more hugs and cheek kissing – and promises to keep in touch – we were in the helicopter and airborne again. As we headed across the island back to the airport, I found myself wondering how long it would be before I relaxed and started breathing normally again. I now suspected it might not happen until after being back in Australia for quite a while. As I pondered this issue, Dom took a phone call.

I saw his jaw tightened as he listened but he said little. After the call, he spoke briefly only to the pilot. He made a couple of phone calls and, by the time he was finished, we were back at the airport. The helicopter set down behind the hangar again. Francesco opened the hangar's rear door and we followed Dom into the building while Francesco held the door open. Dom stowed anything we didn't need with us with the rest of our luggage. The pilot and Angelique were already on board.

There was a loud rumble. I was mesmerised as Francesco opened the whole rear wall of the hangar. I hadn't noticed that the small door we had used wasn't set into a wall, but was a part of one of a pair of much larger doors. As the wall opened completely, Francesco joined us in the plane, closing the cabin door behind him. We taxied out through the rear hangar doors and onto the runway. There was a delay of a couple of minutes waiting for clearance to take-off. Then we were in the air. It took only a few minutes to reach cruising altitude. Crete was somewhere in our wake. Was this the last leg of our journey? I felt it time for more questions. "Where's our next stop?"

"England," Dom answered economically.

"What about refuelling?"

"No need with this plane. We can do it in one hop."

"Uhmm, I'm still carrying the Glock. How am I going to get that through customs?"

"Customs won't be a problem. We will land at a private airfield just outside York. One of the British agencies – I don't remember which one – they all start with a letter – will have a car waiting to take you to your addresses in York."

"Then what happens for you lot?" Troy asked.

"We will refuel at the airfield and fly back to Italy."

"It will be late by the time you arrive back," Troy observed.

"Not too late, and we are all taking tomorrow off."

I remained curious about what agency Dom and his merry men worked for, but he would only volunteer that they were members of

Interpol. Not surprisingly perhaps, conversation eventually came round to Tito and the whole situation we were embroiled in over the past week or so. Dom filled in some of the blanks for us.

"Tito also was a member of Interpol. His recent position was a secondment to head up the special taskforce to counteract illegal trafficking in cultural material. He was so passionate about it, nobody suspected him. However, over time, it became apparent that something was not right. Eventually, it was obvious we had a leak – or worse – either in the taskforce itself or closely associated with it. We needed a contact on Favignana for what was to happen there. They sent me over. Not only was I supposed to be your contact and look after you, I was to watch for anything that might shed light on why the taskforce was not doing so well. It wasn't until Favignana that any suspicion fell on Tito. A few little things happened – or didn't happen – that linked only to Tito. He was the only one who had the information to have instigated those incidents that occurred there."

Dom took a deep breath at the end of his delivery, shrugged and sat back in his seat. I considered what he said. It seemed things could have ended very differently for Troy and I. I didn't really want to dwell on it as I remembered the hole blasted in the passenger's seat of our hire car in Sicily. Dom hadn't finished; he continued his story.

"I have to say, Sonny, your instincts are finely honed."

"…Except I got it very wrong about your role in the whole thing. I could have gotten both of us shot in Messina if you hadn't come along."

"Ah, yes, that was another example of someone on the inside driving it. Only Tito and I knew you had a weapon – and could use it. That is why the gunman went to your side of the car first. The female, thanks to that hat, was easy to identify as being the passenger. Normally, the gunman would go for the driver first. He needed to eliminate the danger before taking care of Troy. You know, if you ever want to move to this side of the world, I'm sure our organisation would welcome you."

"No thanks. I have a good business back home. I like what I do and I like where I live. No offence, Troy, but I can't wait to get home."

It had been a long day and I was starting to feel weary when we heard the announcement that we had started our descent and would soon land in England. Francesco disembarked first, followed by Dom. We were to wait. The two men on the ground became tense as a car made its way towards the aircraft. It stopped a few metres away and the passenger – in a suit and tie – got out and stood beside the car.

He announced himself. I saw Dom relax. He beckoned us down. Francesco was loading our luggage into the car's boot with the help of the driver. Angelique joined us on the runway.

Everyone seemed anxious for us to leave. We thanked everyone and said our final farewells. Dom slipped a business card into my hand as we hugged and I promised to contact him so he would have my contact details. He whispered in my ear. "Hang on to that illegal piece of hand luggage until you are ready to leave England and then throw it in the river or someplace where it won't be found."

I suggested he take it back with him... after all, it did belong to Interpol. He insisted I keep it until I left England. I got a clear message that we might not yet be able to consider ourselves safe. I chose not to share that with Troy... no point in making him nervous again. As we walked to the car, I told Dom how disappointed I was that we lost track of the contents of the container and weren't able to make any inroads into the network. He laughed and carefully worded his reply.

"We did not lose that box, thanks to the work you did. We might not have shut down the whole network – only time will tell – but we certainly crippled it. And we had some help from Tito who is very keen to be helpful in return for a slightly less severe sentence."

Within minutes, we were in the car and on our way into York. Troy asked my plans for tomorrow.

"Book my flight home, go to Kings Manor to finalise my studies and say goodbye to Geoff Featherstone and anyone from the museum crew who might be around. I should go back to the car yard to take advantage of the buy-back arrangement on my car and talk to the real estate people about vacating the flat. When I can take care of those last couple of things will depend on when I fly out."

"Okay, how about we meet up at Kings Manor for lunch tomorrow – say 12:30?"

The car took me home first. Troy helped me carry my luggage upstairs and waited while I let myself in. Then he was gone. Alone at last, I unpacked and set up my computer. I remembered the airline had a 24-hour service for flight bookings, so I tried my luck. After all the rigmarole of pushing buttons in response to prompts, I finally spoke to a bookings officer.

The first flight available was Friday morning. I took it. As it was now Tuesday evening, that allowed two whole days to clean the flat and do everything else before heading home. I needed to let James know what was happening but first, I had an overwhelming desire for a fish and chips dinner. A stroll to the fish and chips shop up the street would do me good after sitting around for most of the day in planes and helicopters.

I was about halfway to the shop when a figure loomed up beside me. I made to move over to let him pass but he grabbed my arm and started dragging me towards a dark alley a short distance up ahead. I stifled my urge to struggle and offered no resistance, telling myself to remember my training. His grip loosened slightly. I spun round on my heel to face him, driving my right fist hard into his midriff. The impact caused him to double over and lose his grip on my arm. I locked both hands together and brought them up hard under his chin, sending him sprawling backwards onto the pavement. A vivid memory of having done something similar on Favignana flashed before my eyes.

He was stunned by the fall, but struggled to remove something from under his jacket. I assumed he was going for a weapon. He lost interest in whatever it was after my boot found his family jewels. The Glock Dominic gave me on Favignana was in my bag. In a split second, it was out and I had a two-handed bead on him.

Out of the darkness, two figures in tracksuits converged at speed on my little tableau. Shit! Three is a bit many to cope with – even though one of them isn't feeling too frisky right now. I moved a couple of steps away from the man on the pavement so I was out of striking range of arms or legs, and raised the Glock in the direction of the two newcomers.

Bloody hell! They both reached into the inner pockets of their jackets. Then they were flashing their badges. I lowered my weapon and they ran to the man on the ground. One handcuffed him while the other spoke on a radio. A car materialised from nowhere and slid to a stop beside the curb. The bloke in handcuffs was bundled into the back of the car. As one of the tracksuit-clad guys was about to follow him in, I cleared my throat.

"You might want to get him checked out. I think the nature of his injuries might curtail his social life for a while."

Both men grinned. The one holding the car door open adopted a serious tone for his response. "I thought he was in too much agony to have done nothing more than bitten his lip when you smacked him one under the chin."

There was more grinning by those in tracksuits as one of them slid into the car. The door slammed and the car sped off, leaving me with the other bloke in a tracksuit. I eyed him off.

"Stewart isn't it? Weren't you and your recently departed mate at the airfield earlier today? You drove us back into York."

"Yes, ma'am, and I am now going to escort you back to your flat."

"No you're not. I'm going to get fish and chips for dinner."

"You know, I could go a fish and chips dinner myself."

Each carrying our own dinner package, we returned to the flat. While I rustled up plates and cutlery, Stewart announced he would be staying the night.

"Not bloody likely, mate! This place has one bedroom and it's mine... alone."

"Relax, I will be out here. One of us will be on guard duty until you leave. When is that by the way?"

I told him I was leaving Friday morning and protested the need for a guard.

"We think the man tonight was a lone wolf but we can't be sure because we don't know – yet – why he was here or who sent him. So, until you leave, we will be unobtrusive but we will be around at all times."

There seemed little point in protesting, so we ate and I cleaned up. I told him to amuse himself as I had emails to deal with. He promptly turned on the TV and settled back. I took a shower before emailing James. When I returned, Stewart was engrossed in some 'shoot-'em-up' western movie.

Chapter 21

I hadn't read a couple of emails from James. I read them both – twice. Something was not right. The emails were chatty enough and didn't contain anything alarming, but I sensed something 'off' about them. Stewart cut across my thoughts.

"Sonny, what's up?"

"Eh? Nothing. Why?"

"You were frowning; looking a bit concerned. Anything I should know about?"

"Oh, no; just emails from home from my business partner."

"Is everything okay?"

"Well, yes, but I sense something is not quite right. I'm probably imagining it."

"I wouldn't bet on that after what I've heard about your finely honed 'gut instinct'."

I laughed awkwardly and concentrated on my emails, not wanting to continue that discussion any further. While I was about it, I sent Dom an email detailing tonight's excitement. Then I took myself off for an early night. It seemed like the day had been at least as long as a week and it felt as though I hadn't slept a wink during that time. I slept soundly, dreamt badly and woke early completely disorientated by the different surroundings

Stewart was brewing coffee and its aroma greeted me as I opened my eyes. After breakfast, there were a few domestic chores and much killing of time until a respectable hour to go to Kings Manor. My car protested a bit when I tried to start it but eventually decided to cooperate.

I caught up with various people, said goodbyes and received glowing reports from my lecturers before dropping in at the museum. There were only a couple of people working in the backroom of the museum, so goodbyes there were swift. Then, with nothing else to do, I went to wait for Troy for lunch. I was early but Troy was already waiting for me. We lingered long over lunch, our conversation roaming over all manner of topics. After a couple of hours, it was time to go. We arranged that Troy would pick me up this evening and we would head to one of the local pubs for dinner. My 'shadow' came along too – in his car – and sat a couple of tables away as we dined in the snug of a nearby pub.

*****

The next two days went by in a blur. Domestic chores, in readiness for vacating the flat, managed to occupy much of Wednesday. Stewart stayed in the flat on Tuesday night, but it appeared no one replaced him on Wednesday. That was until I went down the street to get something for lunch. At the bottom of the stairs, a tall, thin redheaded man introduced himself as Bryon and said he would be accompanying me to wherever I might be going. Oh, joy. His skin was so pale. It looked almost transparent, that appearance supported by the boniness of his face and hands, which were the only bits I could see. His eyebrows and lashes were so pale as to appear non-existent. Poor bloke couldn't help it I suppose, but he just looked eerie.

Troy brought take-away and we ate in my flat on Wednesday night. Stewart had the good grace not to appear until after Troy left. In accordance with the plans put in place the previous night, Troy arrived at my flat at nine o'clock the next morning. He followed me to the car dealership where the buy-back process for my car happened swiftly and without trauma. Now without a car, Troy became my chauffeur.

My next port of call was the real estate agent. I completed paperwork associated with relinquishing the flat, and arranged for them to inspect the place and collect the keys later in the afternoon. Next stop was the bank to get some cash to tide me over until I left the country. By then it was lunchtime. Armed with sandwiches and coffee from a little deli, we sat on a rug under the trees in a local park. We ate and yarned until nearly two o'clock, the appointed time for the real estate agent to visit the flat.

She was late, which was good as it gave me time to move all my stuff from the flat to Troy's car. There wasn't much to move, but I felt a slight emotional twinge seeing the place devoid of my stuff. When the agent did arrive, the formalities took only about ten minutes, and then I was homeless. We argued about where I would spend Thursday night. Troy wanted me to stay at his place. No strings attached he assured me. My intention always was to stay at the same hotel as I stayed in when I arrived. In the end, I won the debate. Troy dropped me at the hotel and went back to Kings Manor for the rest of the afternoon. I was idly checking out the lobby area while waiting for the lift, when I spotted Bryon talking agitatedly to the receptionist.

Troy came back that evening. We dined at a nearby restaurant and – surprise, surprise – Stewart also dined just a few tables away from us. It was a lovely meal – a lovely evening – but, by the end of it, we were both a bit melancholy. We drove back to the hotel in relative silence. I said a speedy goodnight and hurried into the building. This was becoming ridiculous. It must be the effect of too much wine.

Eight o'clock the next morning, Troy knocked on my door as arranged. I spent a disturbed night, and he looked like he had too. He loaded my gear into his car while I checked out. Stewart observed from a lounge chair in the corner of the lobby. I went over to him and told him we were off to the airport. I asked that, if he was not going to follow us to the airport, could I give him something now. He assured me he would be seeing me off at the airport. Oh good, that's wonderful!

After the usual nonsense of trying to find a parking space, we parked and made our way across to the terminal. When we arrived at the entrance, Stewart was already waiting for us. Obviously, they have some special parking arrangement that doesn't involve the grief that mere mortals have to endure to find somewhere to park at an airport. Stewart accompanied us to the restaurant where we intended having breakfast. He ordered raisin toast and coffee, despatched it quickly when it finally arrived, and then announced he would leave us, but would be staying close by.

I opened my bag under the table and spoke to Stewart as he was about to get up.

"Do you have large pockets in that jacket?"

"Eh, what do you mean by 'large'?"

"I have something to give you. It's a bit weighty and reasonably large, but I don't think I'll be able to get it through the scanner in my baggage."

I saw the lights come on as comprehension of what I was talking about dawned on him. I touched him gently on the knee under the table and he held out his hand. I passed him a parcel camouflaged in some second-hand gift wrap paper.

"It was a gift from Dominic," I said cryptically. He nodded and slipped into his pocket, then left the table. As he walked away, I noticed that the left-hand side of his jacket sagged a bit. I dealt with my luggage, seat allocation (no hassles when you're travelling Business Class) and passport check, then we went through security to wait in my departure lounge. There was about an hour to kill before the boarding call for my flight. The emotion lingered from the previous night. It seemed strange that people with such a brief acquaintance should become so close as to feel such a wrench at parting. We spent the time discussing our futures.

Troy received word that he was likely to be elevated to a full professor when the academic board met early next term. He had a couple of reports to complete to finalise it. His calendar was looking exciting: he would present a paper at a prestigious conference, and ICOM requested his attendance at their Annual General Meeting to receive some award for his work against the illegal trafficking of cultural material. However, all that was in the future, more immediately, he was off to the Orkneys next week to act as an advisor on an excavation site there. Would he go back to Crete and his newly discovered site in the cove? He had an offer to return the next season to supervise work there, but he wasn't sure he would accept it. Somehow, Crete seemed to have lost some of its appeal. Regardless of whatever happened in the future, his excitement at the prospect of not spending more time in the immediate future holed up in academia was almost palpable.

My own story paled in comparison. I was going back to my 'day' job – and was happy to be doing so. James was busy in my absence and had accumulated a backlog of jobs still demanding attention. I discussed the concerns I had after reading James' emails. Troy suggested it probably was no more than guilt feelings at having been away for so long. I didn't buy his theory, but there was no point in arguing. He wanted to know more about what James and I did as private investigators. I invested some time in trying to explain something that was pretty unexciting and defied simple explanation anyway.

I heard my flight called. This had to be quick. However, our hug lasted a tad longer than it should. There were reiterated promises to keep in touch, and I rushed for my plane, struggling with the lump in my throat and fighting back tears. God, Sonny! What is wrong with you? Get it together.

Once we were in the air and things settled down, I emailed James my expected arrival time at Millhaven and asked if he intended to collect me from the airport as arranged before I left. Then I slept. I checked my emails just before we reached Australia. My spirits lifted when I read James' upbeat reply. Perhaps I had read too much into his earlier emails.

Finally, I was back in my home state and it was time to go through the irritating process of transferring from the international to domestic terminal for my flight to Millhaven. I didn't care; I could endure it. I was nearly home.

A strong head wind delayed our arrival at Millhaven by several minutes. I was amongst the last to deplane, preferring to leave in comfort rather than endure prodding and jostling by all those who always seem to be in some incredible hurry to disembark and rush off to whatever their day had in store for them.

Passengers and others were milling around the carousel when I entered the baggage area. They were still unloading luggage from the plane when I disembarked, so there would be a bit of a wait yet before anything appeared on the carousel. I pushed through the throng, scanning the crowd for James. I caught my breath when I saw him.

He had lost weight – a lot of weight – and looked drawn and haggard. His now scrawny neck protruded from the collar of a polo shirt that appeared to be at least three sizes too large for him. I resisted the urge to rush over to him. With great restraint, I smiled widely as I wove my way through the crowd. He threw his arms around me in a bear hug that lasted a few seconds. The rest of him felt as scrawny as his neck looked. I heard the ping of the carousel announcing the arrival of luggage, so I disengaged from James and found a vantage point from which to watch for my bag.

The drive to my house was uneventful with conversation centred on various happenings in the town during my absence. My housesitting friends moved into their new home the previous week, leaving my keys with James. I unloaded my gear and told him I would come to the office as soon as I had taken everything inside. He watched me open the door before driving off.

I didn't bother with unpacking my case after I retrieved James' gift from it. All I did was set up my computer to allow it charge and be ready for use when I returned. The car started with the first turn of the key. I suspect James ran it the previous day to be sure it would. Then I drove the familiar route to our office at James' house. The aromas of coffee brewing and raisin bread toasting met me as I walked in.

We took morning tea through to the office and sat at our desks. James was making no secret of the fact he was pleased I was home, but there was no mention of his current condition. After a few minutes of chat about recent jobs, I decided it was time to broach the subject.

"Okay, James, which weight-loss company have you signed up with?"

"Eh, what do you mean?"

"Whichever one it is, it's doing a damned good job. How much weight have you lost? …And don't tell me it's because you been so busy while I was away."

He squirmed in his chair for a moment, fiddling with the letter opener on his desk before replying. "I haven't been well. I'm afraid you are going to have to pick up the bulk of the workload now you're back. I'm thinking that, as soon as you have settled back in, I might take myself off to visit my daughter and grandchildren in Canada. It probably would only be for a couple of weeks or so. I haven't made any bookings yet, so maybe we should have a look at our pending case load and work out when I could get away."

"How ill, James?" I demanded. It wasn't a dose of the flu. In fact, it was blatantly obvious the news was not going to be good. He opened his mouth to speak but caught my steely look, closed his mouth again and reconsidered his response before speaking.

"…Terminally so. They are trying some new treatment, but I haven't noticed any improvement and I don't believe there will be. If everything goes well, I might have six months."

"Jesus, James, why didn't you tell me? I would have come home straight away."

"And that's why I didn't tell you. You needed the break. I knew you would be shouldering the whole load soon enough."

"You knew about this before I left? … And you didn't say anything. It didn't occur to you that I might want to know?"

"No, I didn't know; not really. I went to the doctor just before you left. He wanted me to have some tests done. By the time I had them done and the results came back, you had been gone a month or more. Then there were more tests and experimental treatment, and that's ongoing. However, they told me that, if this current regime doesn't work, there is nothing else to try."

"Don't worry about the case load. Make your flight bookings for Canada now. I can manage – just as you did while I was away – and I'll probably cope better because I'm not ill. Make the bookings and email your daughter that you're coming."

He went into town to make the booking rather than do it online as he normally would. It gave me time alone to weep and get myself under control again before he returned. That's probably why he went to town. My mind was sluggish. I felt as though I was swimming through molasses. I was jet lagged but I would just have to struggle through it. James' longer than anticipated absence gave me time to go through the pending jobs list and make a few phone calls to get a couple of them started. I made appointments for the afternoon, so that gave me some time to put a few things in place with James before I started the first job. Oh God, I just needed to be busy – very busy. It was happening all over again.

He returned just before lunchtime and brought pies and pasties from our favourite baker. I outlined what I had done in his absence and what my afternoon looked like. He told me his flight to Canada was booked for the end of next week. I would need to come up to speed quickly and try to knock over a few of the smaller jobs waiting for attention.

The ensuing week was a sombre affair. I was busy but still devastated by James' news. He was looking forward to being with his family but worried and tense about whether he would survive the trip. Only a week after I left England to return home, I drove James to the airport and saw him off to Canada. He expected to be away only a couple of weeks, but had an open return ticket in case he chose to stay longer.

*****

Two weeks came and went and I hardly noticed them speeding by. I was busy – very busy – and I hadn't heard from James since a couple of days after his arrival in Canada. I sent him yet another chatty email about how busy I'd been making us lots of money and checked my emails for a response every time I was in the office. The response didn't come until near the end of his third week away. He was booked to return at the end of the following week. There was no health update.

He looked exhausted when I collected him from the airport. I drove him to his GP the next day, but then didn't see anything of him for the next couple of days. The office is in an extension added to his house, so we operate out of a separate wing, which also includes a small kitchenette. When James did emerge from the rest of the house and ventured into the office, he looked more rested.

His news was not good. His GP confirmed the treatment was not having any effect and the specialist had revised his life expectancy down to less than three months. For the next six weeks, he spent as much time as he could in the office taking care of paperwork and generally taking over the administrative function. Then it all became too much and, after a week or so of lying around at home, he entered palliative care.

I visited him at least once every day for the first couple of weeks. If I happened to be passing, I would drop in again just to say hello. He insisted I not tell his daughter what was happening until it was 'all over'. His request not to tell his daughter was difficult to live with, but I did as he asked. Troy and I kept in touch by email right through to the end. Although on the other side of the world, he was a rock supporting me through this most difficult time.

Then it was all over. I made that dreadful call to his daughter. She seemed more composed than I was. Then I rang our solicitor who also handled James' private affairs. I needed to check that we could continue trading although only half of the partnership remained. He confirmed that I could. He also told me that James appointed me his executor, although we wouldn't be able to do much about probate until after receiving a death certificate. Christ, I didn't want to go through this again. I'd already been through it when my husband died. The solicitor asked me to call in to go over a few things. I put off seeing him for a couple of days. I wanted to delay it until after the funeral, but he insisted, saying James' will might contain instructions relating to James' wishes regarding funeral arrangements, so I relented.

The next couple of days were lost in a blue funk. I cancelled a couple of appointments. Although I went to the office, I was incapable of doing anything. The fact that the office was at James' house probably didn't help. I made an appointment with the solicitor for first thing in the morning so I wouldn't have time to dwell on it or come up with a reason to cancel. Nevertheless, I steeled myself as I drove into town. I was uncomfortable about the whole thing. It seemed intrusive of me to be going through James' affairs but, as his secretary showed me into the solicitor's office, I realised there was no one else to do it.

I left the solicitor's numb, my mind in a whirl. James left the business to me. The partnership hadn't been set up for that to happen automatically on the death of either one of us. He left his daughter a substantial sum of money, and set up trust funds for his two grandchildren. His daughter would administer those. His house, cars, boat, everything to do with the business, and a significant amount of what he termed 'operating capital' he left to me. There were also a couple of small bequests to charities.

A simple ceremony preceded James' cremation a couple of days after my visit to the solicitor. His will went for probate several weeks later and the long and sometimes difficult process of deconstructing what was left of his life began. I continued to operate out of the office at James' house. This probably wasn't the best situation for me but, in my own mind, it was easy to justify maintaining the status quo. There was a horrendous caseload to deal with after James' death, probably because I was so slack in the weeks leading up to it. I convinced myself I didn't have time to be cleaning the place out and changing my office arrangements.

Late one afternoon, after following a suspect on foot for several hours, I returned to the office exhausted. It was hot and humid, I was tired and sweaty, and a cold beer had a strong appeal. I took one out onto the deck as the first pink rays of sunset began turning crimson. I raised my bottle in salute to James and all the times we did this in the past... and to Troy for being there for me. The black shapes of a flock of ducks returning home in perfect V-formation glided across the deepening colours. After a couple of minutes, a second lot of about eight birds flapped past. This time, it was just a straggly arrangement of black shapes in no particular formation.

A lump threatened to develop in my throat after my maudlin salute to James. The sight of this last group of birds brought back memories of sitting on the sand with Troy on Crete, watching a similar group of straggly birds flap across the evening sky. That completed the development of the lump in my throat. Tears trickled down my cheeks. Troy and I hadn't made contact in over a week; I needed a friend to talk to now. A quick calculation of time differences and I decided now was a good time to call.

"Hi, I just need a friend to talk to right now. Are you free?"

"Always for you. Are you crying... what's happened?" My sniffling was an obvious give-away.

I briefly explained what brought this on yet again. "...So I just needed the comfort of talking to a friend, a friend who has encountered me like this so often lately." His response was confronting, rather than comforting.

"Why are you still there, Sonny?"

"Yes, I know, I should go home."

"That's not what I'm talking about. What are you waiting for?"

"… Waiting for? I'm not waiting for anything. I've just had a long day." This was not going as expected.

"Who is this I'm speaking to? You are not Sonny, the level-head-ed, practical, business-like person I know."

"Of course, it's me. I'm just having a melancholy moment. I'm not waiting for anything and I will go home straight after this call."

"No Sonny, I meant, what change are you waiting for? You can stay where you are for as long as you like, but it won't bring James back. It won't change anything that's happened. It's time you accepted that, took a hard look at your situation and your future and moved on. You talked about locating your office somewhere else. Why haven't you done so? What is stopping you?"

Taken aback, I found myself devoid of a suitable comeback. This was a different Troy: stern, authoritative, demanding, but not comforting. Although, in retrospect, I had to admit that over the last few months there was another side to Troy. He was still the Troy I knew but there was a strength to him I wasn't aware of before.

"Sonny, are you still there?" I mumbled a something. "You need to get away from those surroundings, find that office somewhere else. If you can't find an office or you can't bring yourself to move, come and stay with me for a while. … But you must break away from there."

After I agreed to think about what he said, the rest of the call took on a more 'normal' tone. The call left me unsettled. I packed up as soon as it ended and headed for home. His comments – his questions – gnawed at me for weeks. Although there was plenty of contact during that time, neither Troy nor I again brought up the subject of my moving out of the office at James' house.

It took about six months – during which time I privately revisited that conversation frequently – but at last, I felt strong enough to initiate changes. With the partnership dissolved, I renamed the business Whittington Investigations and took out a lease on a small office in town. A new large shed erected at my house became home to James' cars and boat and a few other bits and pieces from his house. I kept one car as a work vehicle and put tenants into the house.
*****

It was nearly a year after James' death before everything was finalised and I felt able to come to terms with what had happened to someone who was such a large part of my life for so many years. I would never forget James or the lessons and insights he had imparted over the years.

I had lost an old friend but had gained a new one. Although our time together was short and he remained on the other side of the world, Troy was my rock during those dark days leading up to James' death and the difficult time afterwards. I would forever be grateful for the care and support he gave me. Troy Donaldson had made a lasting impression. Somehow, he was more than a friend, more like a confidante I had known all my life. Regardless of however I might describe him, I knew I wanted Troy Donaldson to remain a part of my life for some time to come.

The End.

About the Author

NEIVE DENIS is the creator of the series featuring the Private Investigator, Sonoma Whittington. Neive Denis is the pen name of a writer who was lured from her usual genre to focus on the mystery and excitement that are a part of Sonoma Whittington's world. Neive came into being specifically for this series and, for the moment at least, intends remaining faithful to only Sonny's stories.

This series of stories tells of the intrigue and scrapes – some on occasion life threatening – that are part of the life of Sonoma Whittington, an Australian Private Investigator based in a Central Queensland coastal city. However, Sonny doesn't confine her escapades to Australia, and that provides Neive with an opportunity to weave some of her other areas of interest into Sonny's hair-raising adventures.

See more about Neive Denis and her work at

www.neivedenis.com

or contact her at
contact@neivedenis.com